comiXOLOGY ORIGINALS

Lost on PLANET EARTH

WRITTEN BY
Magdalene Visaggio

ILLUSTRATED BY
Claudia Aguirre

LETTERED BY
IBD's Zakk Saam

EDITED BY
Joe Corallo

FROM

DEATH RATTLE

DESIGN BY TIM DANIEL

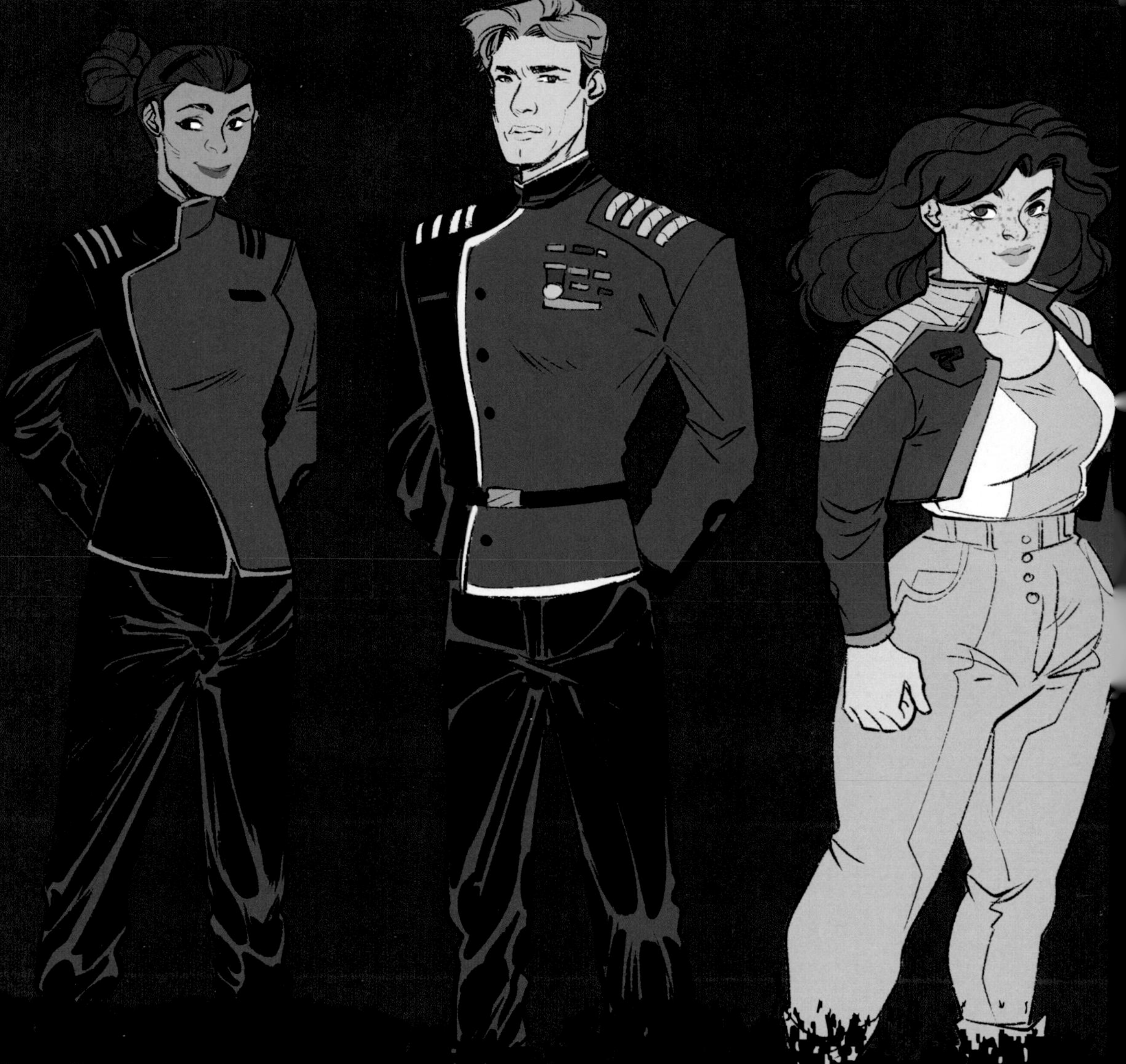

Lost on Planet Earth wasn't supposed to be about any of this.

It started out of some idle affectionate criticism of *Star Trek* I picked up from Ronald D. Moore about how strange it was that everyone in the Federation just wanted to put on a uniform and join the fleet. Even within the *Star Trek* universe, people seemed to understand how insidious and militarized the Federation seemed to be. You have Quark and Garak lamenting the ways it sucks in other cultures with its bubbly assumption that someday the whole galaxy would join in its great self-proclaimed mission of peace, and T'Kuvma accusing the Federation of assimilationism. As Garak put it, at least the Borg tell you what they're going to do. Even Jean-Luc Picard abandoned Starfleet.

There is, then, a pessimism here, because in 2381, the human race might be united, but it is so only in the project of expansion and assimilation, a project every man, woman, and child understands as their responsibility to preserve and carry forward. Citizenship, like in *Starship Troopers,* depends on service—and *everybody* plays their part. Even if that means suppressing your best, truest self.

But every time I tried to write it, it just came out as polemic. Basil would trudge from set piece to set piece and people would explain to her how shitty things were. But there wasn't really a story, and there wasn't really a character. It took embarrassingly long for me to recognize what Basil's story really was: not indicting a system, nor even extricating herself from it, but finding out who she was and what she wanted. It has parallels with my own history in Roman Catholicism, and my slow process of unlearning it. With recognizing the ways I was upholding something destructive. Even more than upholding it. I was carrying it forward.

Lost on
PLANET EARTH

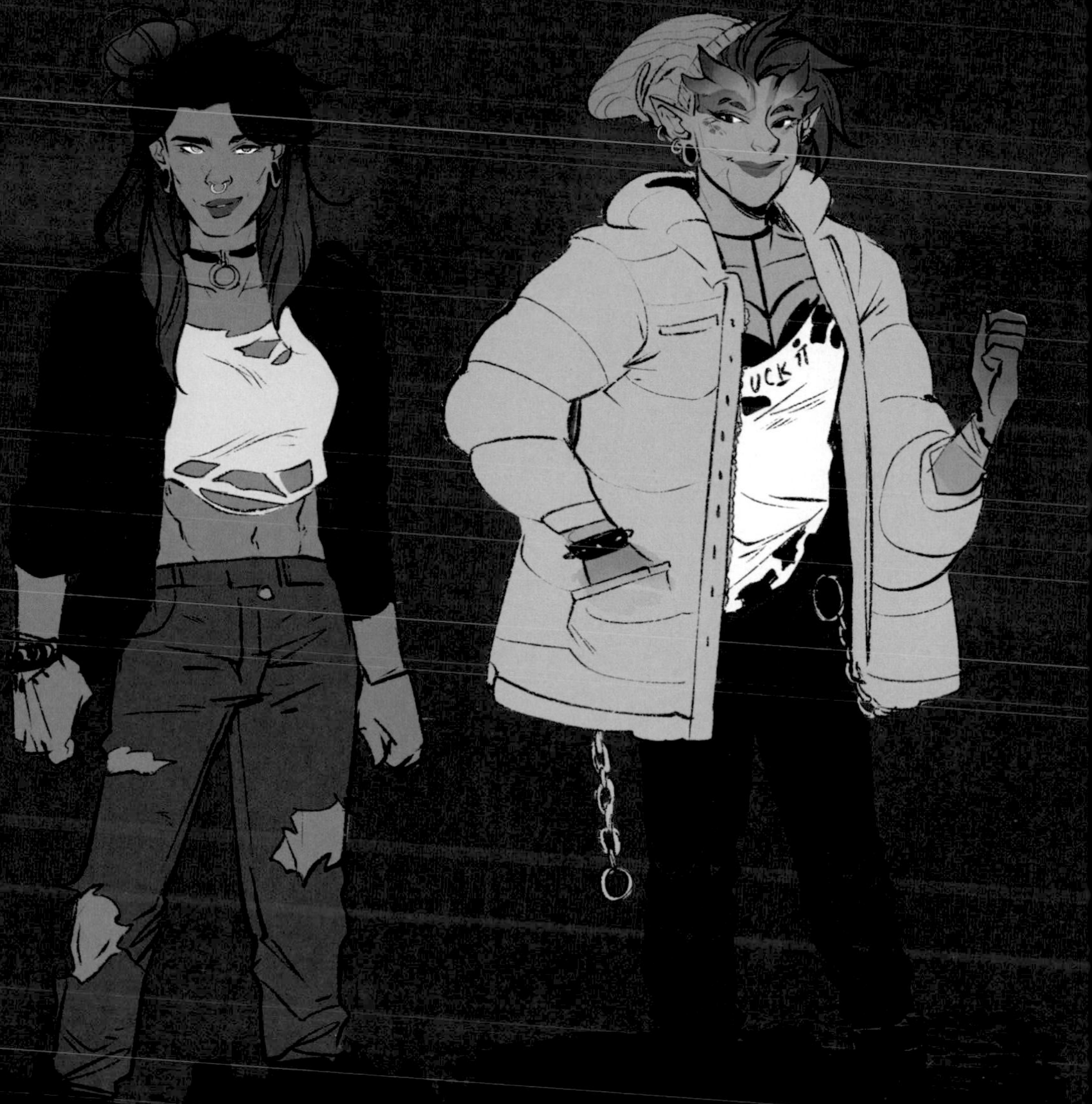
UCK IT

As I write this, two weeks have passed since George Floyd was murdered by police, launching massive nationwide protests and riots in the midst of a pandemic. Across the land, racism is being frankly and unequivocally confronted. I cannot predict the future, as Confederate statues come down across the land, my own hometown of Richmond is removing those that dot Monument Avenue, including the statue of Robert E. Lee I made a point of including in this book (although a judge has blocked it for the next ten days, so we'll see if it actually comes down). It stands as the backdrop to a parade celebrating legendary starship captain Carter Maine, and in doing so is intended to underscore the reactionary nature of this store-brand Federation. The fact that it's become an anachronism so quickly gives me immense reason for hope in the future, and that Basil's world won't come to pass.

But *Lost on Planet Earth* isn't about the future. It's about what it feels like to live right now, at this moment, at this inflection point in history when it can seem like the only things being built are walls. It's about discovering what you want and who you are when everything and everybody tells you not to ask those questions too deeply, or if you do, not to press on them. It's about complicity and running away.

Much of this book rings unpleasantly true right now, with the middle chapter featuring a violent confrontation between police and radicals fighting for their lives in Byrd Park, a place that shares a name with Harry F. Byrd who represented Virginia in the US Senate and advocated for shutting public schools down rather than integrating them, in a city that burned itself to the ground fighting to keep men slaves.

I don't write to convey a message. I don't like being preachy. But I hope, if you find anything in this book, in these times, it's this: you are not beholden to the systems and structures around you. You have a choice. We all do.

We're ***made*** of choices.

Magdalene Visaggio
New York City
June 9, 2020

DARK HORSE TEAM

President and Publisher
MIKE RICHARDSON

Editor
DANIEL CHABON

Assistant Editor
KONNER KNUDSEN

DESIGNER
SKYLER WEISSENFLUH

Digital Art Technician
JASON RICKERD

Neil Hankerson Executive Vice President • Tom Weddle Chief Financial Officer • Randy Stradley Vice President of Publishing • Nick McWhorter Chief Business Development Officer • Dale LaFountain Chief Information Officer • Matt Parkinson Vice President of Marketing • Vanessa Todd-Holmes Vice President of Production and Scheduling • Mark Bernardi Vice President of Book Trade and Digital Sales • Ken Lizzi General Counsel • Dave Marshall Editor in Chief • Davey Estrada Editorial Director • Chris Warner Senior Books Editor • Cary Grazzini Director of Specialty Projects • Lia Ribacchi Art Director • Matt Dryer Director of Digital Art and Prepress • Michael Gombos Senior Director of Licensed Publications • Kari Yadro Director of Custom Programs • Kari Torson Director of International Licensing • Sean Brice Director of Trade Sales

Published by Dark Horse Books
A division of Dark Horse Comics LLC
10956 SE Main Street
Milwaukie, OR 97222

First edition: August 2021
Trade paperback ISBN: 978-1-50672-456-0

10 9 8 7 6 5 4 3 2 1
Printed in China

Comic Shop Locator Service: comicshoplocator.com

LOST ON PLANET EARTH

This volume collects *Lost on Planet Earth* #1–#5.

Library of Congress Cataloging-in-Publication Data

Names: Visaggio, Magdalene, writer. | Aguirre, Claudia, illustrator. |
    Saam, Zakk, letterer.
Title: Lost on planet earth / written by Magdalene Visaggio ; illustrated
    by Claudia Aguirre ; lettered by IBD's Zakk Saam.
Description: First edition. | Milwaukie, OR : Dark Horse Books, 2021. |
    "This volume collects Lost on Planet Earth #1-#5." | Summary: "It's
    2381, and Basil Miranda, on the verge of graduation, knows exactly what
    she's doing with the rest of her life and always has: a primo assignment
    on the best ship in the fleet alongside her best friend in the world.
    She has meticulously prepared herself, and the final Fleet Exam is
    tomorrow. But what if none of that is what she really wants? And why
    hasn't she ever asked herself that before?"-- Provided by publisher.
Identifiers: LCCN 2021003158 | ISBN 9781506724560 (trade paperback)
Subjects: LCSH: Comic books, strips, etc.
Classification: LCC PN6728.L6766 V57 2021 | DDC 741.5/973--dc23
LC record available at https://lccn.loc.gov/2021003158

Chapter **One**

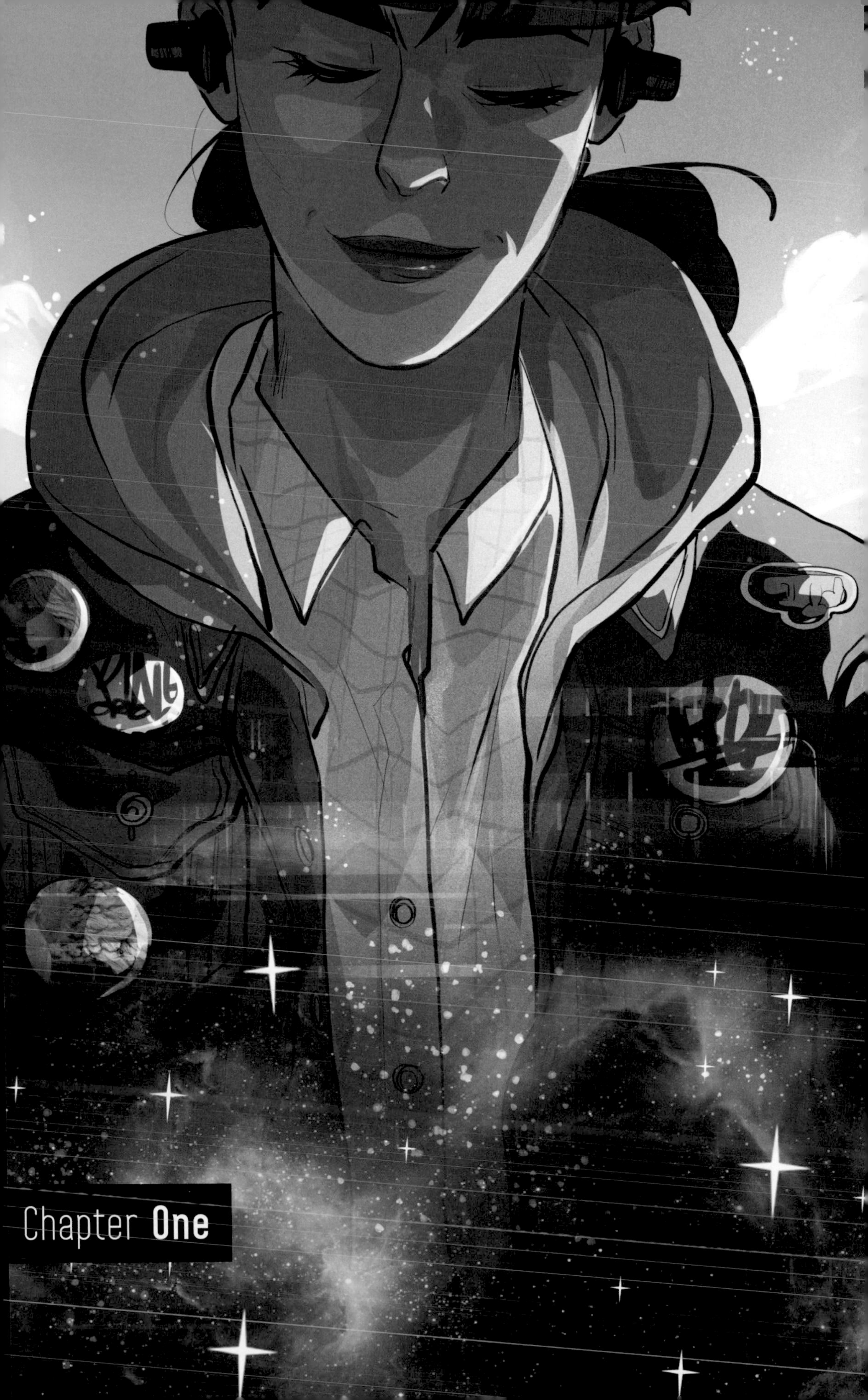

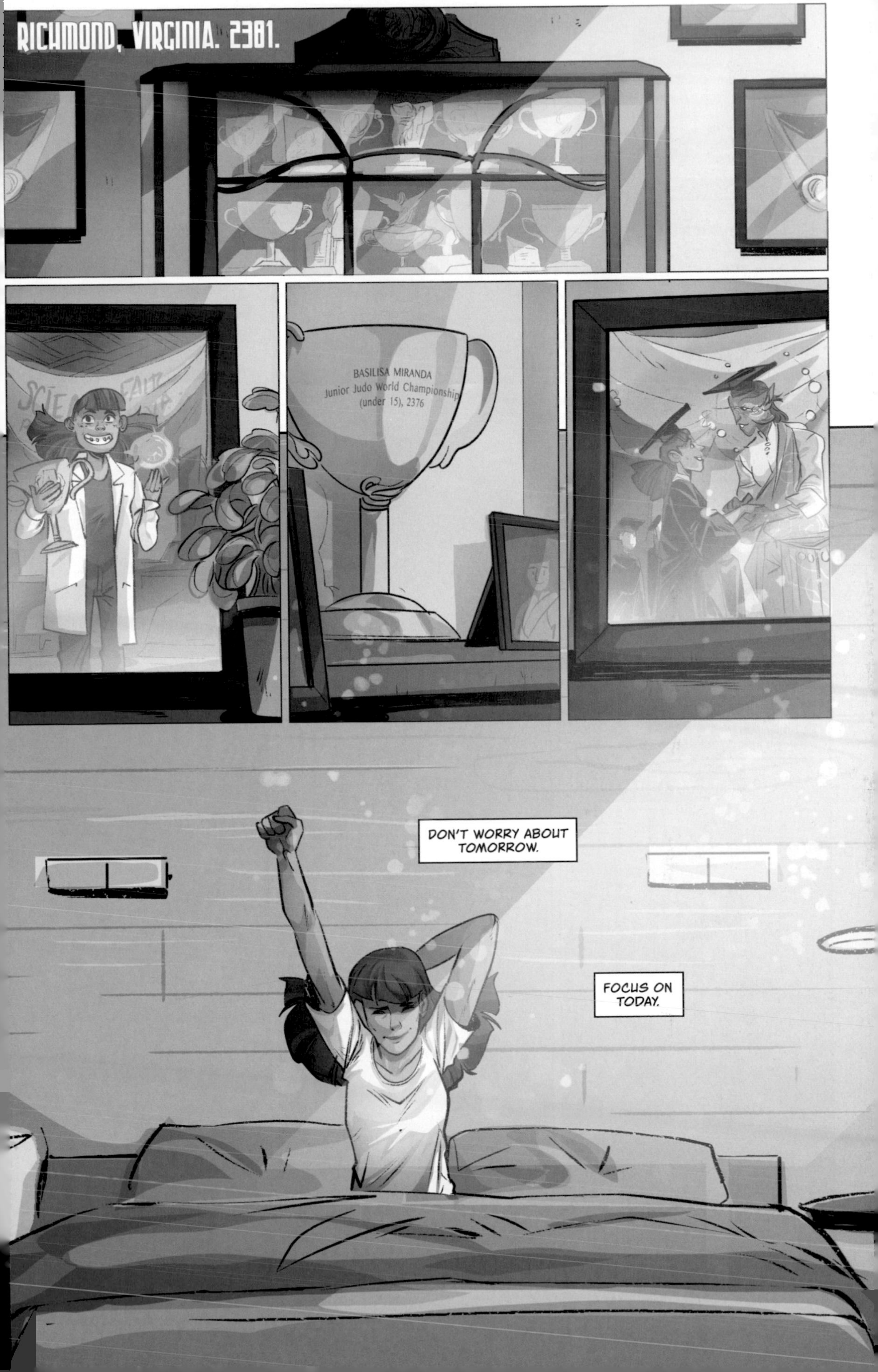
RICHMOND, VIRGINIA. 2381.
BASILISA MIRANDA
Junior Judo World Championship
(under 15), 2376
DON'T WORRY ABOUT TOMORROW.
FOCUS ON TODAY.

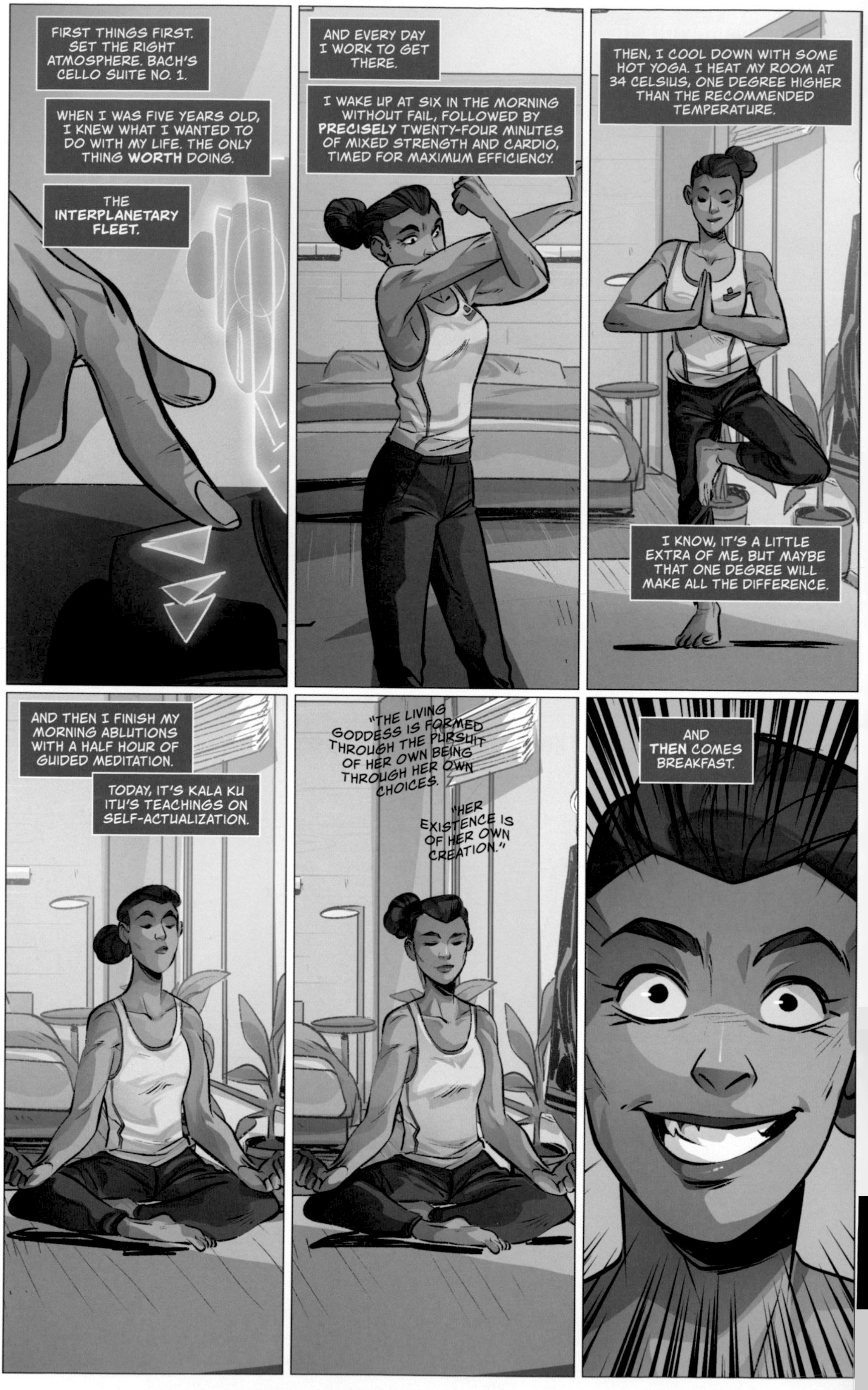

FIRST THINGS FIRST. SET THE RIGHT ATMOSPHERE. BACH'S CELLO SUITE NO. 1.
WHEN I WAS FIVE YEARS OLD, I KNEW WHAT I WANTED TO DO WITH MY LIFE. THE ONLY THING **WORTH** DOING.
THE **INTERPLANETARY FLEET.**
AND EVERY DAY I WORK TO GET THERE.
I WAKE UP AT SIX IN THE MORNING WITHOUT FAIL, FOLLOWED BY **PRECISELY** TWENTY-FOUR MINUTES OF MIXED STRENGTH AND CARDIO, TIMED FOR MAXIMUM EFFICIENCY.
THEN, I COOL DOWN WITH SOME HOT YOGA. I HEAT MY ROOM AT 34 CELSIUS, ONE DEGREE HIGHER THAN THE RECOMMENDED TEMPERATURE.
I KNOW, IT'S A LITTLE EXTRA OF ME, BUT MAYBE THAT ONE DEGREE WILL MAKE ALL THE DIFFERENCE.
AND THEN I FINISH MY MORNING ABLUTIONS WITH A HALF HOUR OF GUIDED MEDITATION.
TODAY, IT'S KALA KU ITU'S TEACHINGS ON SELF-ACTUALIZATION.
"THE LIVING GODDESS IS FORMED THROUGH THE PURSUIT OF HER OWN BEING THROUGH HER OWN CHOICES.
"HER EXISTENCE IS OF HER OWN CREATION."
AND **THEN** COMES BREAKFAST.

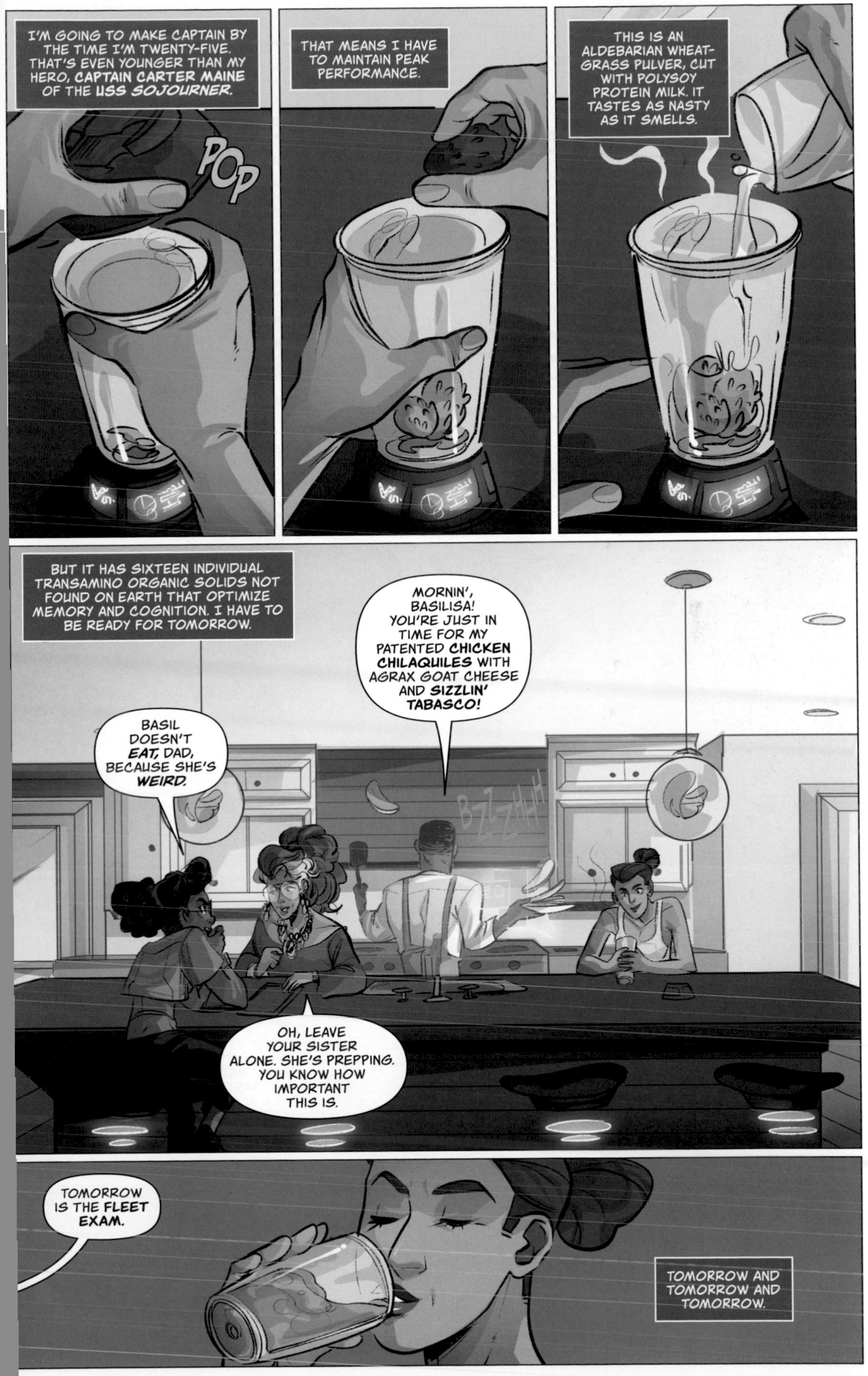
I'M GOING TO MAKE CAPTAIN BY THE TIME I'M TWENTY-FIVE. THAT'S EVEN YOUNGER THAN MY HERO, CAPTAIN CARTER MAINE OF THE USS SOJOURNER.
POP
THAT MEANS I HAVE TO MAINTAIN PEAK PERFORMANCE.
THIS IS AN ALDEBARIAN WHEAT-GRASS PULVER, CUT WITH POLYSOY PROTEIN MILK. IT TASTES AS NASTY AS IT SMELLS.
BUT IT HAS SIXTEEN INDIVIDUAL TRANSAMINO ORGANIC SOLIDS NOT FOUND ON EARTH THAT OPTIMIZE MEMORY AND COGNITION. I HAVE TO BE READY FOR TOMORROW.
MORNIN', BASILISA! YOU'RE JUST IN TIME FOR MY PATENTED CHICKEN CHILAQUILES WITH AGRAX GOAT CHEESE AND SIZZLIN' TABASCO!
BASIL DOESN'T EAT, DAD, BECAUSE SHE'S WEIRD.
BZZZHHH
OH, LEAVE YOUR SISTER ALONE. SHE'S PREPPING. YOU KNOW HOW IMPORTANT THIS IS.
TOMORROW IS THE FLEET EXAM.
TOMORROW AND TOMORROW AND TOMORROW.

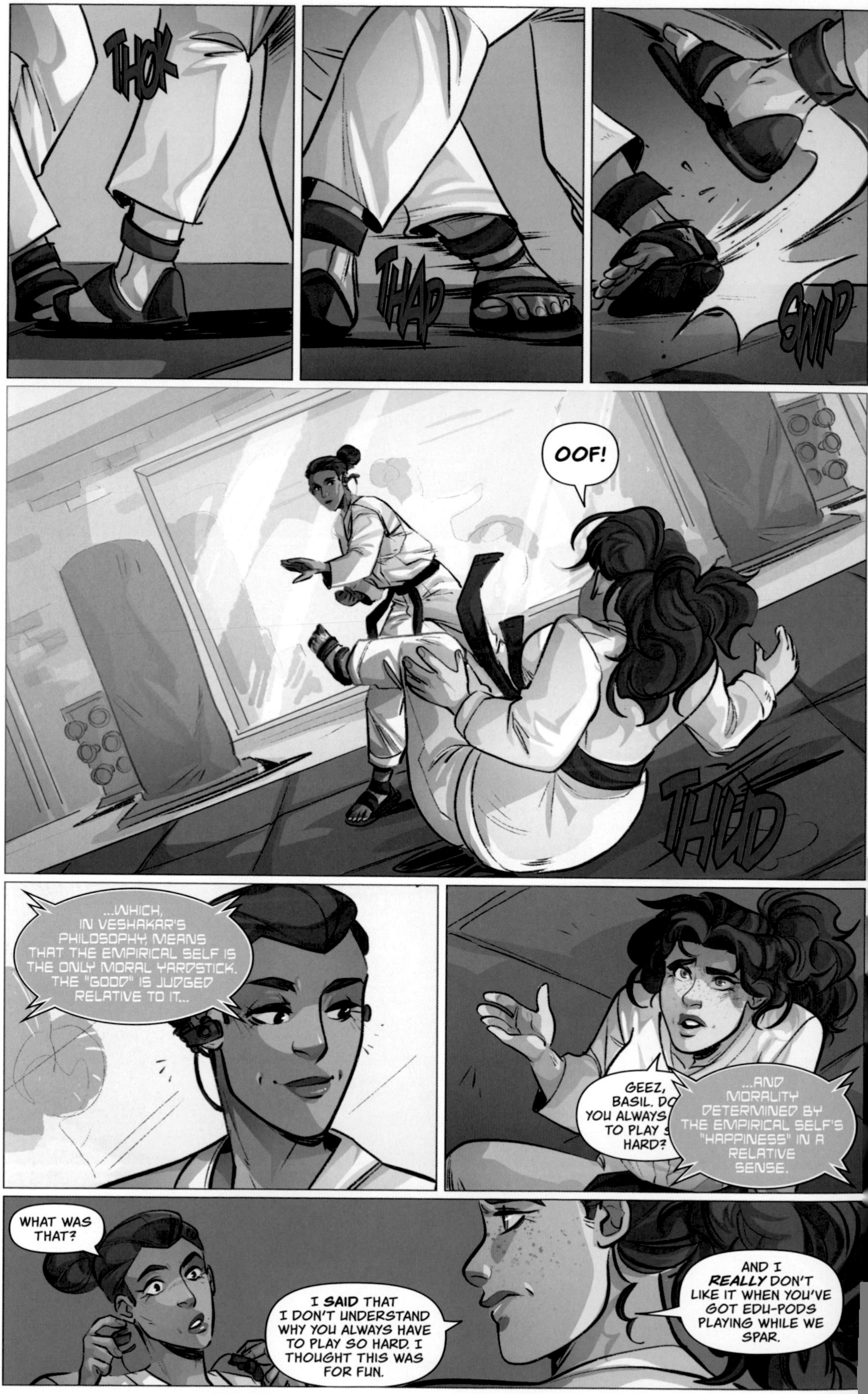
THOK
THAP
SWIP
OOF!
THUD
...WHICH, IN VESHAKAR'S PHILOSOPHY, MEANS THAT THE EMPIRICAL SELF IS THE ONLY MORAL YARDSTICK. THE "GOOD" IS JUDGED RELATIVE TO IT...
GEEZ, BASIL. DO YOU ALWAYS TO PLAY HARD?
...AND MORALITY DETERMINED BY THE EMPIRICAL SELF'S "HAPPINESS" IN A RELATIVE SENSE.
WHAT WAS THAT?
I **SAID** THAT I DON'T UNDERSTAND WHY YOU ALWAYS HAVE TO PLAY SO HARD. I THOUGHT THIS WAS FOR FUN.
AND I ***REALLY*** DON'T LIKE IT WHEN YOU'VE GOT EDU-PODS PLAYING WHILE WE SPAR.

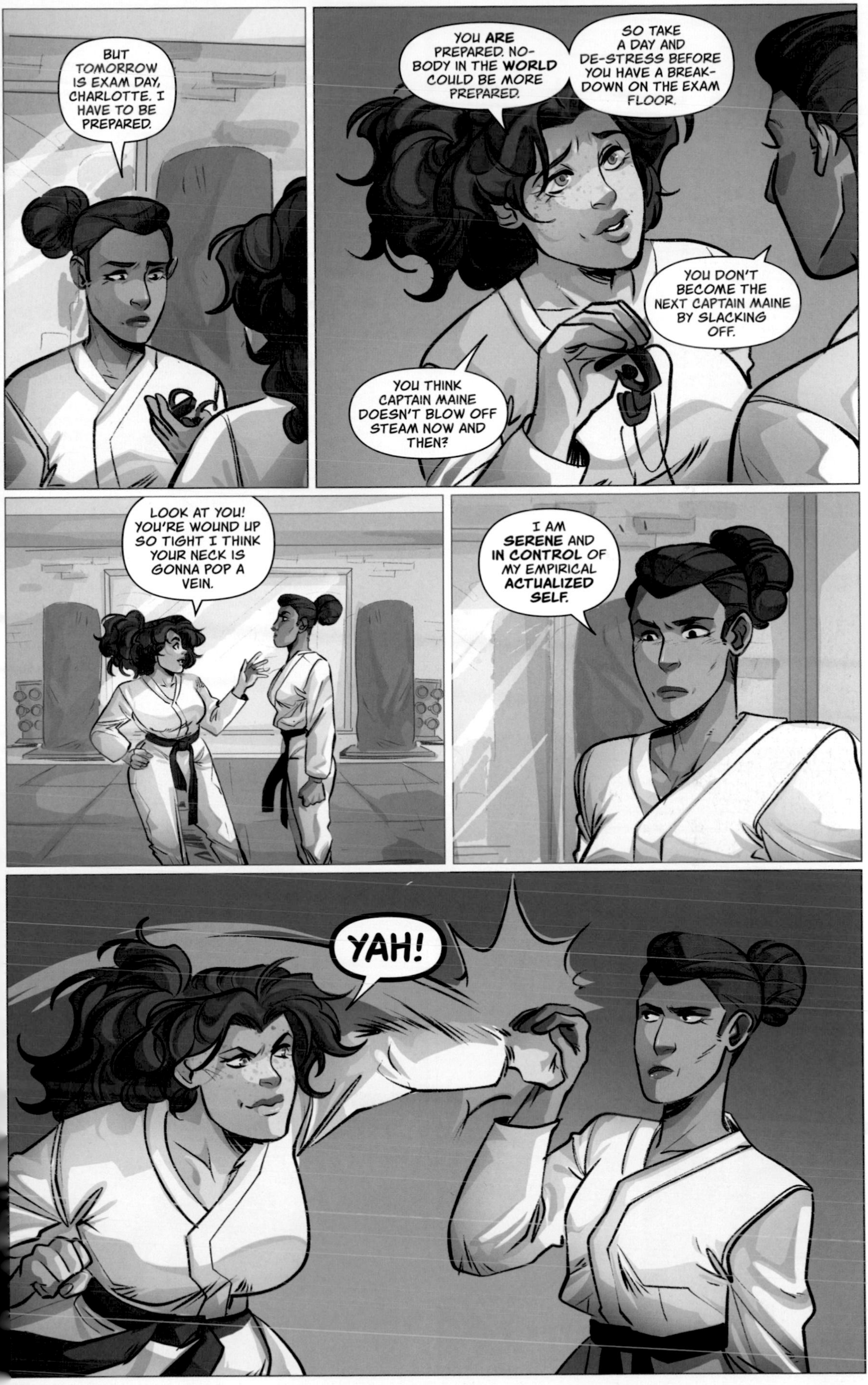
BUT TOMORROW IS EXAM DAY, CHARLOTTE. I HAVE TO BE PREPARED.
YOU ARE PREPARED. NOBODY IN THE WORLD COULD BE MORE PREPARED.
SO TAKE A DAY AND DE-STRESS BEFORE YOU HAVE A BREAKDOWN ON THE EXAM FLOOR.
YOU DON'T BECOME THE NEXT CAPTAIN MAINE BY SLACKING OFF.
YOU THINK CAPTAIN MAINE DOESN'T BLOW OFF STEAM NOW AND THEN?
LOOK AT YOU! YOU'RE WOUND UP SO TIGHT I THINK YOUR NECK IS GONNA POP A VEIN.
I AM SERENE AND IN CONTROL OF MY EMPIRICAL ACTUALIZED SELF.
YAH!

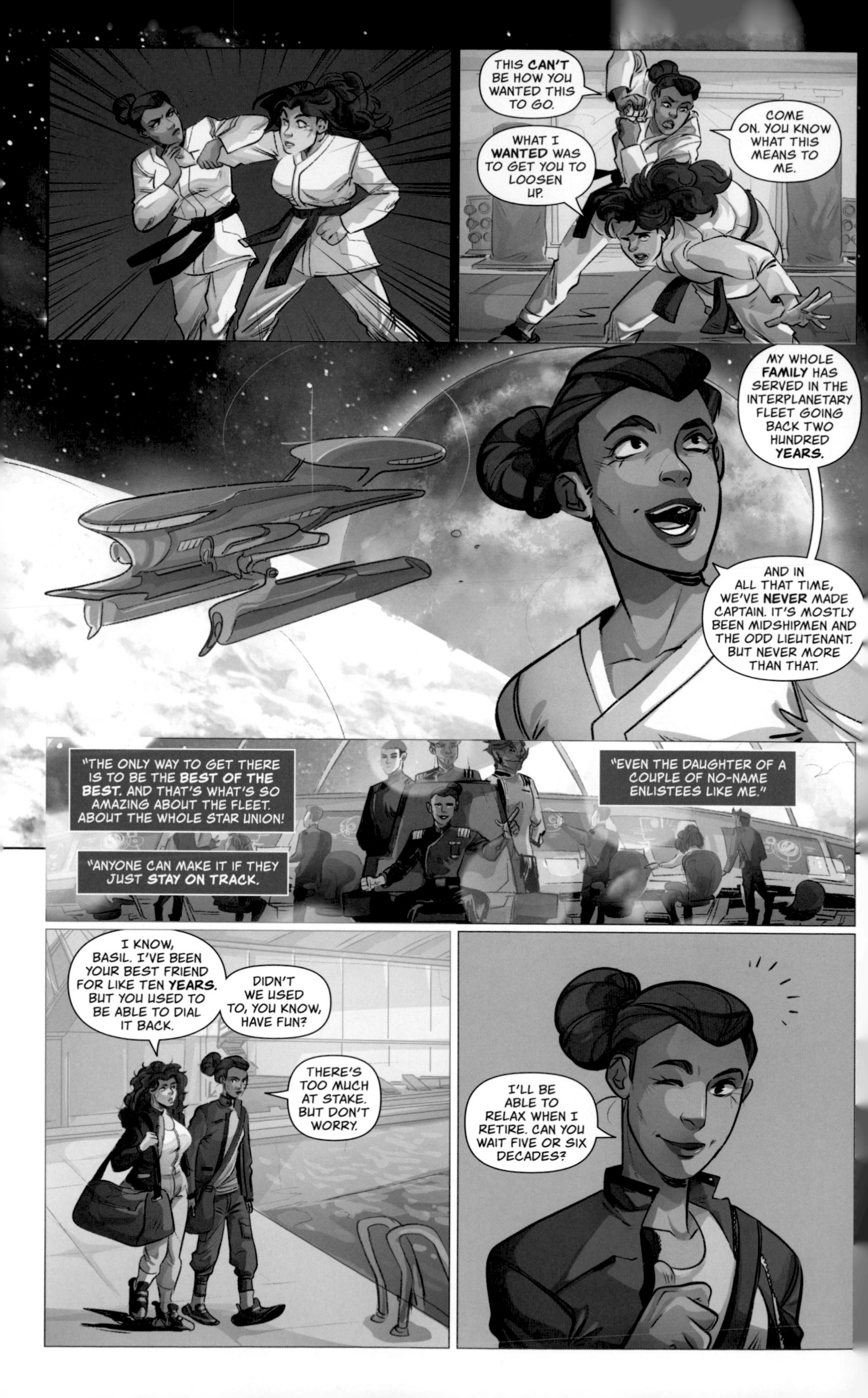
THIS CAN'T BE HOW YOU WANTED THIS TO GO.
WHAT I WANTED WAS TO GET YOU TO LOOSEN UP.
COME ON. YOU KNOW WHAT THIS MEANS TO ME.
MY WHOLE FAMILY HAS SERVED IN THE INTERPLANETARY FLEET GOING BACK TWO HUNDRED YEARS.
AND IN ALL THAT TIME, WE'VE NEVER MADE CAPTAIN. IT'S MOSTLY BEEN MIDSHIPMEN AND THE ODD LIEUTENANT. BUT NEVER MORE THAN THAT.
"THE ONLY WAY TO GET THERE IS TO BE THE BEST OF THE BEST. AND THAT'S WHAT'S SO AMAZING ABOUT THE FLEET. ABOUT THE WHOLE STAR UNION!
"ANYONE CAN MAKE IT IF THEY JUST STAY ON TRACK.
"EVEN THE DAUGHTER OF A COUPLE OF NO-NAME ENLISTEES LIKE ME."
I KNOW, BASIL. I'VE BEEN YOUR BEST FRIEND FOR LIKE TEN YEARS. BUT YOU USED TO BE ABLE TO DIAL IT BACK.
DIDN'T WE USED TO, YOU KNOW, HAVE FUN?
THERE'S TOO MUCH AT STAKE. BUT DON'T WORRY.
I'LL BE ABLE TO RELAX WHEN I RETIRE. CAN YOU WAIT FIVE OR SIX DECADES?

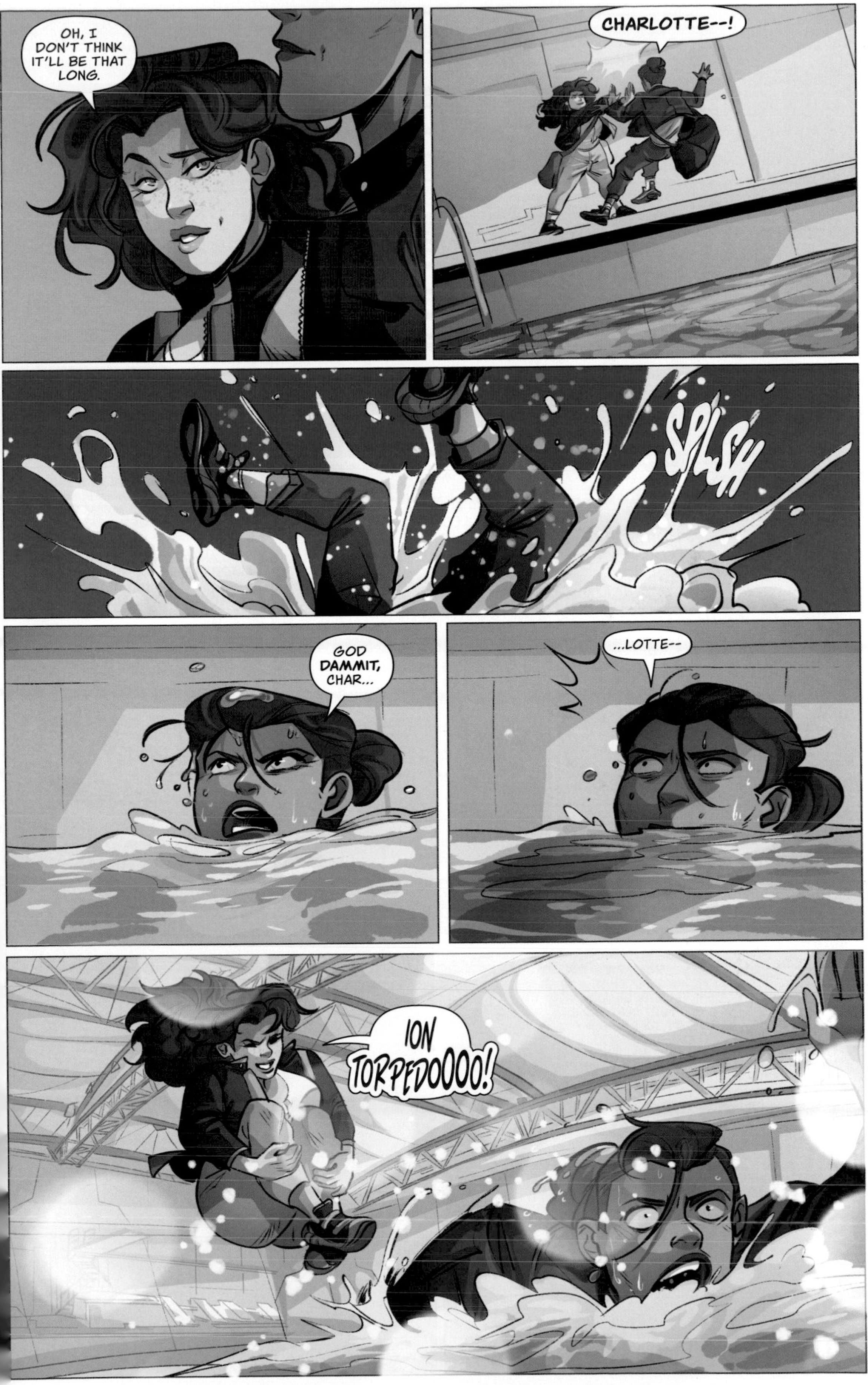
OH, I DON'T THINK IT'LL BE THAT LONG.
CHARLOTTE--!
SPLSH
GOD DAMMIT, CHAR...
...LOTTE--
ION TORPEDOOOO!

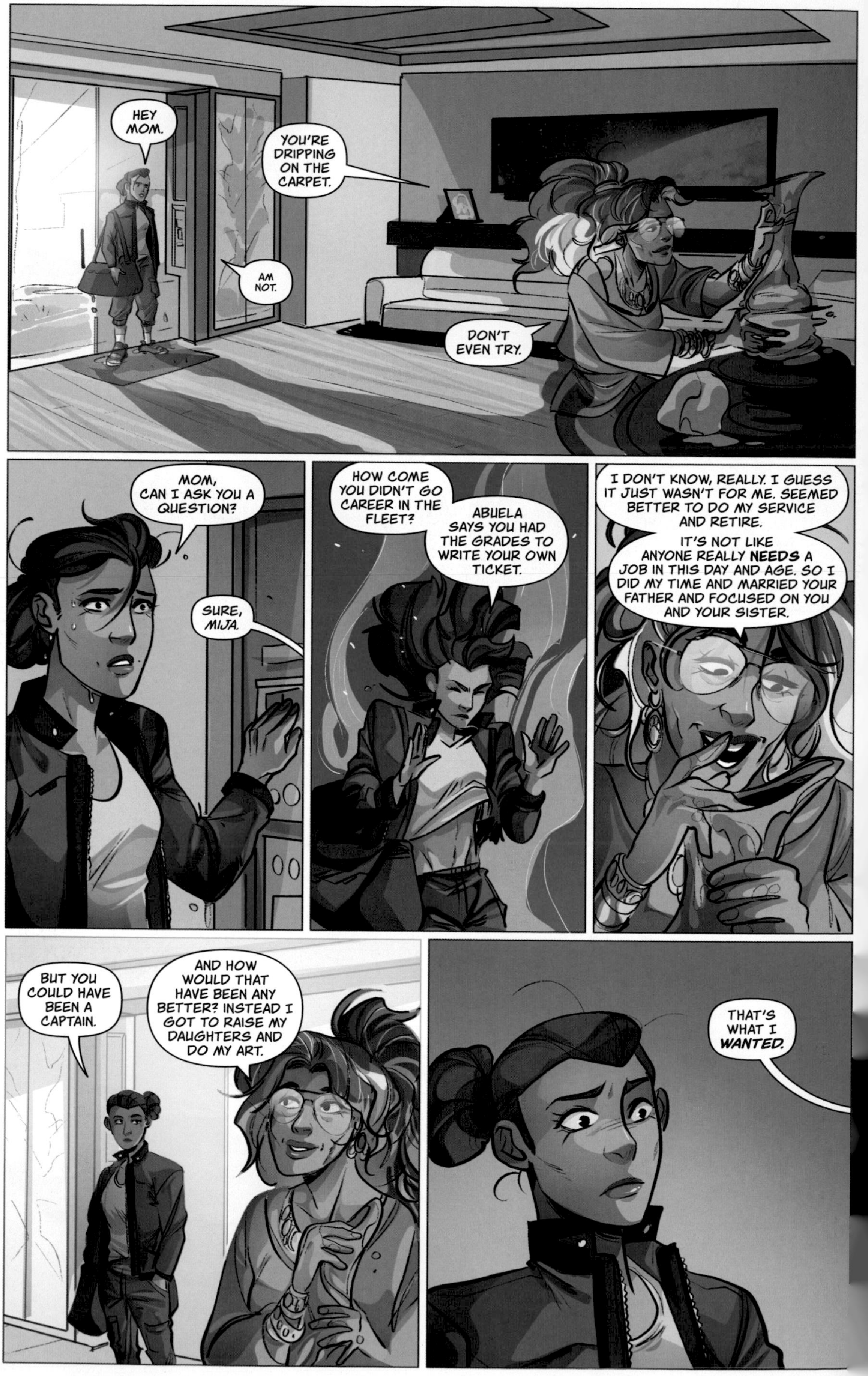
HEY MOM.
YOU'RE DRIPPING ON THE CARPET.
AM NOT.
DON'T EVEN TRY.
MOM, CAN I ASK YOU A QUESTION?
SURE, *MIJA.*
HOW COME YOU DIDN'T GO CAREER IN THE FLEET?
ABUELA SAYS YOU HAD THE GRADES TO WRITE YOUR OWN TICKET.
I DON'T KNOW, REALLY. I GUESS IT JUST WASN'T FOR ME. SEEMED BETTER TO DO MY SERVICE AND RETIRE.
IT'S NOT LIKE ANYONE REALLY **NEEDS** A JOB IN THIS DAY AND AGE. SO I DID MY TIME AND MARRIED YOUR FATHER AND FOCUSED ON YOU AND YOUR SISTER.
BUT YOU COULD HAVE BEEN A CAPTAIN.
AND HOW WOULD THAT HAVE BEEN ANY BETTER? INSTEAD I GOT TO RAISE MY DAUGHTERS AND DO MY ART.
THAT'S WHAT I ***WANTED.***

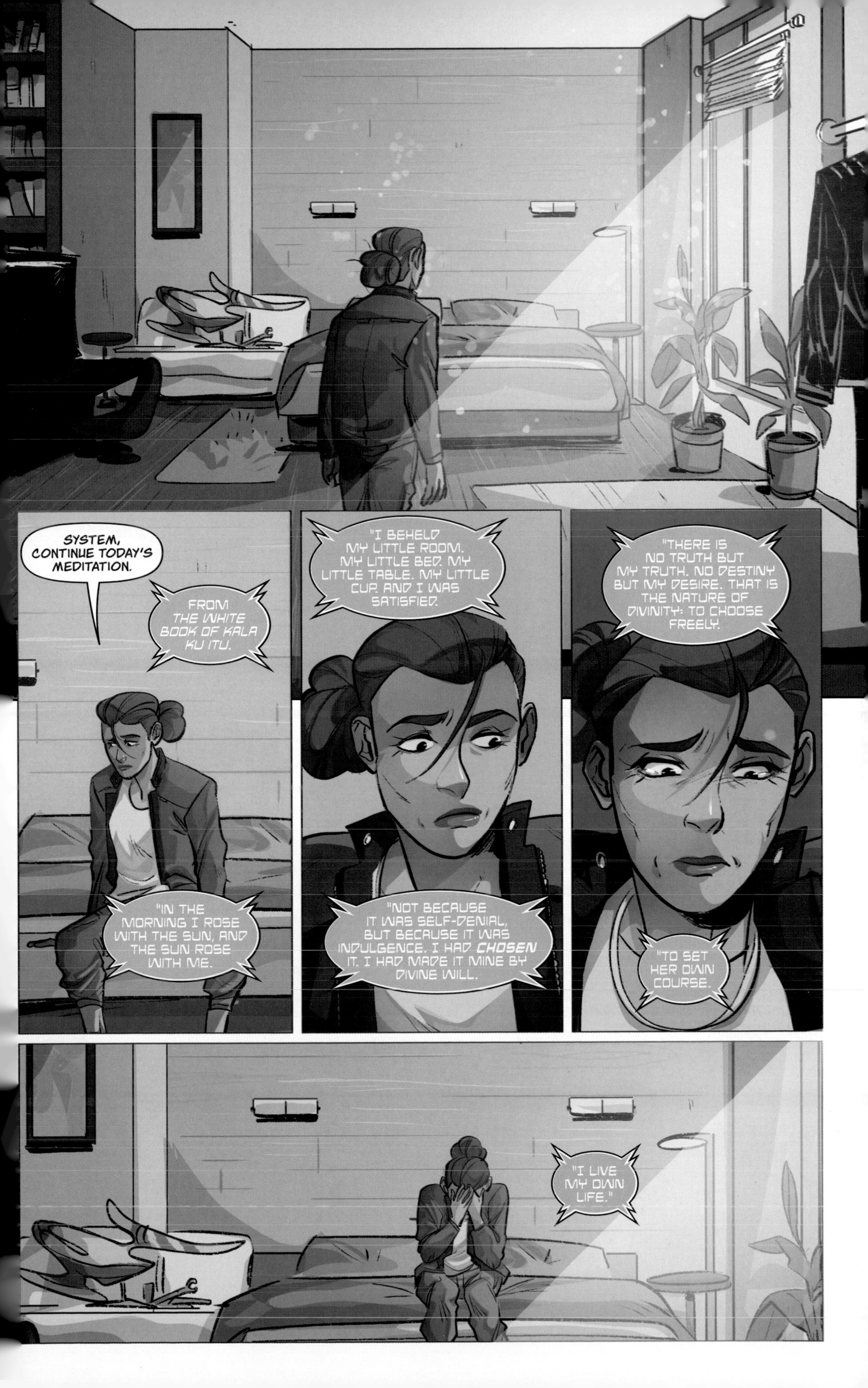
SYSTEM, CONTINUE TODAY'S MEDITATION.
FROM THE WHITE BOOK OF KALA KU ITU.
"IN THE MORNING I ROSE WITH THE SUN, AND THE SUN ROSE WITH ME.
"I BEHELD MY LITTLE ROOM. MY LITTLE BED. MY LITTLE TABLE. MY LITTLE CUP. AND I WAS SATISFIED.
"NOT BECAUSE IT WAS SELF-DENIAL, BUT BECAUSE IT WAS INDULGENCE. I HAD *CHOSEN* IT. I HAD MADE IT MINE BY DIVINE WILL.
"THERE IS NO TRUTH BUT MY TRUTH. NO DESTINY BUT MY DESIRE. THAT IS THE NATURE OF DIVINITY: TO CHOOSE FREELY.
"TO SET HER OWN COURSE.
"I LIVE MY OWN LIFE."

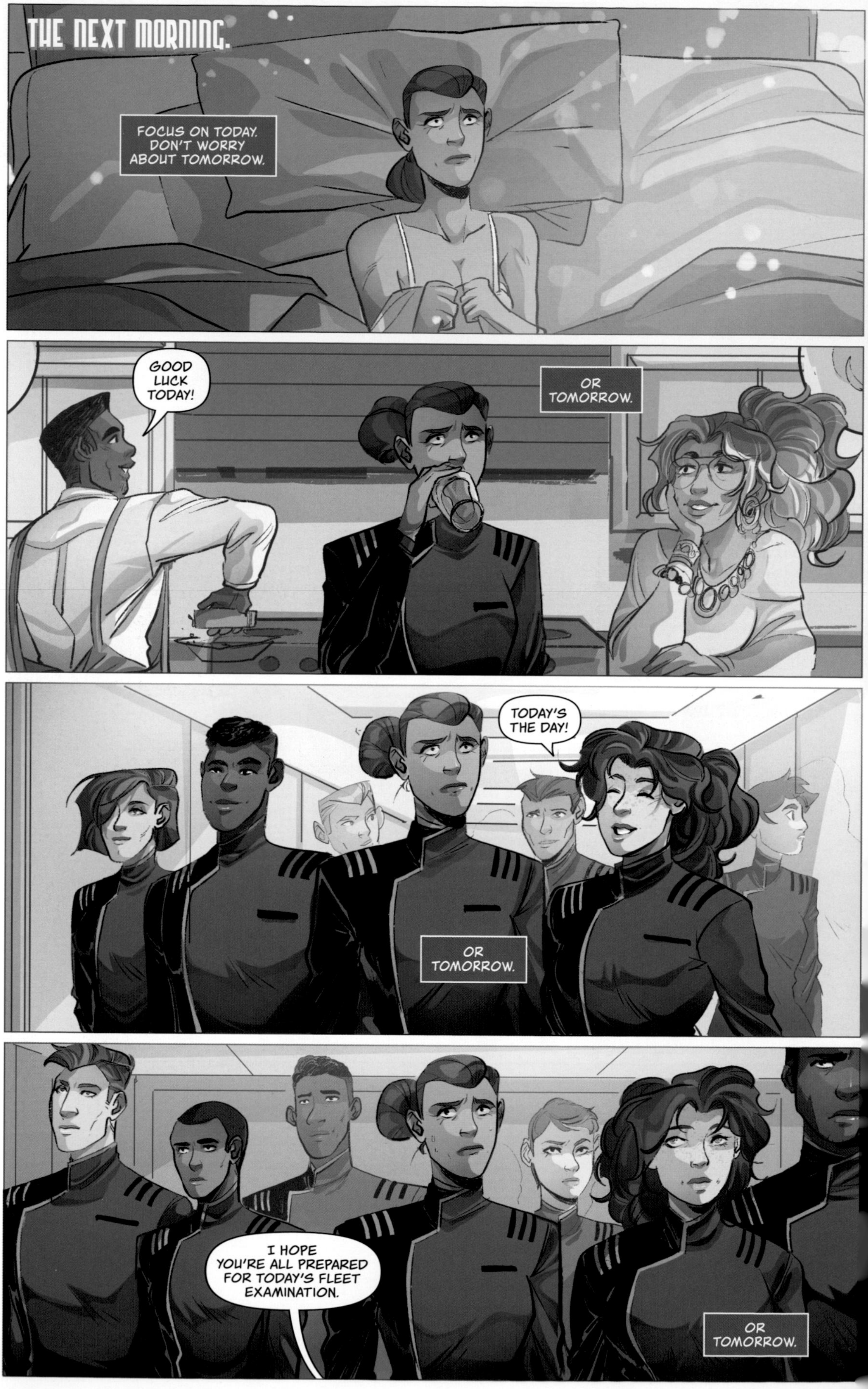
THE NEXT MORNING.
FOCUS ON TODAY. DON'T WORRY ABOUT TOMORROW.
GOOD LUCK TODAY!
OR TOMORROW.
TODAY'S THE DAY!
OR TOMORROW.
I HOPE YOU'RE ALL PREPARED FOR TODAY'S FLEET EXAMINATION.
OR TOMORROW.

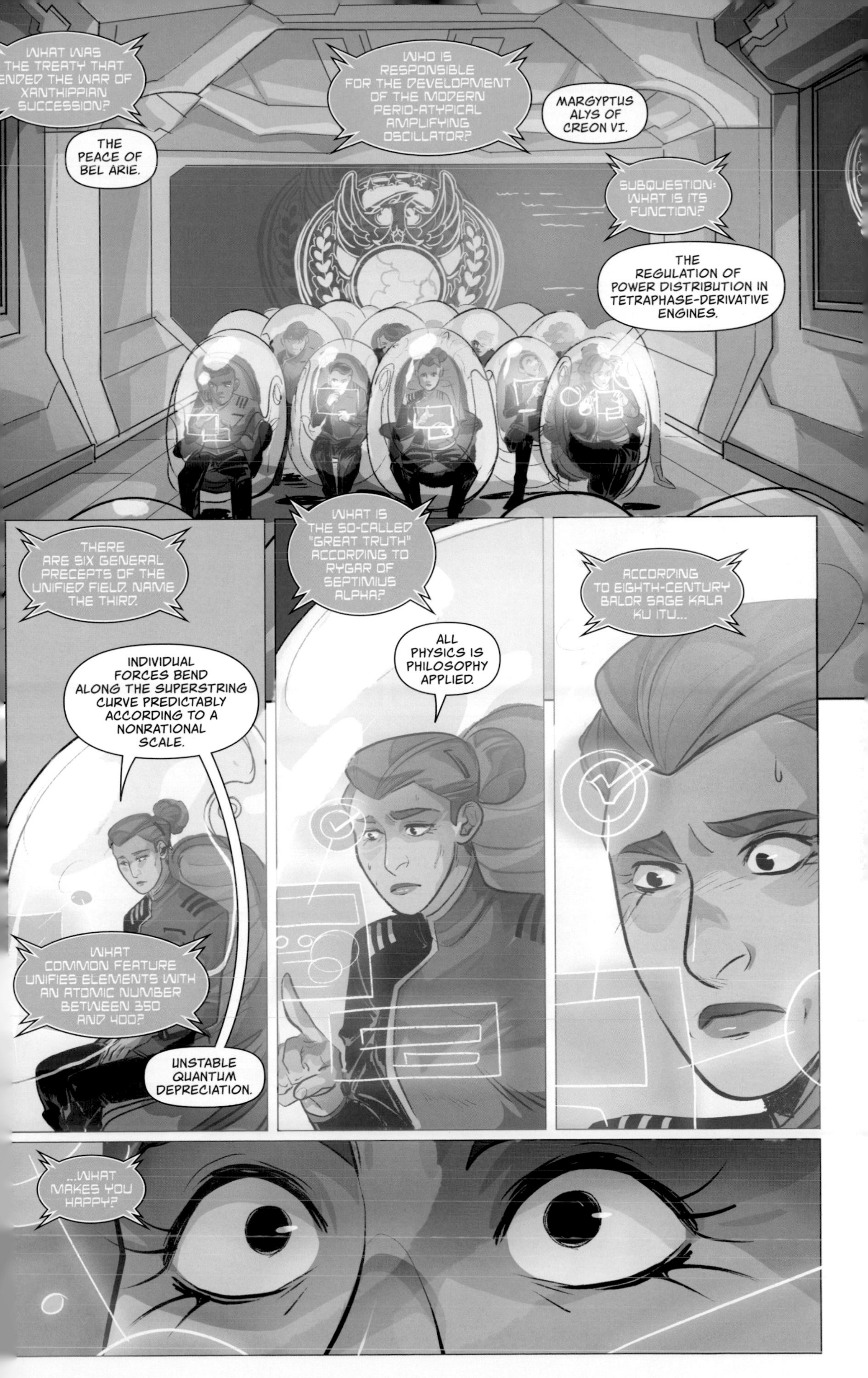
WHAT WAS THE TREATY THAT ENDED THE WAR OF XANTHIPPIAN SUCCESSION?
THE PEACE OF BEL ARIE.
WHO IS RESPONSIBLE FOR THE DEVELOPMENT OF THE MODERN PERIO-ATYPICAL AMPLIFYING OSCILLATOR?
MARGYPTUS ALYS OF CREON VI.
SUBQUESTION: WHAT IS ITS FUNCTION?
THE REGULATION OF POWER DISTRIBUTION IN TETRAPHASE-DERIVATIVE ENGINES.
THERE ARE SIX GENERAL PRECEPTS OF THE UNIFIED FIELD. NAME THE THIRD.
INDIVIDUAL FORCES BEND ALONG THE SUPERSTRING CURVE PREDICTABLY ACCORDING TO A NONRATIONAL SCALE.
WHAT COMMON FEATURE UNIFIES ELEMENTS WITH AN ATOMIC NUMBER BETWEEN 350 AND 400?
UNSTABLE QUANTUM DEPRECIATION.
WHAT IS THE SO-CALLED "GREAT TRUTH" ACCORDING TO RYGAR OF SEPTIMIUS ALPHA?
ALL PHYSICS IS PHILOSOPHY APPLIED.
ACCORDING TO EIGHTH-CENTURY BALOR SAGE KALA KU ITU...
...WHAT MAKES YOU HAPPY?

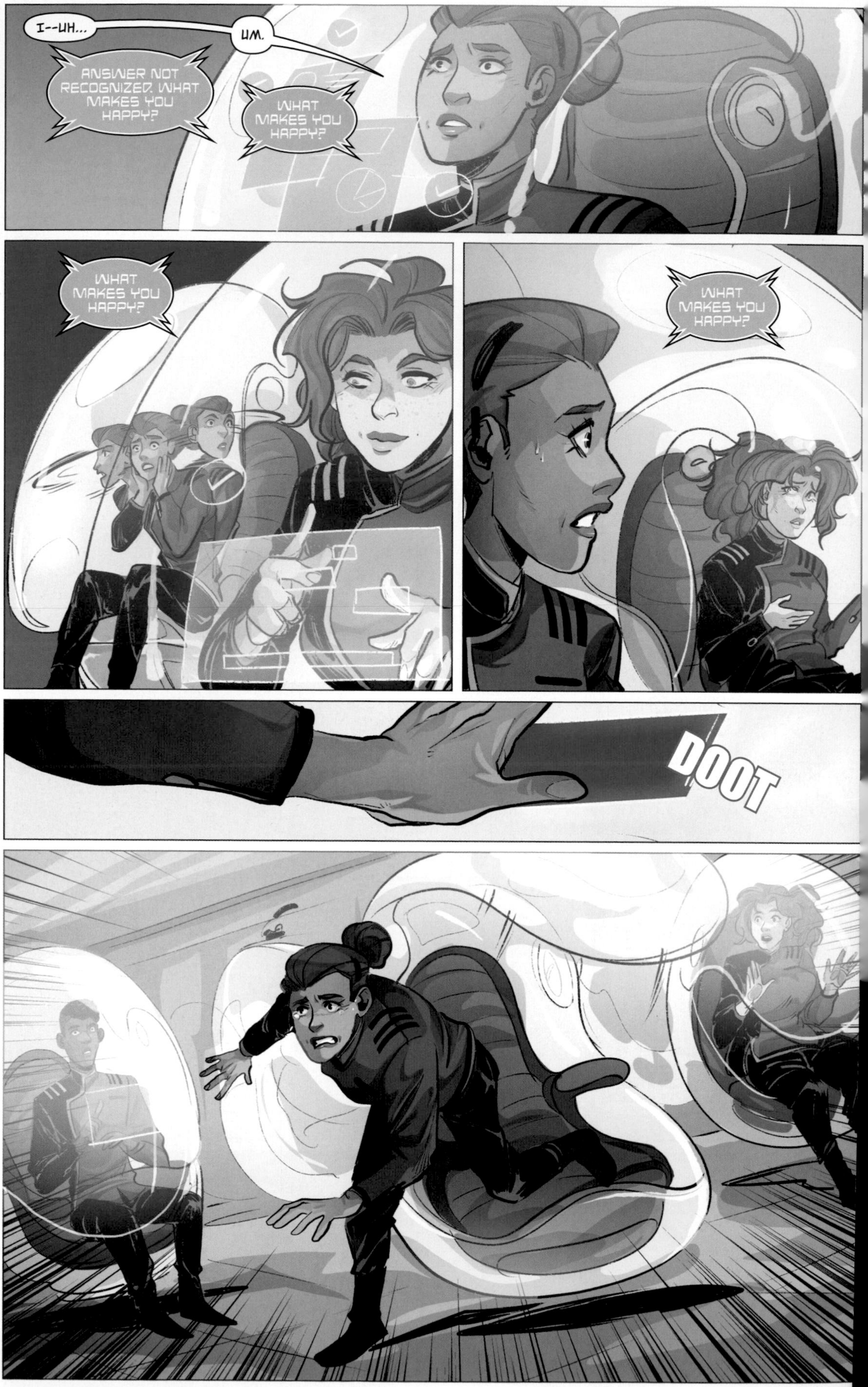
I--UH...
UM.
ANSWER NOT RECOGNIZED. WHAT MAKES YOU HAPPY?
WHAT MAKES YOU HAPPY?
WHAT MAKES YOU HAPPY?
WHAT MAKES YOU HAPPY?
DOOT

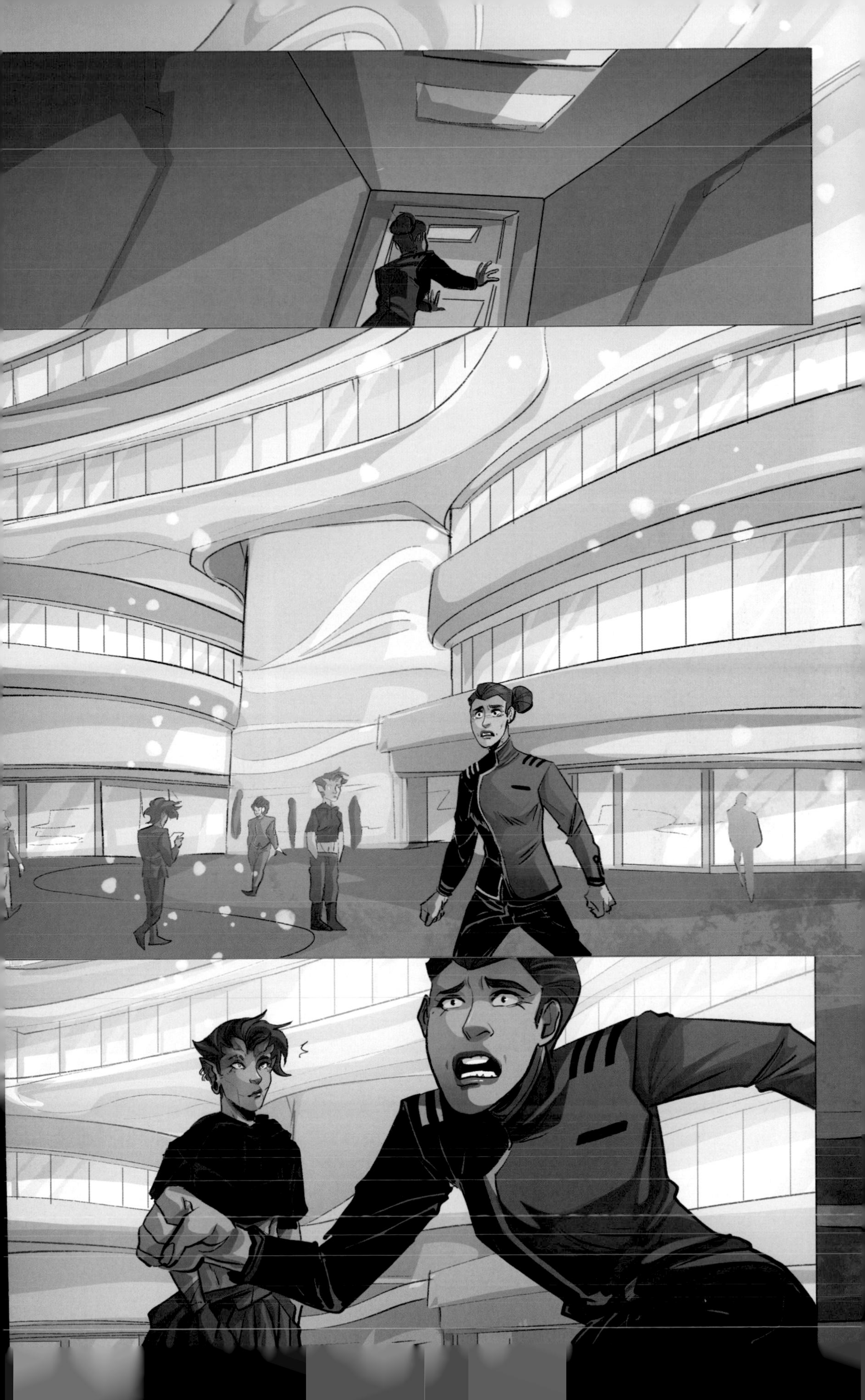

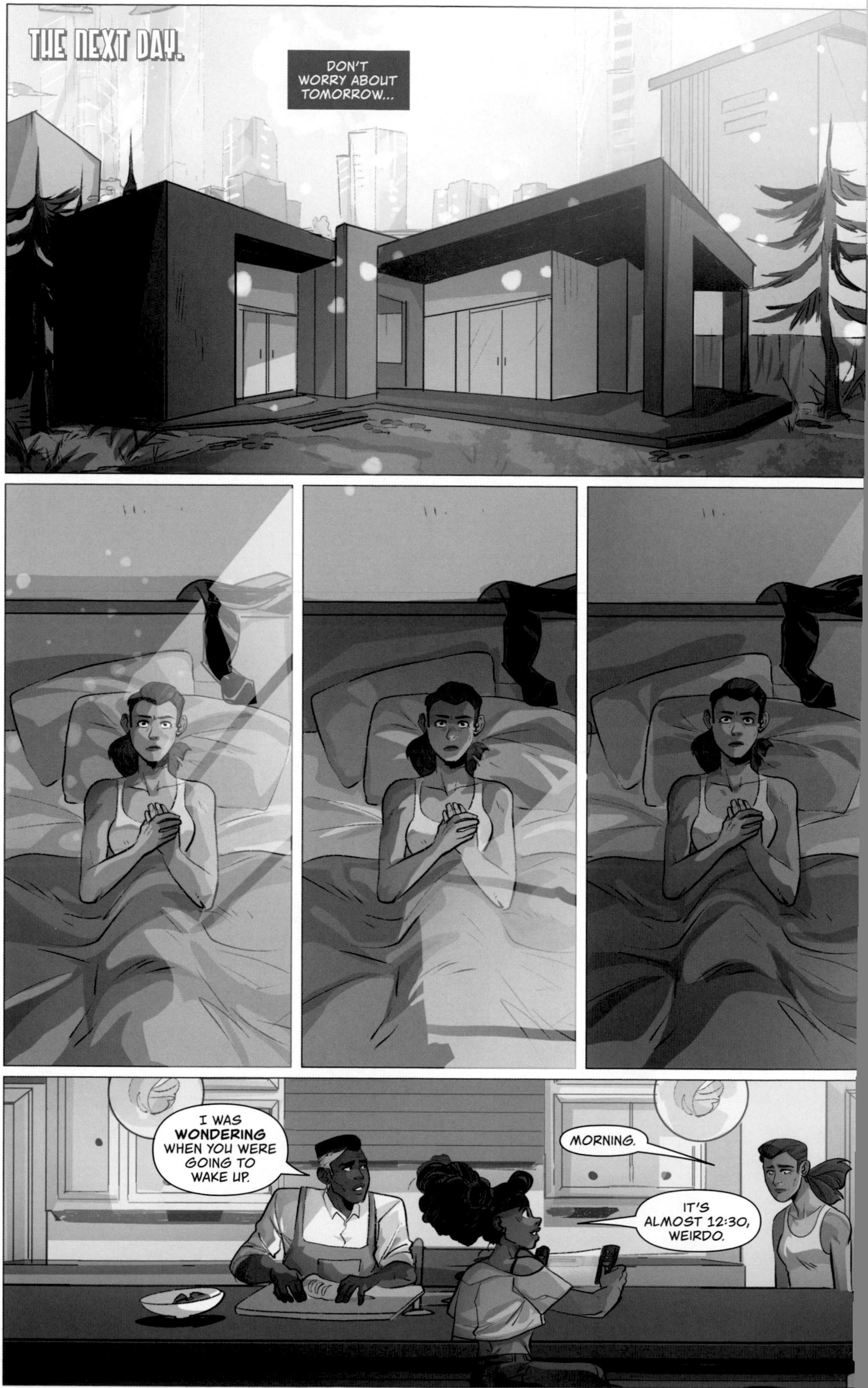
THE NEXT DAY.
DON'T WORRY ABOUT TOMORROW...
I WAS WONDERING WHEN YOU WERE GOING TO WAKE UP.
MORNING.
IT'S ALMOST 12:30, WEIRDO.

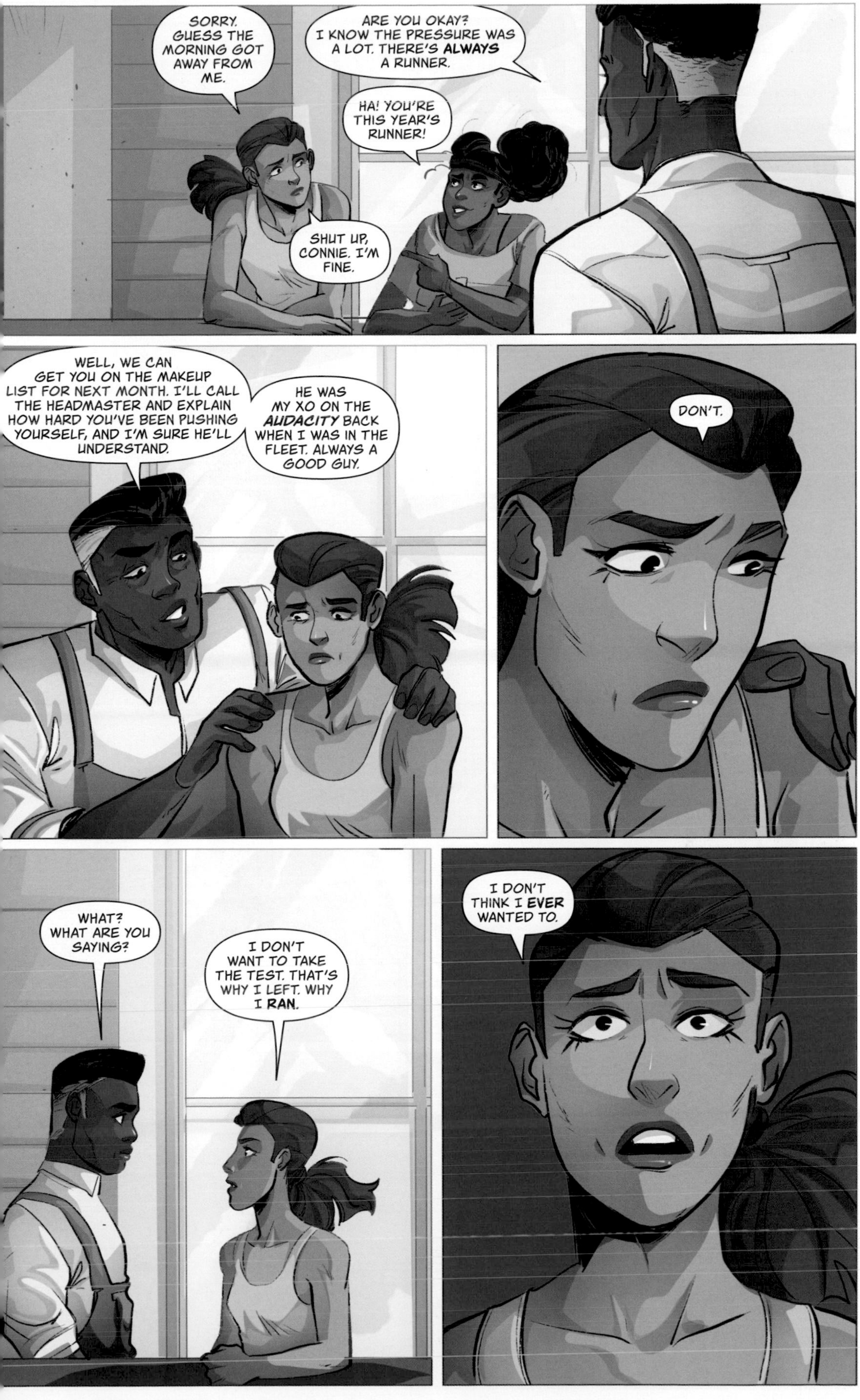
SORRY. GUESS THE MORNING GOT AWAY FROM ME.
ARE YOU OKAY? I KNOW THE PRESSURE WAS A LOT. THERE'S **ALWAYS** A RUNNER.
HA! YOU'RE THIS YEAR'S RUNNER!
SHUT UP, CONNIE. I'M FINE.
WELL, WE CAN GET YOU ON THE MAKEUP LIST FOR NEXT MONTH. I'LL CALL THE HEADMASTER AND EXPLAIN HOW HARD YOU'VE BEEN PUSHING YOURSELF, AND I'M SURE HE'LL UNDERSTAND.
HE WAS MY XO ON THE ***AUDACITY*** BACK WHEN I WAS IN THE FLEET. ALWAYS A GOOD GUY.
DON'T.
WHAT? WHAT ARE YOU SAYING?
I DON'T WANT TO TAKE THE TEST. THAT'S WHY I LEFT. WHY I **RAN**.
I DON'T THINK I **EVER** WANTED TO.

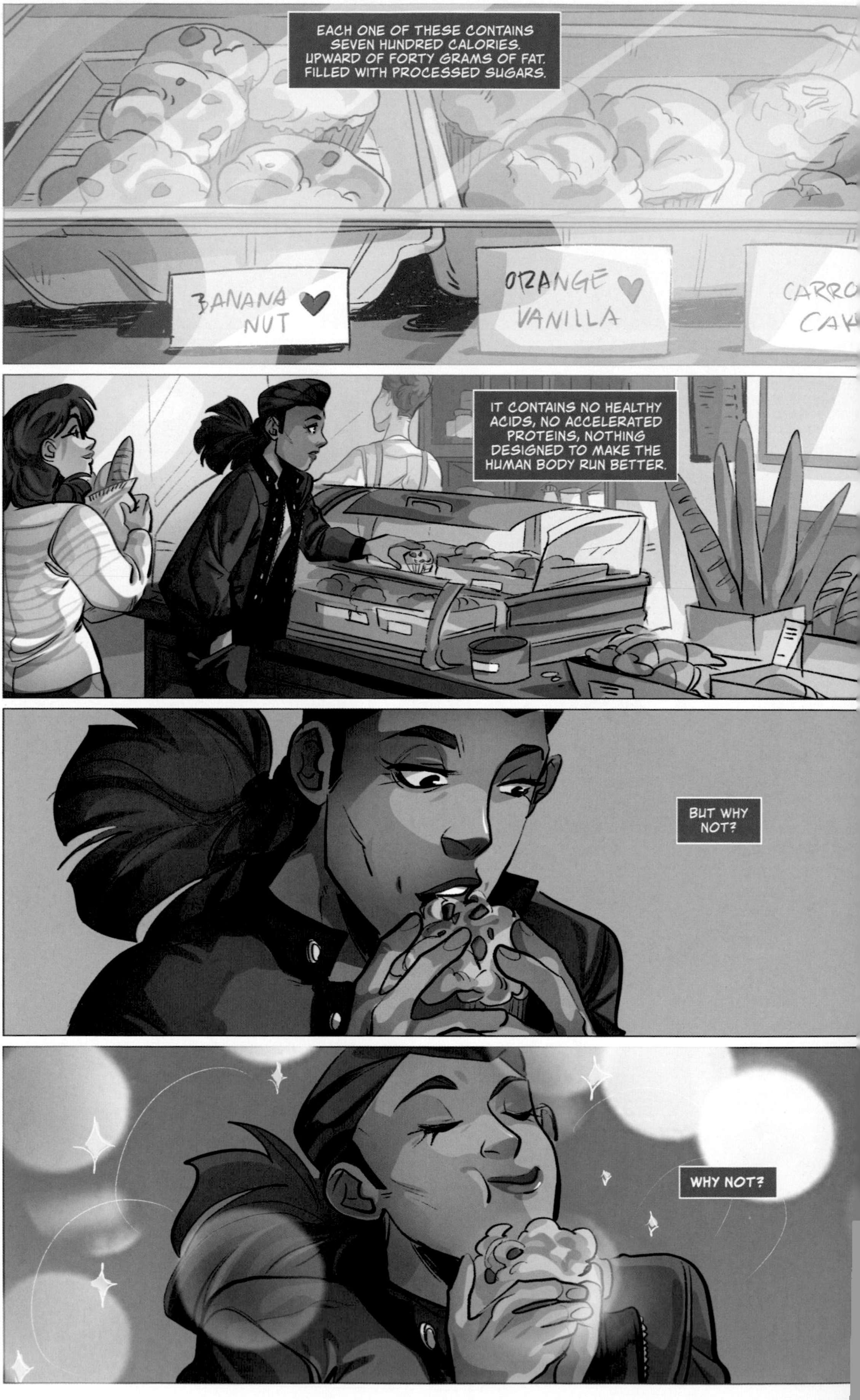
EACH ONE OF THESE CONTAINS SEVEN HUNDRED CALORIES. UPWARD OF FORTY GRAMS OF FAT. FILLED WITH PROCESSED SUGARS.
BANANA NUT
ORANGE VANILLA
IT CONTAINS NO HEALTHY ACIDS, NO ACCELERATED PROTEINS, NOTHING DESIGNED TO MAKE THE HUMAN BODY RUN BETTER.
BUT WHY NOT?
WHY NOT?

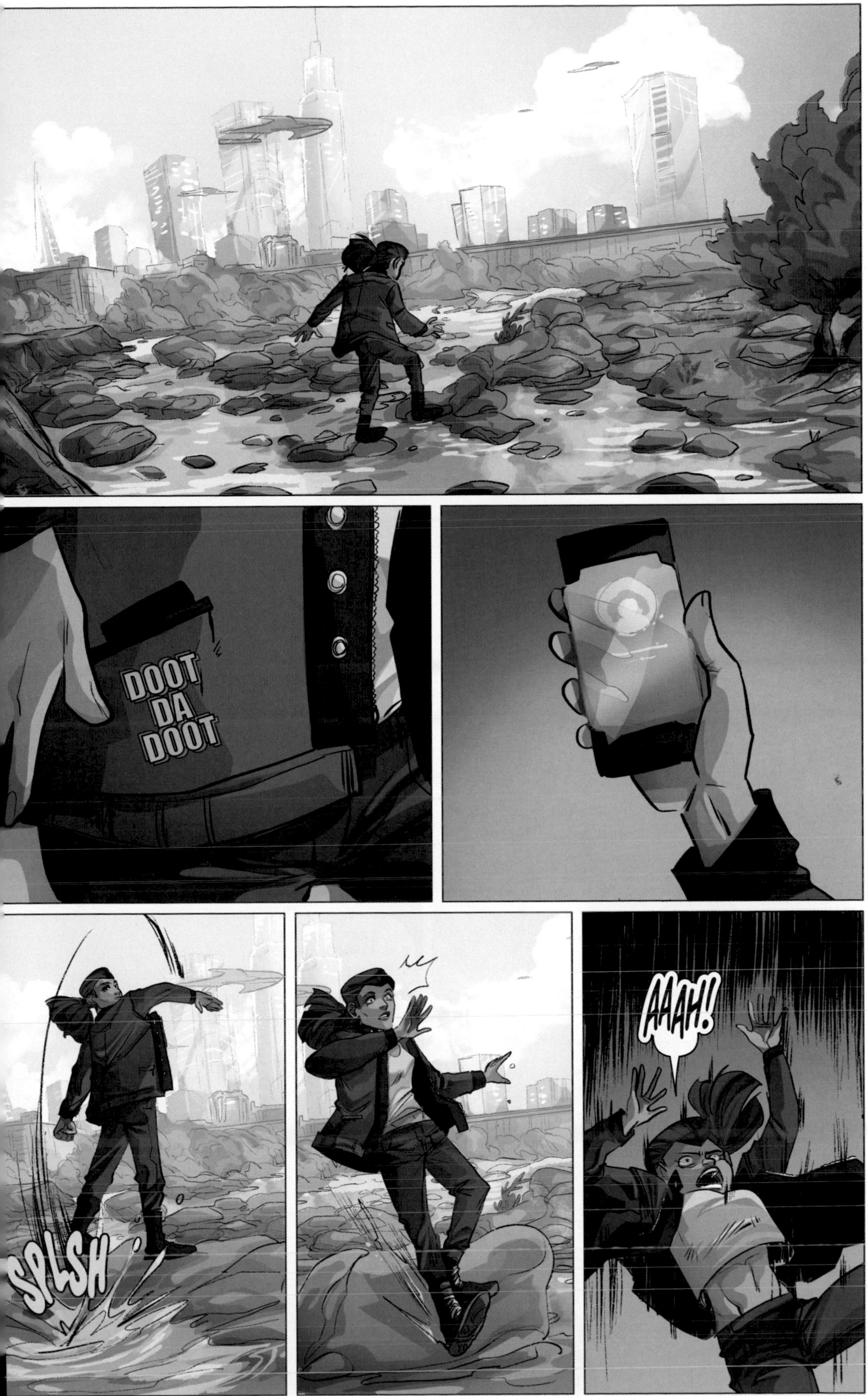
DOOT
DA
DOOT
SPLSH
AAAH!

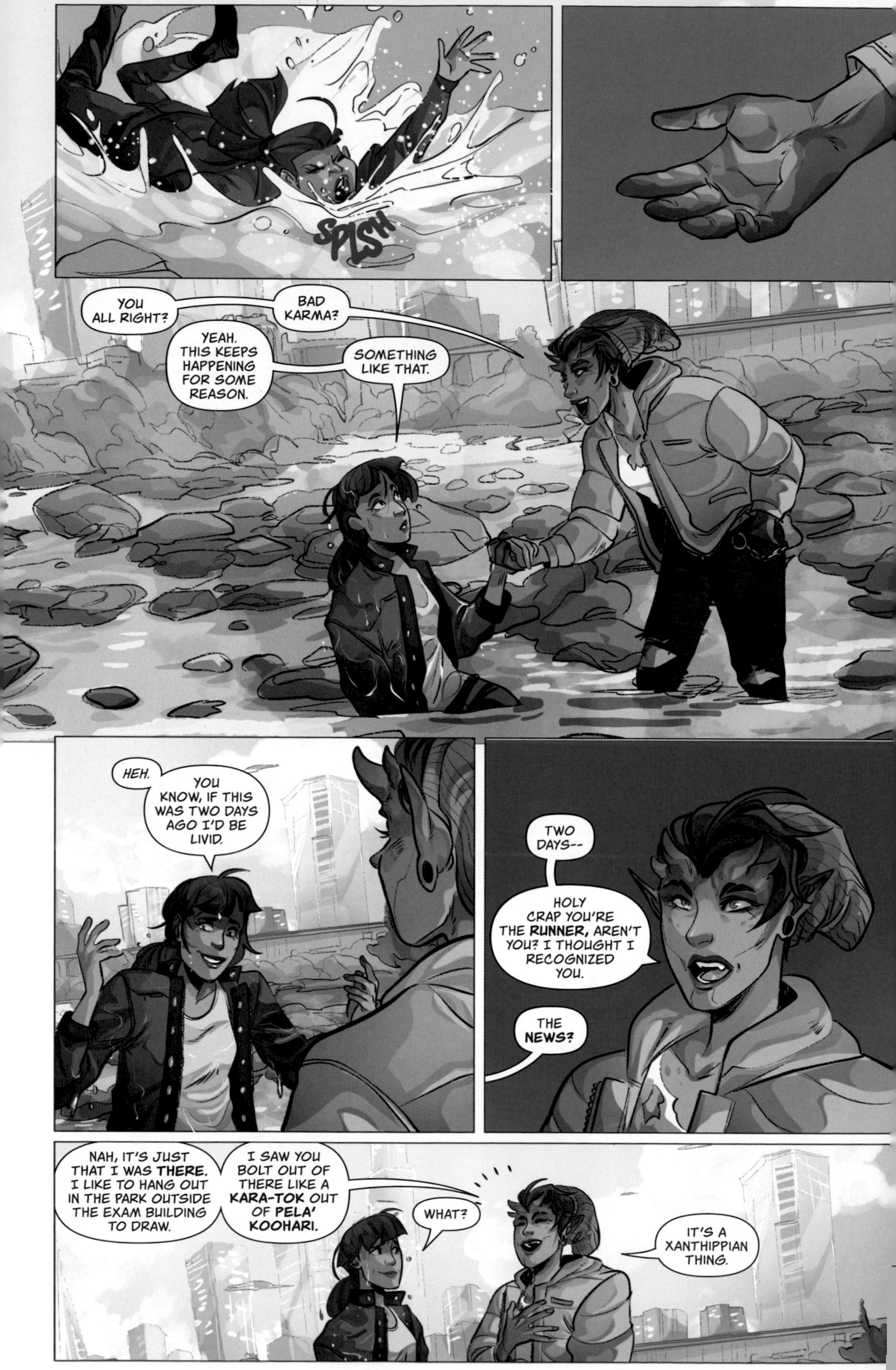
SPLSH
YOU ALL RIGHT?
BAD KARMA?
YEAH. THIS KEEPS HAPPENING FOR SOME REASON.
SOMETHING LIKE THAT.
HEH.
YOU KNOW, IF THIS WAS TWO DAYS AGO I'D BE LIVID.
TWO DAYS--
HOLY CRAP YOU'RE THE RUNNER, AREN'T YOU? I THOUGHT I RECOGNIZED YOU.
THE NEWS?
NAH, IT'S JUST THAT I WAS THERE. I LIKE TO HANG OUT IN THE PARK OUTSIDE THE EXAM BUILDING TO DRAW.
I SAW YOU BOLT OUT OF THERE LIKE A KARA-TOK OUT OF PELA' KOOHARI.
WHAT?
IT'S A XANTHIPPIAN THING.

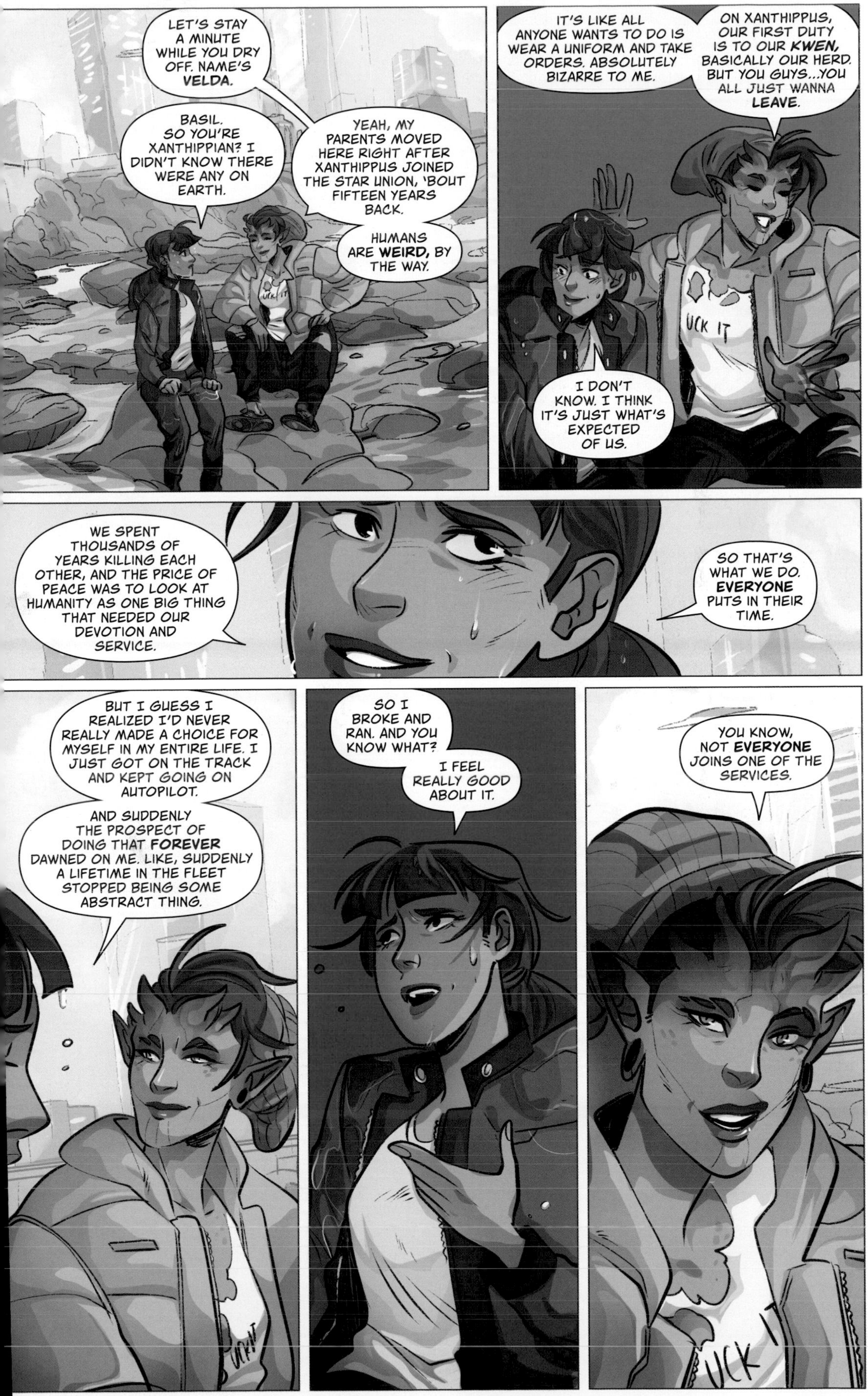
LET'S STAY A MINUTE WHILE YOU DRY OFF. NAME'S **VELDA.**
BASIL. SO YOU'RE XANTHIPPIAN? I DIDN'T KNOW THERE WERE ANY ON EARTH.
YEAH, MY PARENTS MOVED HERE RIGHT AFTER XANTHIPPUS JOINED THE STAR UNION, 'BOUT FIFTEEN YEARS BACK.
HUMANS ARE **WEIRD,** BY THE WAY.
UCK IT
IT'S LIKE ALL ANYONE WANTS TO DO IS WEAR A UNIFORM AND TAKE ORDERS. ABSOLUTELY BIZARRE TO ME.
ON XANTHIPPUS, OUR FIRST DUTY IS TO OUR **KWEN,** BASICALLY OUR HERD. BUT YOU GUYS...YOU ALL JUST WANNA **LEAVE.**
UCK IT
I DON'T KNOW. I THINK IT'S JUST WHAT'S EXPECTED OF US.
WE SPENT THOUSANDS OF YEARS KILLING EACH OTHER, AND THE PRICE OF PEACE WAS TO LOOK AT HUMANITY AS ONE BIG THING THAT NEEDED OUR DEVOTION AND SERVICE.
SO THAT'S WHAT WE DO. **EVERYONE** PUTS IN THEIR TIME.
BUT I GUESS I REALIZED I'D NEVER REALLY MADE A CHOICE FOR MYSELF IN MY ENTIRE LIFE. I JUST GOT ON THE TRACK AND KEPT GOING ON AUTOPILOT.
AND SUDDENLY THE PROSPECT OF DOING THAT **FOREVER** DAWNED ON ME. LIKE, SUDDENLY A LIFETIME IN THE FLEET STOPPED BEING SOME ABSTRACT THING.
UCK IT
SO I BROKE AND RAN. AND YOU KNOW WHAT?
I FEEL REALLY GOOD ABOUT IT.
YOU KNOW, NOT **EVERYONE** JOINS ONE OF THE SERVICES.
UCK IT

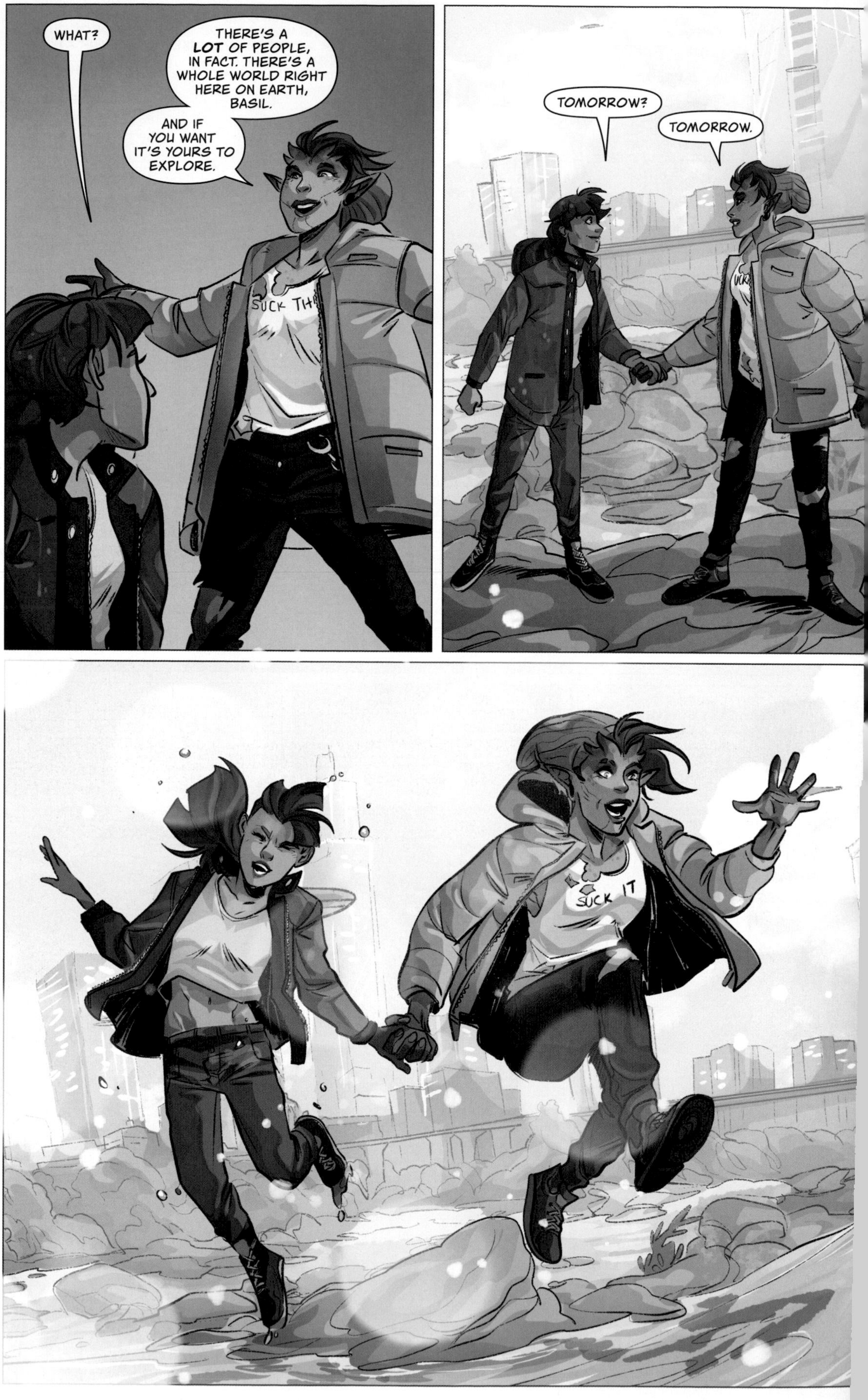
WHAT?
THERE'S A LOT OF PEOPLE, IN FACT. THERE'S A WHOLE WORLD RIGHT HERE ON EARTH, BASIL.
AND IF YOU WANT IT'S YOURS TO EXPLORE.
SUCK TH
TOMORROW?
TOMORROW.
SUCK IT

Chapter **Two**

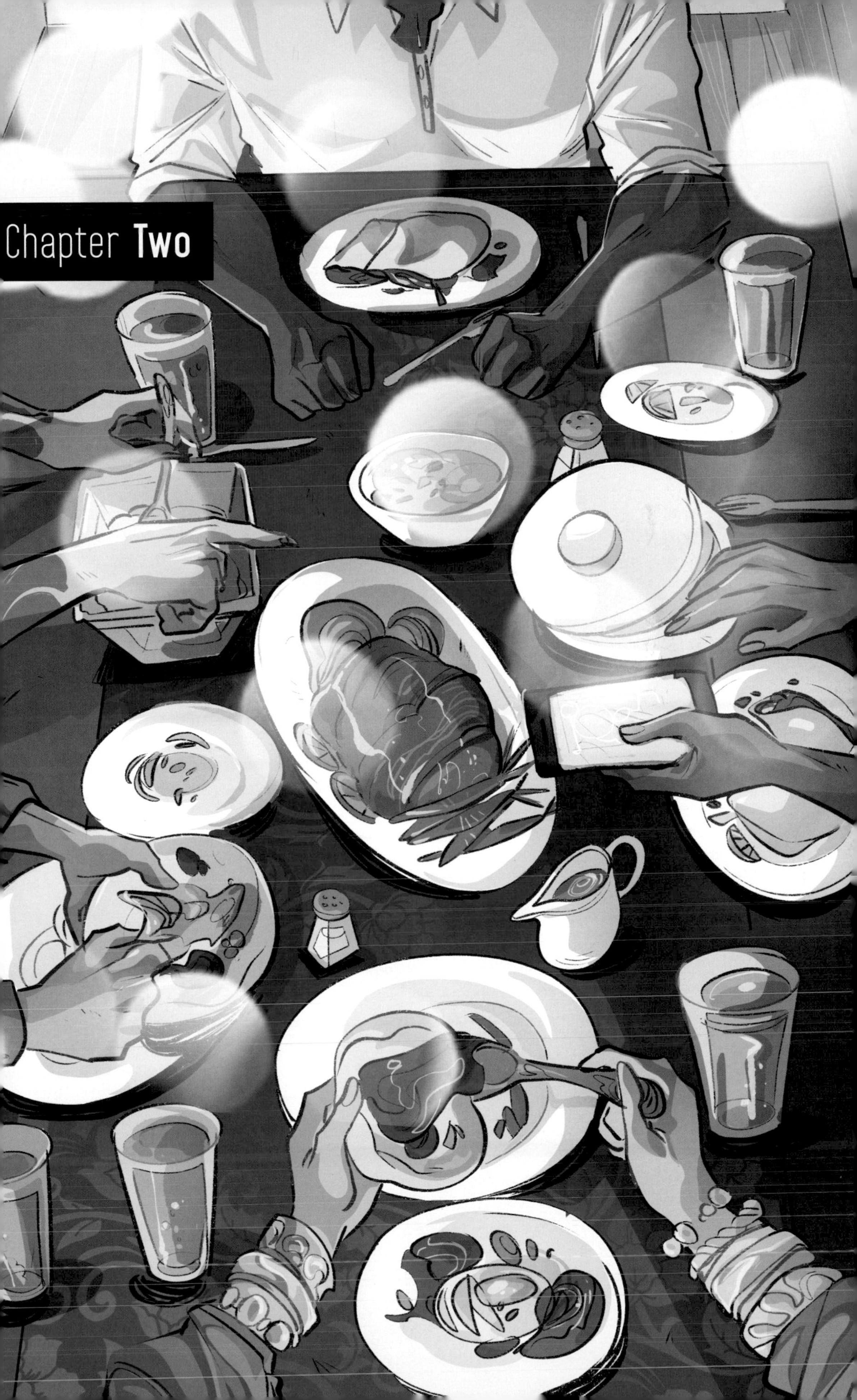

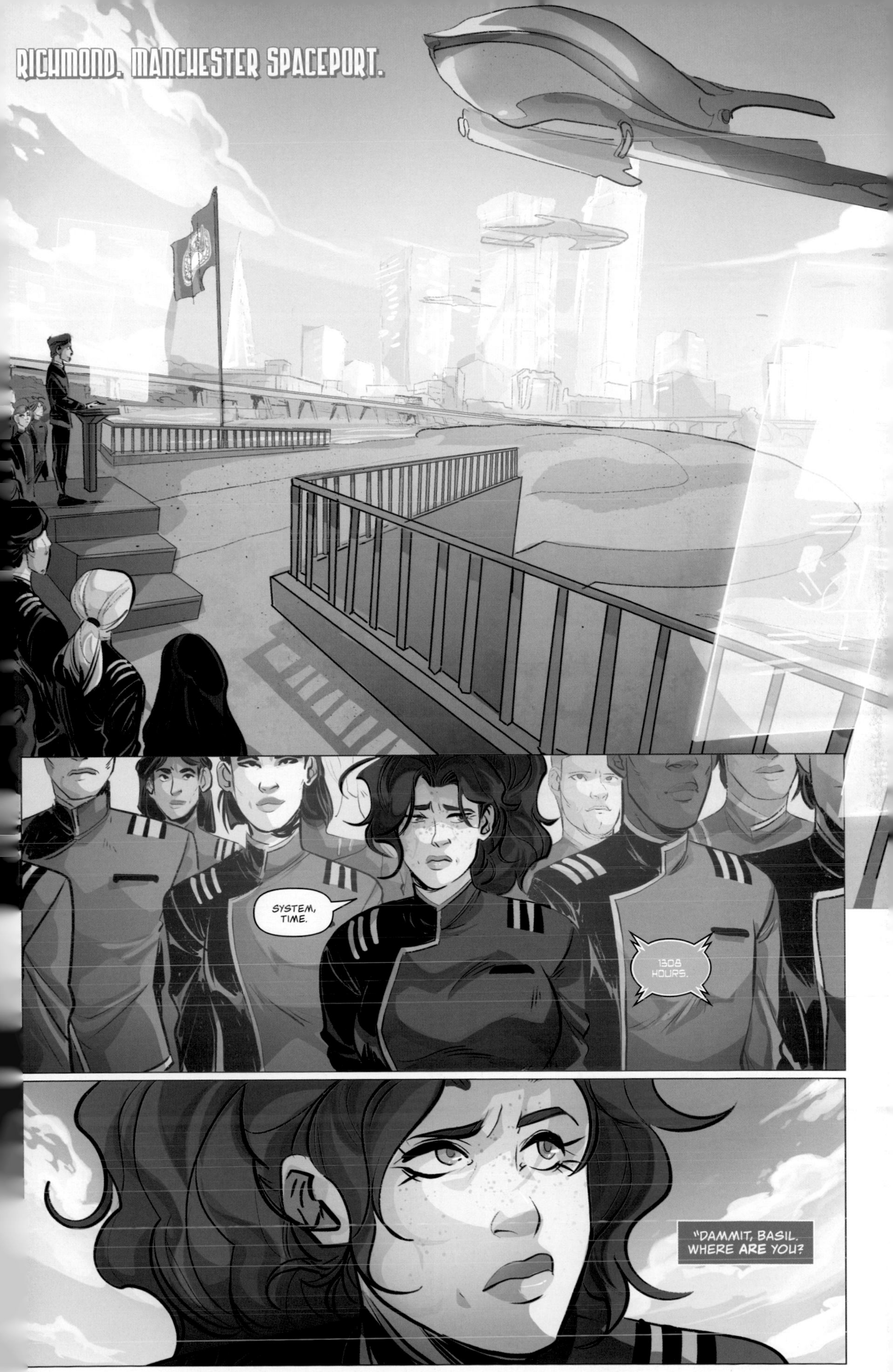
RICHMOND. MANCHESTER SPACEPORT.
SYSTEM, TIME.
1308 HOURS.
"DAMMIT, BASIL. WHERE ARE YOU?

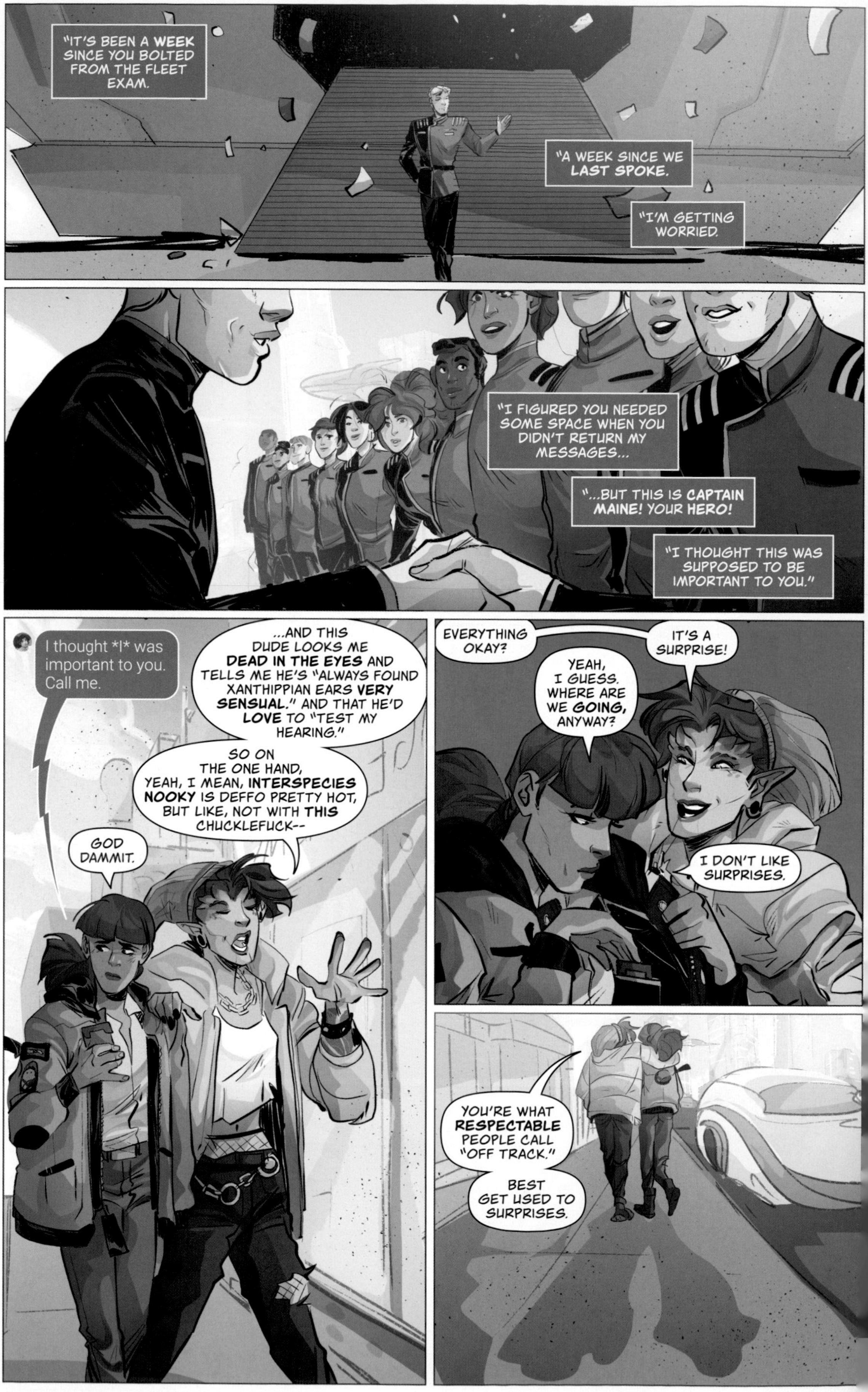
"IT'S BEEN A WEEK SINCE YOU BOLTED FROM THE FLEET EXAM.
"A WEEK SINCE WE LAST SPOKE.
"I'M GETTING WORRIED.
"I FIGURED YOU NEEDED SOME SPACE WHEN YOU DIDN'T RETURN MY MESSAGES...
"...BUT THIS IS CAPTAIN MAINE! YOUR HERO!
"I THOUGHT THIS WAS SUPPOSED TO BE IMPORTANT TO YOU."
I thought *I* was important to you. Call me.
...AND THIS DUDE LOOKS ME DEAD IN THE EYES AND TELLS ME HE'S "ALWAYS FOUND XANTHIPPIAN EARS VERY SENSUAL." AND THAT HE'D LOVE TO "TEST MY HEARING."
SO ON THE ONE HAND, YEAH, I MEAN, INTERSPECIES NOOKY IS DEFFO PRETTY HOT, BUT LIKE, NOT WITH THIS CHUCKLEFUCK--
GOD DAMMIT.
EVERYTHING OKAY?
IT'S A SURPRISE!
YEAH, I GUESS. WHERE ARE WE GOING, ANYWAY?
I DON'T LIKE SURPRISES.
YOU'RE WHAT RESPECTABLE PEOPLE CALL "OFF TRACK."
BEST GET USED TO SURPRISES.

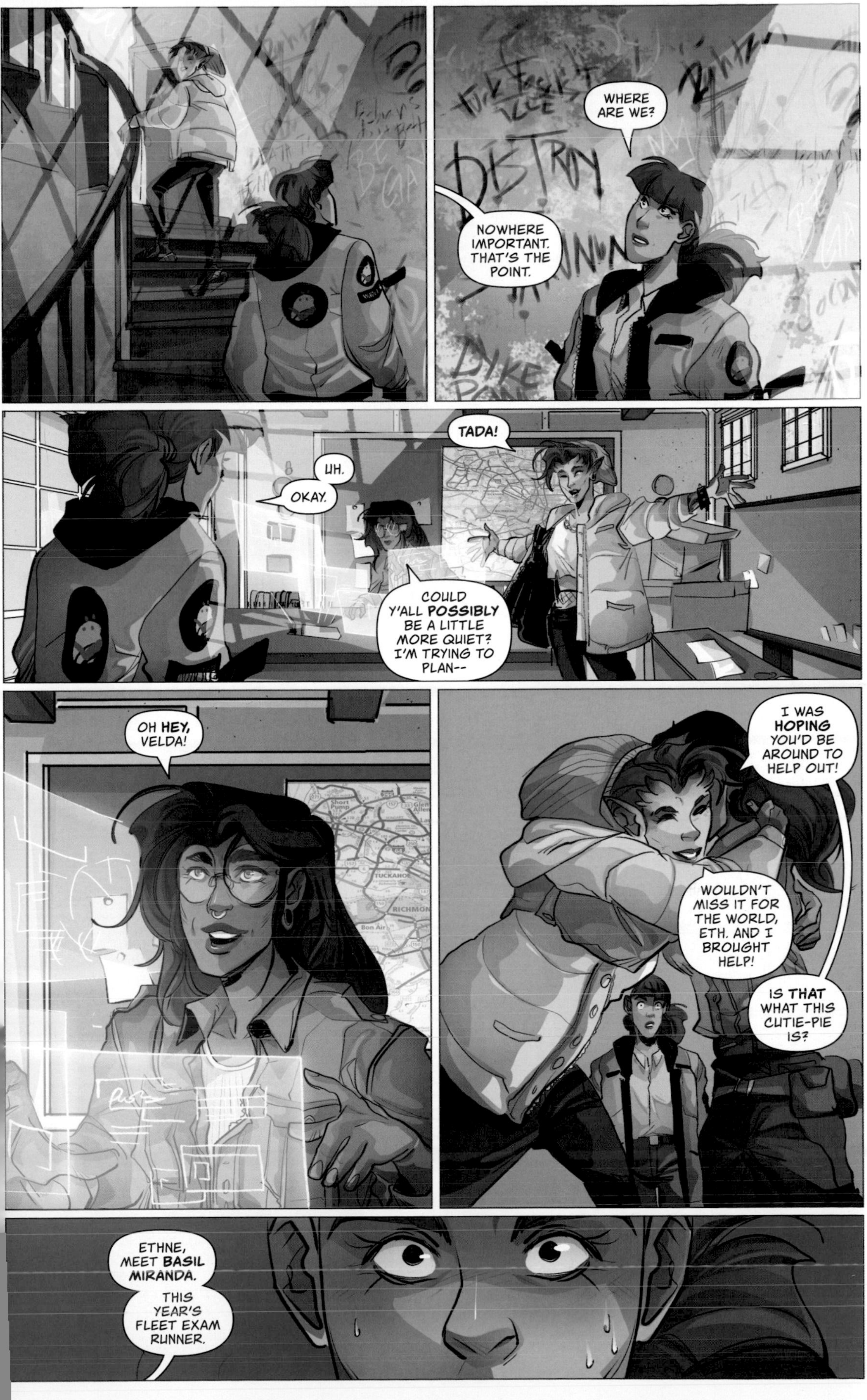

WHERE ARE WE?
NOWHERE IMPORTANT. THAT'S THE POINT.
DESTROY
DYKE
TADA!
UH.
OKAY.
COULD Y'ALL **POSSIBLY** BE A LITTLE MORE QUIET? I'M TRYING TO PLAN--
OH **HEY,** VELDA!
I WAS **HOPING** YOU'D BE AROUND TO HELP OUT!
WOULDN'T MISS IT FOR THE WORLD, ETH. AND I BROUGHT HELP!
IS **THAT** WHAT THIS CUTIE-PIE IS?
ETHNE, MEET **BASIL MIRANDA.**
THIS YEAR'S FLEET EXAM RUNNER.

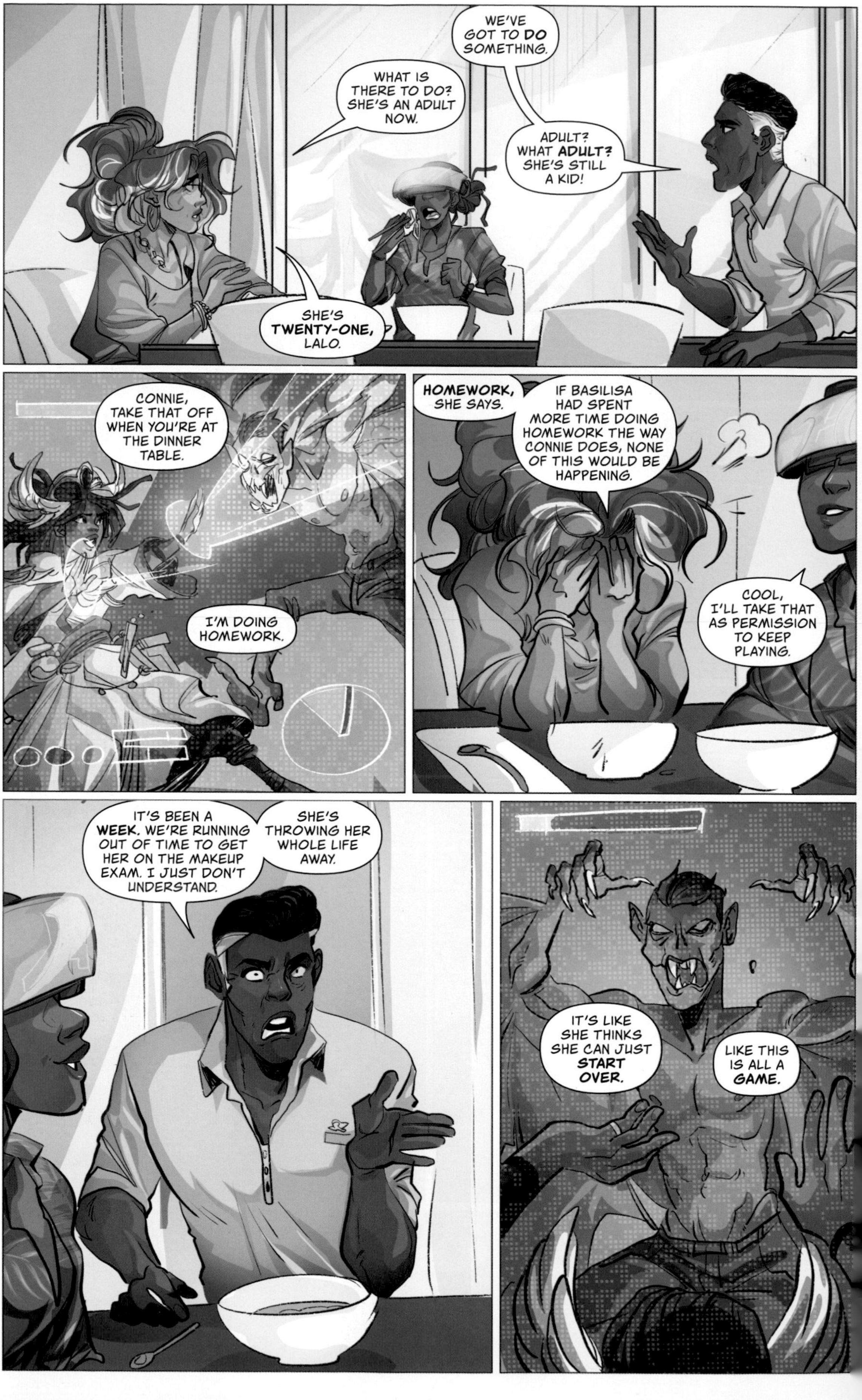
WHAT IS THERE TO DO? SHE'S AN ADULT NOW.
WE'VE GOT TO DO SOMETHING.
ADULT? WHAT ADULT? SHE'S STILL A KID!
SHE'S TWENTY-ONE, LALO.
CONNIE, TAKE THAT OFF WHEN YOU'RE AT THE DINNER TABLE.
I'M DOING HOMEWORK.
HOMEWORK, SHE SAYS.
IF BASILISA HAD SPENT MORE TIME DOING HOMEWORK THE WAY CONNIE DOES, NONE OF THIS WOULD BE HAPPENING.
COOL, I'LL TAKE THAT AS PERMISSION TO KEEP PLAYING.
IT'S BEEN A WEEK. WE'RE RUNNING OUT OF TIME TO GET HER ON THE MAKEUP EXAM. I JUST DON'T UNDERSTAND.
SHE'S THROWING HER WHOLE LIFE AWAY.
IT'S LIKE SHE THINKS SHE CAN JUST START OVER.
LIKE THIS IS ALL A GAME.

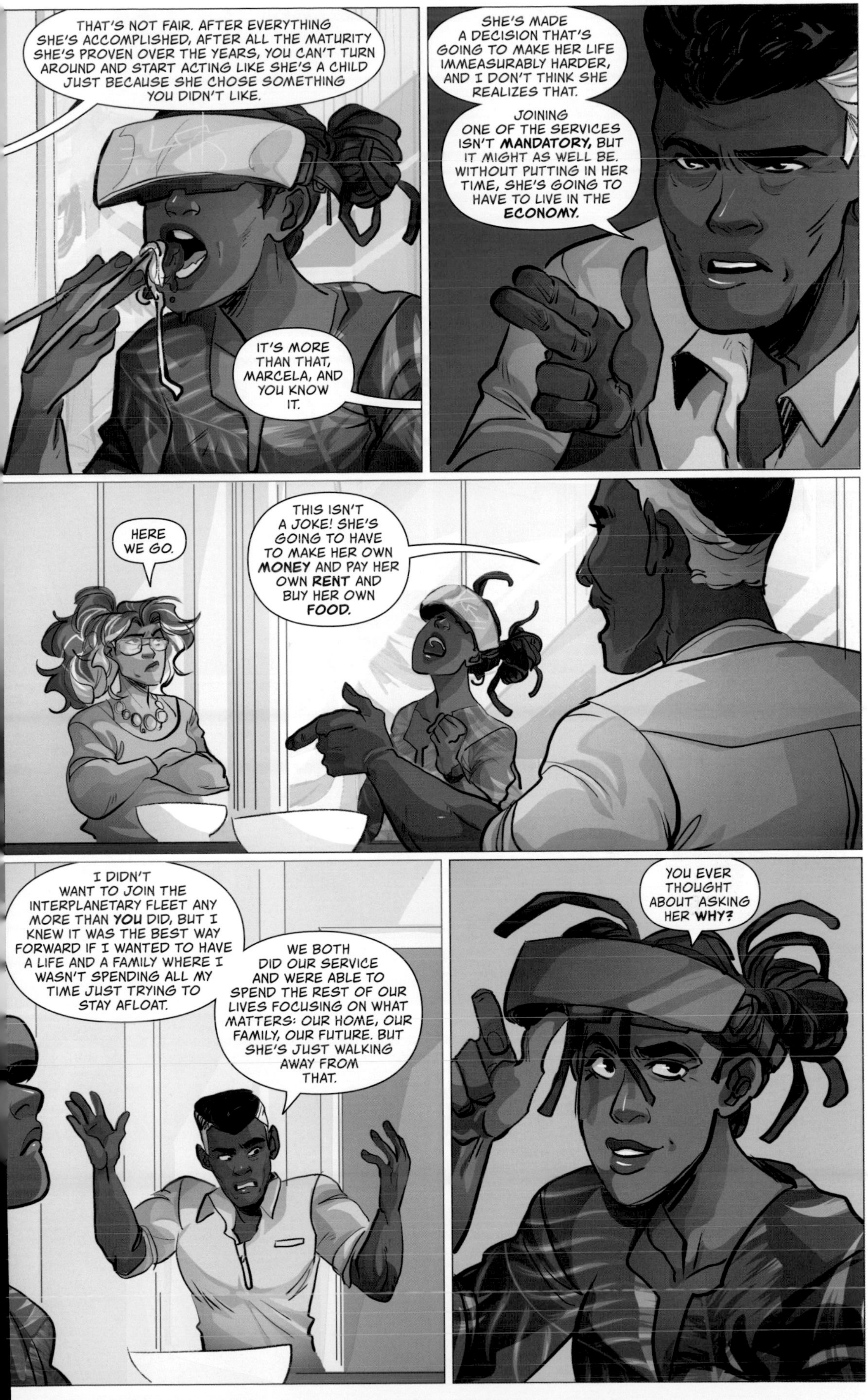
THAT'S NOT FAIR. AFTER EVERYTHING SHE'S ACCOMPLISHED, AFTER ALL THE MATURITY SHE'S PROVEN OVER THE YEARS, YOU CAN'T TURN AROUND AND START ACTING LIKE SHE'S A CHILD JUST BECAUSE SHE CHOSE SOMETHING YOU DIDN'T LIKE.
IT'S MORE THAN THAT, MARCELA, AND YOU KNOW IT.
SHE'S MADE A DECISION THAT'S GOING TO MAKE HER LIFE IMMEASURABLY HARDER, AND I DON'T THINK SHE REALIZES THAT.
JOINING ONE OF THE SERVICES ISN'T **MANDATORY,** BUT IT MIGHT AS WELL BE. WITHOUT PUTTING IN HER TIME, SHE'S GOING TO HAVE TO LIVE IN THE **ECONOMY.**
HERE WE GO.
THIS ISN'T A JOKE! SHE'S GOING TO HAVE TO MAKE HER OWN **MONEY** AND PAY HER OWN **RENT** AND BUY HER OWN **FOOD.**
I DIDN'T WANT TO JOIN THE INTERPLANETARY FLEET ANY MORE THAN **YOU** DID, BUT I KNEW IT WAS THE BEST WAY FORWARD IF I WANTED TO HAVE A LIFE AND A FAMILY WHERE I WASN'T SPENDING ALL MY TIME JUST TRYING TO STAY AFLOAT.
WE BOTH DID OUR SERVICE AND WERE ABLE TO SPEND THE REST OF OUR LIVES FOCUSING ON WHAT MATTERS: OUR HOME, OUR FAMILY, OUR FUTURE. BUT SHE'S JUST WALKING AWAY FROM THAT.
YOU EVER THOUGHT ABOUT ASKING HER **WHY?**

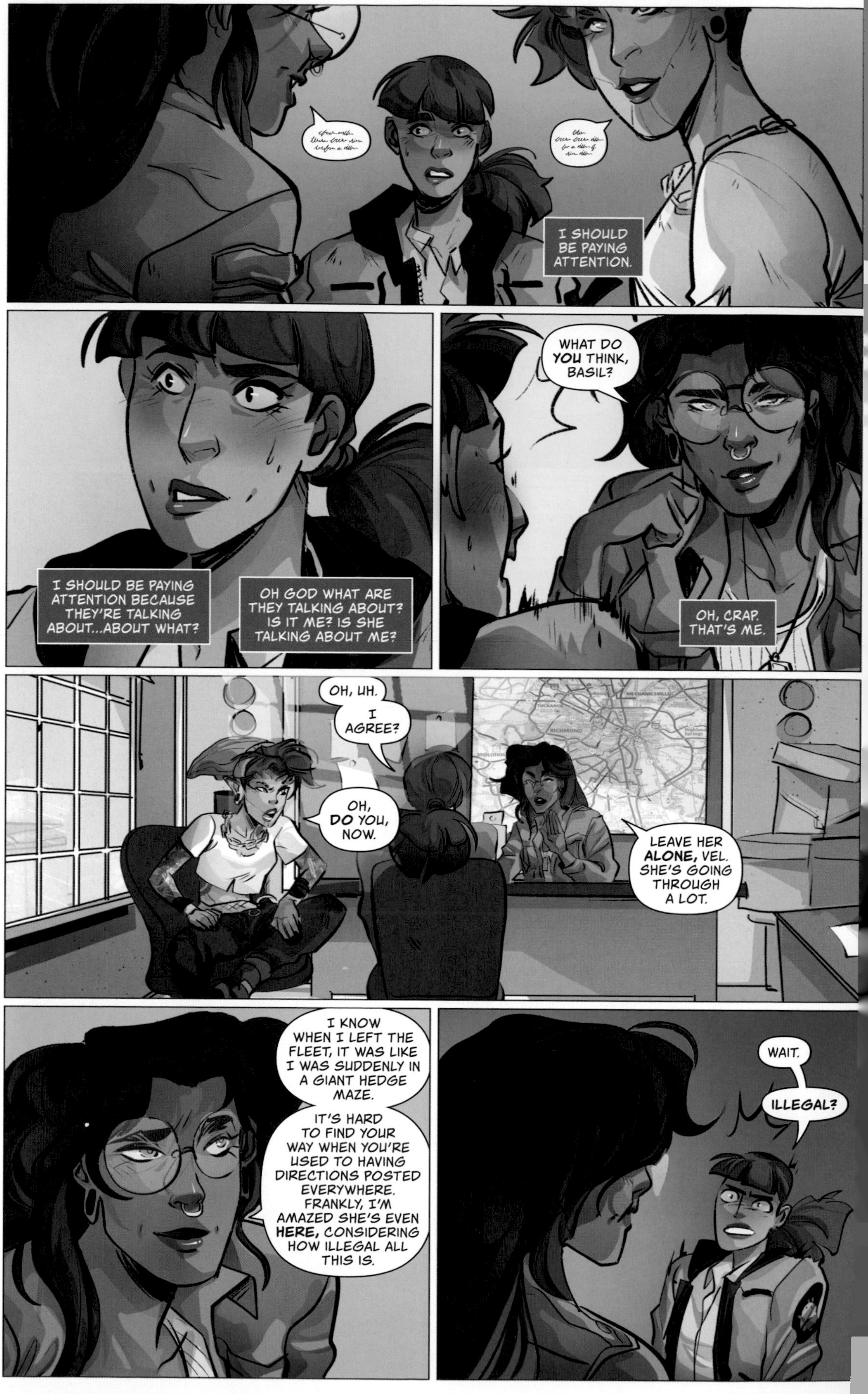
I SHOULD BE PAYING ATTENTION.
I SHOULD BE PAYING ATTENTION BECAUSE THEY'RE TALKING ABOUT...ABOUT WHAT?
OH GOD WHAT ARE THEY TALKING ABOUT? IS IT ME? IS SHE TALKING ABOUT ME?
WHAT DO YOU THINK, BASIL?
OH, CRAP. THAT'S ME.
OH, UH.
I AGREE?
OH, DO YOU, NOW.
LEAVE HER ALONE, VEL. SHE'S GOING THROUGH A LOT.
I KNOW WHEN I LEFT THE FLEET, IT WAS LIKE I WAS SUDDENLY IN A GIANT HEDGE MAZE.
IT'S HARD TO FIND YOUR WAY WHEN YOU'RE USED TO HAVING DIRECTIONS POSTED EVERYWHERE. FRANKLY, I'M AMAZED SHE'S EVEN HERE, CONSIDERING HOW ILLEGAL ALL THIS IS.
WAIT.
ILLEGAL?

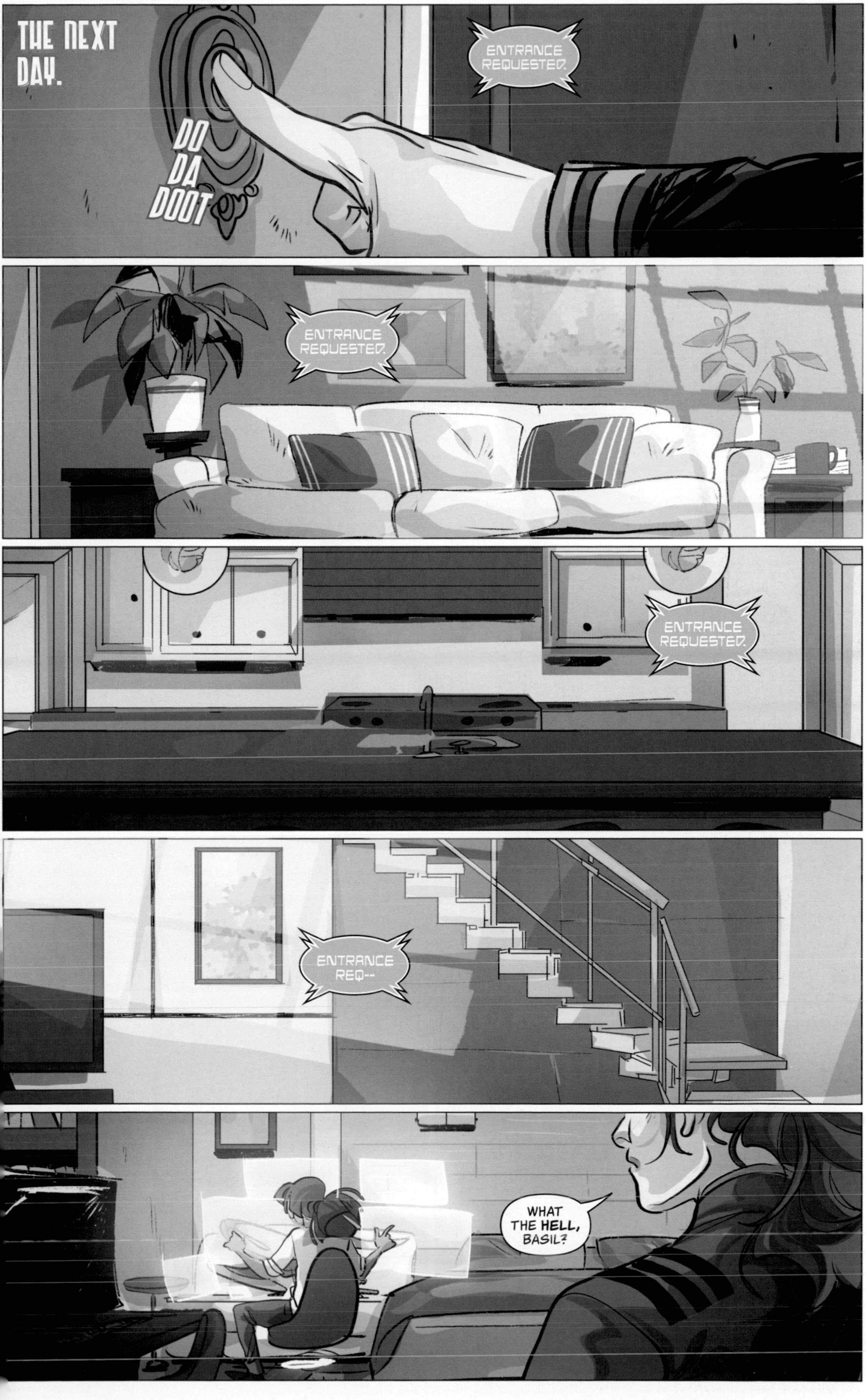
THE NEXT DAY.
ENTRANCE REQUESTED.
DO DA DOOT
ENTRANCE REQUESTED.
ENTRANCE REQUESTED.
ENTRANCE REQ--
WHAT THE HELL, BASIL?

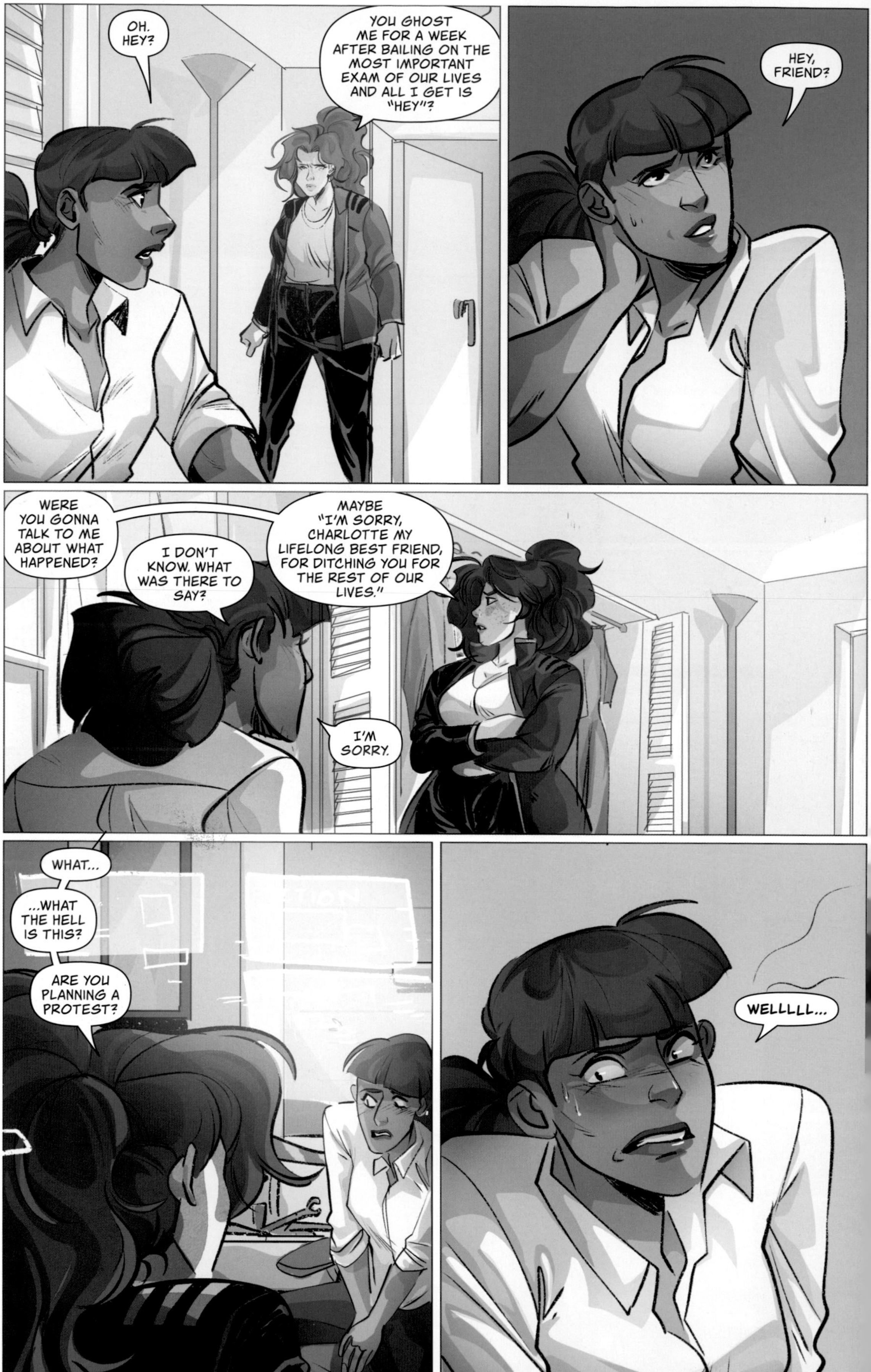
OH. HEY?
YOU GHOST ME FOR A WEEK AFTER BAILING ON THE MOST IMPORTANT EXAM OF OUR LIVES AND ALL I GET IS "HEY"?
HEY, FRIEND?
WERE YOU GONNA TALK TO ME ABOUT WHAT HAPPENED?
MAYBE "I'M SORRY, CHARLOTTE MY LIFELONG BEST FRIEND, FOR DITCHING YOU FOR THE REST OF OUR LIVES."
I DON'T KNOW. WHAT WAS THERE TO SAY?
I'M SORRY.
WHAT...
...WHAT THE HELL IS THIS?
ARE YOU PLANNING A PROTEST?
WELLLLL...

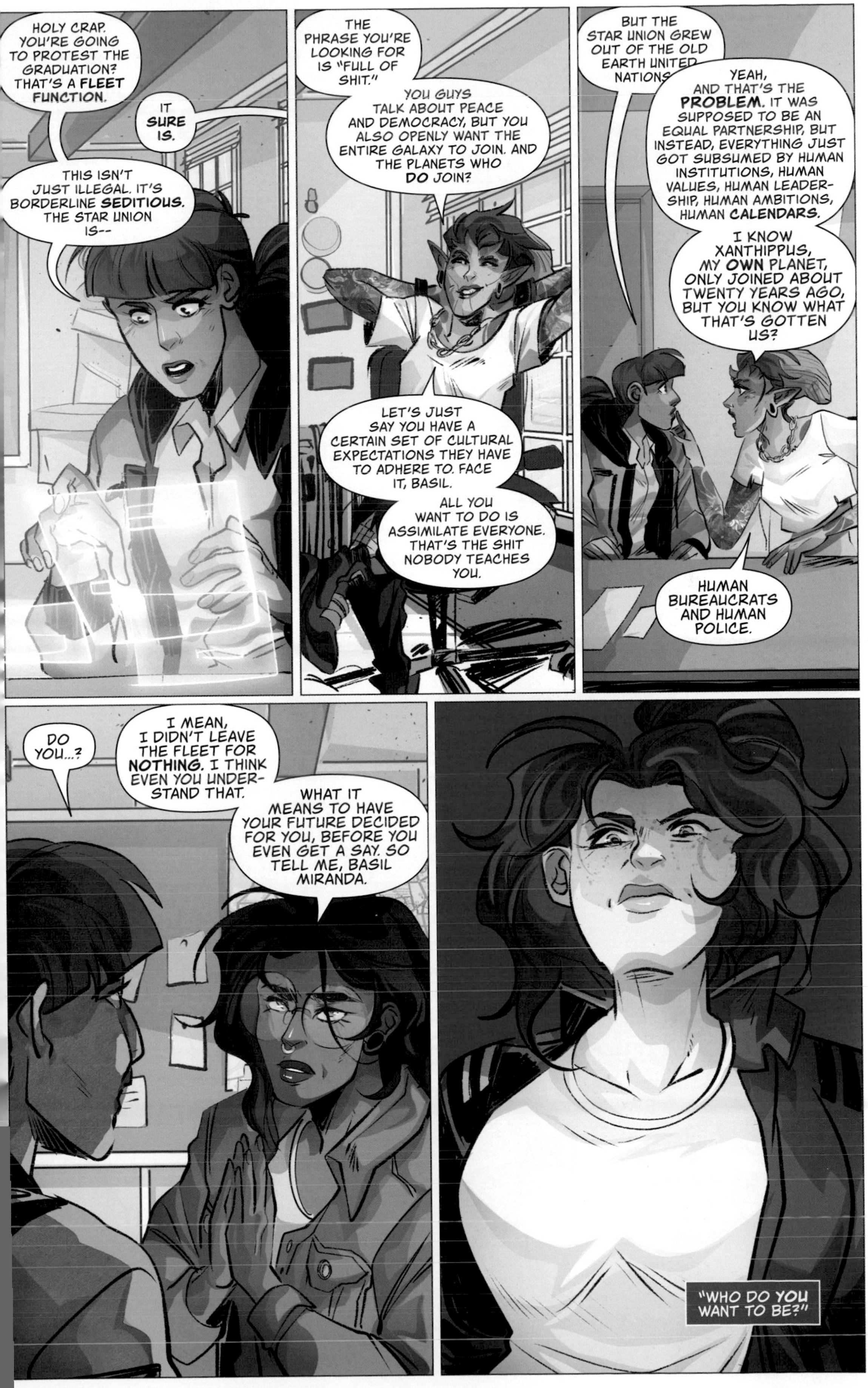
HOLY CRAP. YOU'RE GOING TO PROTEST THE GRADUATION? THAT'S A FLEET FUNCTION.
IT SURE IS.
THIS ISN'T JUST ILLEGAL. IT'S BORDERLINE SEDITIOUS. THE STAR UNION IS--
THE PHRASE YOU'RE LOOKING FOR IS "FULL OF SHIT."
YOU GUYS TALK ABOUT PEACE AND DEMOCRACY, BUT YOU ALSO OPENLY WANT THE ENTIRE GALAXY TO JOIN. AND THE PLANETS WHO DO JOIN?
LET'S JUST SAY YOU HAVE A CERTAIN SET OF CULTURAL EXPECTATIONS THEY HAVE TO ADHERE TO. FACE IT, BASIL.
ALL YOU WANT TO DO IS ASSIMILATE EVERYONE. THAT'S THE SHIT NOBODY TEACHES YOU.
BUT THE STAR UNION GREW OUT OF THE OLD EARTH UNITED NATIONS.
YEAH, AND THAT'S THE PROBLEM. IT WAS SUPPOSED TO BE AN EQUAL PARTNERSHIP, BUT INSTEAD, EVERYTHING JUST GOT SUBSUMED BY HUMAN INSTITUTIONS, HUMAN VALUES, HUMAN LEADERSHIP, HUMAN AMBITIONS, HUMAN CALENDARS.
I KNOW XANTHIPPUS, MY OWN PLANET, ONLY JOINED ABOUT TWENTY YEARS AGO, BUT YOU KNOW WHAT THAT'S GOTTEN US?
HUMAN BUREAUCRATS AND HUMAN POLICE.
DO YOU...?
I MEAN, I DIDN'T LEAVE THE FLEET FOR NOTHING. I THINK EVEN YOU UNDERSTAND THAT.
WHAT IT MEANS TO HAVE YOUR FUTURE DECIDED FOR YOU, BEFORE YOU EVEN GET A SAY. SO TELL ME, BASIL MIRANDA.
"WHO DO YOU WANT TO BE?"

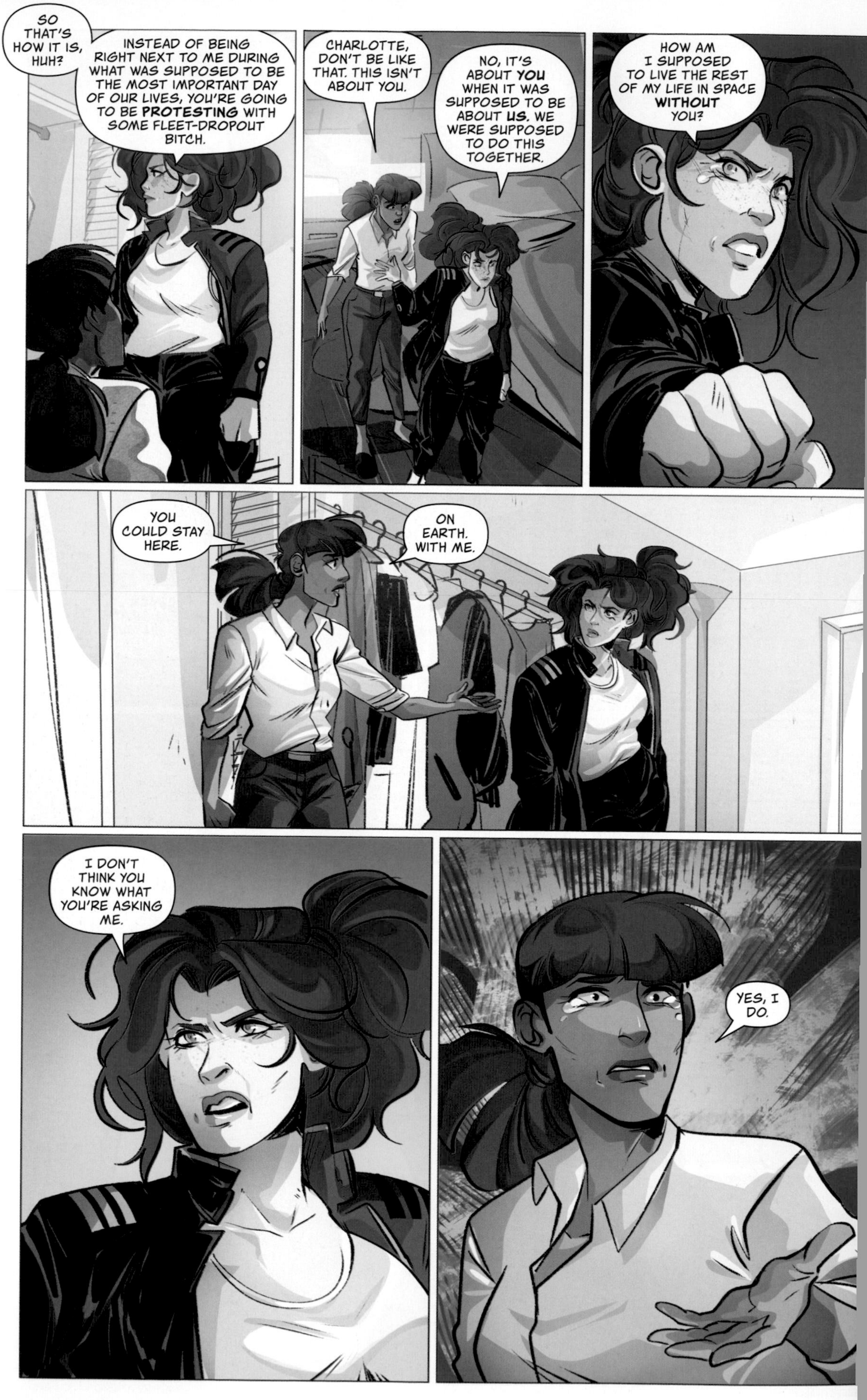
SO THAT'S HOW IT IS, HUH?
INSTEAD OF BEING RIGHT NEXT TO ME DURING WHAT WAS SUPPOSED TO BE THE MOST IMPORTANT DAY OF OUR LIVES, YOU'RE GOING TO BE **PROTESTING** WITH SOME FLEET-DROPOUT BITCH.
CHARLOTTE, DON'T BE LIKE THAT. THIS ISN'T ABOUT YOU.
NO, IT'S ABOUT **YOU** WHEN IT WAS SUPPOSED TO BE ABOUT **US.** WE WERE SUPPOSED TO DO THIS TOGETHER.
HOW AM I SUPPOSED TO LIVE THE REST OF MY LIFE IN SPACE **WITHOUT** YOU?
YOU COULD STAY HERE.
ON EARTH. WITH ME.
I DON'T THINK YOU KNOW WHAT YOU'RE ASKING ME.
YES, I DO.

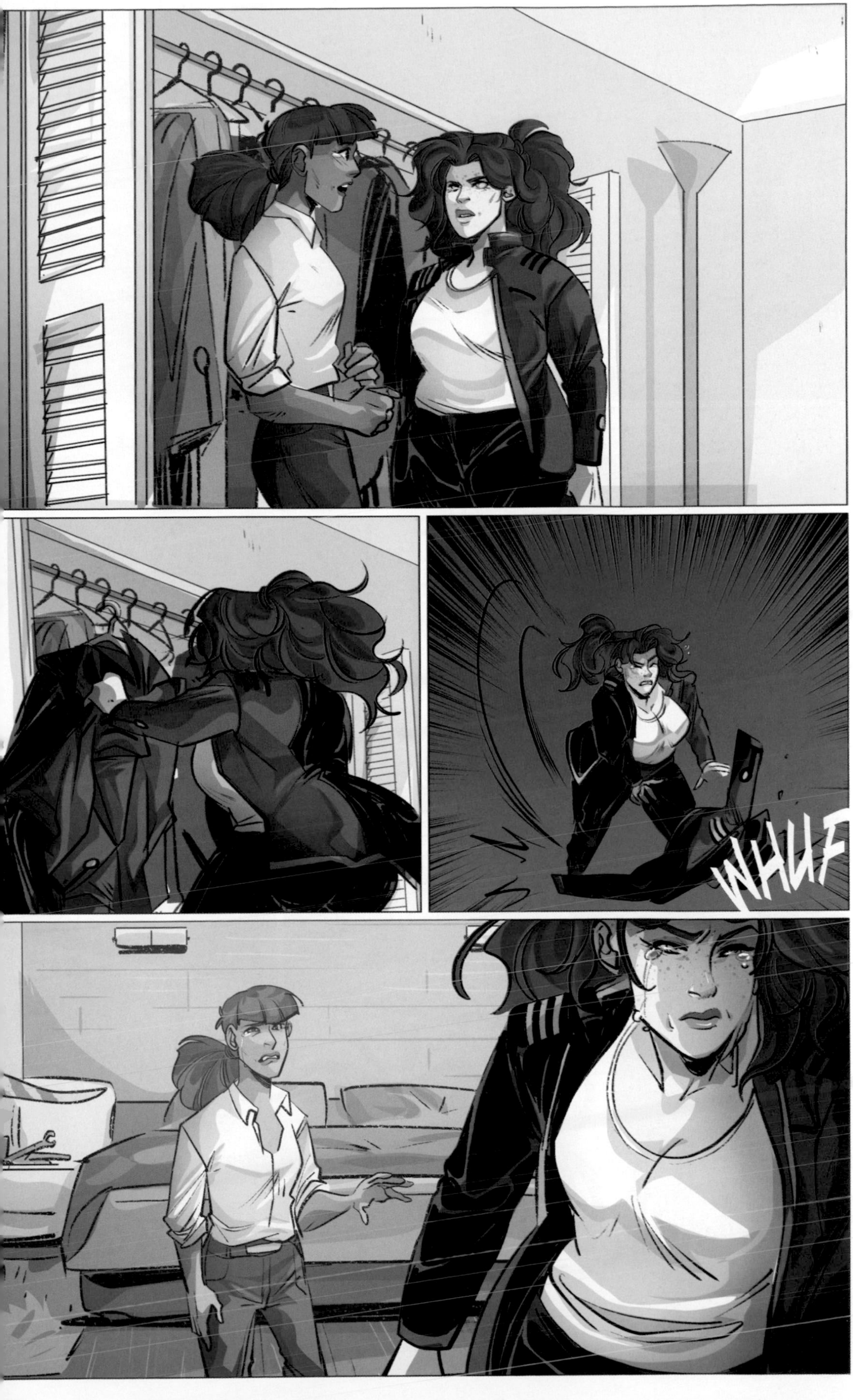
WHUF

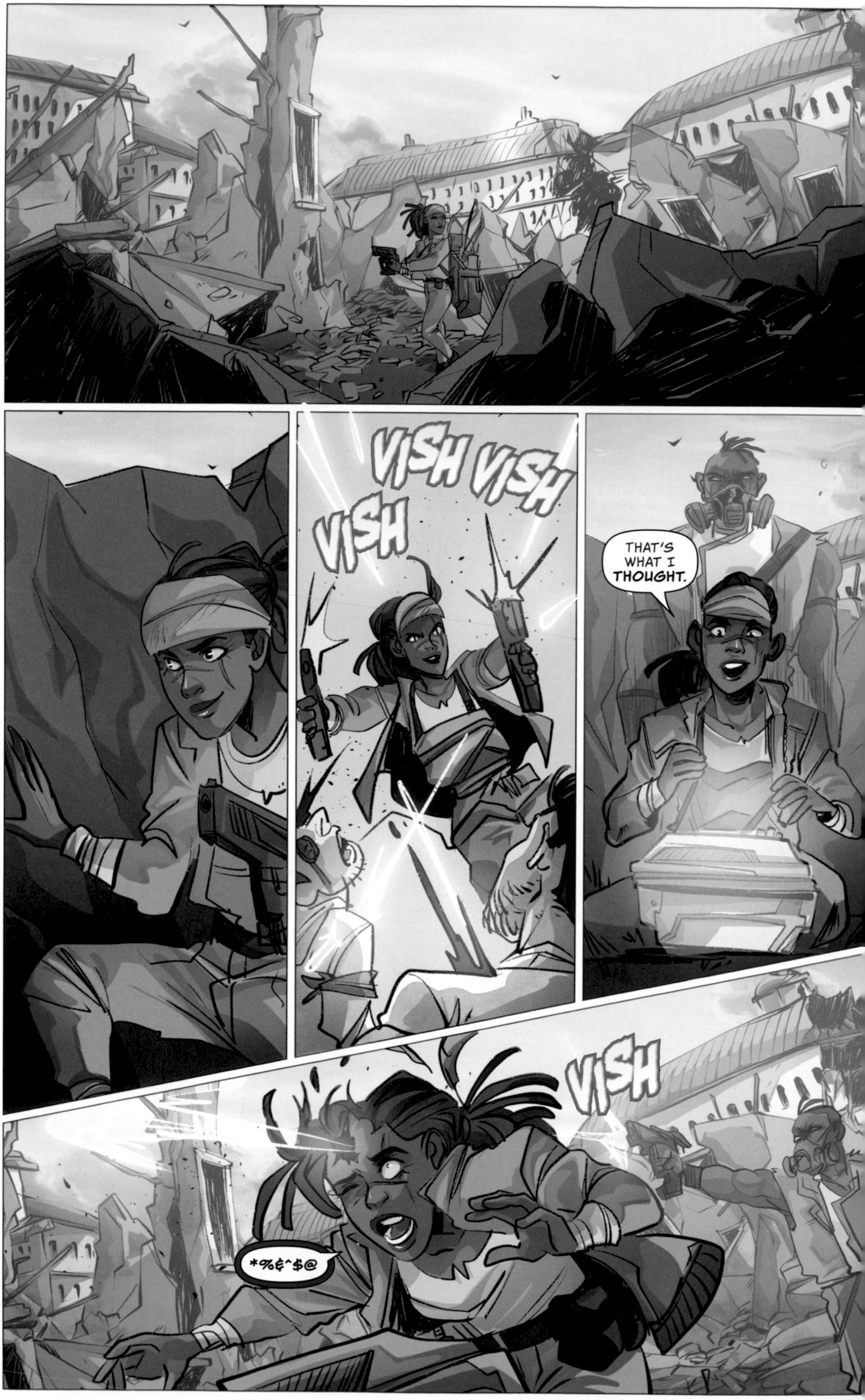
VISH VISH
VISH
THAT'S WHAT I THOUGHT.
VISH
*%¢^$@

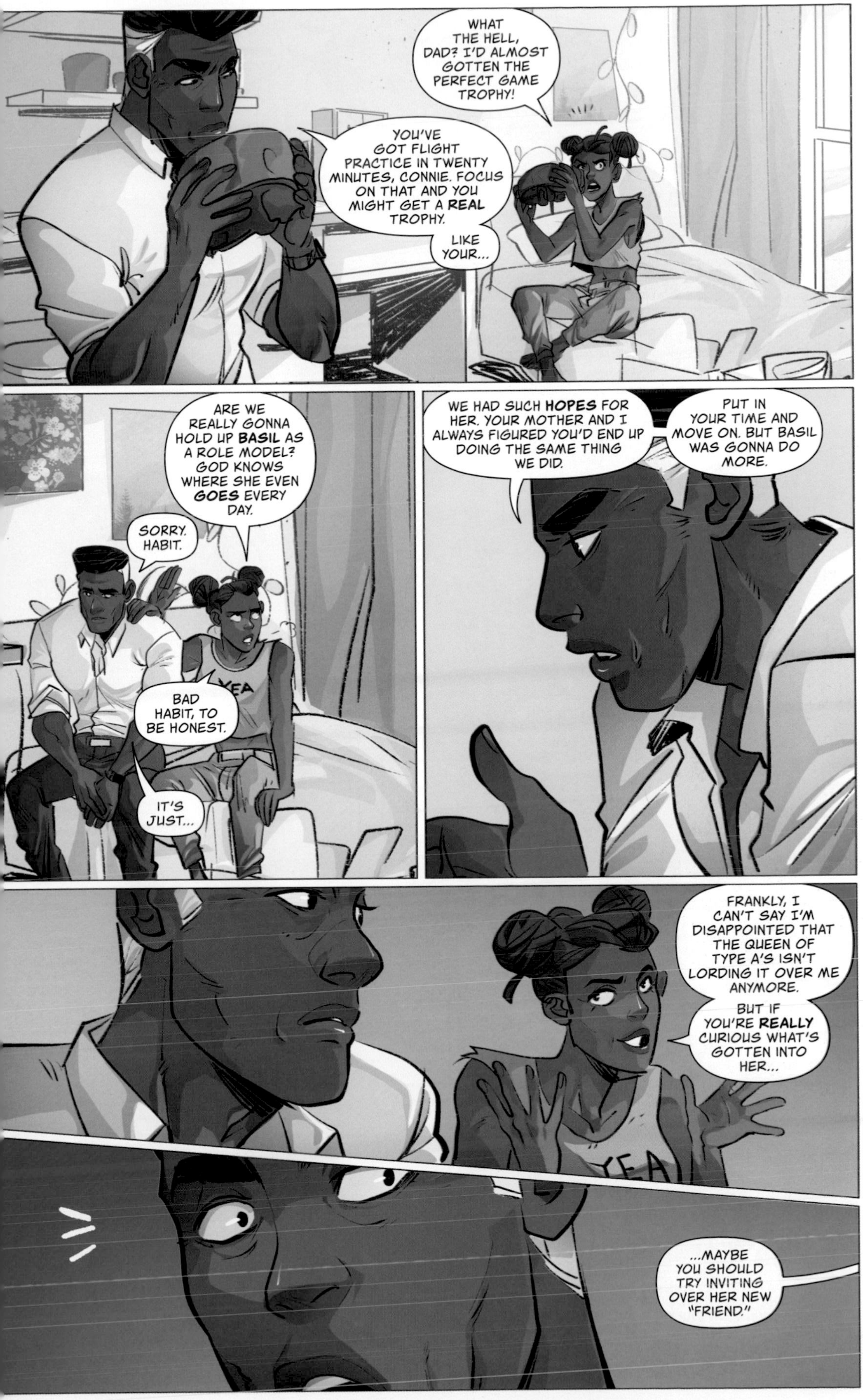
WHAT THE HELL, DAD? I'D ALMOST GOTTEN THE PERFECT GAME TROPHY!
YOU'VE GOT FLIGHT PRACTICE IN TWENTY MINUTES, CONNIE. FOCUS ON THAT AND YOU MIGHT GET A **REAL** TROPHY.
LIKE YOUR...
ARE WE REALLY GONNA HOLD UP **BASIL** AS A ROLE MODEL? GOD KNOWS WHERE SHE EVEN **GOES** EVERY DAY.
SORRY. HABIT.
YEA
BAD HABIT, TO BE HONEST.
IT'S JUST...
WE HAD SUCH **HOPES** FOR HER. YOUR MOTHER AND I ALWAYS FIGURED YOU'D END UP DOING THE SAME THING WE DID.
PUT IN YOUR TIME AND MOVE ON. BUT BASIL WAS GONNA DO MORE.
FRANKLY, I CAN'T SAY I'M DISAPPOINTED THAT THE QUEEN OF TYPE A'S ISN'T LORDING IT OVER ME ANYMORE.
BUT IF YOU'RE **REALLY** CURIOUS WHAT'S GOTTEN INTO HER...
YEA
...MAYBE YOU SHOULD TRY INVITING OVER HER NEW "FRIEND."

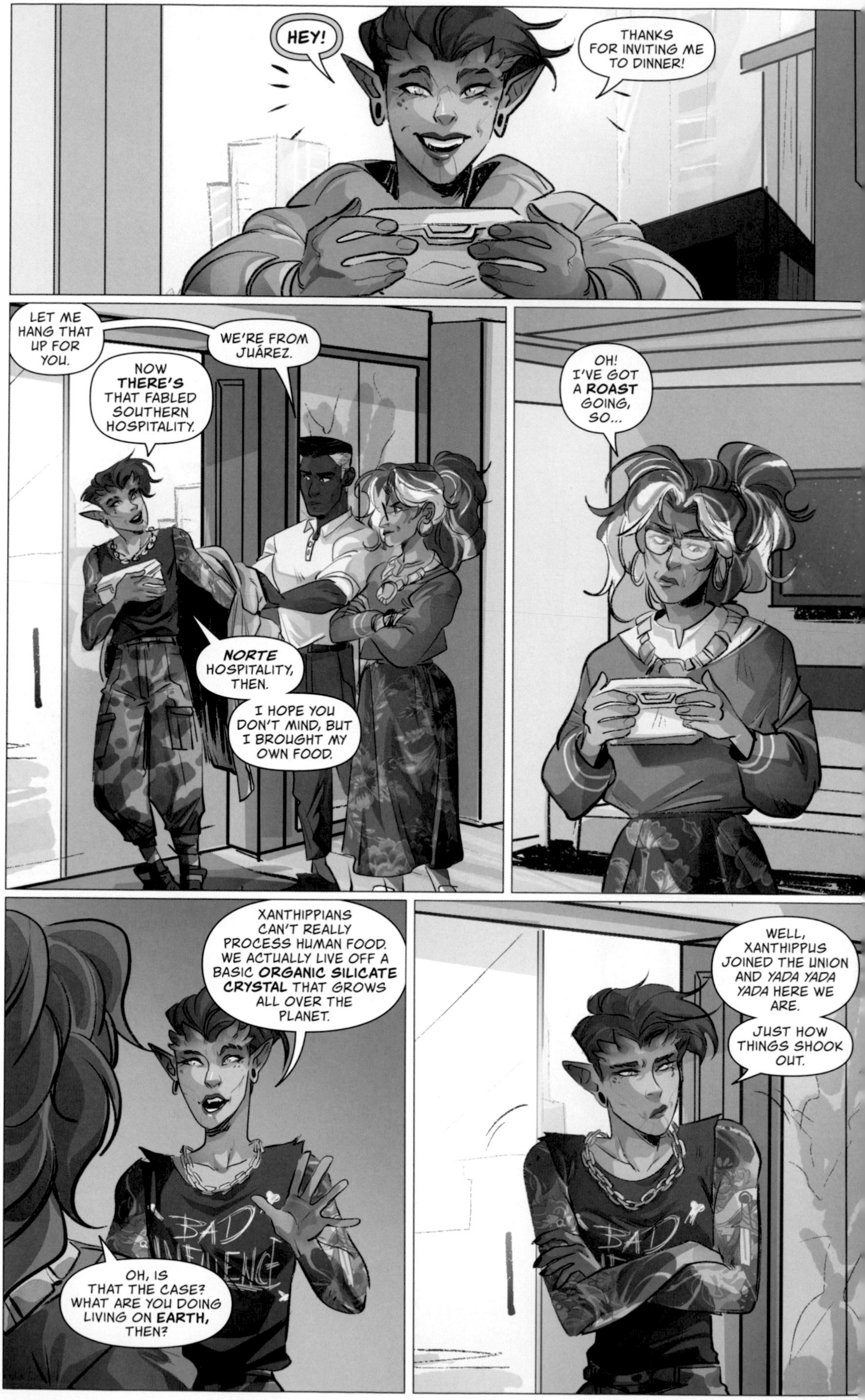
HEY!
THANKS FOR INVITING ME TO DINNER!
LET ME HANG THAT UP FOR YOU.
NOW **THERE'S** THAT FABLED SOUTHERN HOSPITALITY.
WE'RE FROM JUÁREZ.
NORTE HOSPITALITY, THEN.
I HOPE YOU DON'T MIND, BUT I BROUGHT MY OWN FOOD.
OH! I'VE GOT A **ROAST** GOING, SO...
XANTHIPPIANS CAN'T REALLY PROCESS HUMAN FOOD. WE ACTUALLY LIVE OFF A BASIC **ORGANIC SILICATE CRYSTAL** THAT GROWS ALL OVER THE PLANET.
OH, IS THAT THE CASE? WHAT ARE YOU DOING LIVING ON **EARTH,** THEN?
WELL, XANTHIPPUS JOINED THE UNION AND *YADA YADA YADA* HERE WE ARE.
JUST HOW THINGS SHOOK OUT.

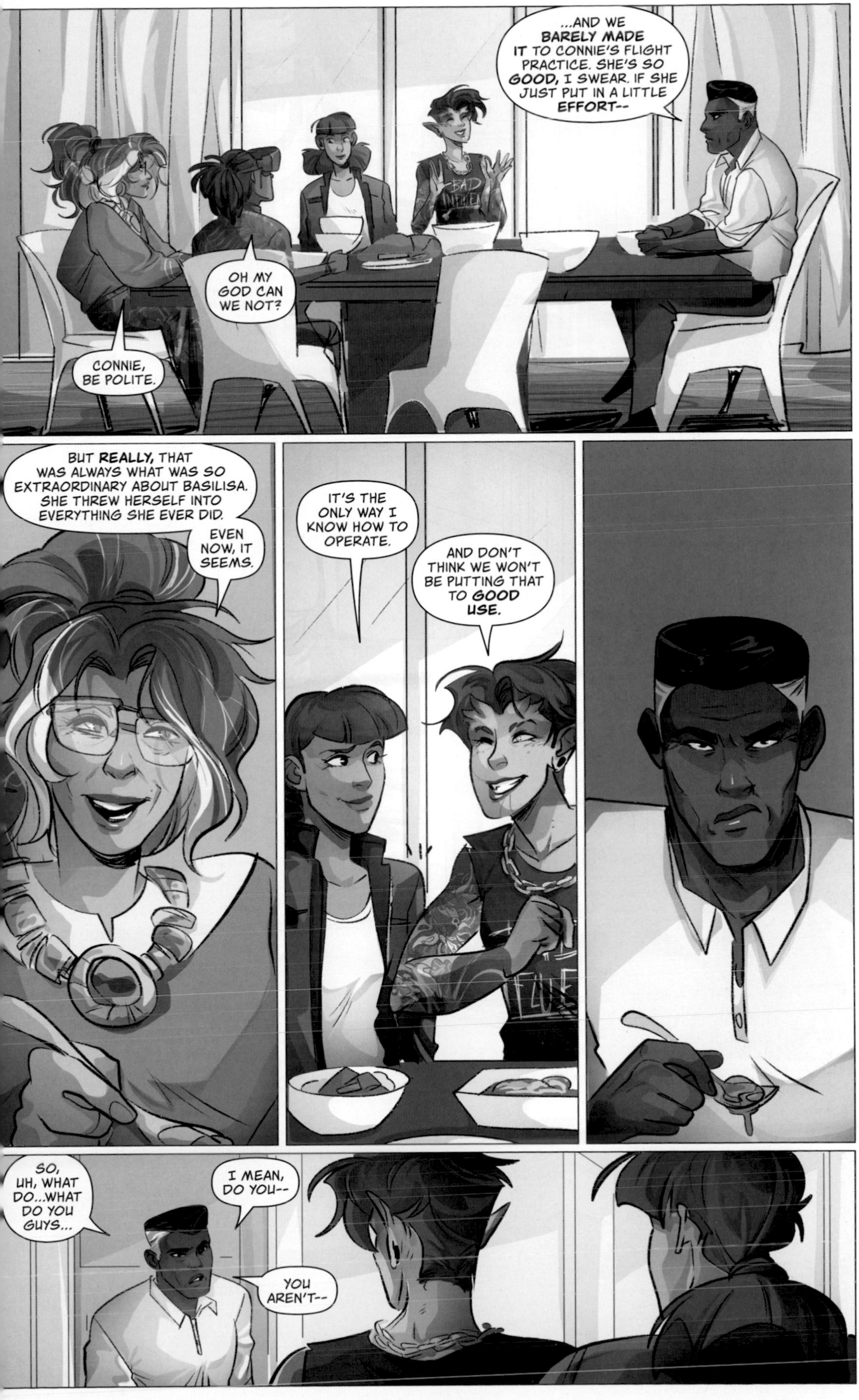
...AND WE BARELY MADE IT TO CONNIE'S FLIGHT PRACTICE. SHE'S SO GOOD, I SWEAR. IF SHE JUST PUT IN A LITTLE EFFORT--
OH MY GOD CAN WE NOT?
CONNIE, BE POLITE.
BUT REALLY, THAT WAS ALWAYS WHAT WAS SO EXTRAORDINARY ABOUT BASILISA. SHE THREW HERSELF INTO EVERYTHING SHE EVER DID.
EVEN NOW, IT SEEMS.
IT'S THE ONLY WAY I KNOW HOW TO OPERATE.
AND DON'T THINK WE WON'T BE PUTTING THAT TO GOOD USE.
SO, UH, WHAT DO...WHAT DO YOU GUYS...
I MEAN, DO YOU--
YOU AREN'T--

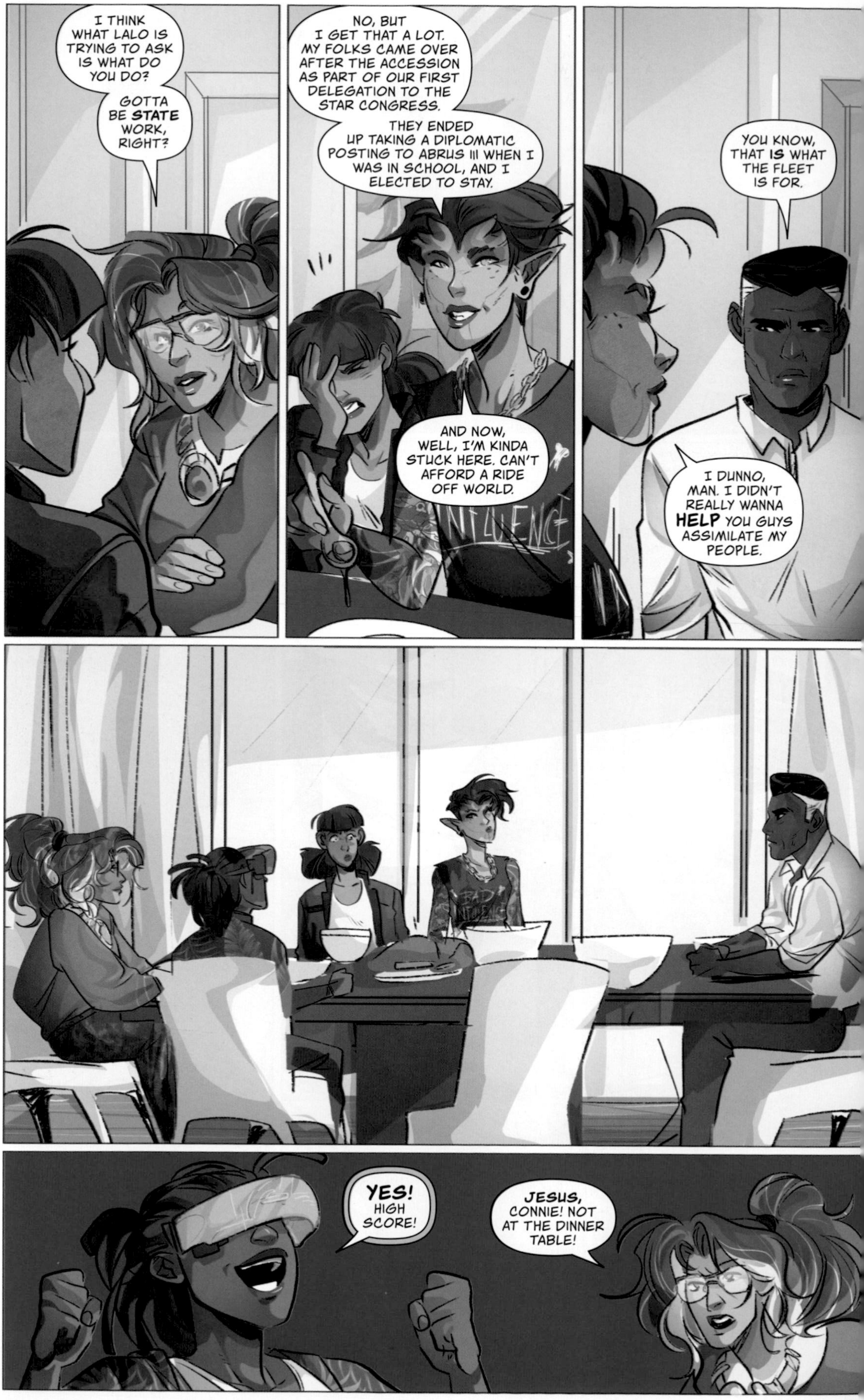

I THINK WHAT LALO IS TRYING TO ASK IS WHAT DO YOU DO?
GOTTA BE **STATE** WORK, RIGHT?
NO, BUT I GET THAT A LOT. MY FOLKS CAME OVER AFTER THE ACCESSION AS PART OF OUR FIRST DELEGATION TO THE STAR CONGRESS.
THEY ENDED UP TAKING A DIPLOMATIC POSTING TO ABRUS III WHEN I WAS IN SCHOOL, AND I ELECTED TO STAY.
AND NOW, WELL, I'M KINDA STUCK HERE. CAN'T AFFORD A RIDE OFF WORLD.
YOU KNOW, THAT **IS** WHAT THE FLEET IS FOR.
I DUNNO, MAN. I DIDN'T REALLY WANNA **HELP** YOU GUYS ASSIMILATE MY PEOPLE.
YES! HIGH SCORE!
JESUS, CONNIE! NOT AT THE DINNER TABLE!

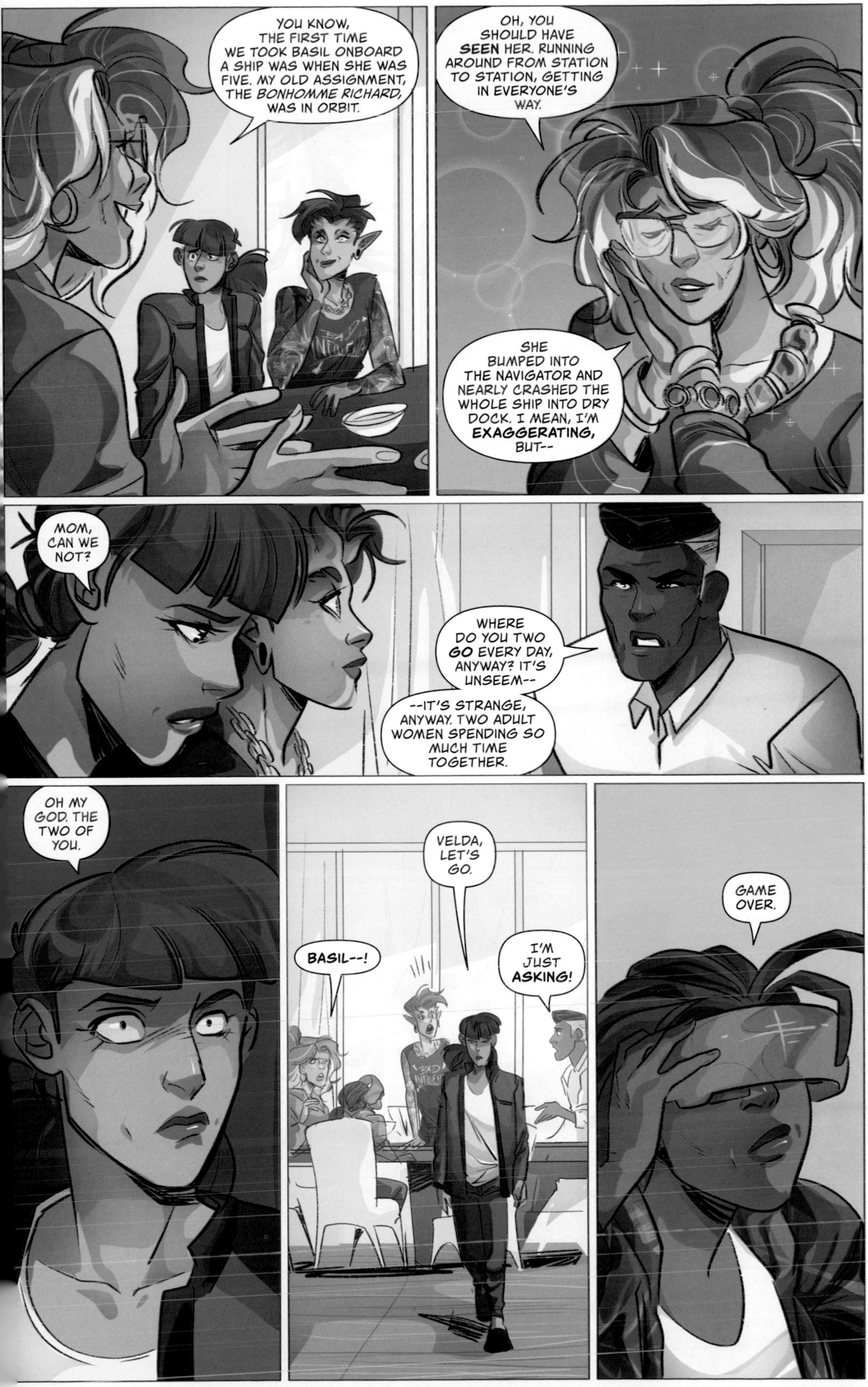
YOU KNOW, THE FIRST TIME WE TOOK BASIL ONBOARD A SHIP WAS WHEN SHE WAS FIVE. MY OLD ASSIGNMENT, THE *BONHOMME RICHARD,* WAS IN ORBIT.
OH, YOU SHOULD HAVE **SEEN** HER. RUNNING AROUND FROM STATION TO STATION, GETTING IN EVERYONE'S WAY.
SHE BUMPED INTO THE NAVIGATOR AND NEARLY CRASHED THE WHOLE SHIP INTO DRY DOCK. I MEAN, I'M **EXAGGERATING,** BUT--
MOM, CAN WE NOT?
WHERE DO YOU TWO **GO** EVERY DAY, ANYWAY? IT'S UNSEEM--
--IT'S STRANGE, ANYWAY. TWO ADULT WOMEN SPENDING SO MUCH TIME TOGETHER.
OH MY GOD. THE TWO OF YOU.
VELDA, LET'S GO.
BASIL--!
I'M JUST **ASKING!**
GAME OVER.

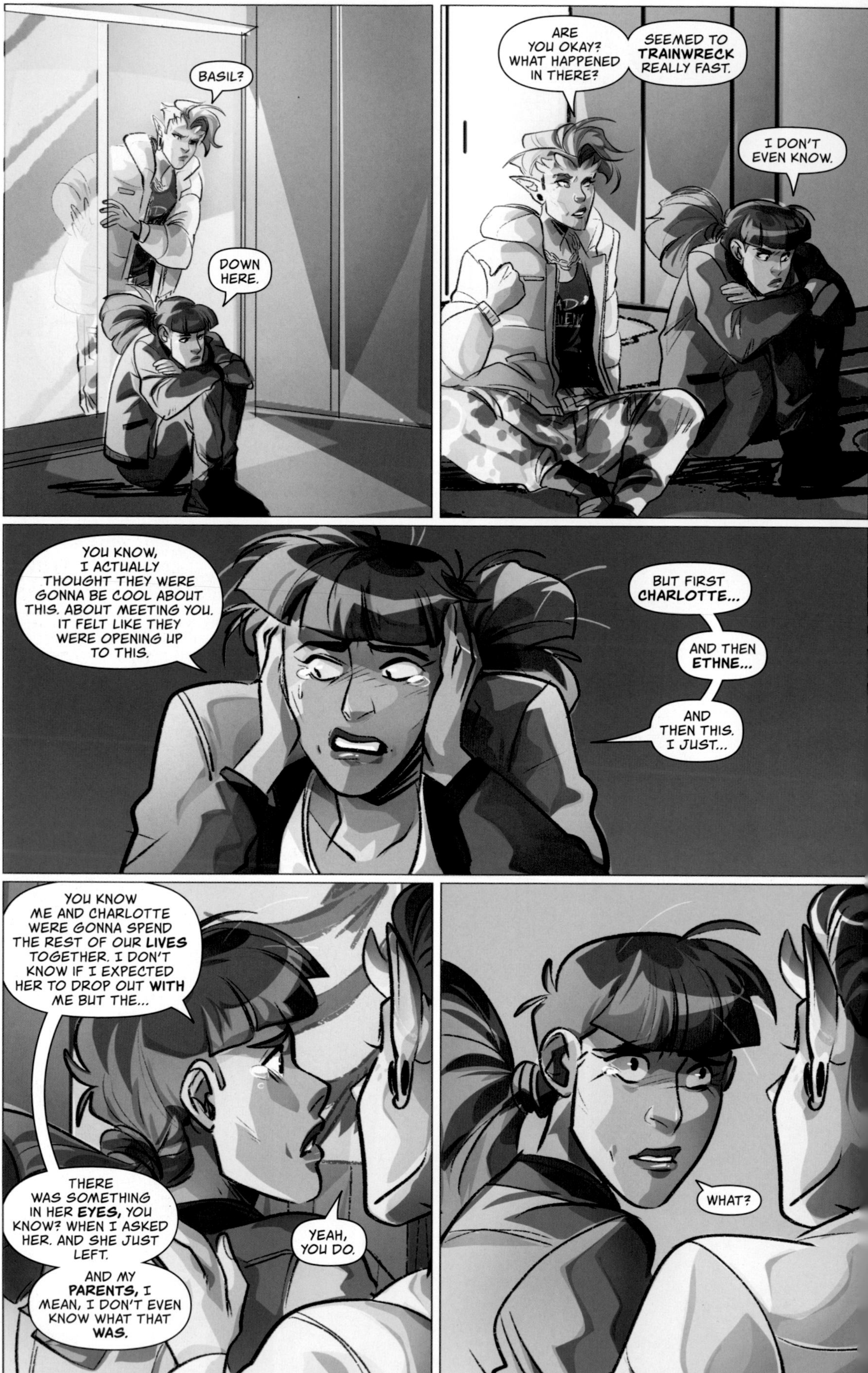
BASIL?
DOWN HERE.
ARE YOU OKAY? WHAT HAPPENED IN THERE?
SEEMED TO **TRAINWRECK** REALLY FAST.
I DON'T EVEN KNOW.
YOU KNOW, I ACTUALLY THOUGHT THEY WERE GONNA BE COOL ABOUT THIS. ABOUT MEETING YOU. IT FELT LIKE THEY WERE OPENING UP TO THIS.
BUT FIRST **CHARLOTTE...**
AND THEN **ETHNE...**
AND THEN THIS. I JUST...
YOU KNOW ME AND CHARLOTTE WERE GONNA SPEND THE REST OF OUR **LIVES** TOGETHER. I DON'T KNOW IF I EXPECTED HER TO DROP OUT **WITH** ME BUT THE...
THERE WAS SOMETHING IN HER **EYES,** YOU KNOW? WHEN I ASKED HER. AND SHE JUST LEFT.
AND MY **PARENTS,** I MEAN, I DON'T EVEN KNOW WHAT THAT **WAS.**
YEAH, YOU DO.
WHAT?

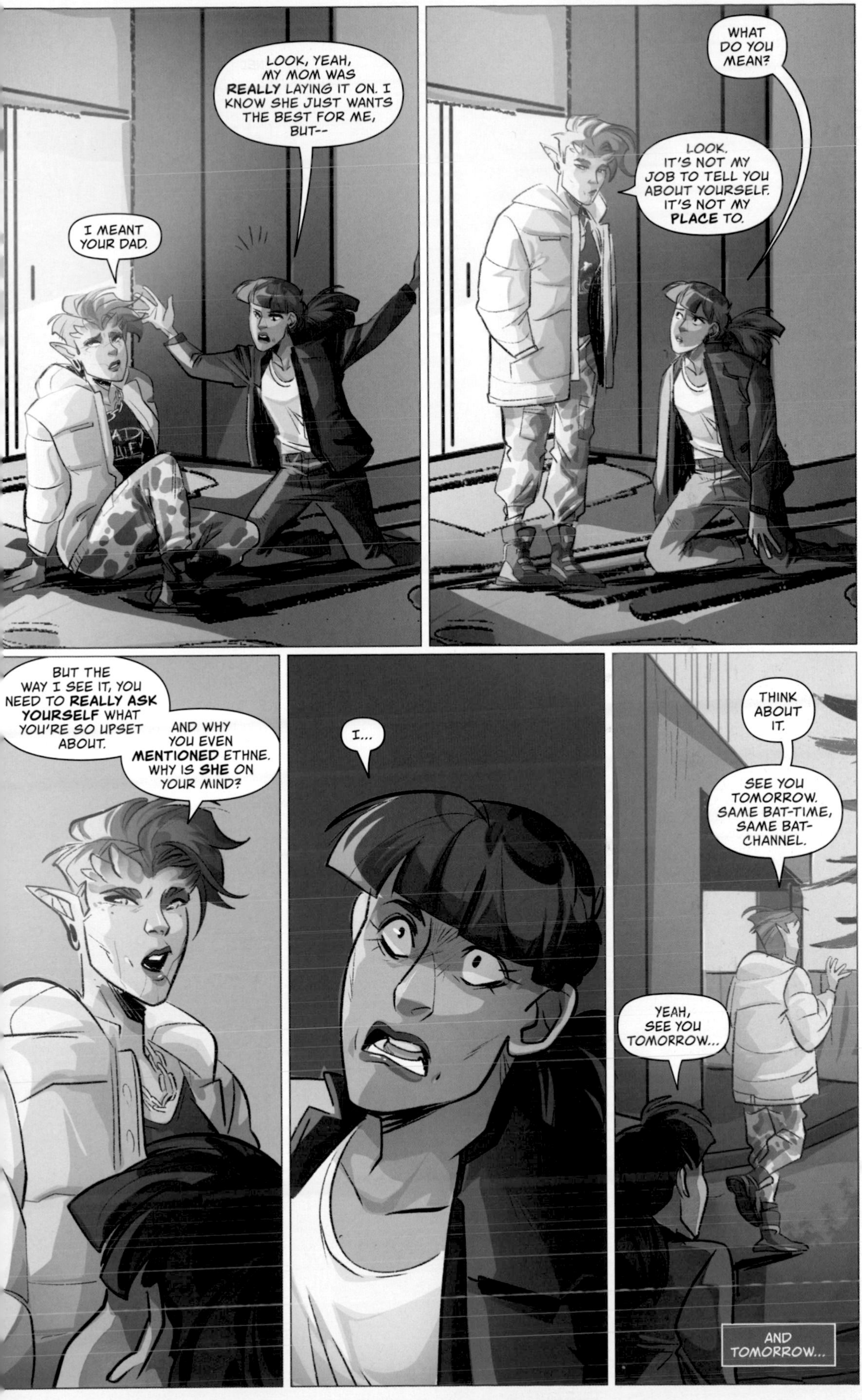
LOOK, YEAH, MY MOM WAS REALLY LAYING IT ON. I KNOW SHE JUST WANTS THE BEST FOR ME, BUT--
I MEANT YOUR DAD.
WHAT DO YOU MEAN?
LOOK. IT'S NOT MY JOB TO TELL YOU ABOUT YOURSELF. IT'S NOT MY PLACE TO.
BUT THE WAY I SEE IT, YOU NEED TO REALLY ASK YOURSELF WHAT YOU'RE SO UPSET ABOUT.
AND WHY YOU EVEN MENTIONED ETHNE. WHY IS SHE ON YOUR MIND?
I...
THINK ABOUT IT.
SEE YOU TOMORROW. SAME BAT-TIME, SAME BAT-CHANNEL.
YEAH, SEE YOU TOMORROW...
AND TOMORROW...

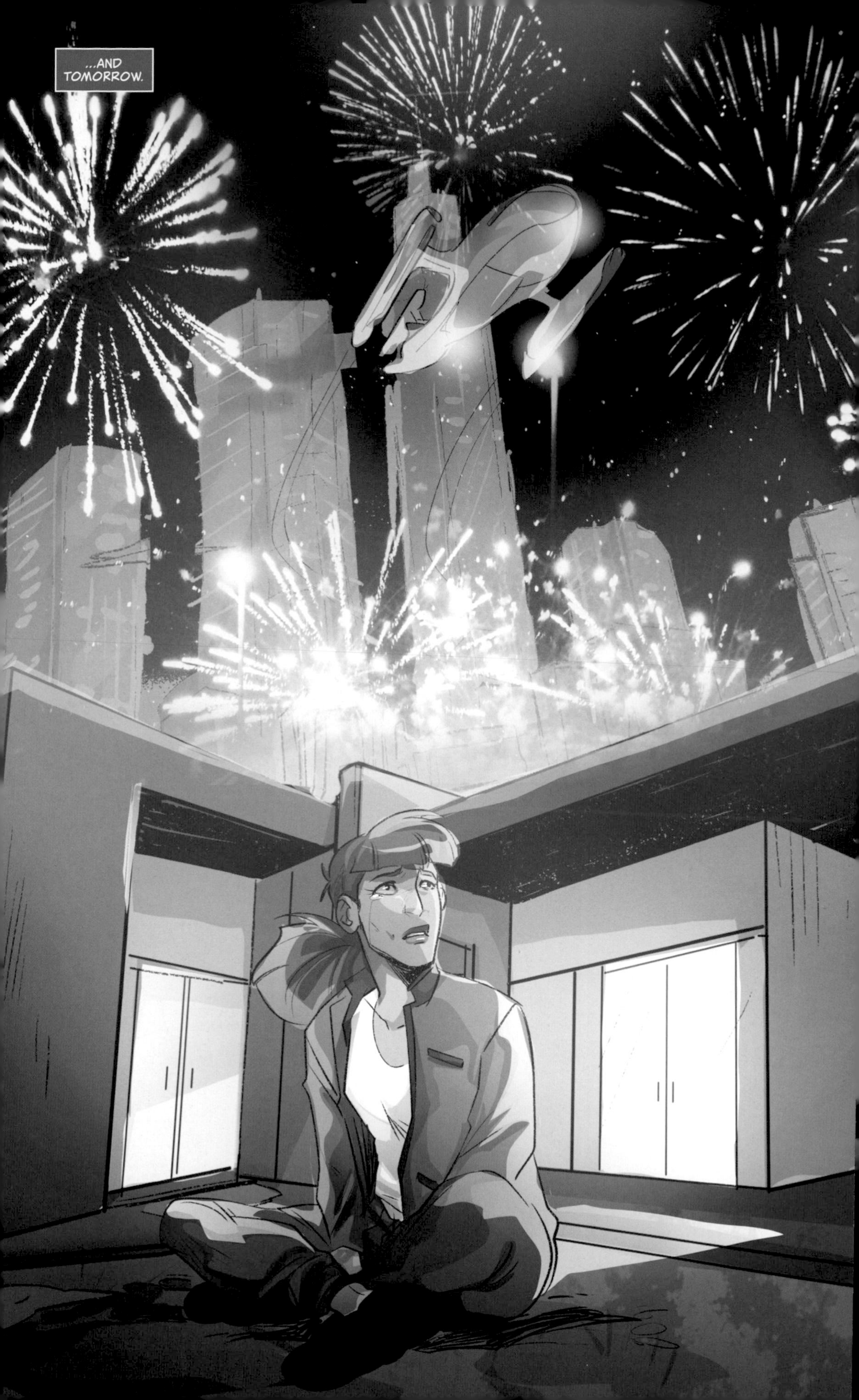
...AND TOMORROW.

Chapter Three

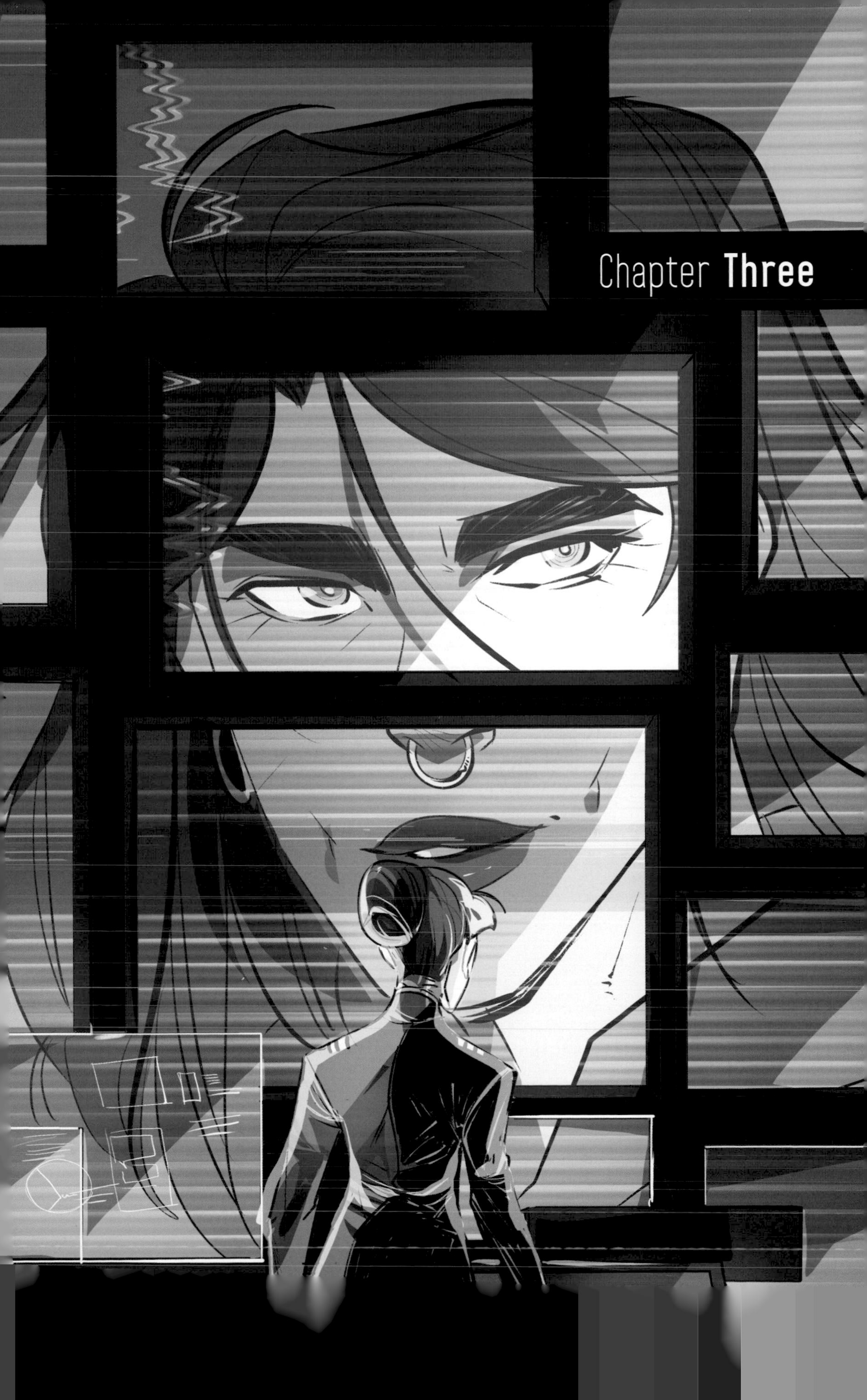

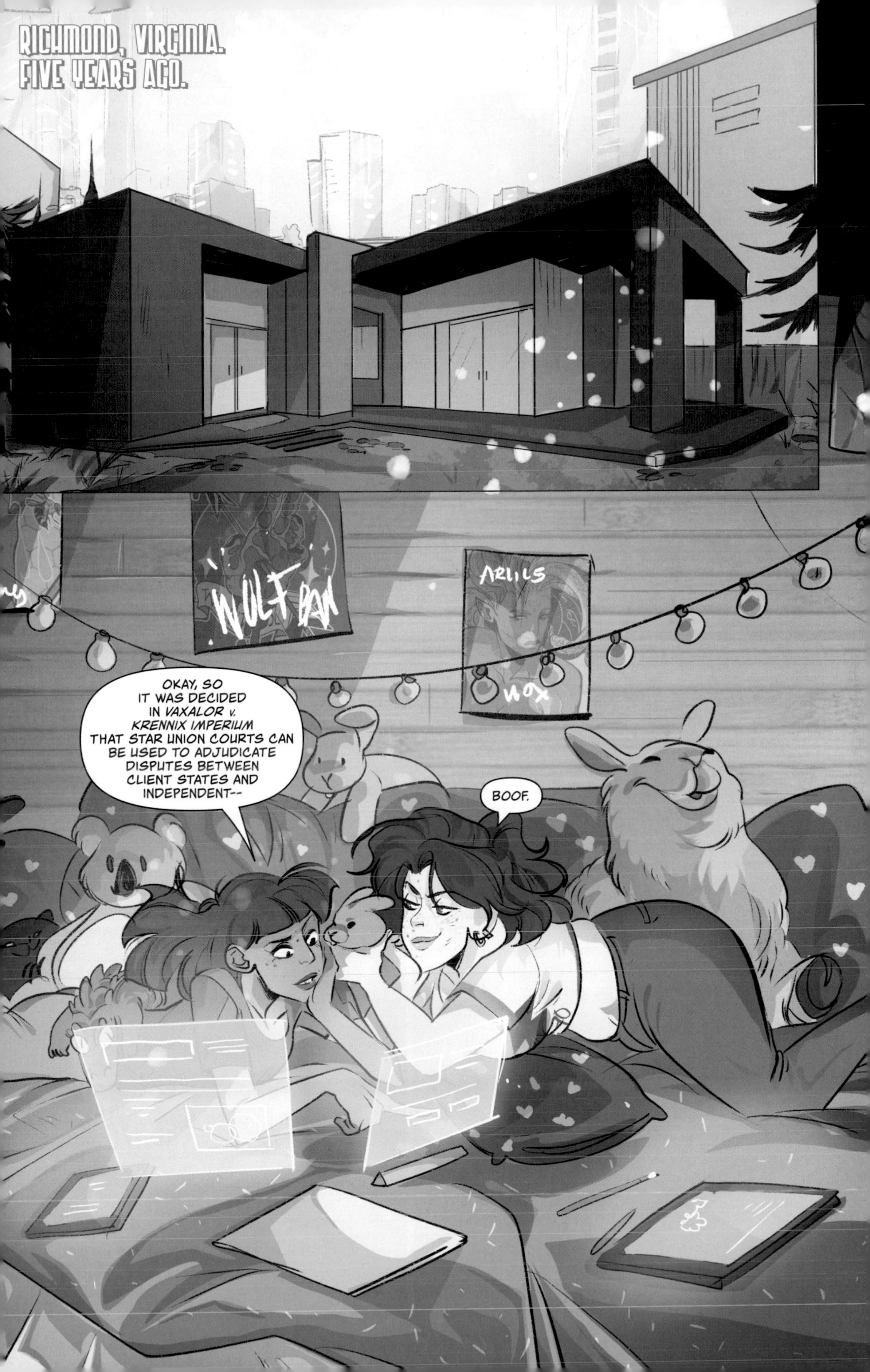
RICHMOND, VIRGINIA.
FIVE YEARS AGO.
WOLF BAN
ARLILS
VOX
OKAY, SO IT WAS DECIDED IN *VAXALOR v. KRENNIX IMPERIUM* THAT STAR UNION COURTS CAN BE USED TO ADJUDICATE DISPUTES BETWEEN CLIENT STATES AND INDEPENDENT--
BOOF.

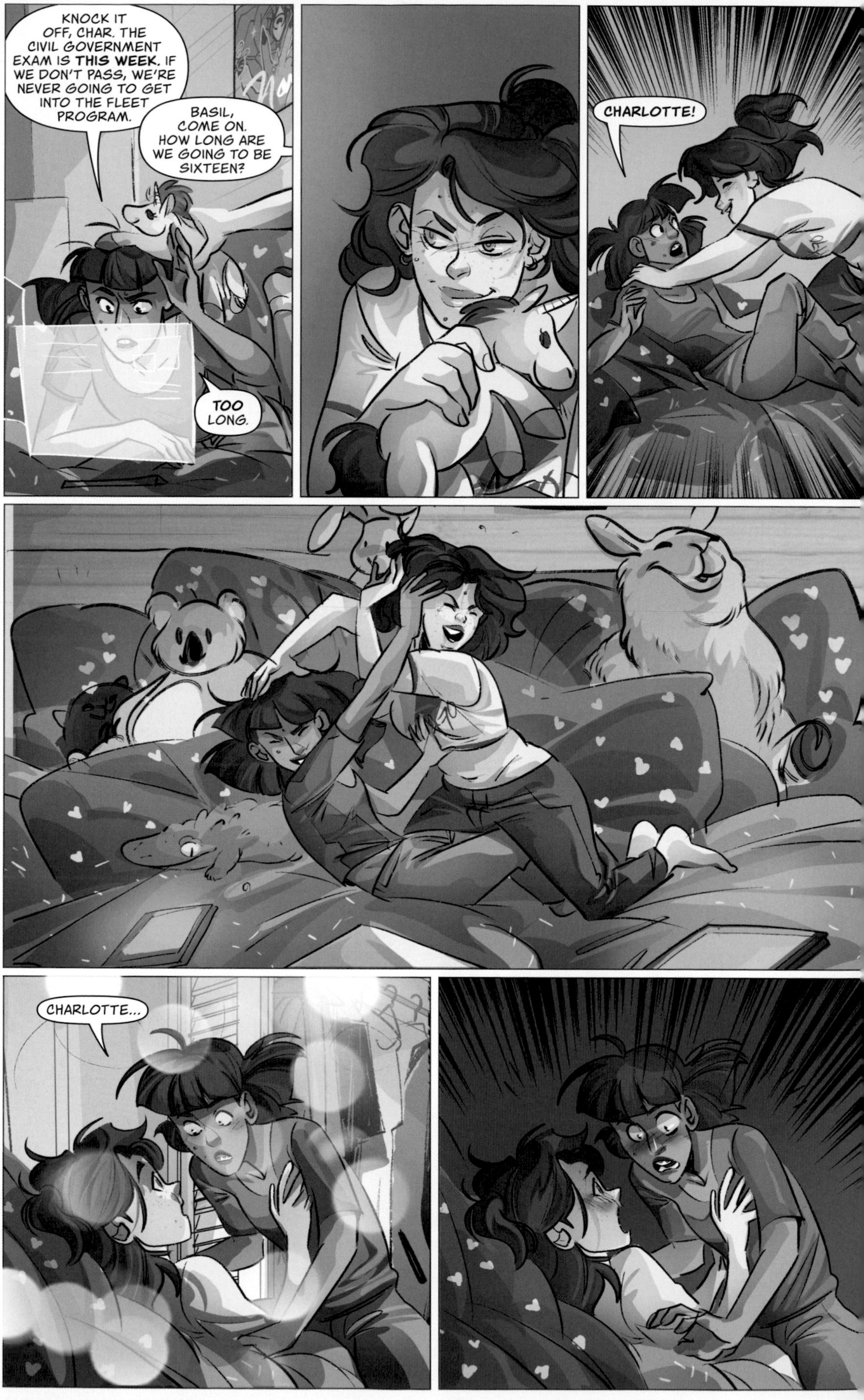
KNOCK IT OFF, CHAR. THE CIVIL GOVERNMENT EXAM IS **THIS WEEK.** IF WE DON'T PASS, WE'RE NEVER GOING TO GET INTO THE FLEET PROGRAM.
BASIL, COME ON. HOW LONG ARE WE GOING TO BE SIXTEEN?
TOO LONG.
CHARLOTTE!
CHARLOTTE...

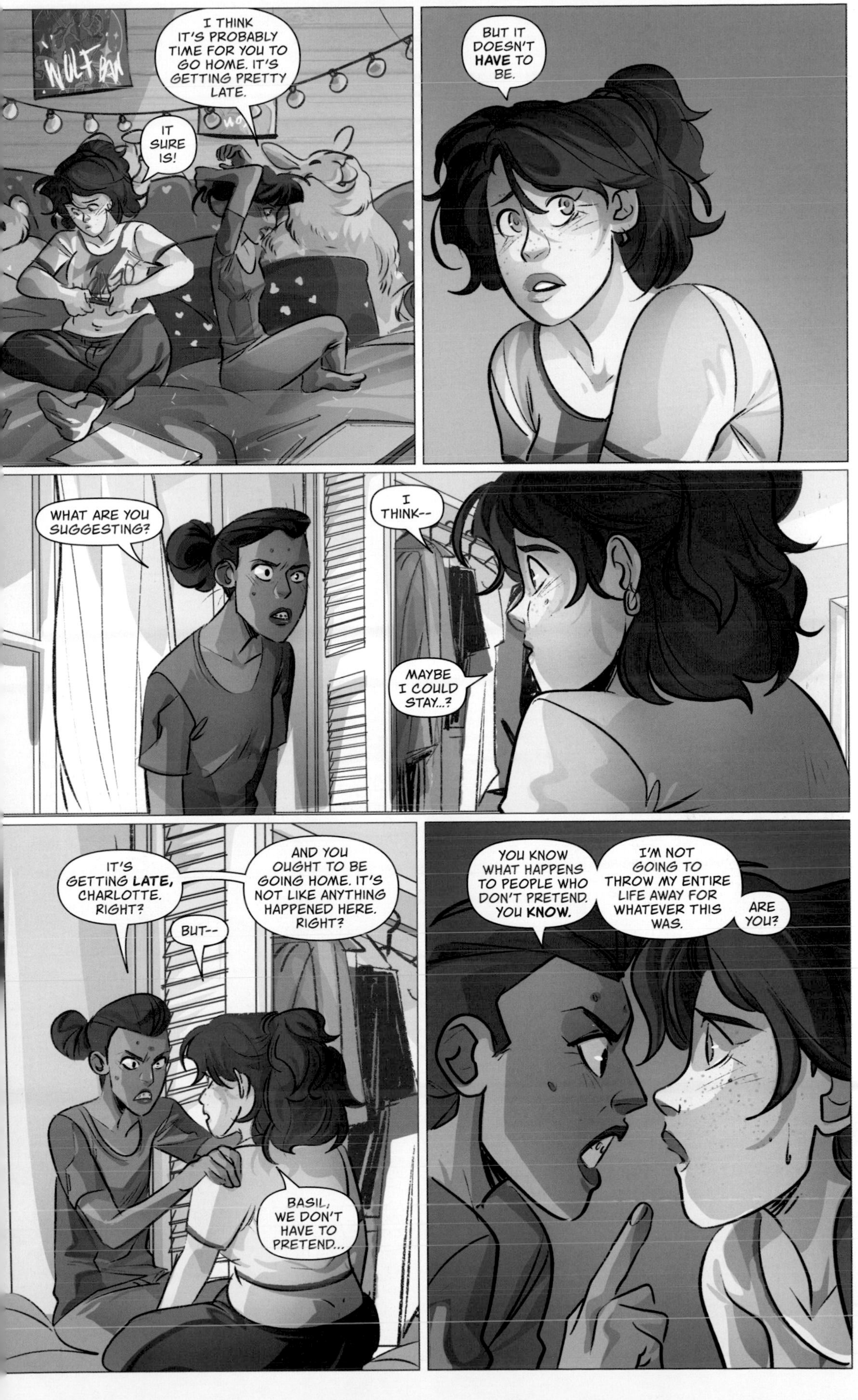

I THINK IT'S PROBABLY TIME FOR YOU TO GO HOME. IT'S GETTING PRETTY LATE.
IT SURE IS!
BUT IT DOESN'T **HAVE** TO BE.
WHAT ARE YOU SUGGESTING?
I THINK--
MAYBE I COULD STAY...?
IT'S GETTING **LATE,** CHARLOTTE. RIGHT?
AND YOU OUGHT TO BE GOING HOME. IT'S NOT LIKE ANYTHING HAPPENED HERE. RIGHT?
BUT--
BASIL, WE DON'T HAVE TO PRETEND...
YOU KNOW WHAT HAPPENS TO PEOPLE WHO DON'T PRETEND. YOU **KNOW.**
I'M NOT GOING TO THROW MY ENTIRE LIFE AWAY FOR WHATEVER THIS WAS.
ARE YOU?

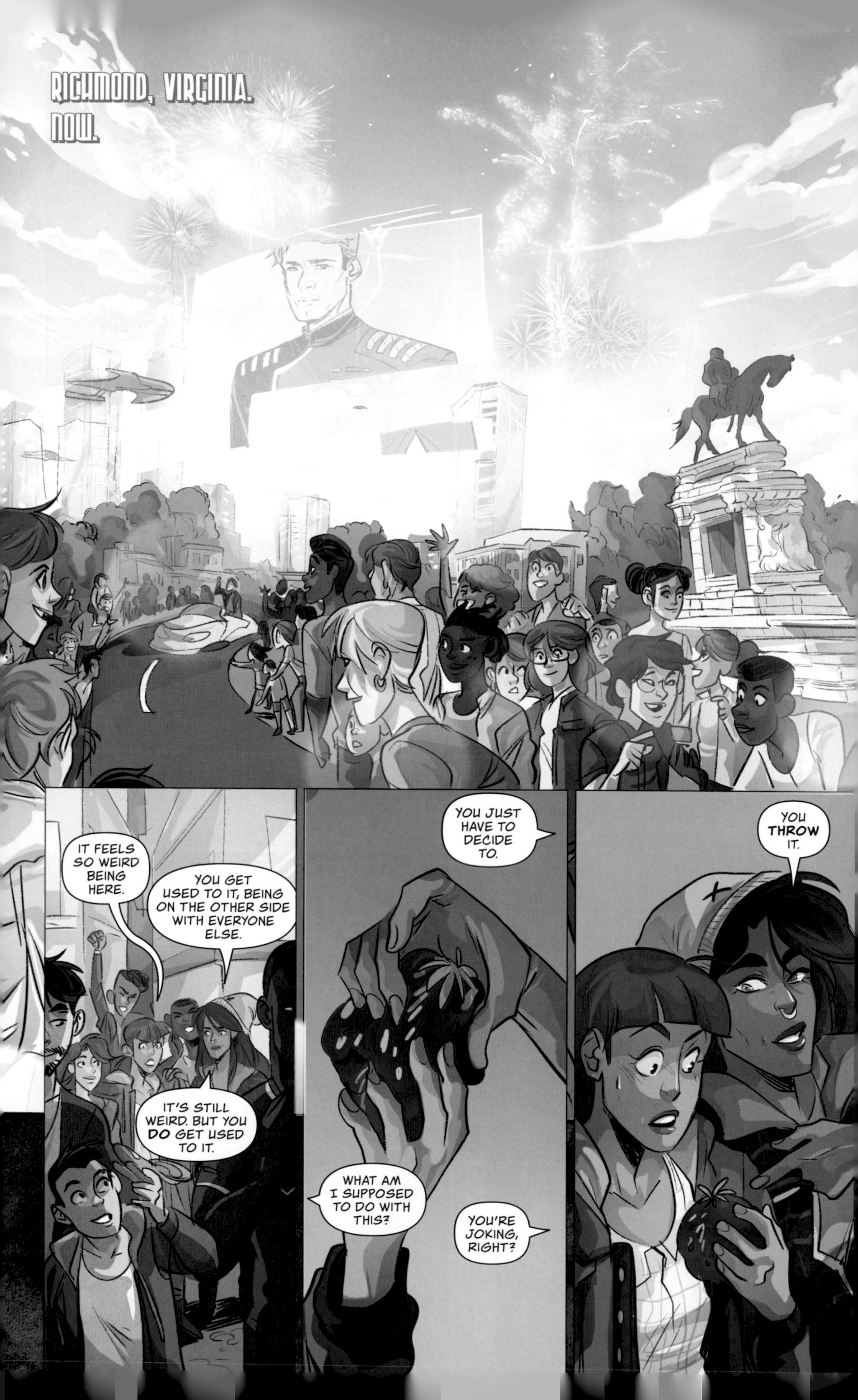
RICHMOND, VIRGINIA.
NOW.
IT FEELS SO WEIRD BEING HERE.
YOU GET USED TO IT, BEING ON THE OTHER SIDE WITH EVERYONE ELSE.
IT'S STILL WEIRD. BUT YOU DO GET USED TO IT.
YOU JUST HAVE TO DECIDE TO.
WHAT AM I SUPPOSED TO DO WITH THIS?
YOU'RE JOKING, RIGHT?
YOU THROW IT.

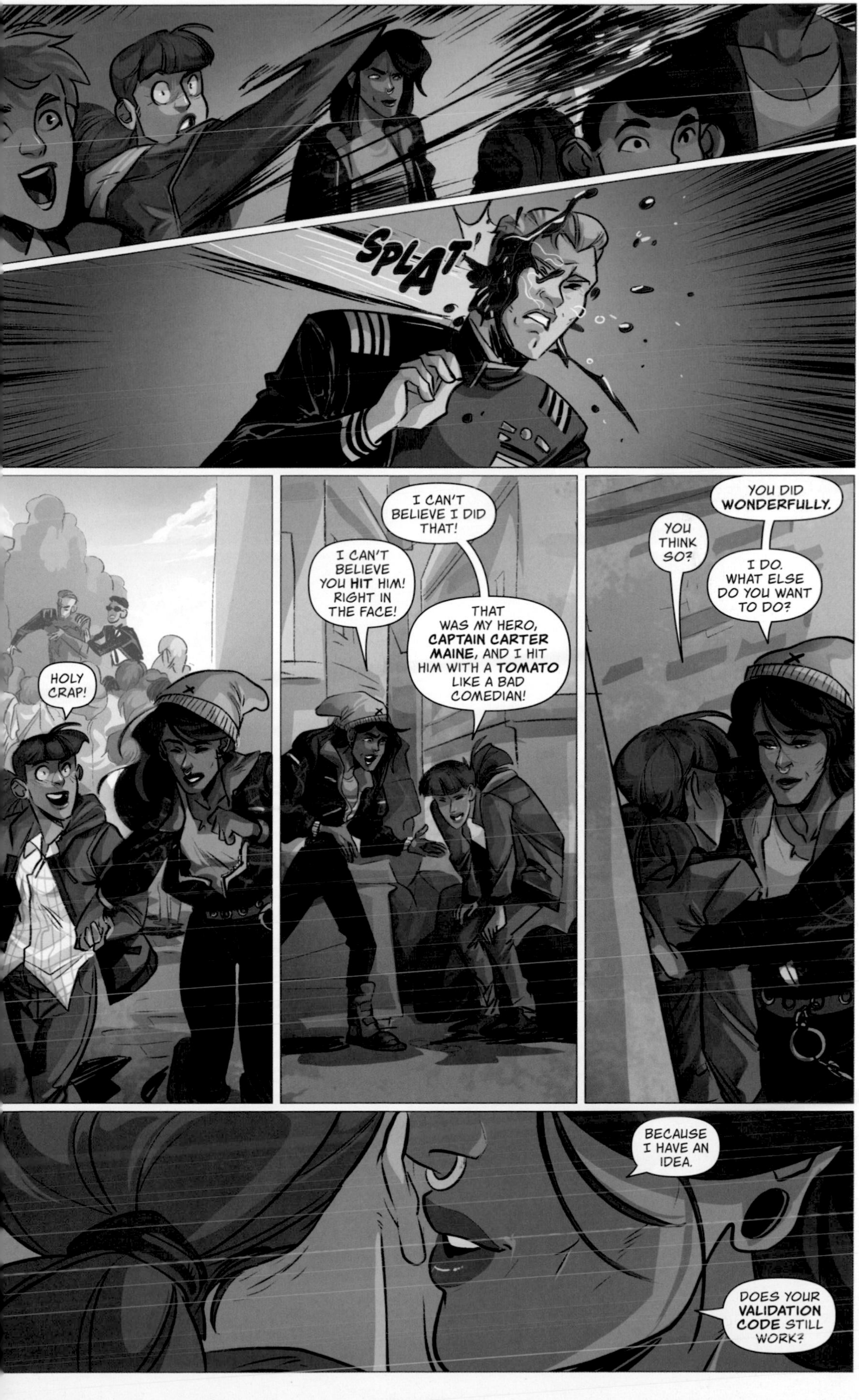

SPLAT!
HOLY CRAP!
I CAN'T BELIEVE YOU HIT HIM! RIGHT IN THE FACE!
I CAN'T BELIEVE I DID THAT!
THAT WAS MY HERO, CAPTAIN CARTER MAINE, AND I HIT HIM WITH A TOMATO LIKE A BAD COMEDIAN!
YOU DID WONDERFULLY.
YOU THINK SO?
I DO. WHAT ELSE DO YOU WANT TO DO?
BECAUSE I HAVE AN IDEA.
DOES YOUR VALIDATION CODE STILL WORK?

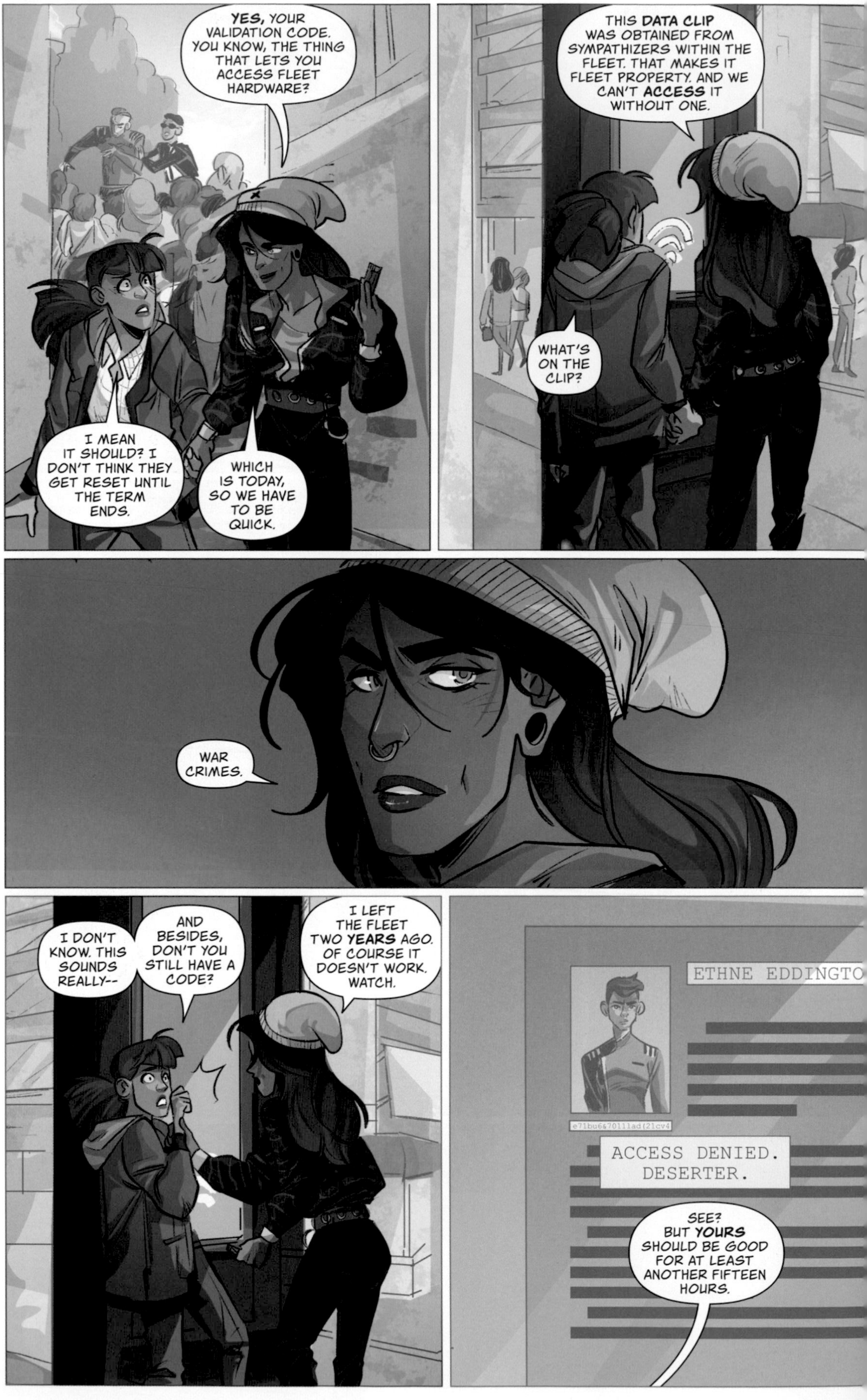
YES, YOUR VALIDATION CODE. YOU KNOW, THE THING THAT LETS YOU ACCESS FLEET HARDWARE?
I MEAN IT SHOULD? I DON'T THINK THEY GET RESET UNTIL THE TERM ENDS.
WHICH IS TODAY, SO WE HAVE TO BE QUICK.
THIS DATA CLIP WAS OBTAINED FROM SYMPATHIZERS WITHIN THE FLEET. THAT MAKES IT FLEET PROPERTY. AND WE CAN'T ACCESS IT WITHOUT ONE.
WHAT'S ON THE CLIP?
WAR CRIMES.
I DON'T KNOW. THIS SOUNDS REALLY--
AND BESIDES, DON'T YOU STILL HAVE A CODE?
I LEFT THE FLEET TWO YEARS AGO. OF COURSE IT DOESN'T WORK. WATCH.
ETHNE EDDINGTO
e71bu6&70111ad(21cv4
ACCESS DENIED. DESERTER.
SEE? BUT YOURS SHOULD BE GOOD FOR AT LEAST ANOTHER FIFTEEN HOURS.

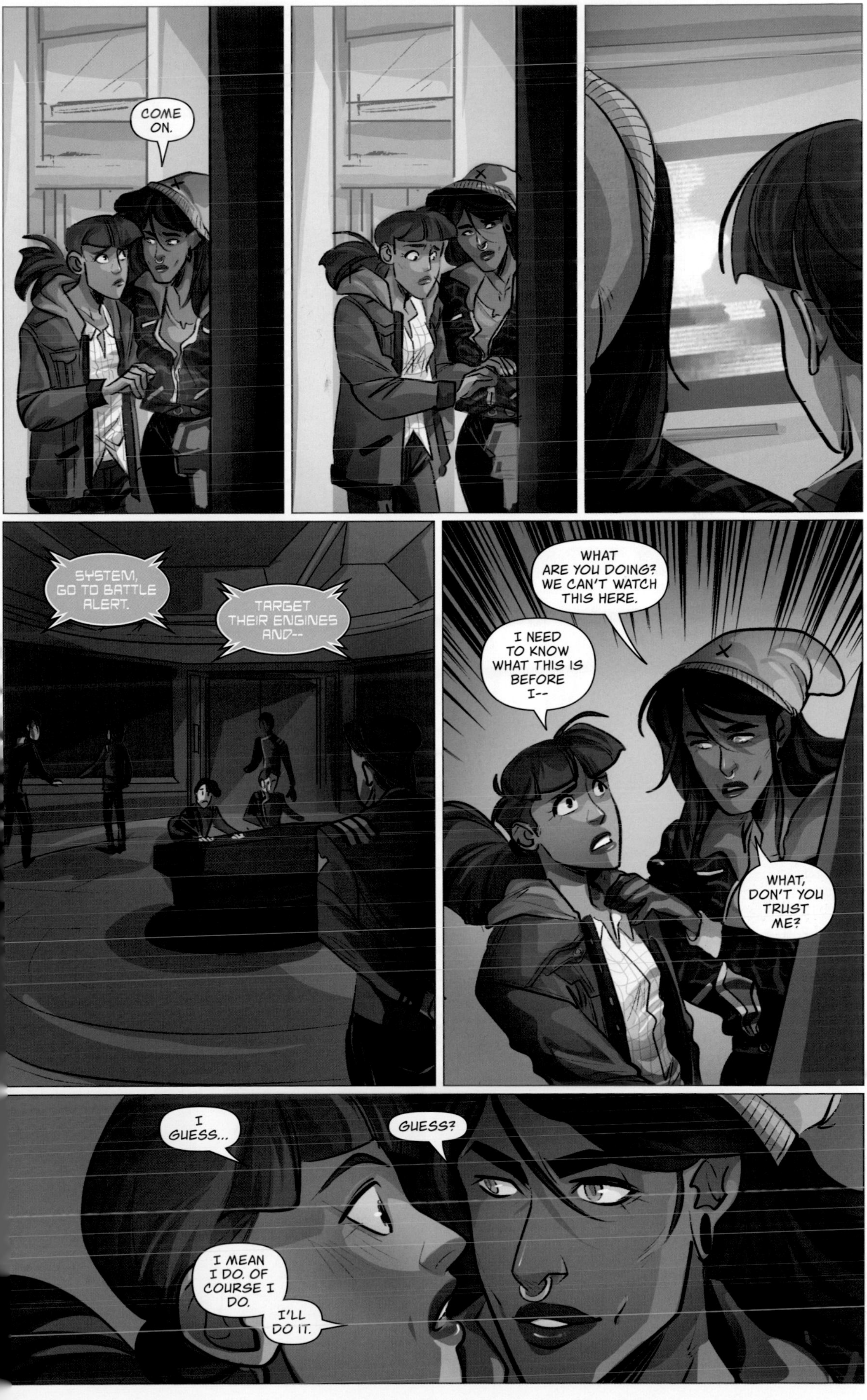
COME ON.
SYSTEM, GO TO BATTLE ALERT.
TARGET THEIR ENGINES AND--
WHAT ARE YOU DOING? WE CAN'T WATCH THIS HERE.
I NEED TO KNOW WHAT THIS IS BEFORE I--
WHAT, DON'T YOU TRUST ME?
I GUESS...
GUESS?
I MEAN I DO. OF COURSE I DO.
I'LL DO IT.

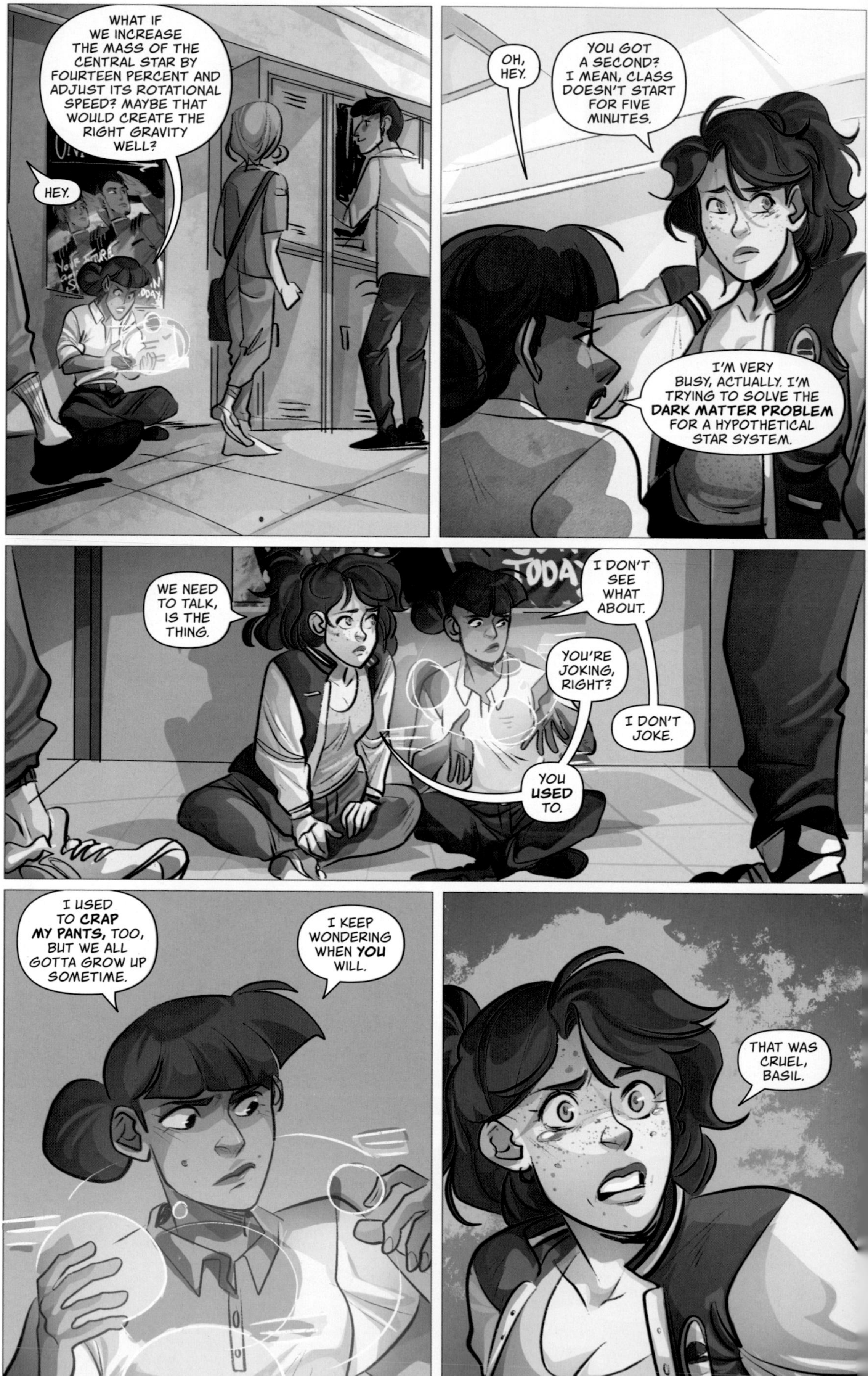
WHAT IF WE INCREASE THE MASS OF THE CENTRAL STAR BY FOURTEEN PERCENT AND ADJUST ITS ROTATIONAL SPEED? MAYBE THAT WOULD CREATE THE RIGHT GRAVITY WELL?
HEY.
OH, HEY.
YOU GOT A SECOND? I MEAN, CLASS DOESN'T START FOR FIVE MINUTES.
I'M VERY BUSY, ACTUALLY. I'M TRYING TO SOLVE THE **DARK MATTER PROBLEM** FOR A HYPOTHETICAL STAR SYSTEM.
WE NEED TO TALK, IS THE THING.
I DON'T SEE WHAT ABOUT.
YOU'RE JOKING, RIGHT?
I DON'T JOKE.
YOU **USED** TO.
I USED TO **CRAP MY PANTS,** TOO, BUT WE ALL GOTTA GROW UP SOMETIME.
I KEEP WONDERING WHEN **YOU** WILL.
THAT WAS CRUEL, BASIL.

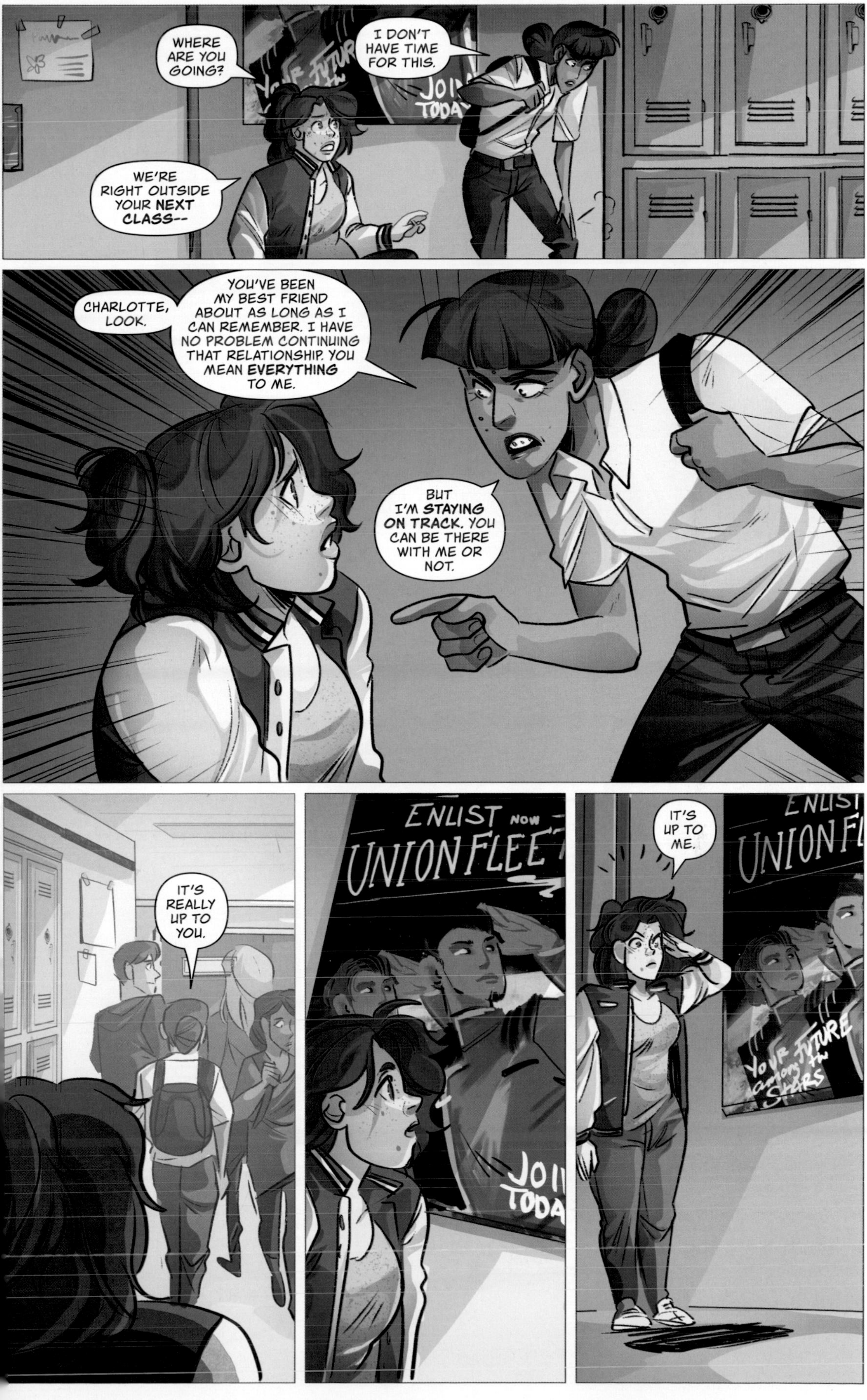

WHERE ARE YOU GOING?
I DON'T HAVE TIME FOR THIS.
WE'RE RIGHT OUTSIDE YOUR **NEXT CLASS**--
CHARLOTTE, LOOK.
YOU'VE BEEN MY BEST FRIEND ABOUT AS LONG AS I CAN REMEMBER. I HAVE NO PROBLEM CONTINUING THAT RELATIONSHIP. YOU MEAN **EVERYTHING** TO ME.
BUT I'M **STAYING ON TRACK**. YOU CAN BE THERE WITH ME OR NOT.
IT'S REALLY UP TO YOU.
ENLIST NOW
UNION FLEET
JOIN TODAY
IT'S UP TO ME.
YOUR FUTURE among the STARS

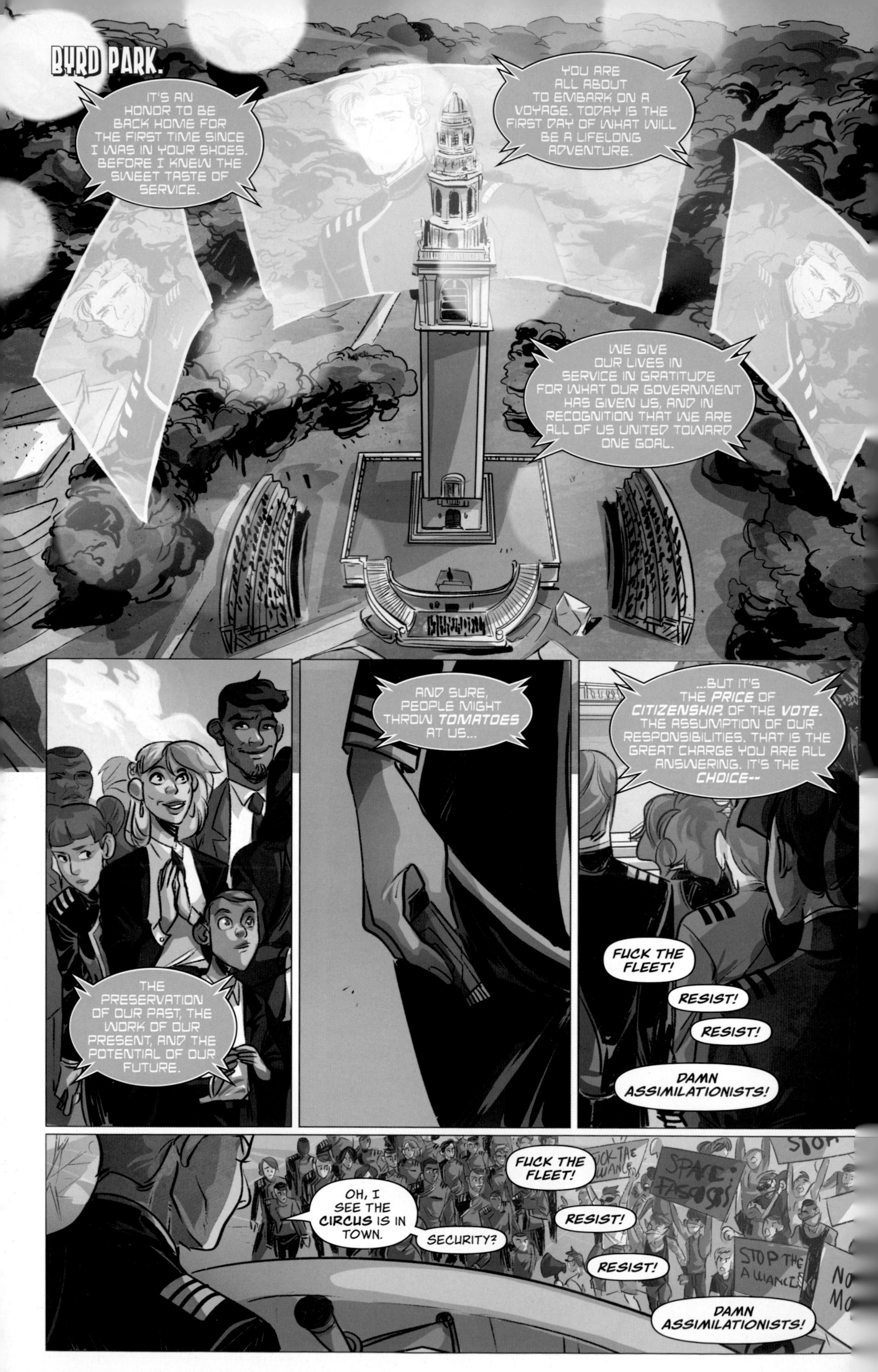
BYRD PARK.
IT'S AN HONOR TO BE BACK HOME FOR THE FIRST TIME SINCE I WAS IN YOUR SHOES. BEFORE I KNEW THE SWEET TASTE OF SERVICE.
YOU ARE ALL ABOUT TO EMBARK ON A VOYAGE. TODAY IS THE FIRST DAY OF WHAT WILL BE A LIFELONG ADVENTURE.
WE GIVE OUR LIVES IN SERVICE IN GRATITUDE FOR WHAT OUR GOVERNMENT HAS GIVEN US, AND IN RECOGNITION THAT WE ARE ALL OF US UNITED TOWARD ONE GOAL.
THE PRESERVATION OF OUR PAST, THE WORK OF OUR PRESENT, AND THE POTENTIAL OF OUR FUTURE.
AND SURE, PEOPLE MIGHT THROW *TOMATOES* AT US...
...BUT IT'S THE *PRICE* OF *CITIZENSHIP*, OF THE *VOTE*. THE ASSUMPTION OF OUR RESPONSIBILITIES. THAT IS THE GREAT CHARGE YOU ARE ALL ANSWERING. IT'S THE *CHOICE*--
FUCK THE FLEET!
RESIST!
RESIST!
DAMN ASSIMILATIONISTS!
OH, I SEE THE **CIRCUS** IS IN TOWN.
SECURITY?
FUCK THE FLEET!
RESIST!
RESIST!
DAMN ASSIMILATIONISTS!

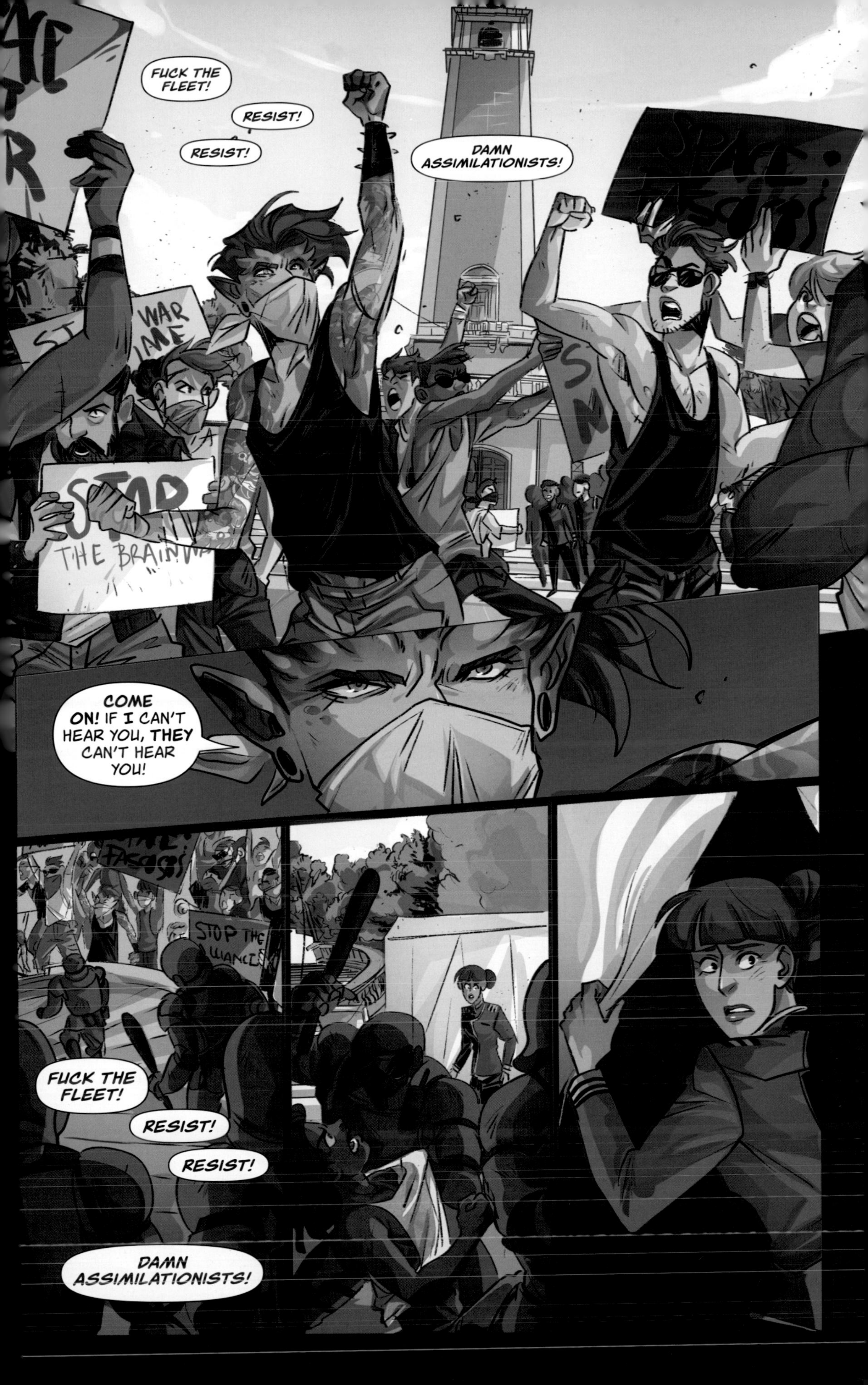
FUCK THE FLEET!
RESIST!
RESIST!
DAMN ASSIMILATIONISTS!
COME ON! IF I CAN'T HEAR YOU, THEY CAN'T HEAR YOU!
FUCK THE FLEET!
RESIST!
RESIST!
DAMN ASSIMILATIONISTS!

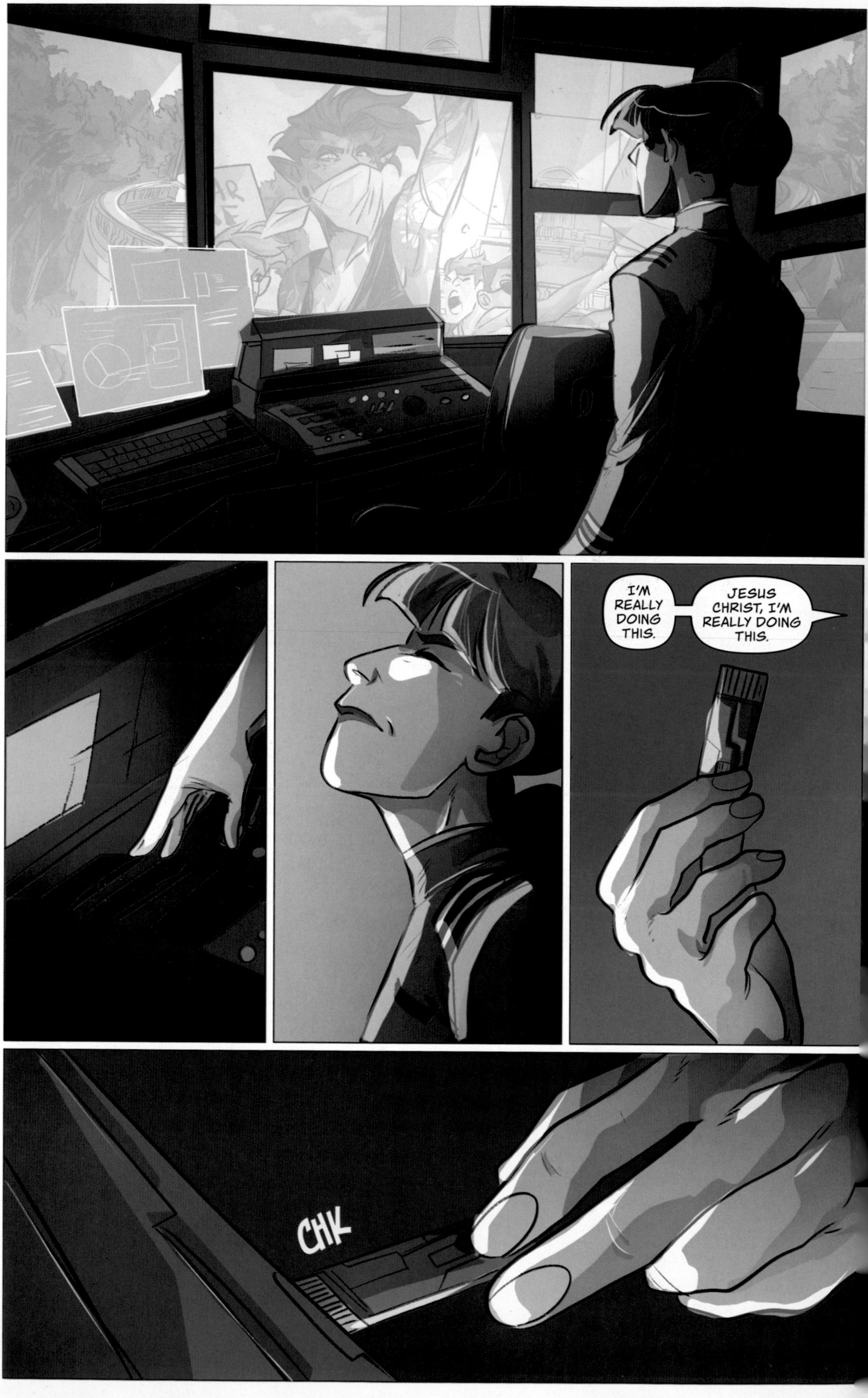
I'M REALLY DOING THIS.
JESUS CHRIST, I'M REALLY DOING THIS.
CHK

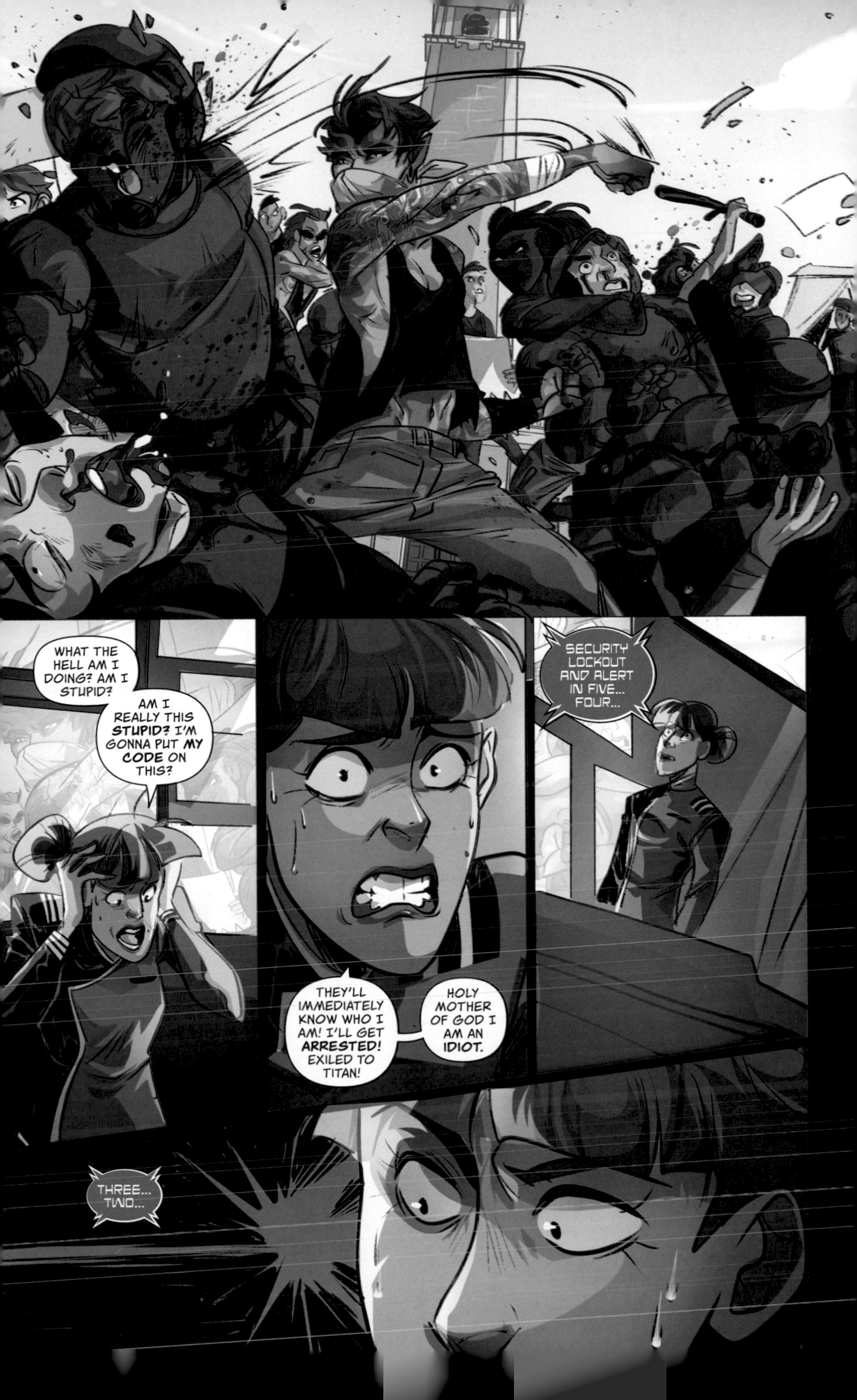

WHAT THE HELL AM I DOING? AM I STUPID?
AM I REALLY THIS **STUPID?** I'M GONNA PUT **MY CODE** ON THIS?
THEY'LL IMMEDIATELY KNOW WHO I AM! I'LL GET **ARRESTED!** EXILED TO TITAN!
HOLY MOTHER OF GOD I AM AN **IDIOT.**
SECURITY LOCKOUT AND ALERT IN FIVE... FOUR...
THREE... TWO...

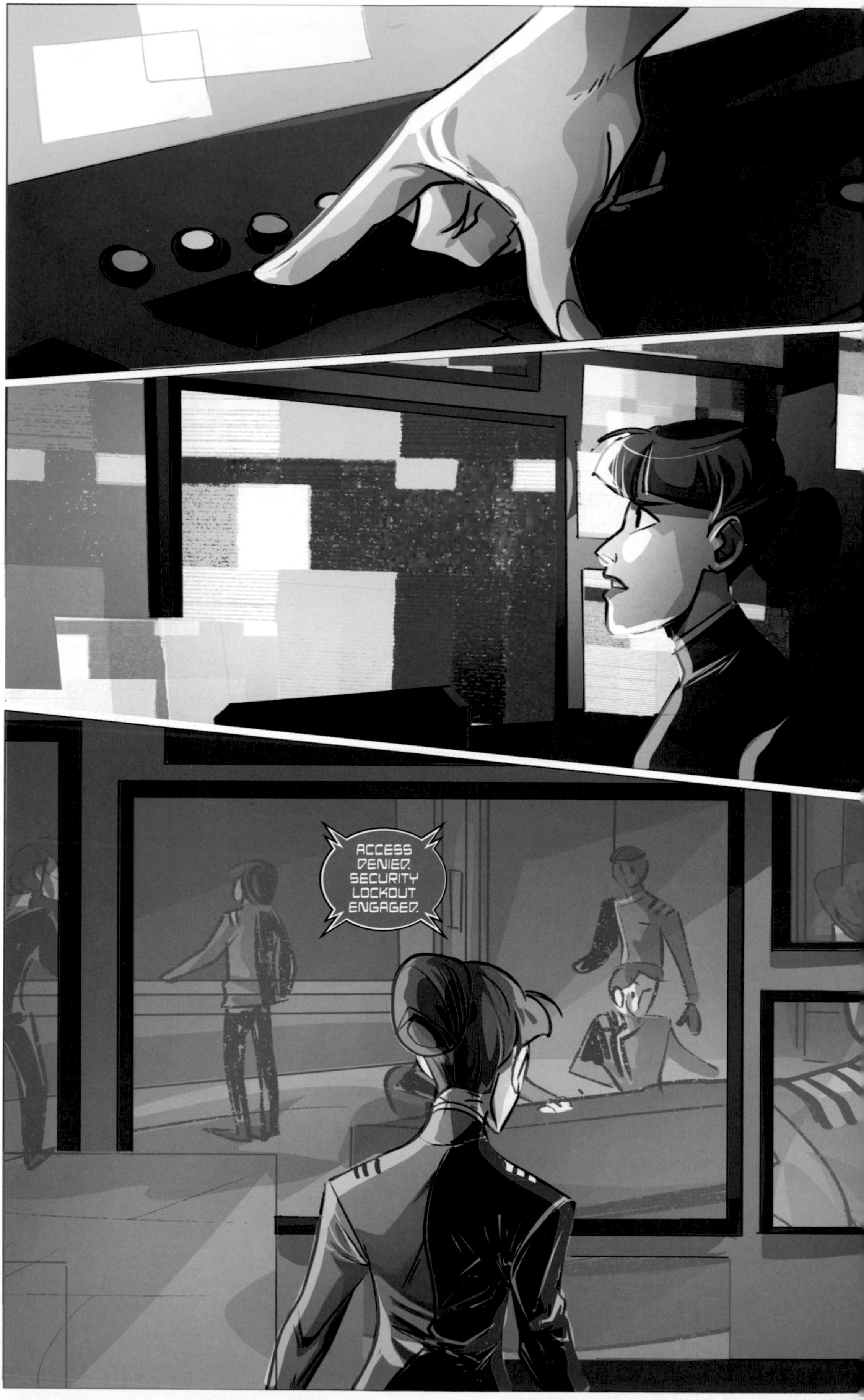
ACCESS DENIED. SECURITY LOCKOUT ENGAGED.

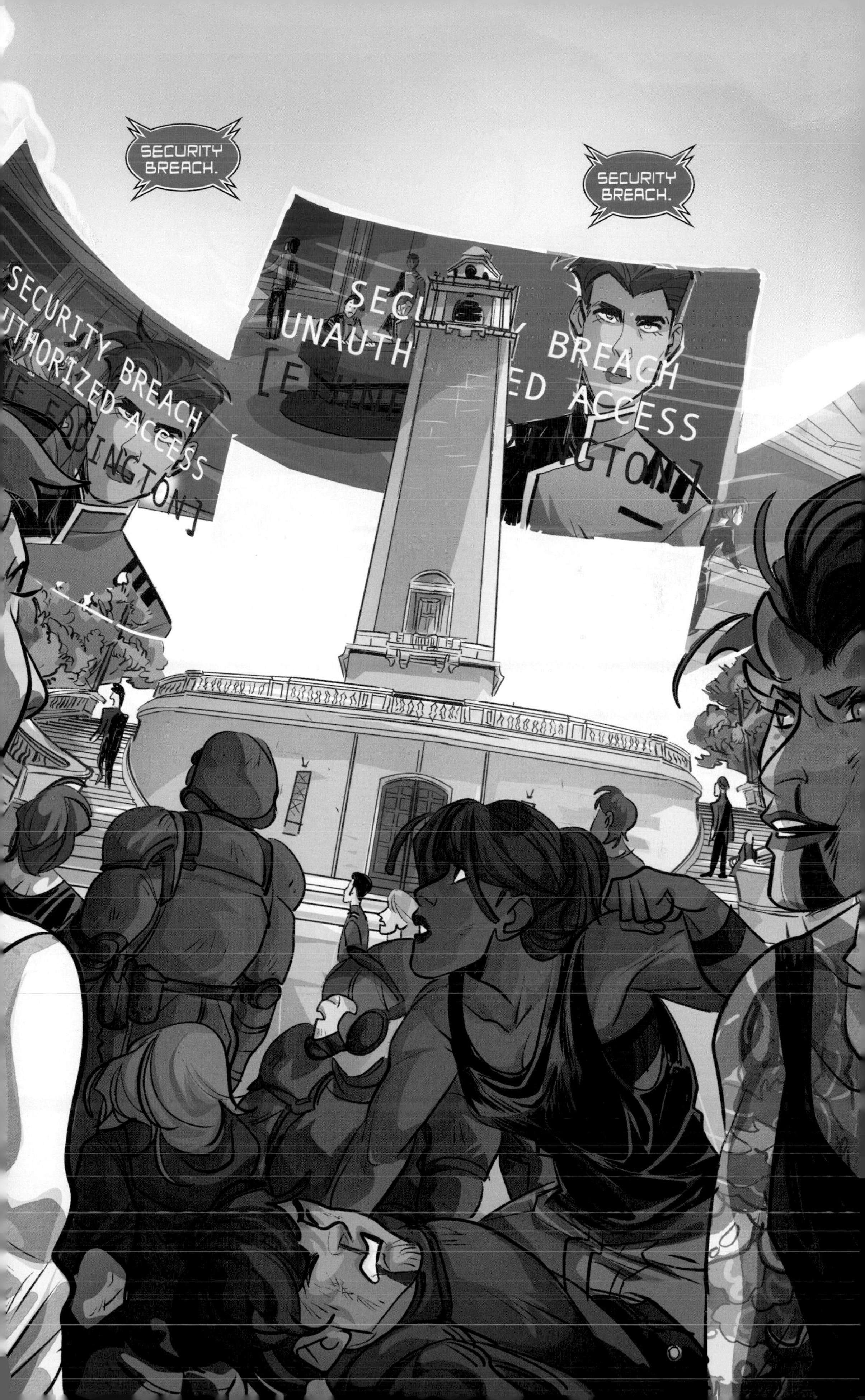
SECURITY BREACH.
SECURITY BREACH.
SECURITY BREACH

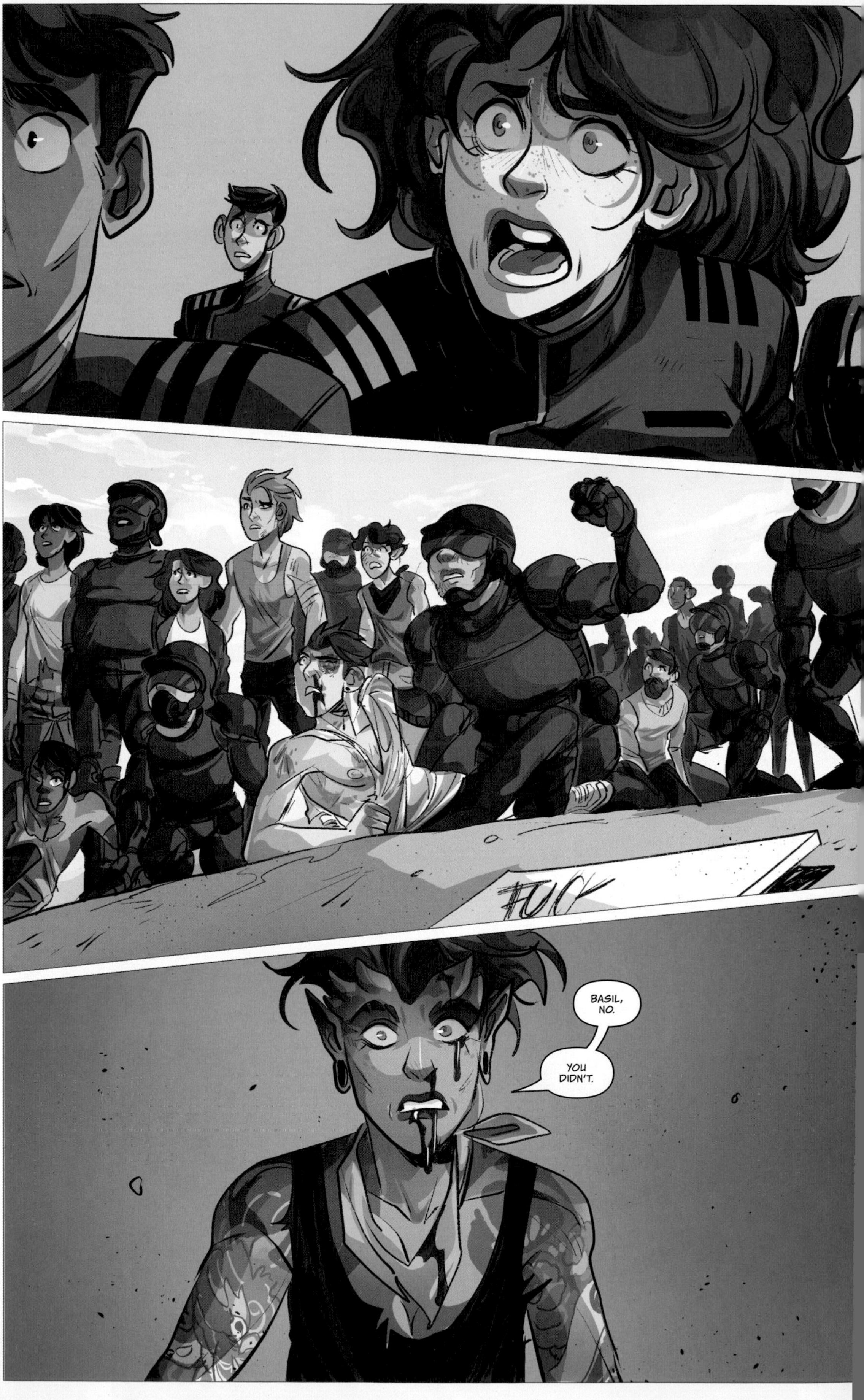
FUCK
BASIL, NO.
YOU DIDN'T.

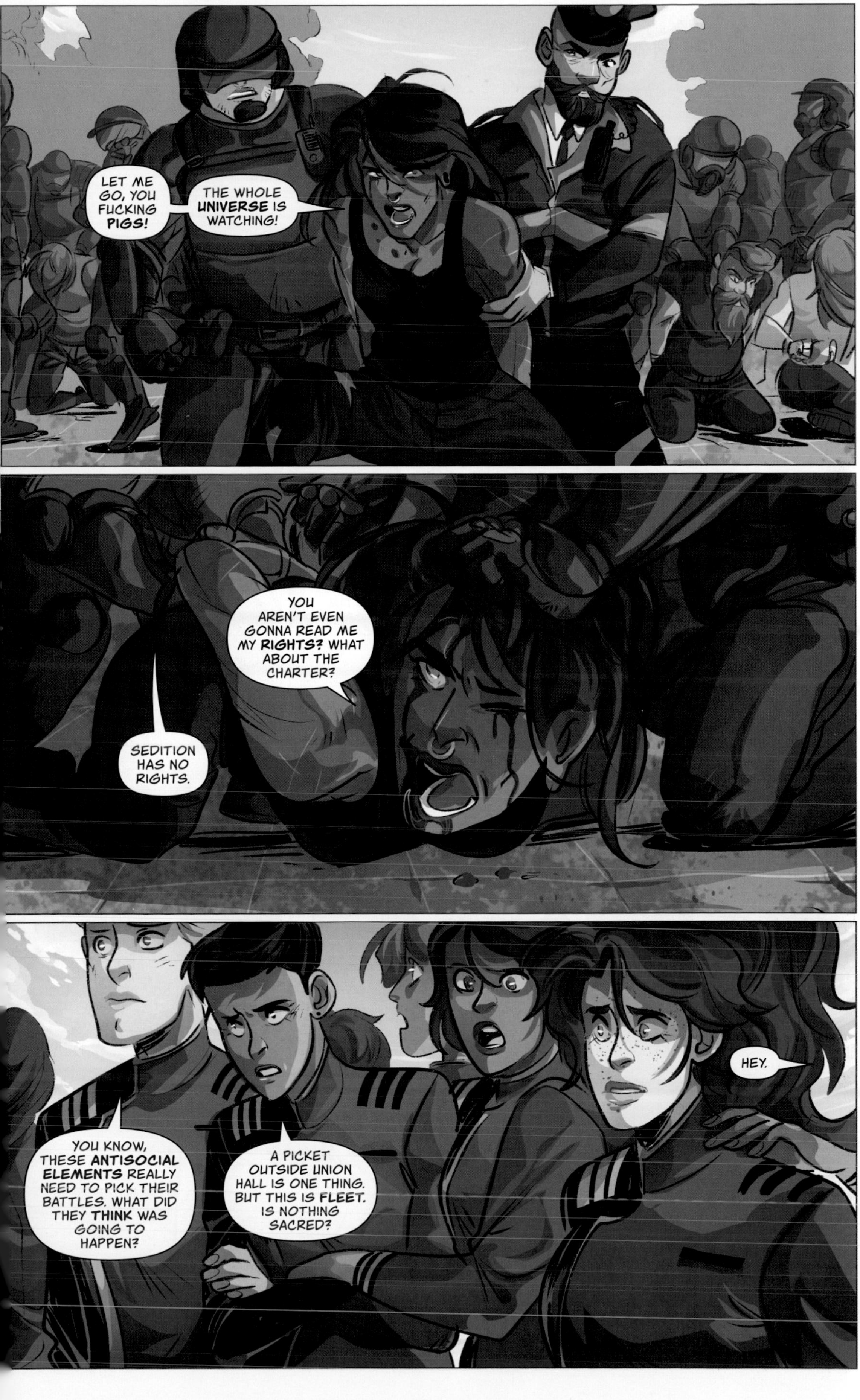

LET ME GO, YOU FUCKING PIGS!
THE WHOLE UNIVERSE IS WATCHING!
YOU AREN'T EVEN GONNA READ ME MY RIGHTS? WHAT ABOUT THE CHARTER?
SEDITION HAS NO RIGHTS.
HEY.
YOU KNOW, THESE ANTISOCIAL ELEMENTS REALLY NEED TO PICK THEIR BATTLES. WHAT DID THEY THINK WAS GOING TO HAPPEN?
A PICKET OUTSIDE UNION HALL IS ONE THING. BUT THIS IS FLEET. IS NOTHING SACRED?

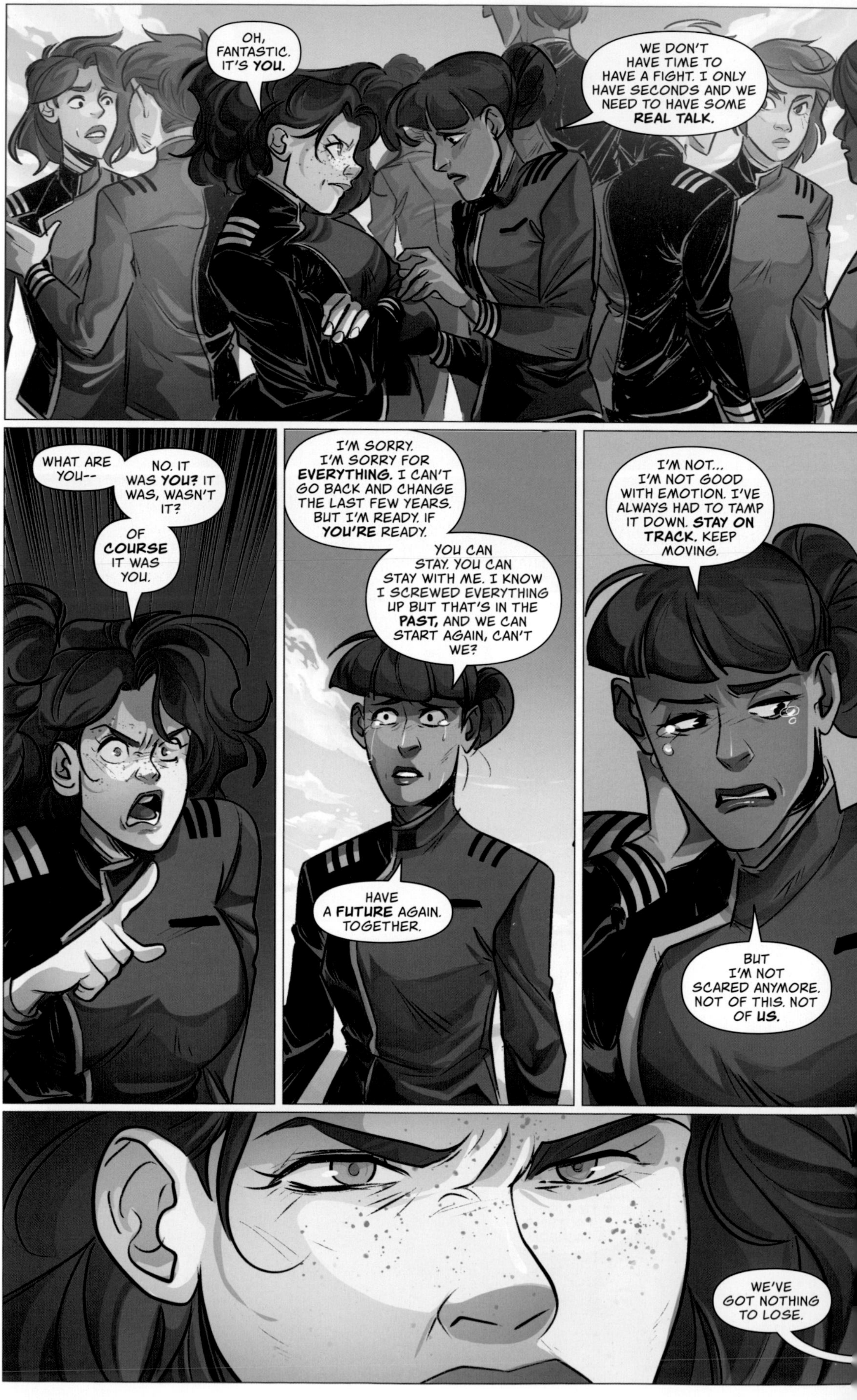
OH, FANTASTIC. IT'S YOU.
WE DON'T HAVE TIME TO HAVE A FIGHT. I ONLY HAVE SECONDS AND WE NEED TO HAVE SOME REAL TALK.
WHAT ARE YOU--
NO. IT WAS YOU? IT WAS, WASN'T IT?
OF COURSE IT WAS YOU.
I'M SORRY. I'M SORRY FOR EVERYTHING. I CAN'T GO BACK AND CHANGE THE LAST FEW YEARS. BUT I'M READY. IF YOU'RE READY.
YOU CAN STAY. YOU CAN STAY WITH ME. I KNOW I SCREWED EVERYTHING UP BUT THAT'S IN THE PAST, AND WE CAN START AGAIN, CAN'T WE?
HAVE A FUTURE AGAIN. TOGETHER.
I'M NOT... I'M NOT GOOD WITH EMOTION. I'VE ALWAYS HAD TO TAMP IT DOWN. STAY ON TRACK. KEEP MOVING.
BUT I'M NOT SCARED ANYMORE. NOT OF THIS. NOT OF US.
WE'VE GOT NOTHING TO LOSE.

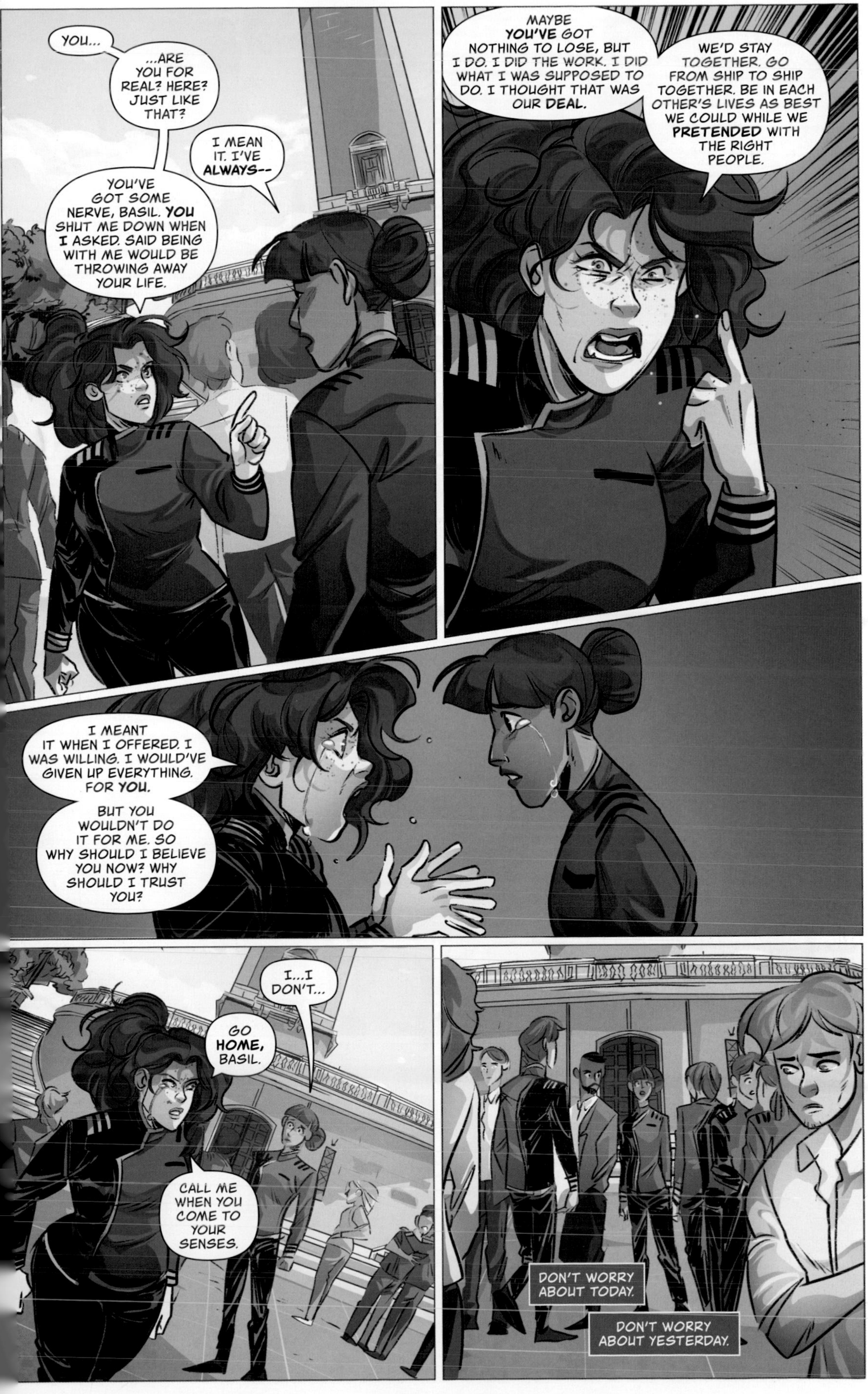
YOU...
...ARE YOU FOR REAL? HERE? JUST LIKE THAT?
I MEAN IT. I'VE **ALWAYS--**
YOU'VE GOT SOME NERVE, BASIL. **YOU** SHUT ME DOWN WHEN **I** ASKED. SAID BEING WITH ME WOULD BE THROWING AWAY YOUR LIFE.
MAYBE **YOU'VE** GOT NOTHING TO LOSE, BUT I DO. I DID THE WORK. I DID WHAT I WAS SUPPOSED TO DO. I THOUGHT THAT WAS OUR **DEAL.**
WE'D STAY TOGETHER. GO FROM SHIP TO SHIP TOGETHER. BE IN EACH OTHER'S LIVES AS BEST WE COULD WHILE WE **PRETENDED** WITH THE RIGHT PEOPLE.
I MEANT IT WHEN I OFFERED. I WAS WILLING. I WOULD'VE GIVEN UP EVERYTHING. FOR **YOU.**
BUT YOU WOULDN'T DO IT FOR ME. SO WHY SHOULD I BELIEVE YOU NOW? WHY SHOULD I TRUST YOU?
I...I DON'T...
GO **HOME,** BASIL.
CALL ME WHEN YOU COME TO YOUR SENSES.
DON'T WORRY ABOUT TODAY.
DON'T WORRY ABOUT YESTERDAY.

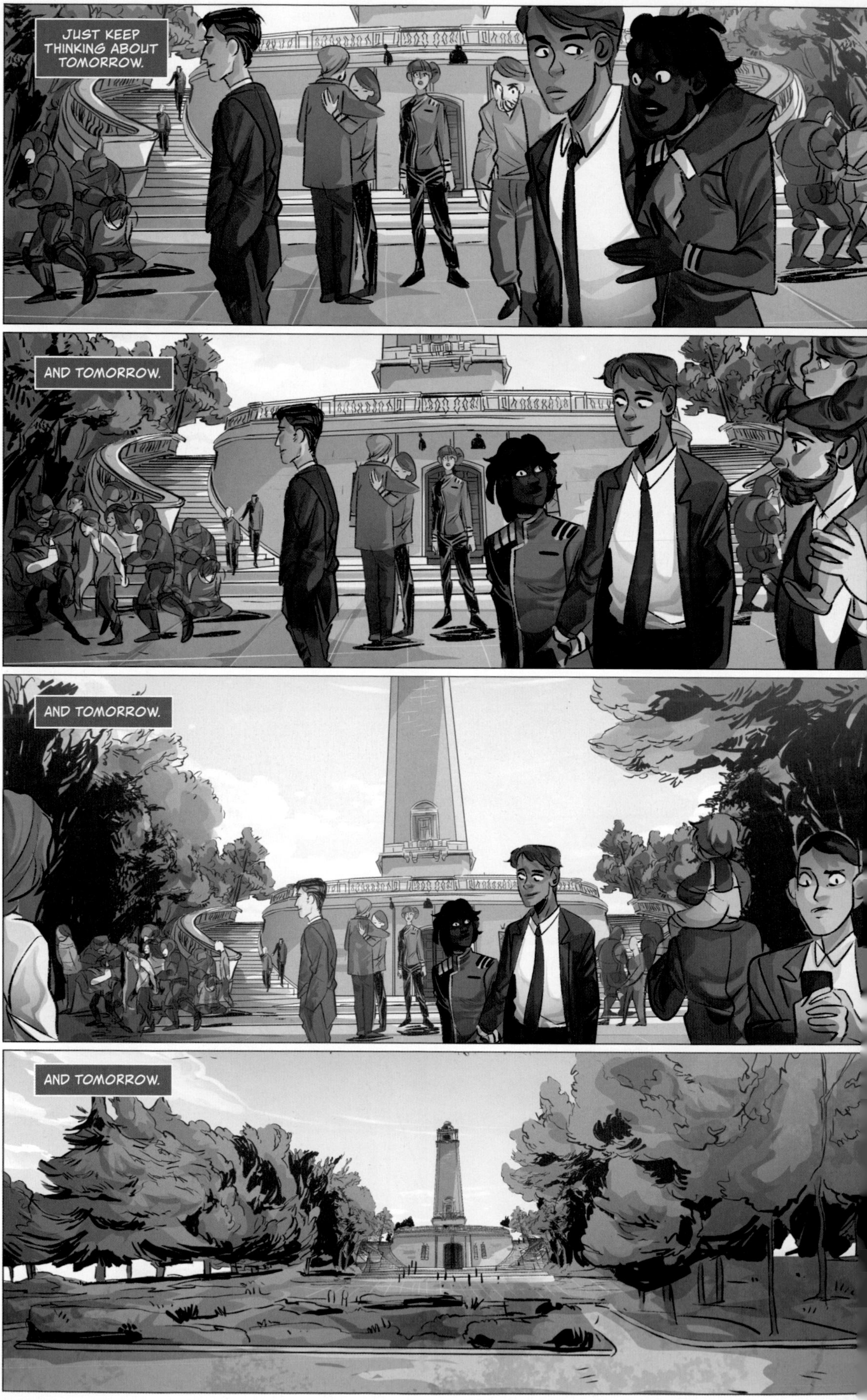
JUST KEEP THINKING ABOUT TOMORROW.
AND TOMORROW.
AND TOMORROW.
AND TOMORROW.

hapter **Four**

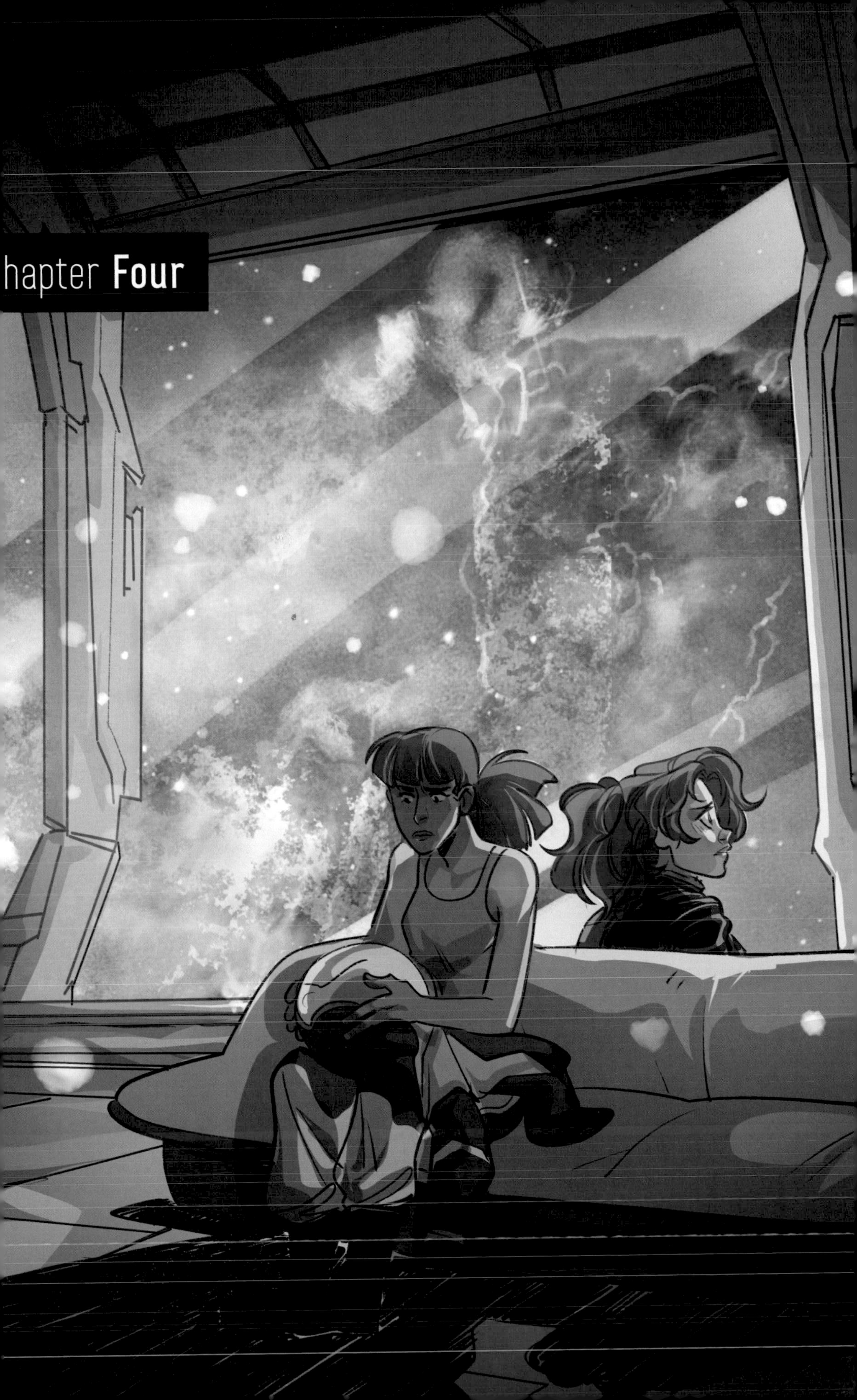

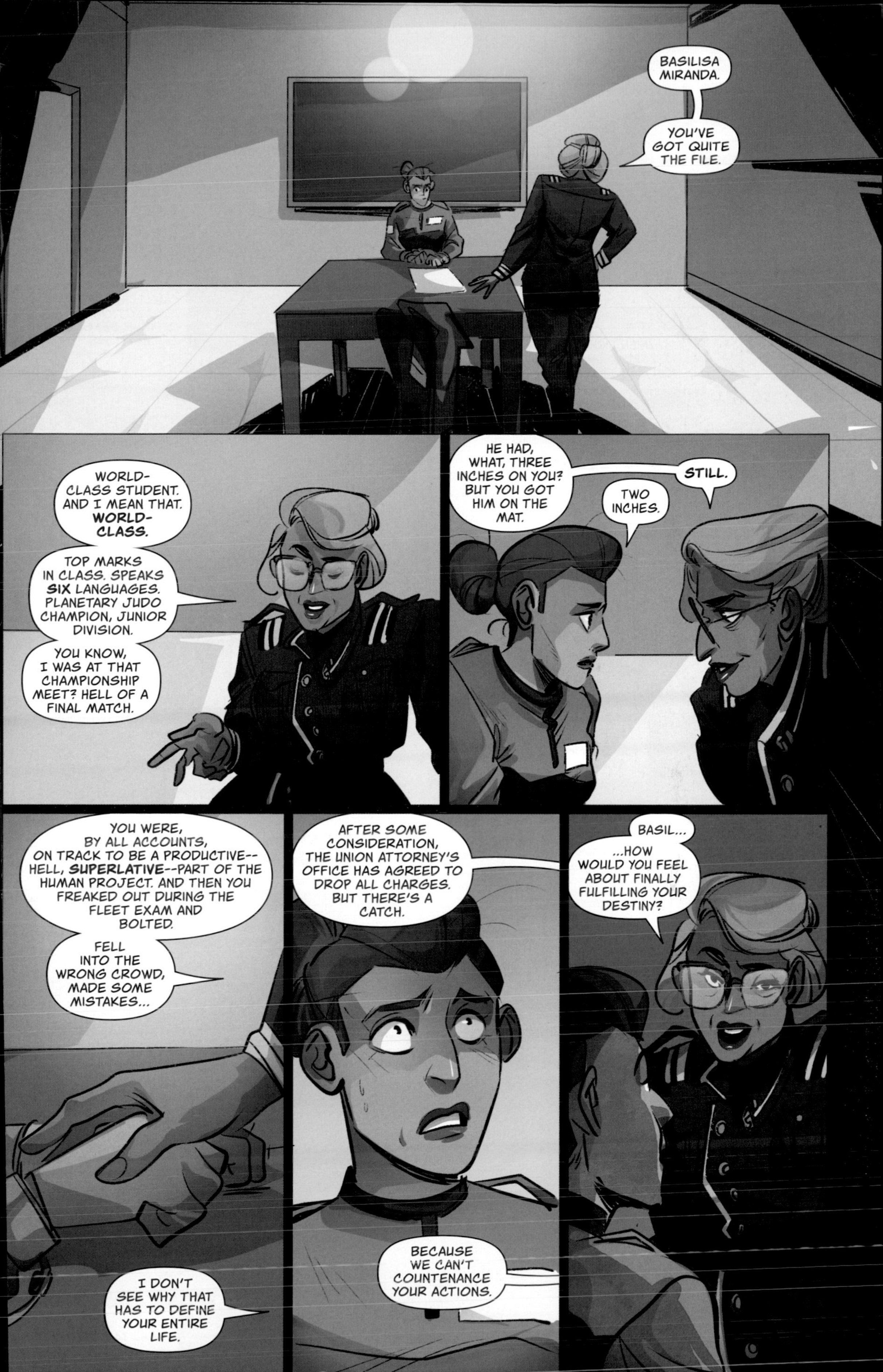
BASILISA MIRANDA.
YOU'VE GOT QUITE THE FILE.
WORLD-CLASS STUDENT. AND I MEAN THAT. **WORLD-CLASS.**
TOP MARKS IN CLASS. SPEAKS **SIX** LANGUAGES. PLANETARY JUDO CHAMPION, JUNIOR DIVISION.
YOU KNOW, I WAS AT THAT CHAMPIONSHIP MEET? HELL OF A FINAL MATCH.
HE HAD, WHAT, THREE INCHES ON YOU? BUT YOU GOT HIM ON THE MAT.
TWO INCHES.
STILL.
YOU WERE, BY ALL ACCOUNTS, ON TRACK TO BE A PRODUCTIVE--HELL, **SUPERLATIVE**--PART OF THE HUMAN PROJECT. AND THEN YOU FREAKED OUT DURING THE FLEET EXAM AND BOLTED.
FELL INTO THE WRONG CROWD, MADE SOME MISTAKES...
I DON'T SEE WHY THAT HAS TO DEFINE YOUR ENTIRE LIFE.
AFTER SOME CONSIDERATION, THE UNION ATTORNEY'S OFFICE HAS AGREED TO DROP ALL CHARGES. BUT THERE'S A CATCH.
BECAUSE WE CAN'T COUNTENANCE YOUR ACTIONS.
BASIL...
...HOW WOULD YOU FEEL ABOUT FINALLY FULFILLING YOUR DESTINY?

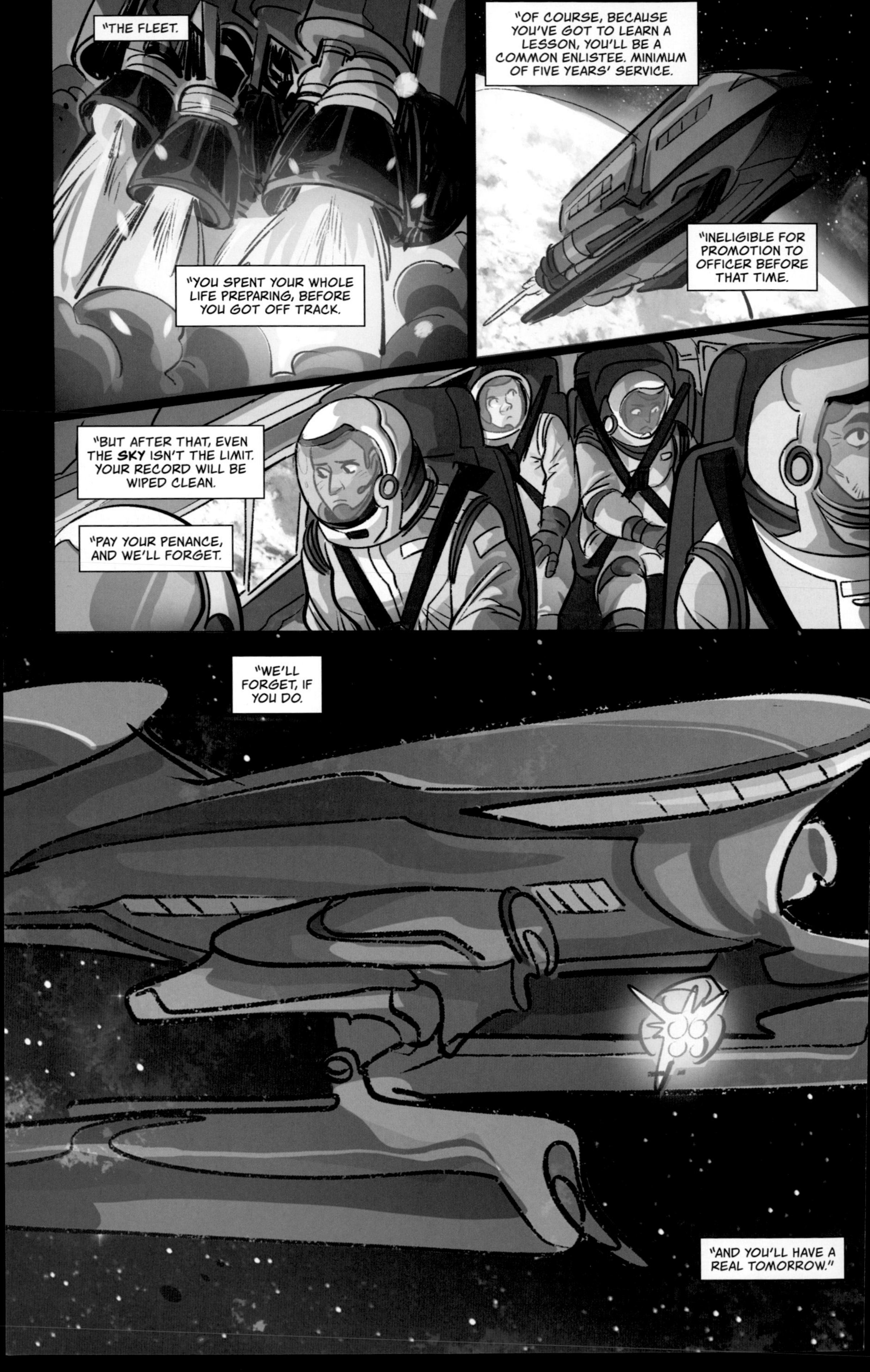
"THE FLEET.
"YOU SPENT YOUR WHOLE LIFE PREPARING, BEFORE YOU GOT OFF TRACK.
"OF COURSE, BECAUSE YOU'VE GOT TO LEARN A LESSON, YOU'LL BE A COMMON ENLISTEE. MINIMUM OF FIVE YEARS' SERVICE.
"INELIGIBLE FOR PROMOTION TO OFFICER BEFORE THAT TIME.
"BUT AFTER THAT, EVEN THE SKY ISN'T THE LIMIT. YOUR RECORD WILL BE WIPED CLEAN.
"PAY YOUR PENANCE, AND WE'LL FORGET.
"WE'LL FORGET, IF YOU DO.
"AND YOU'LL HAVE A REAL TOMORROW."

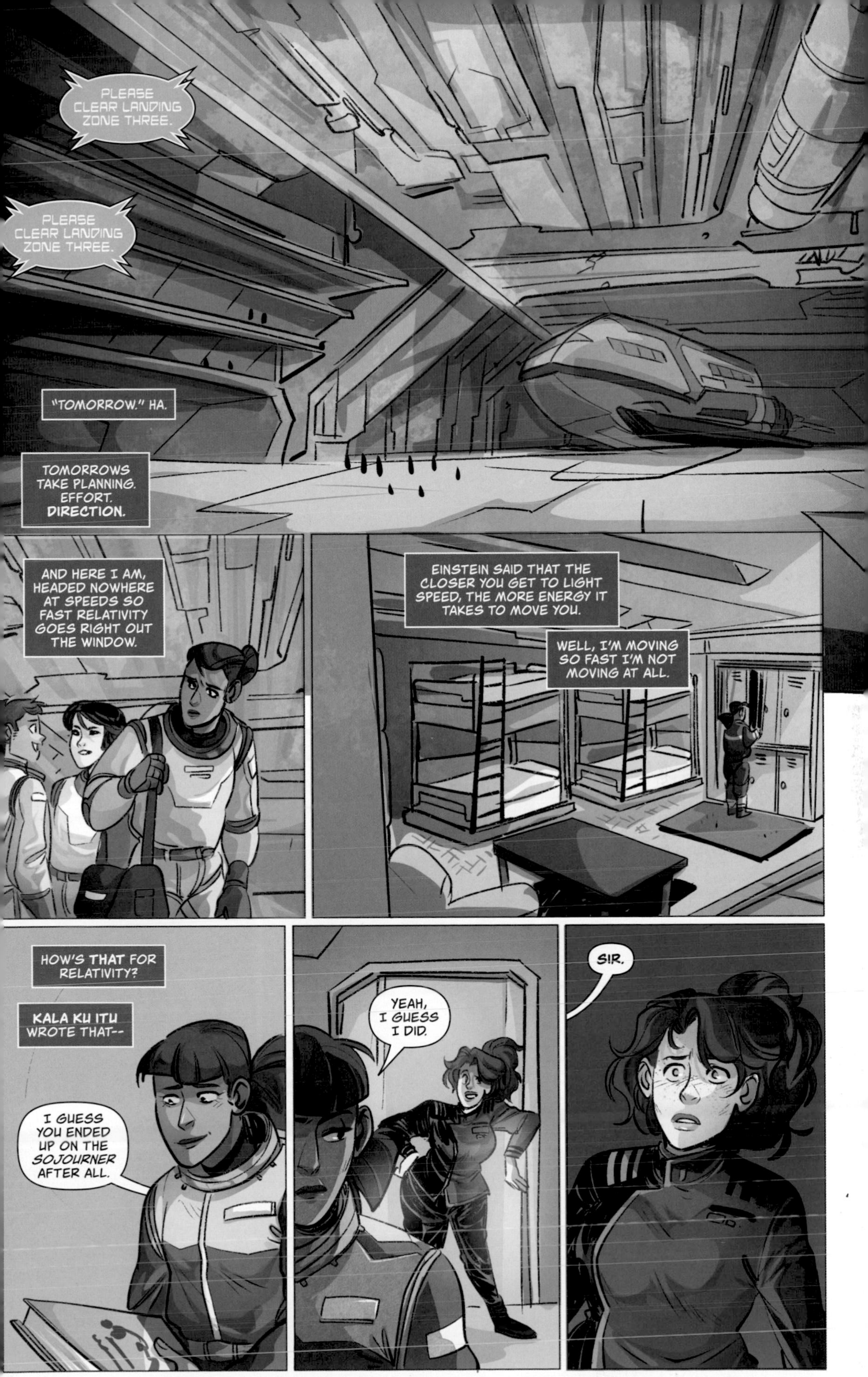
PLEASE CLEAR LANDING ZONE THREE.
PLEASE CLEAR LANDING ZONE THREE.
"TOMORROW." HA.
TOMORROWS TAKE PLANNING. EFFORT. DIRECTION.
AND HERE I AM, HEADED NOWHERE AT SPEEDS SO FAST RELATIVITY GOES RIGHT OUT THE WINDOW.
EINSTEIN SAID THAT THE CLOSER YOU GET TO LIGHT SPEED, THE MORE ENERGY IT TAKES TO MOVE YOU.
WELL, I'M MOVING SO FAST I'M NOT MOVING AT ALL.
HOW'S THAT FOR RELATIVITY?
KALA KU ITU WROTE THAT--
I GUESS YOU ENDED UP ON THE SOJOURNER AFTER ALL.
YEAH, I GUESS I DID.
SIR.

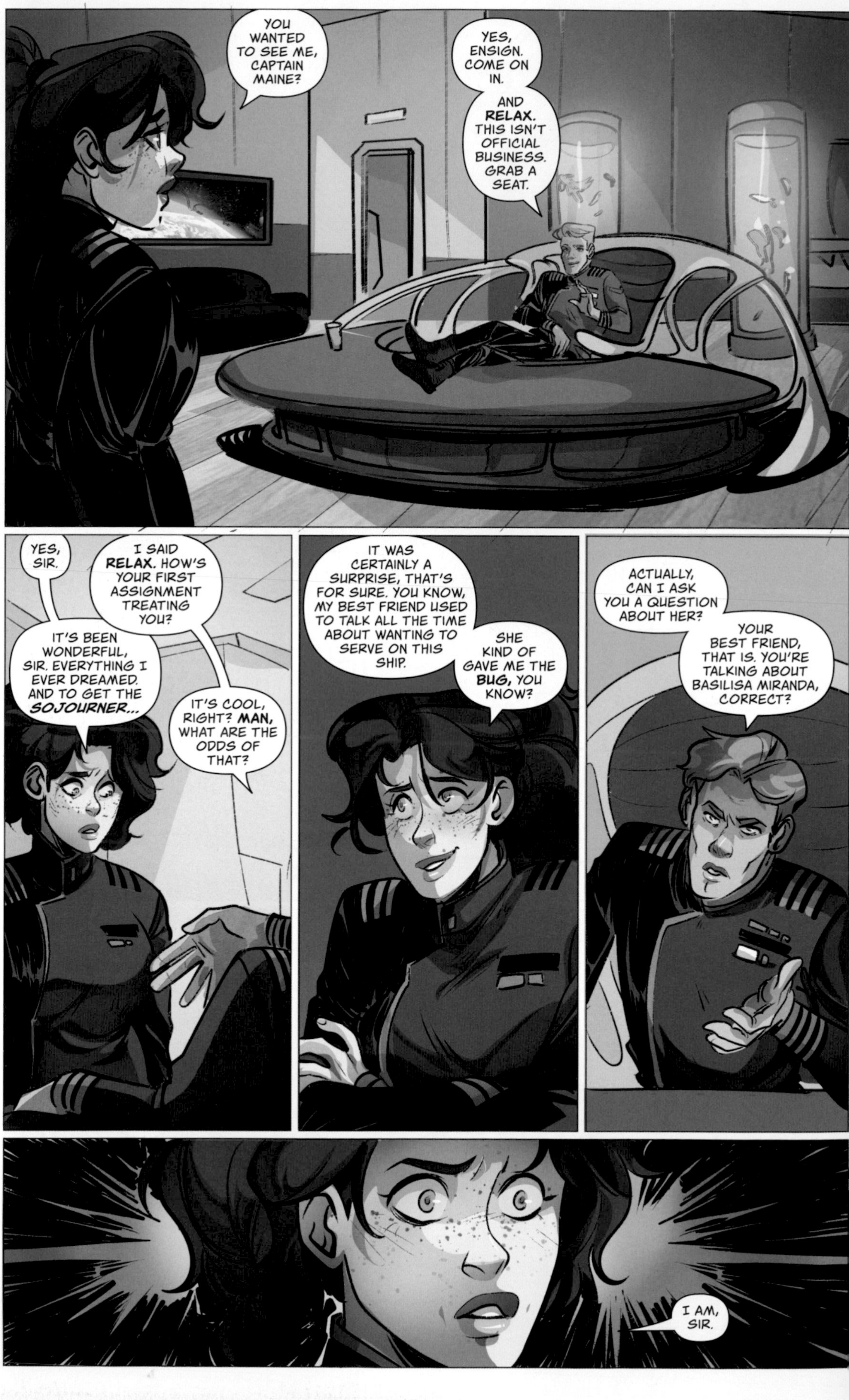
YOU WANTED TO SEE ME, CAPTAIN MAINE?
YES, ENSIGN. COME ON IN.
AND **RELAX.** THIS ISN'T OFFICIAL BUSINESS. GRAB A SEAT.
YES, SIR.
I SAID **RELAX.** HOW'S YOUR FIRST ASSIGNMENT TREATING YOU?
IT'S BEEN WONDERFUL, SIR. EVERYTHING I EVER DREAMED. AND TO GET THE ***SOJOURNER...***
IT'S COOL, RIGHT? **MAN,** WHAT ARE THE ODDS OF THAT?
IT WAS CERTAINLY A SURPRISE, THAT'S FOR SURE. YOU KNOW, MY BEST FRIEND USED TO TALK ALL THE TIME ABOUT WANTING TO SERVE ON THIS SHIP.
SHE KIND OF GAVE ME THE **BUG,** YOU KNOW?
ACTUALLY, CAN I ASK YOU A QUESTION ABOUT HER?
YOUR BEST FRIEND, THAT IS. YOU'RE TALKING ABOUT BASILISA MIRANDA, CORRECT?
I AM, SIR.

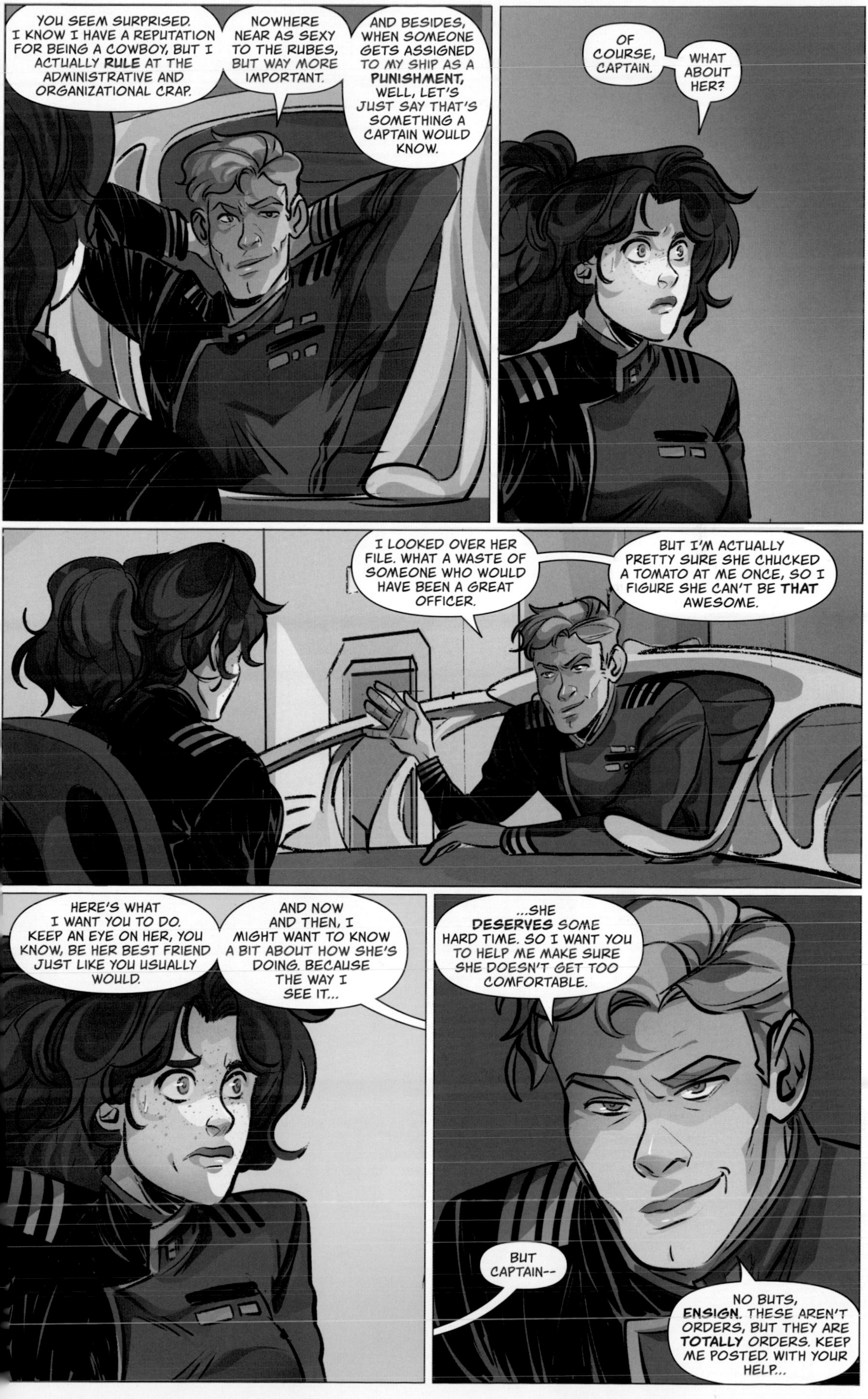
YOU SEEM SURPRISED. I KNOW I HAVE A REPUTATION FOR BEING A COWBOY, BUT I ACTUALLY **RULE** AT THE ADMINISTRATIVE AND ORGANIZATIONAL CRAP.
NOWHERE NEAR AS SEXY TO THE RUBES, BUT WAY MORE IMPORTANT.
AND BESIDES, WHEN SOMEONE GETS ASSIGNED TO MY SHIP AS A **PUNISHMENT,** WELL, LET'S JUST SAY THAT'S SOMETHING A CAPTAIN WOULD KNOW.
OF COURSE, CAPTAIN.
WHAT ABOUT HER?
I LOOKED OVER HER FILE. WHAT A WASTE OF SOMEONE WHO WOULD HAVE BEEN A GREAT OFFICER.
BUT I'M ACTUALLY PRETTY SURE SHE CHUCKED A TOMATO AT ME ONCE, SO I FIGURE SHE CAN'T BE **THAT** AWESOME.
HERE'S WHAT I WANT YOU TO DO. KEEP AN EYE ON HER, YOU KNOW, BE HER BEST FRIEND JUST LIKE YOU USUALLY WOULD.
AND NOW AND THEN, I MIGHT WANT TO KNOW A BIT ABOUT HOW SHE'S DOING. BECAUSE THE WAY I SEE IT...
...SHE **DESERVES** SOME HARD TIME. SO I WANT YOU TO HELP ME MAKE SURE SHE DOESN'T GET TOO COMFORTABLE.
BUT CAPTAIN--
NO BUTS, **ENSIGN.** THESE AREN'T ORDERS, BUT THEY ARE **TOTALLY** ORDERS. KEEP ME POSTED. WITH YOUR HELP...

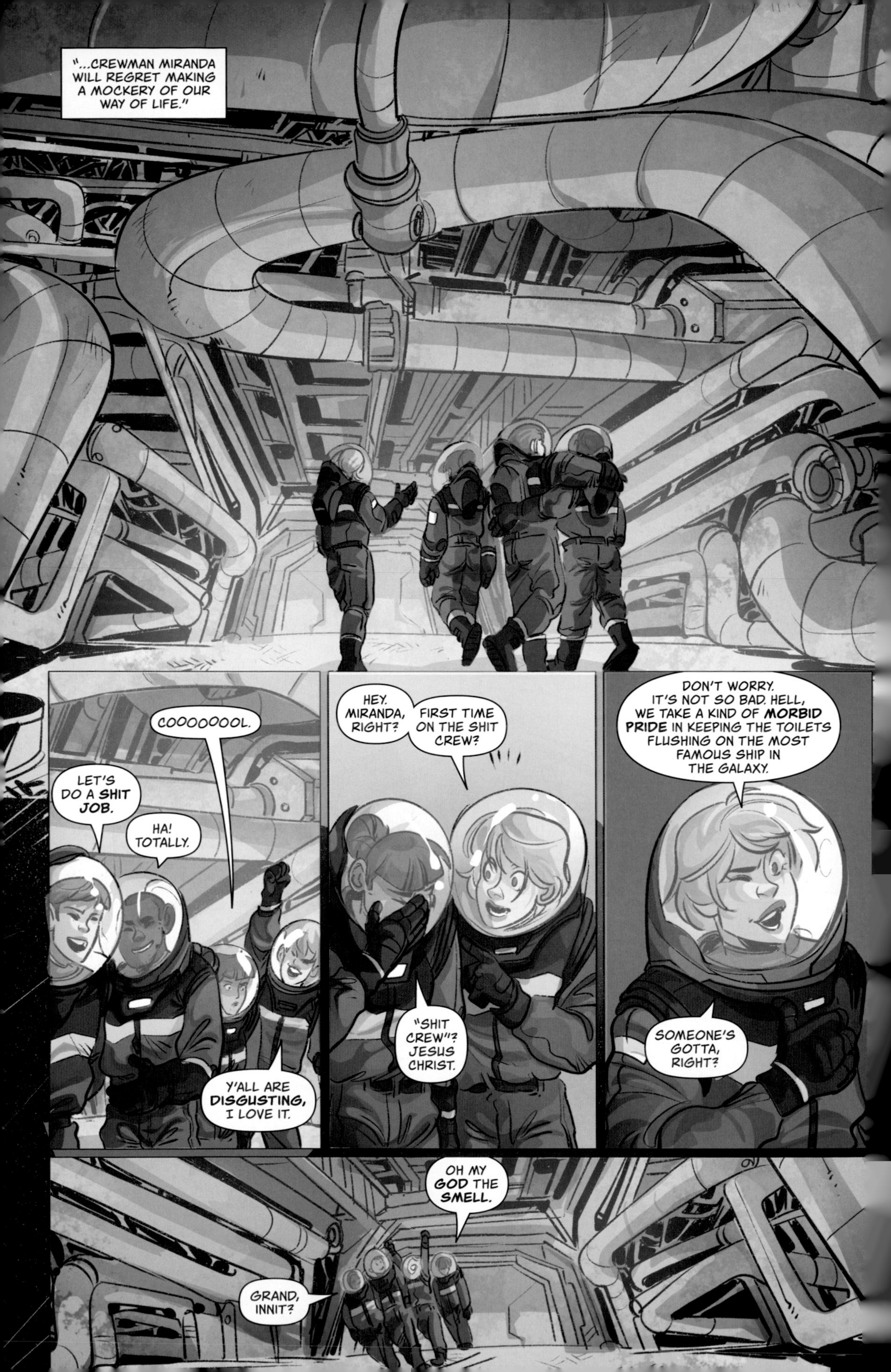
"...CREWMAN MIRANDA WILL REGRET MAKING A MOCKERY OF OUR WAY OF LIFE."
COOOOOOOL.
LET'S DO A **SHIT JOB**.
HA! TOTALLY.
Y'ALL ARE **DISGUSTING,** I LOVE IT.
HEY. MIRANDA, RIGHT?
FIRST TIME ON THE SHIT CREW?
"SHIT CREW"? JESUS CHRIST.
DON'T WORRY. IT'S NOT SO BAD. HELL, WE TAKE A KIND OF **MORBID PRIDE** IN KEEPING THE TOILETS FLUSHING ON THE MOST FAMOUS SHIP IN THE GALAXY.
SOMEONE'S GOTTA, RIGHT?
OH MY **GOD** THE **SMELL.**
GRAND, INNIT?

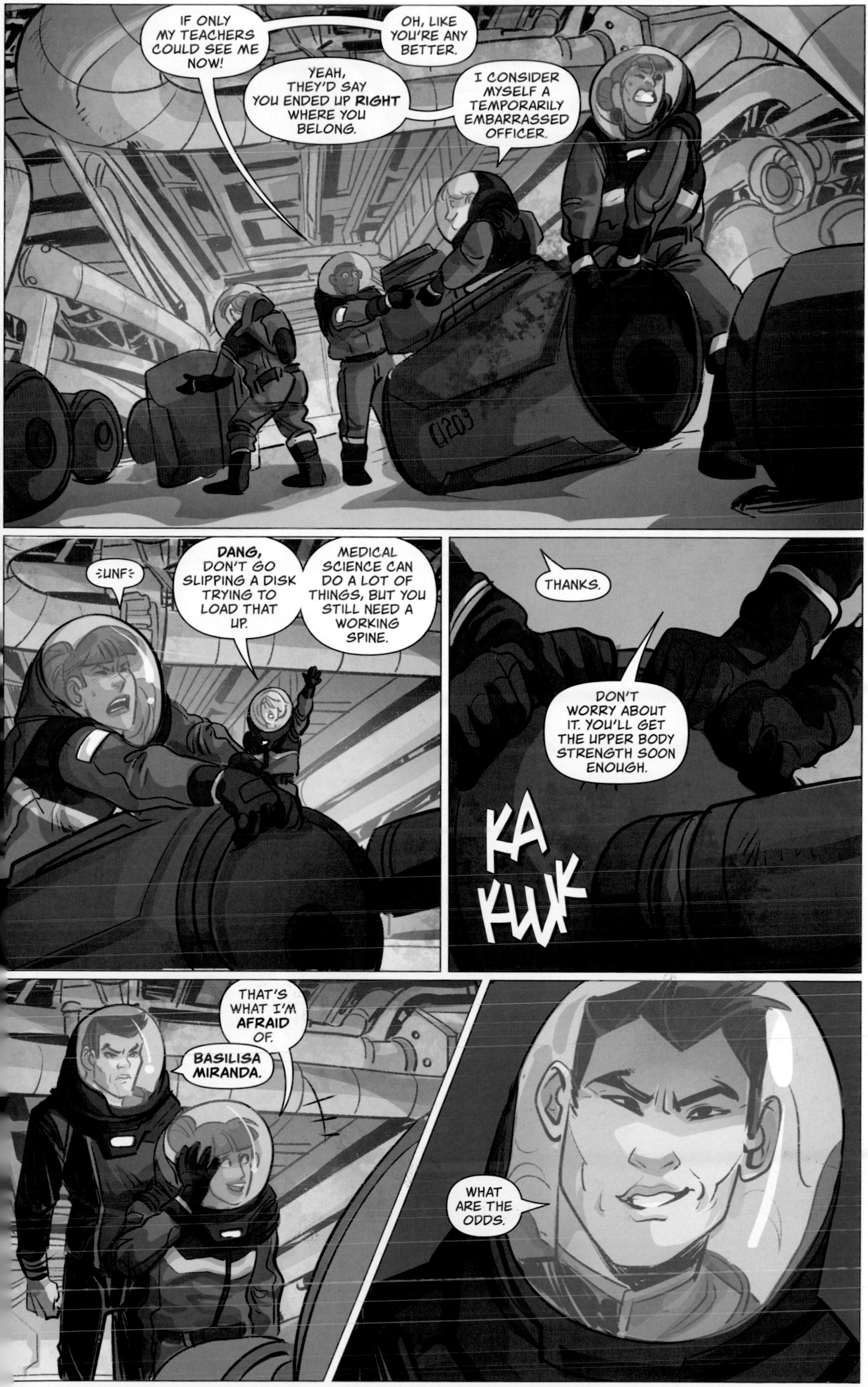
IF ONLY MY TEACHERS COULD SEE ME NOW!
OH, LIKE YOU'RE ANY BETTER.
YEAH, THEY'D SAY YOU ENDED UP **RIGHT** WHERE YOU BELONG.
I CONSIDER MYSELF A TEMPORARILY EMBARRASSED OFFICER.
C1203
UNF
DANG, DON'T GO SLIPPING A DISK TRYING TO LOAD THAT UP.
MEDICAL SCIENCE CAN DO A LOT OF THINGS, BUT YOU STILL NEED A WORKING SPINE.
THANKS.
DON'T WORRY ABOUT IT. YOU'LL GET THE UPPER BODY STRENGTH SOON ENOUGH.
KA KWK
THAT'S WHAT I'M **AFRAID** OF.
BASILISA MIRANDA.
WHAT ARE THE ODDS.

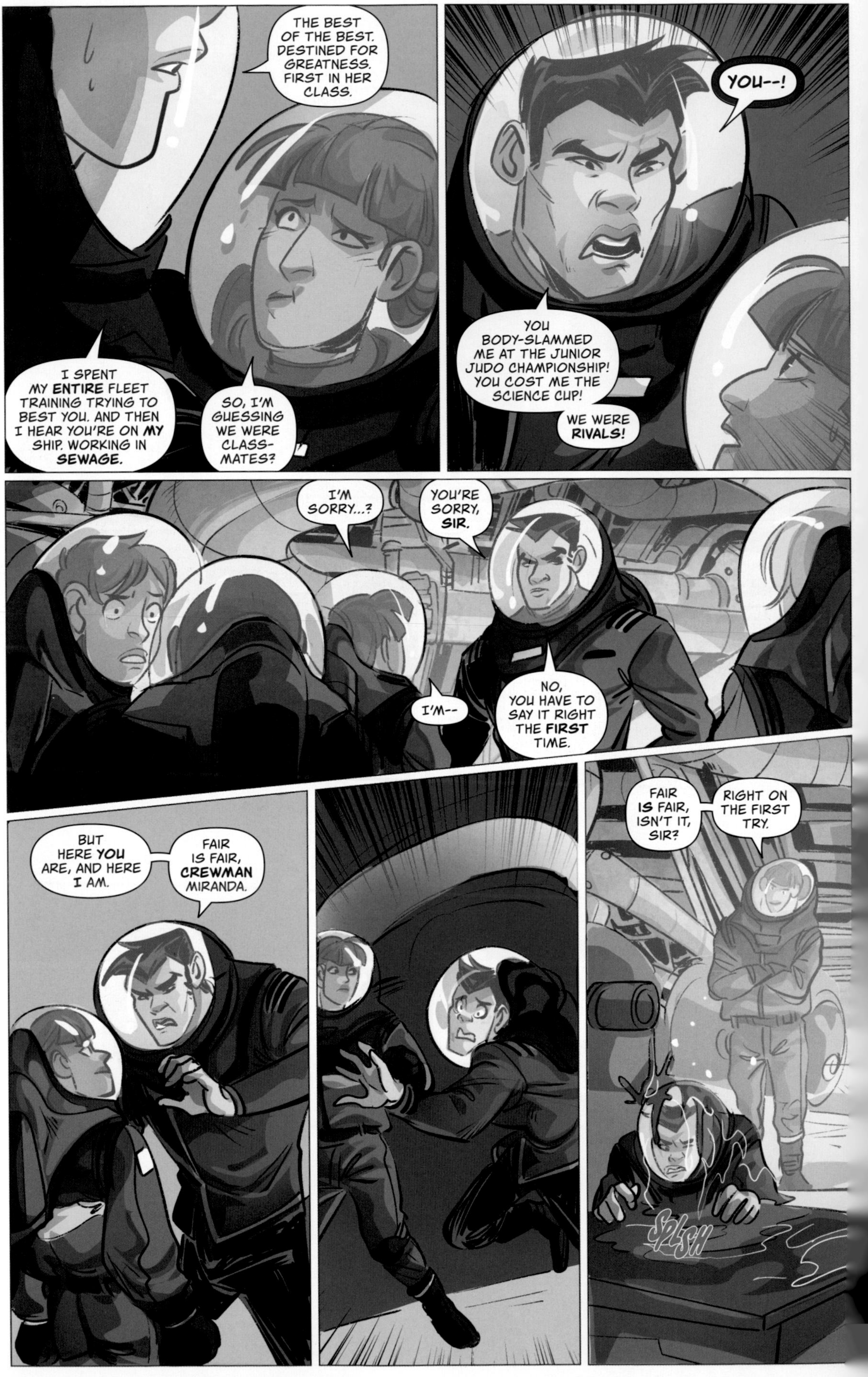
THE BEST OF THE BEST. DESTINED FOR GREATNESS. FIRST IN HER CLASS.
I SPENT MY **ENTIRE** FLEET TRAINING TRYING TO BEST YOU. AND THEN I HEAR YOU'RE ON **MY** SHIP. WORKING IN **SEWAGE.**
SO, I'M GUESSING WE WERE CLASS-MATES?
YOU--!
YOU BODY-SLAMMED ME AT THE JUNIOR JUDO CHAMPIONSHIP! YOU COST ME THE SCIENCE CUP!
WE WERE **RIVALS!**
I'M SORRY...?
YOU'RE SORRY, **SIR.**
I'M--
NO, YOU HAVE TO SAY IT RIGHT THE **FIRST** TIME.
BUT HERE **YOU** ARE, AND HERE **I** AM.
FAIR IS FAIR, **CREWMAN** MIRANDA.
FAIR **IS** FAIR, ISN'T IT, SIR?
RIGHT ON THE FIRST TRY.
SPLSH

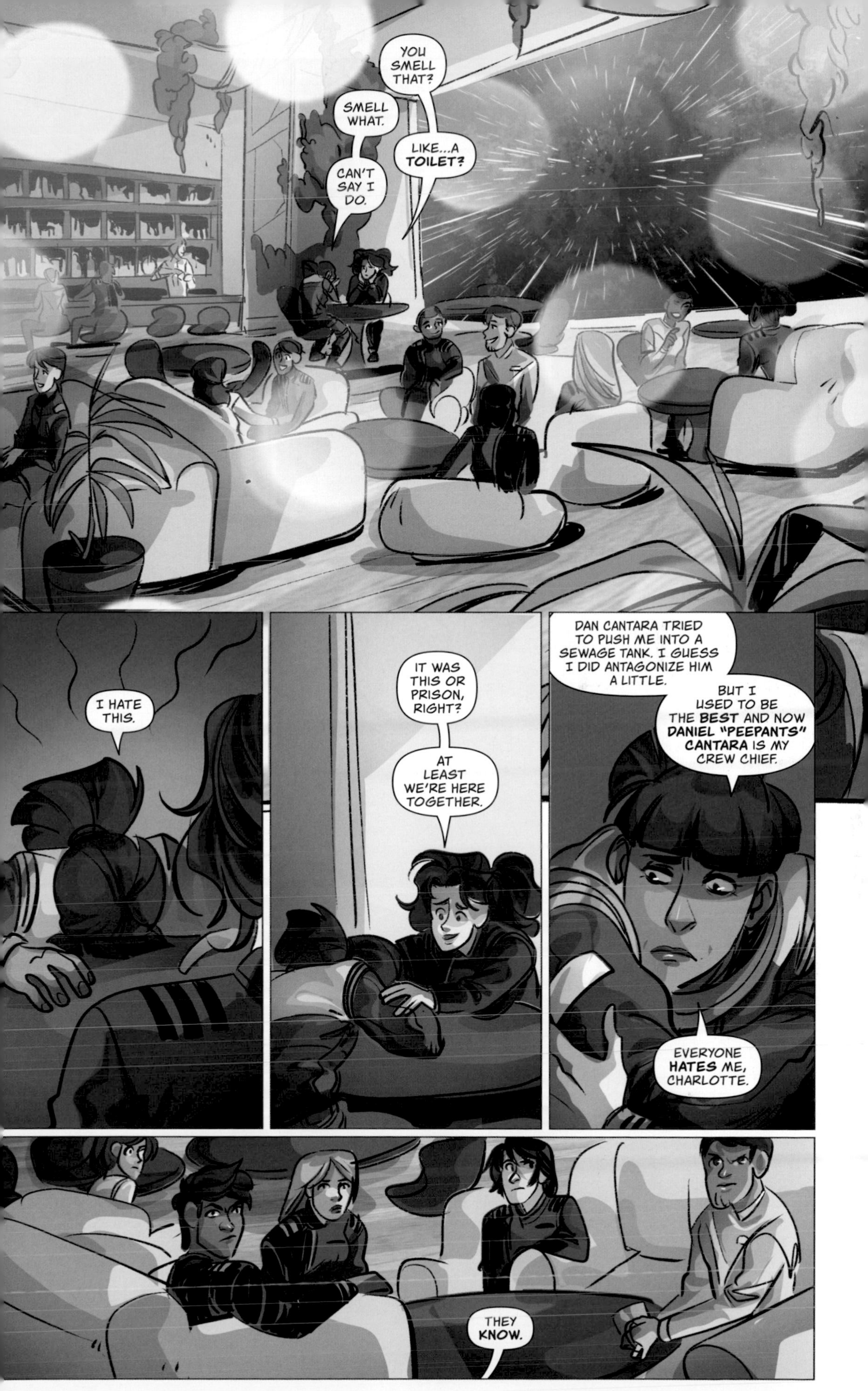
YOU SMELL THAT?
SMELL WHAT.
LIKE...A TOILET?
CAN'T SAY I DO.
I HATE THIS.
IT WAS THIS OR PRISON, RIGHT?
AT LEAST WE'RE HERE TOGETHER.
DAN CANTARA TRIED TO PUSH ME INTO A SEWAGE TANK. I GUESS I DID ANTAGONIZE HIM A LITTLE.
BUT I USED TO BE THE BEST AND NOW DANIEL "PEEPANTS" CANTARA IS MY CREW CHIEF.
EVERYONE HATES ME, CHARLOTTE.
THEY KNOW.

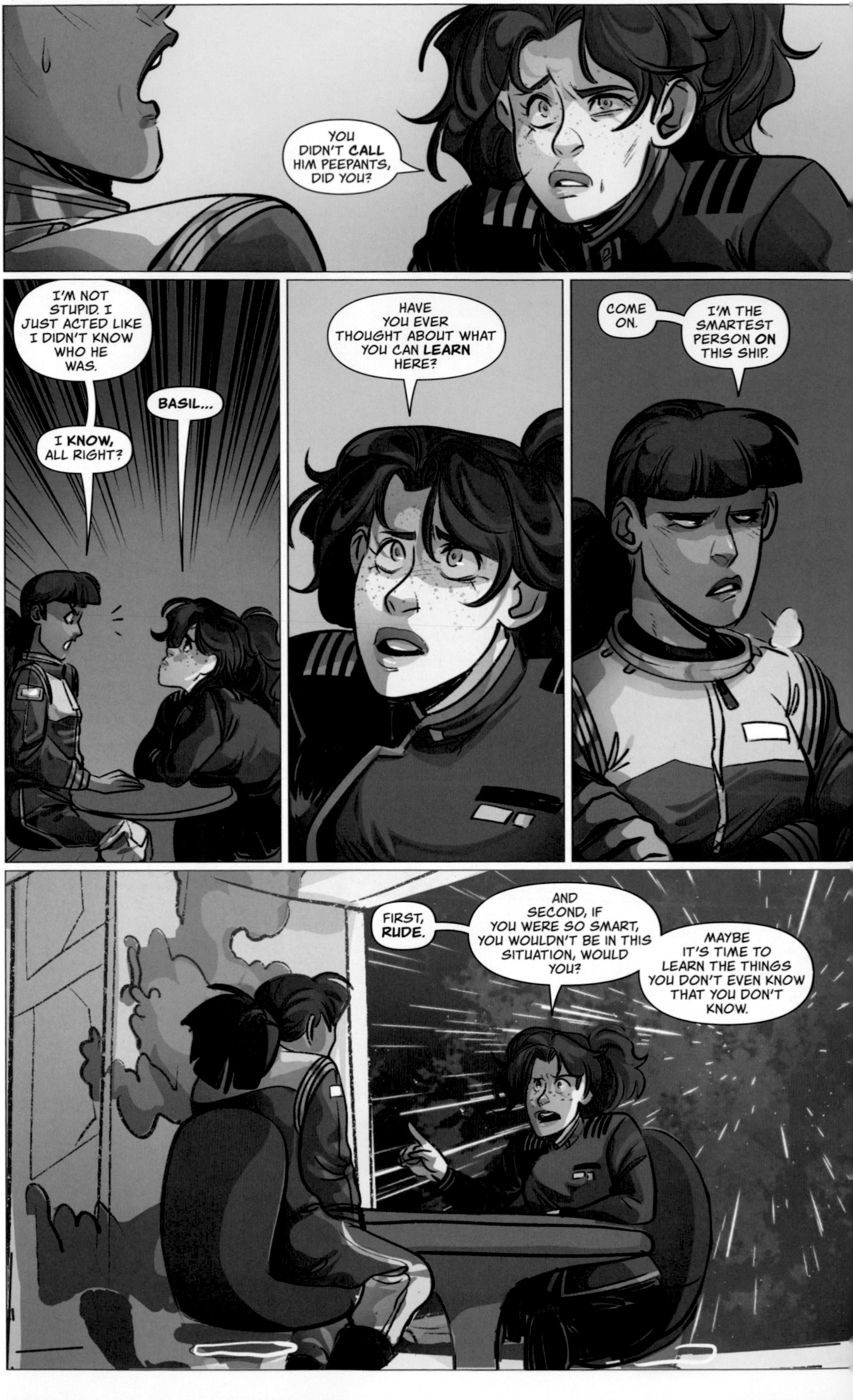
YOU DIDN'T CALL HIM PEEPANTS, DID YOU?
I'M NOT STUPID. I JUST ACTED LIKE I DIDN'T KNOW WHO HE WAS.
BASIL...
I KNOW, ALL RIGHT?
HAVE YOU EVER THOUGHT ABOUT WHAT YOU CAN LEARN HERE?
COME ON.
I'M THE SMARTEST PERSON ON THIS SHIP.
FIRST, RUDE.
AND SECOND, IF YOU WERE SO SMART, YOU WOULDN'T BE IN THIS SITUATION, WOULD YOU?
MAYBE IT'S TIME TO LEARN THE THINGS YOU DON'T EVEN KNOW THAT YOU DON'T KNOW.

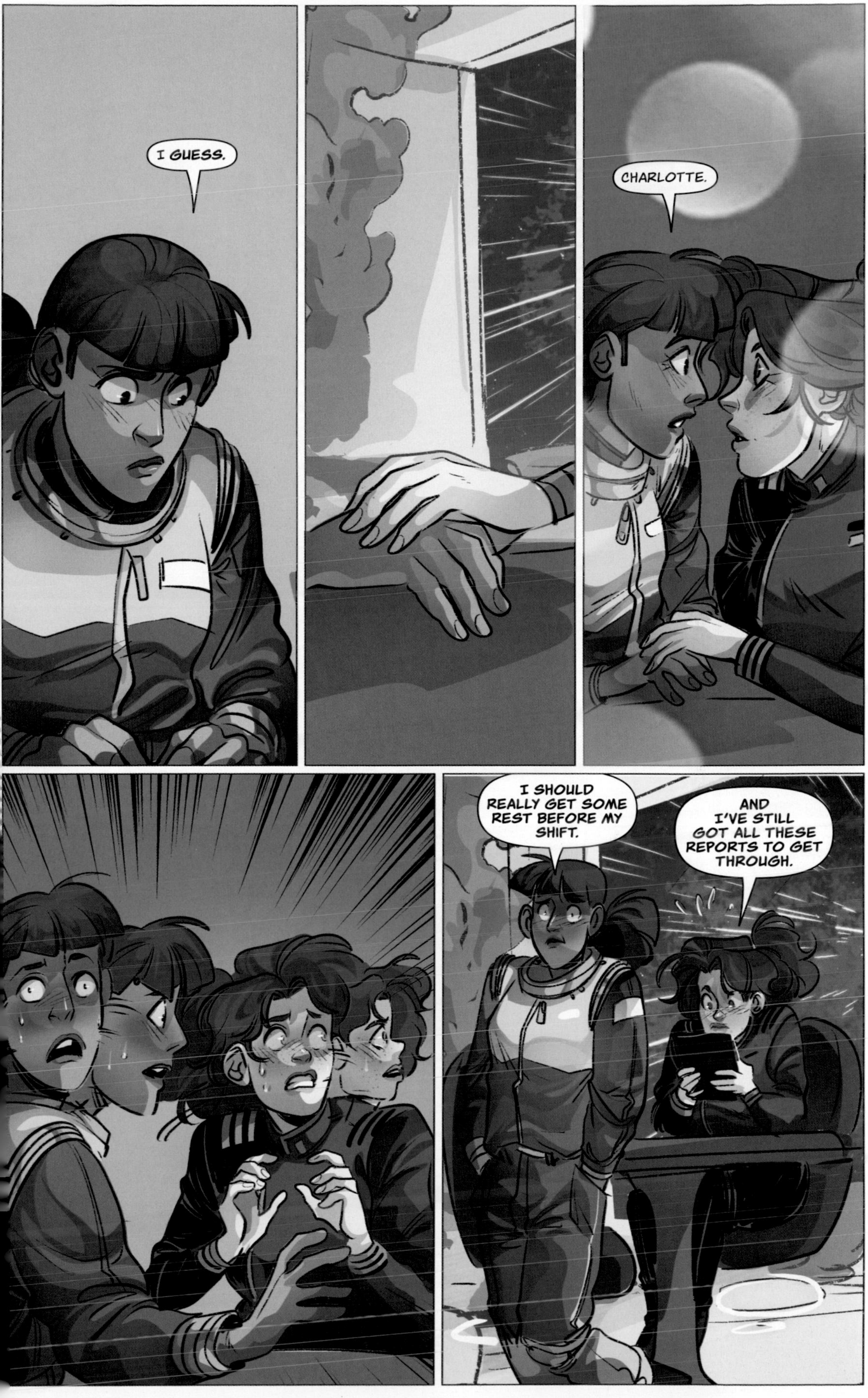
I GUESS.
CHARLOTTE.
I SHOULD REALLY GET SOME REST BEFORE MY SHIFT.
AND I'VE STILL GOT ALL THESE REPORTS TO GET THROUGH.

DOOT DOOT

ENTER.

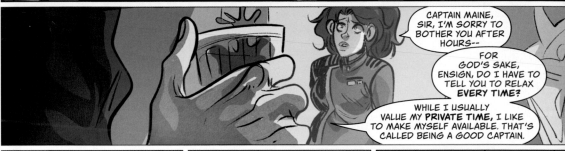

CAPTAIN MAINE, SIR, I'M SORRY TO BOTHER YOU AFTER HOURS--

FOR GOD'S SAKE, ENSIGN, DO I HAVE TO TELL YOU TO RELAX **EVERY TIME?**

WHILE I USUALLY VALUE MY **PRIVATE TIME,** I LIKE TO MAKE MYSELF AVAILABLE. THAT'S CALLED BEING A GOOD CAPTAIN.

I WAS HOPING WE COULD TALK ABOUT CREWMAN MIRANDA--

I DON'T DRINK, SIR. ABOUT MIRA--

I BET YOU'RE EXCITED ABOUT YOUR FIRST MISSION. YOU'RE LUCKY, TOO. I HEAR MARGARTEN IS A LOVELY COLONY. NIGHTCAP?

OF COURSE YOU DON'T. YOU'RE A NEW, YOUNG OFFICER. HEALTHY BODY, HEALTHY MIND. BUT YOU'RE NOT ON EARTH, MS. DEEGAN.

I BET YOU'D LIKE **SCOTCH.**

BOTTOMS UP, ENSIGN.

BOTTOMS UP.

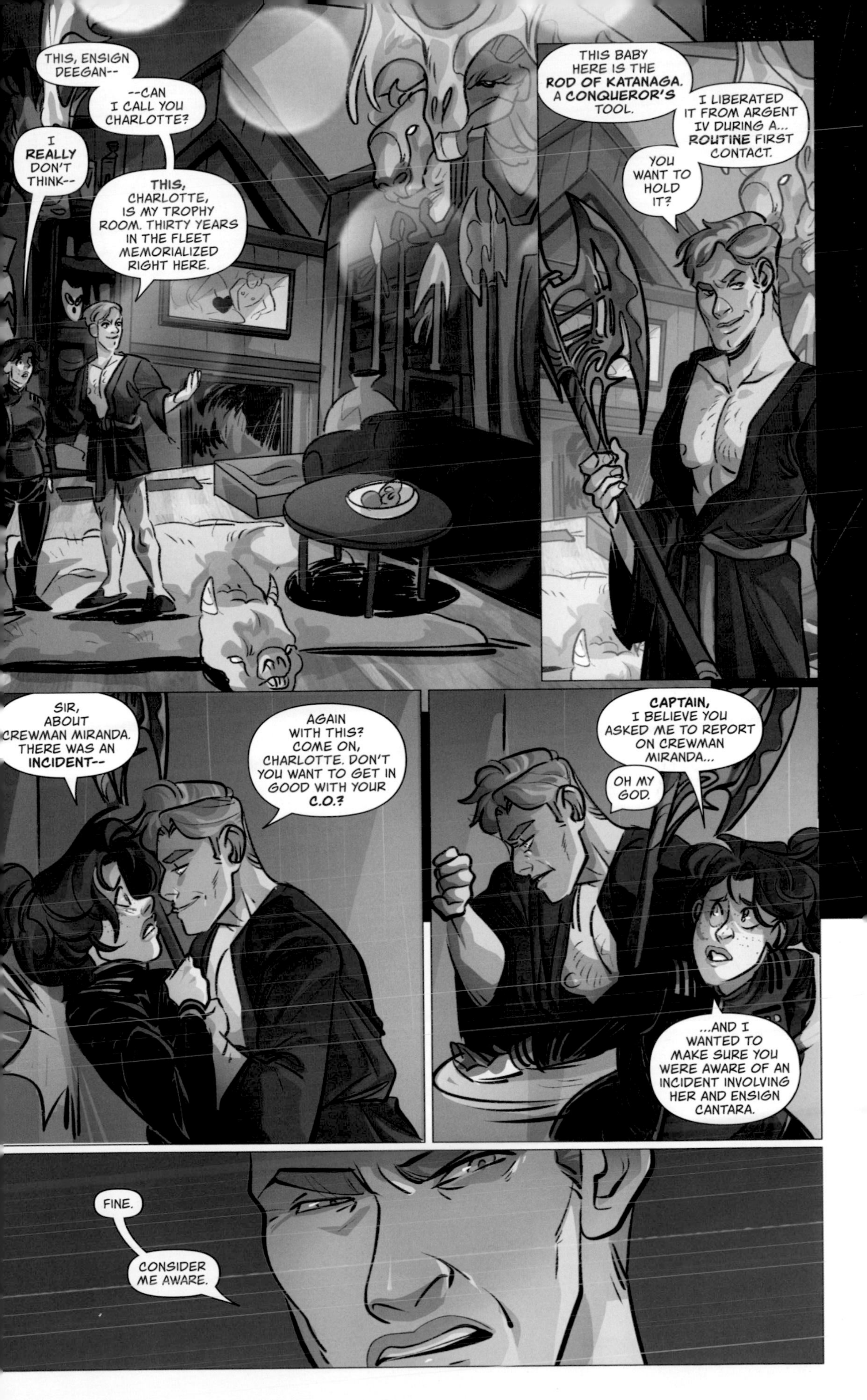
THIS, ENSIGN DEEGAN--
--CAN I CALL YOU CHARLOTTE?
I REALLY DON'T THINK--
THIS, CHARLOTTE, IS MY TROPHY ROOM. THIRTY YEARS IN THE FLEET MEMORIALIZED RIGHT HERE.
THIS BABY HERE IS THE ROD OF KATANAGA. A CONQUEROR'S TOOL.
I LIBERATED IT FROM ARGENT IV DURING A... ROUTINE FIRST CONTACT.
YOU WANT TO HOLD IT?
SIR, ABOUT CREWMAN MIRANDA. THERE WAS AN INCIDENT--
AGAIN WITH THIS? COME ON, CHARLOTTE. DON'T YOU WANT TO GET IN GOOD WITH YOUR C.O.?
CAPTAIN, I BELIEVE YOU ASKED ME TO REPORT ON CREWMAN MIRANDA...
OH MY GOD.
...AND I WANTED TO MAKE SURE YOU WERE AWARE OF AN INCIDENT INVOLVING HER AND ENSIGN CANTARA.
FINE.
CONSIDER ME AWARE.

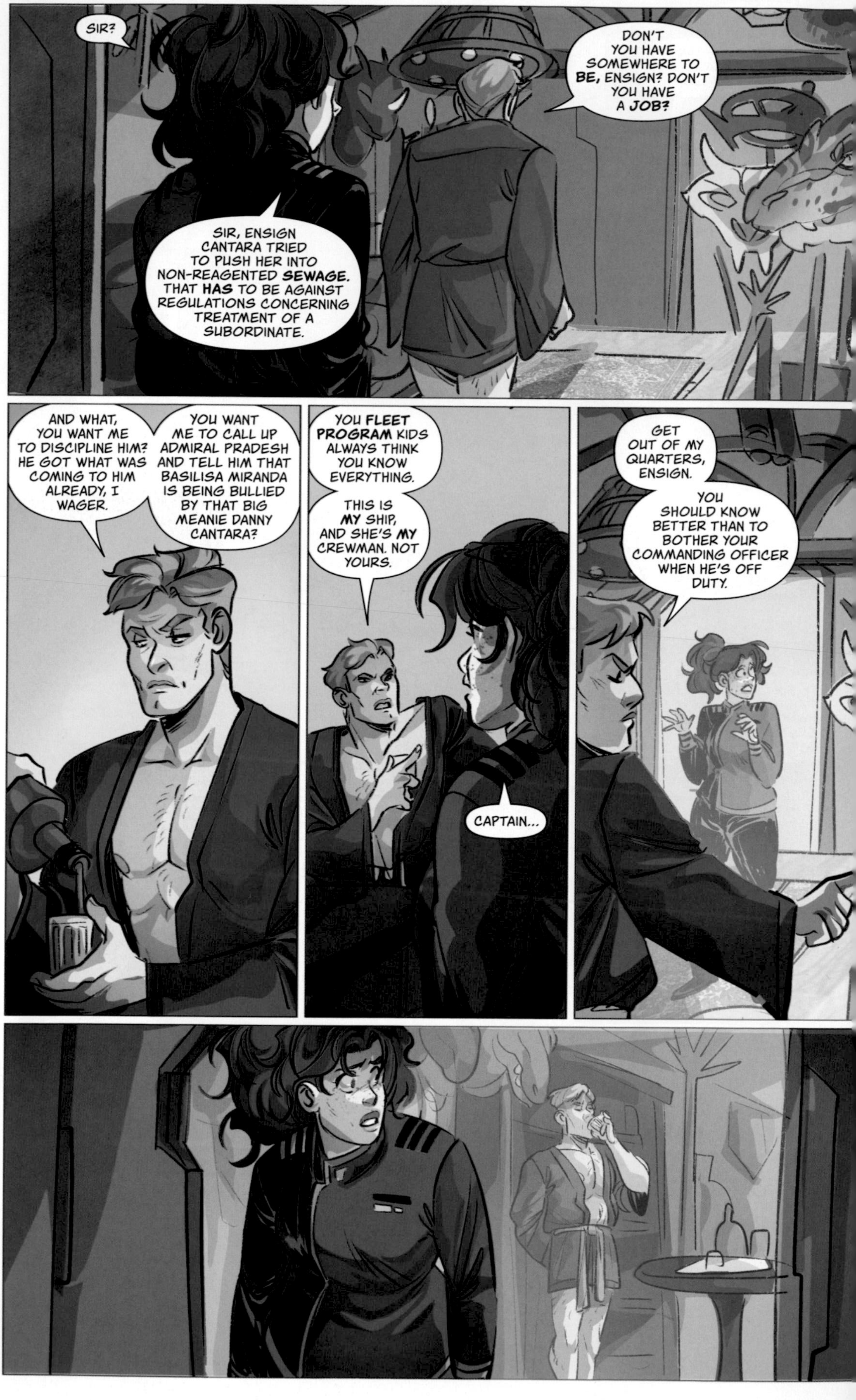
SIR?
DON'T YOU HAVE SOMEWHERE TO BE, ENSIGN? DON'T YOU HAVE A JOB?
SIR, ENSIGN CANTARA TRIED TO PUSH HER INTO NON-REAGENTED SEWAGE. THAT HAS TO BE AGAINST REGULATIONS CONCERNING TREATMENT OF A SUBORDINATE.
AND WHAT, YOU WANT ME TO DISCIPLINE HIM? HE GOT WHAT WAS COMING TO HIM ALREADY, I WAGER.
YOU WANT ME TO CALL UP ADMIRAL PRADESH AND TELL HIM THAT BASILISA MIRANDA IS BEING BULLIED BY THAT BIG MEANIE DANNY CANTARA?
YOU FLEET PROGRAM KIDS ALWAYS THINK YOU KNOW EVERYTHING.
THIS IS MY SHIP, AND SHE'S MY CREWMAN. NOT YOURS.
CAPTAIN...
GET OUT OF MY QUARTERS, ENSIGN.
YOU SHOULD KNOW BETTER THAN TO BOTHER YOUR COMMANDING OFFICER WHEN HE'S OFF DUTY.

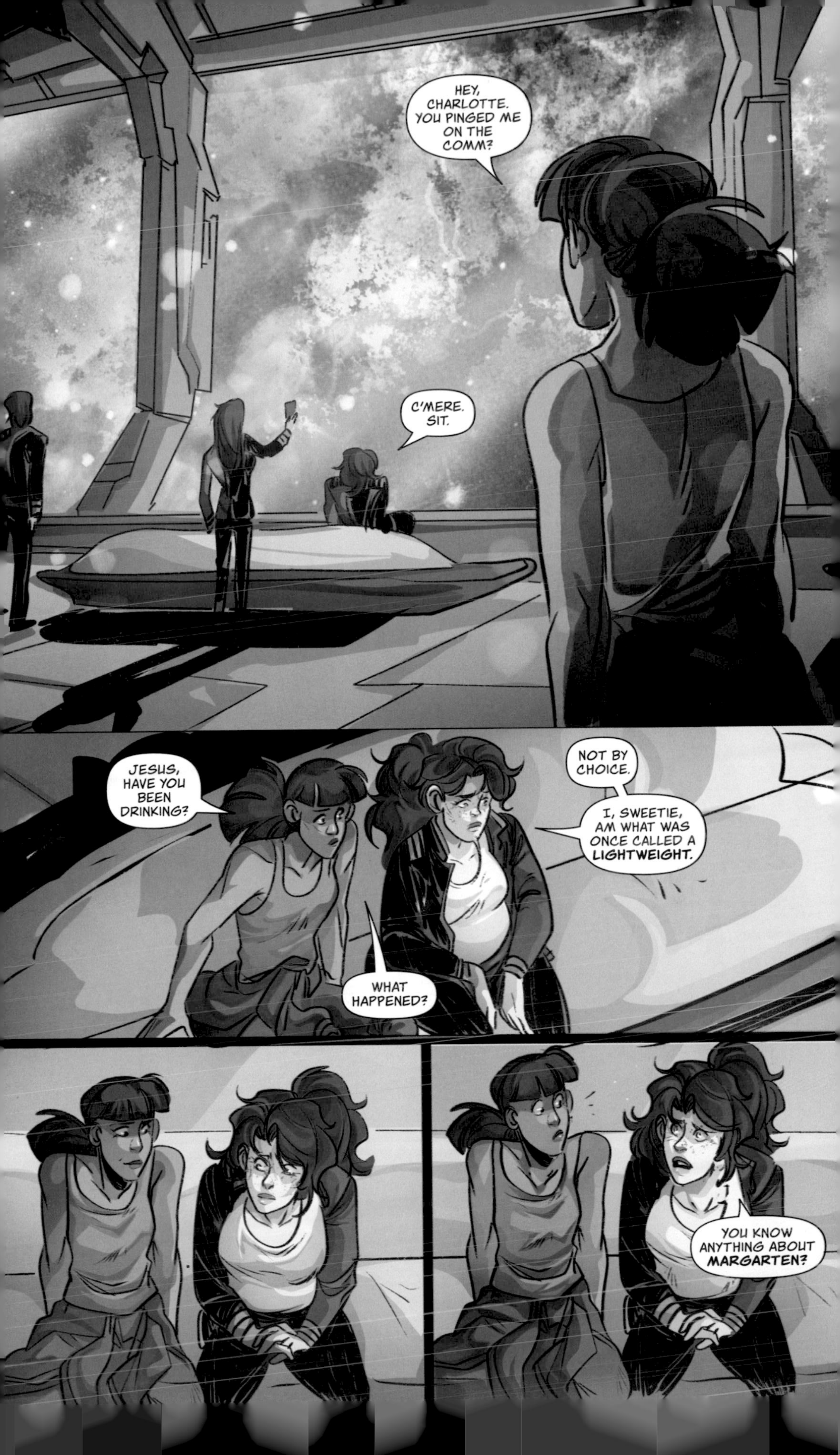

HEY, CHARLOTTE. YOU PINGED ME ON THE COMM?
C'MERE. SIT.
JESUS, HAVE YOU BEEN DRINKING?
NOT BY CHOICE.
I, SWEETIE, AM WHAT WAS ONCE CALLED A **LIGHTWEIGHT.**
WHAT HAPPENED?
YOU KNOW ANYTHING ABOUT **MARGARTEN?**

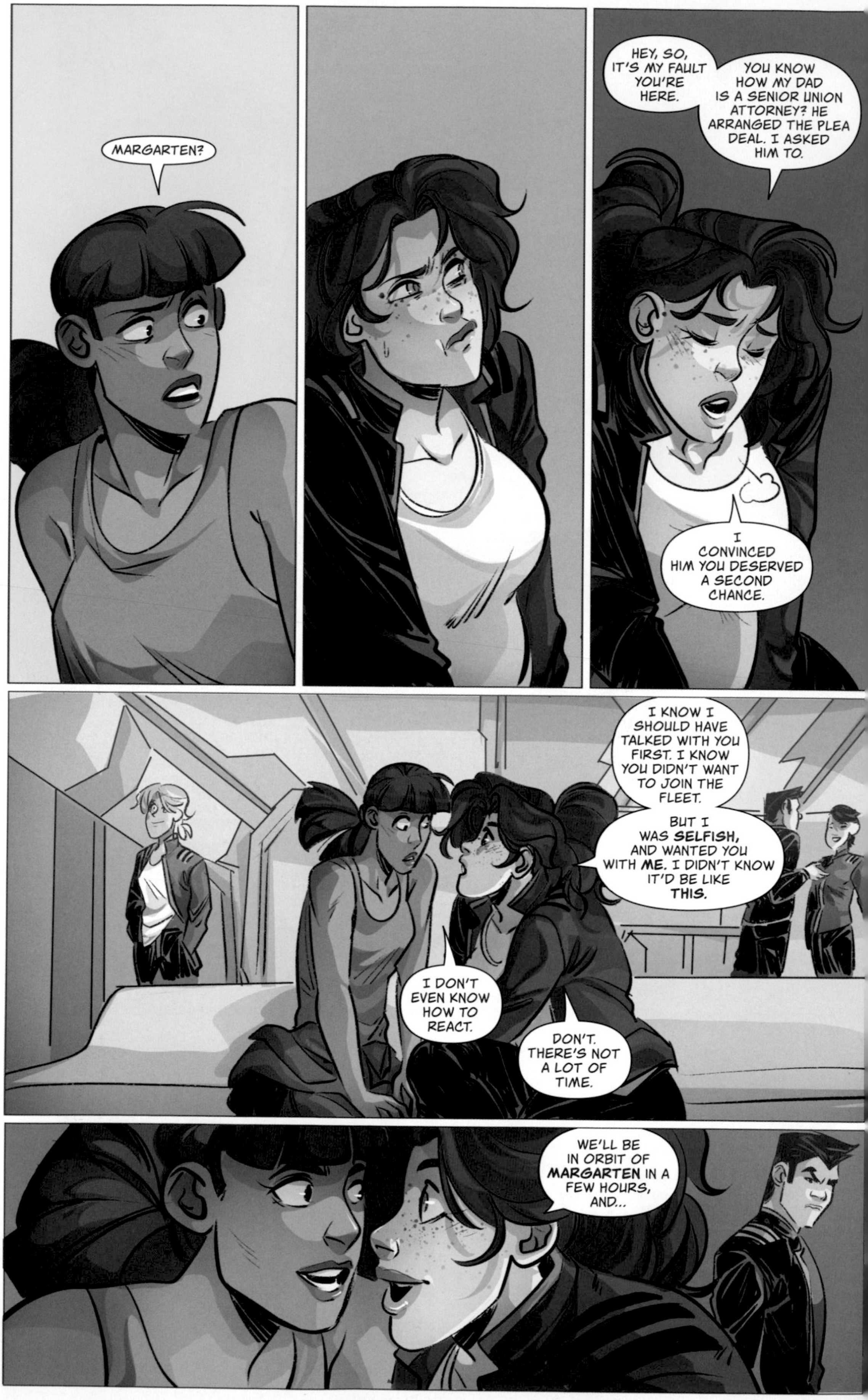
MARGARTEN?
HEY, SO, IT'S MY FAULT YOU'RE HERE.
YOU KNOW HOW MY DAD IS A SENIOR UNION ATTORNEY? HE ARRANGED THE PLEA DEAL. I ASKED HIM TO.
I CONVINCED HIM YOU DESERVED A SECOND CHANCE.
I KNOW I SHOULD HAVE TALKED WITH YOU FIRST. I KNOW YOU DIDN'T WANT TO JOIN THE FLEET.
BUT I WAS SELFISH, AND WANTED YOU WITH ME. I DIDN'T KNOW IT'D BE LIKE THIS.
I DON'T EVEN KNOW HOW TO REACT.
DON'T. THERE'S NOT A LOT OF TIME.
WE'LL BE IN ORBIT OF MARGARTEN IN A FEW HOURS, AND...

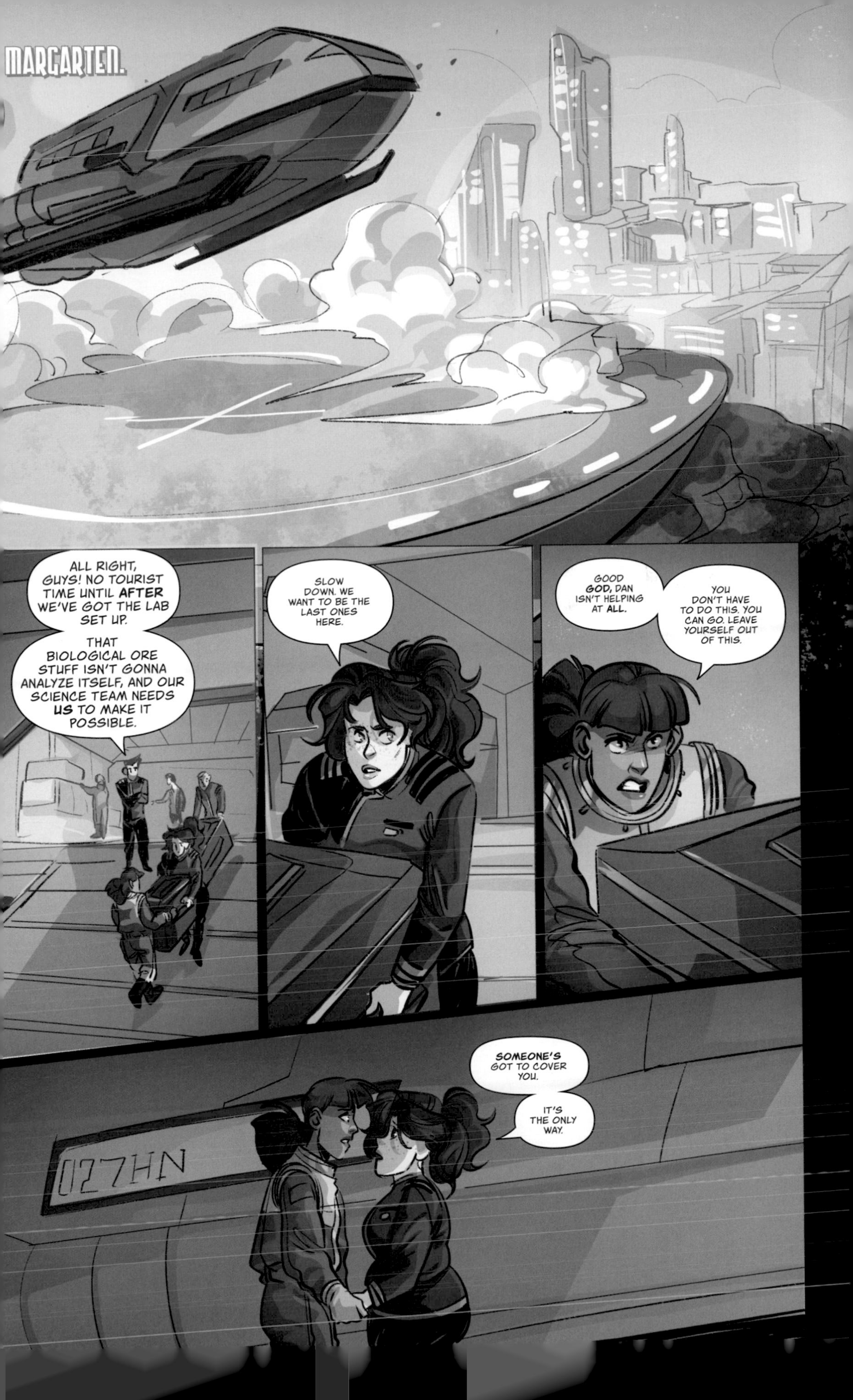
MARGARTEN.
ALL RIGHT, GUYS! NO TOURIST TIME UNTIL **AFTER** WE'VE GOT THE LAB SET UP.
THAT BIOLOGICAL ORE STUFF ISN'T GONNA ANALYZE ITSELF, AND OUR SCIENCE TEAM NEEDS **US** TO MAKE IT POSSIBLE.
SLOW DOWN. WE WANT TO BE THE LAST ONES HERE.
GOOD **GOD,** DAN ISN'T HELPING AT **ALL.**
YOU DON'T HAVE TO DO THIS. YOU CAN GO. LEAVE YOURSELF OUT OF THIS.
SOMEONE'S GOT TO COVER YOU.
IT'S THE ONLY WAY.
027HN

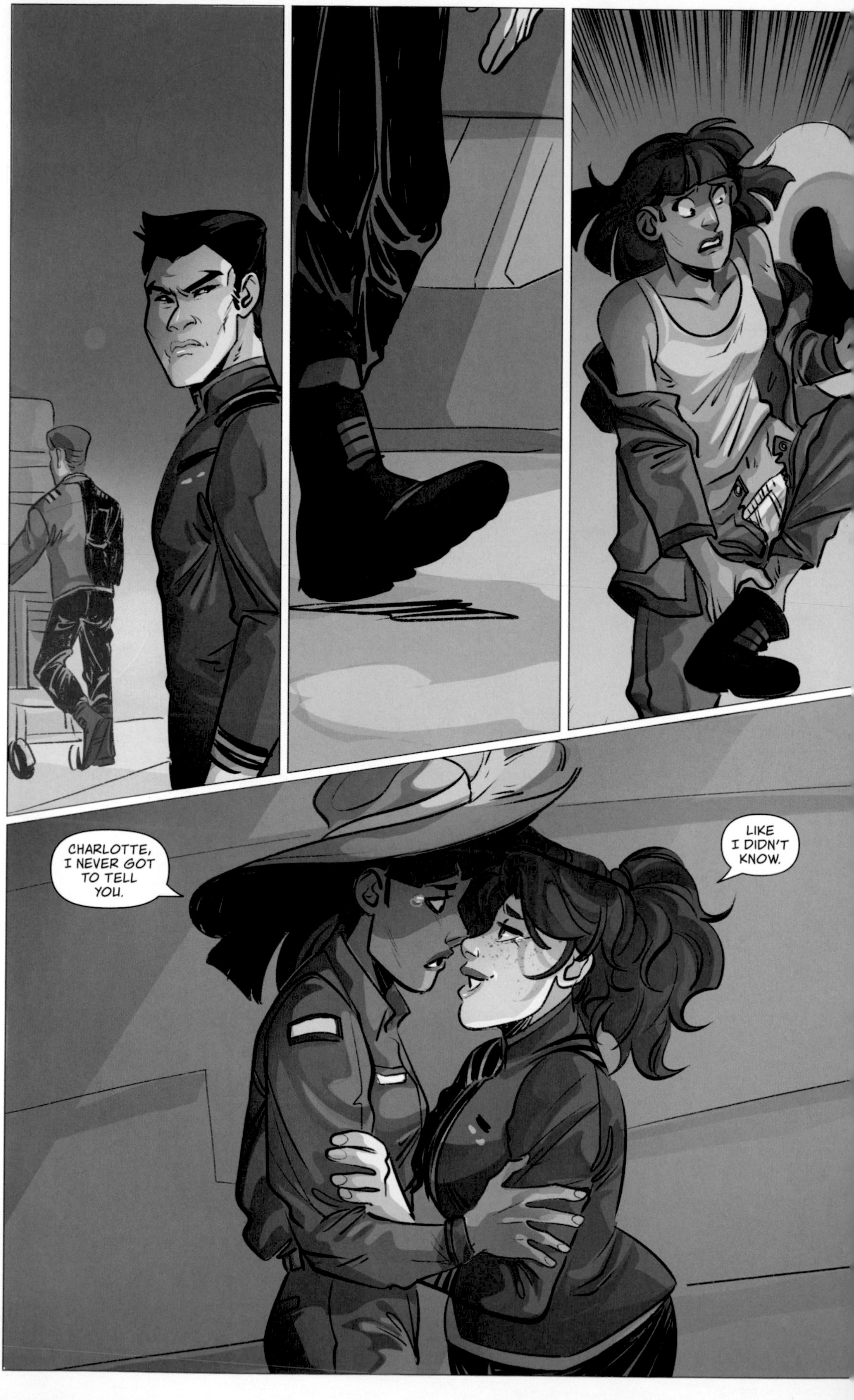
CHARLOTTE, I NEVER GOT TO TELL YOU.
LIKE I DIDN'T KNOW.

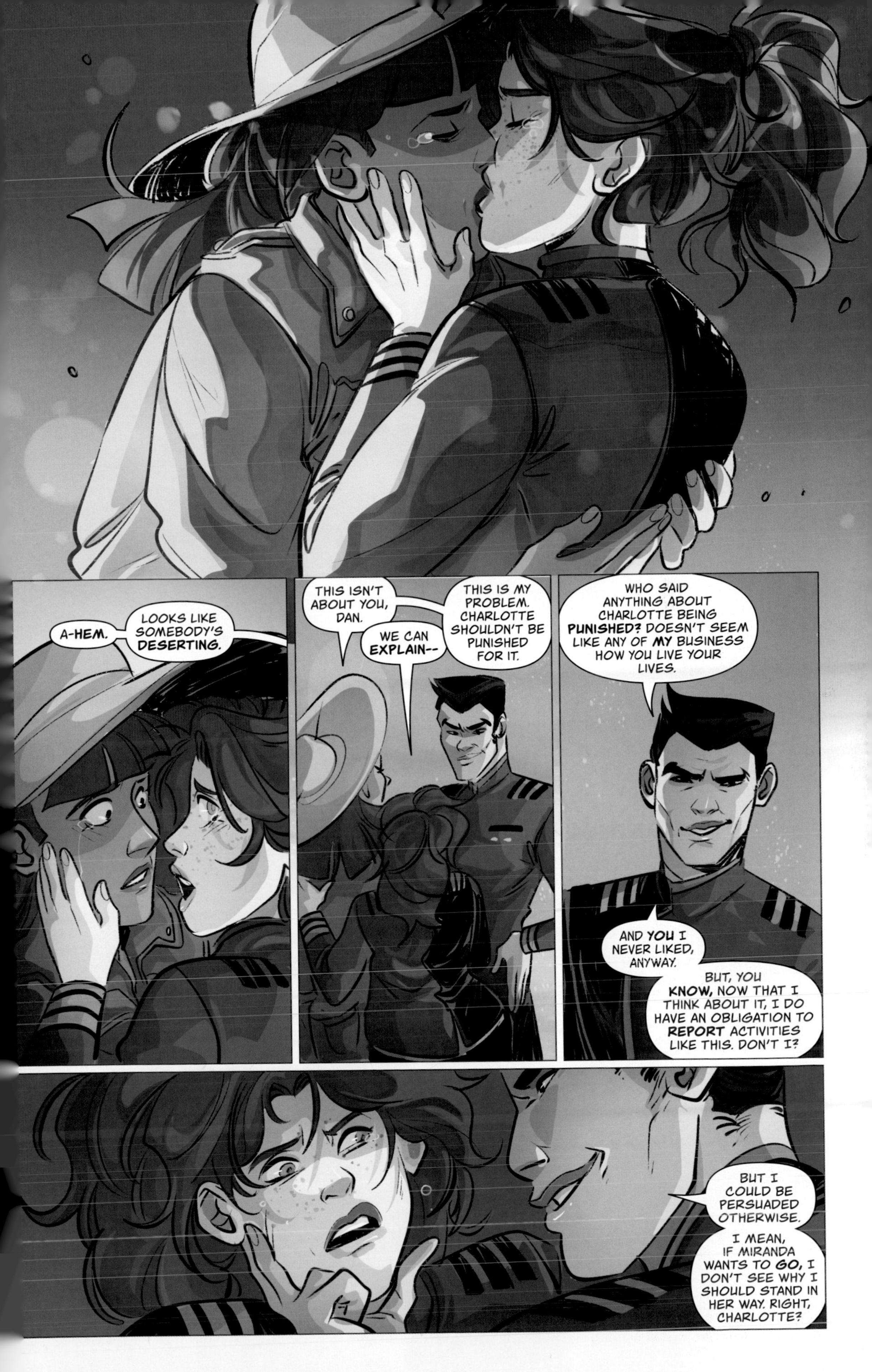
A-HEM.
LOOKS LIKE SOMEBODY'S DESERTING.
THIS ISN'T ABOUT YOU, DAN.
THIS IS MY PROBLEM. CHARLOTTE SHOULDN'T BE PUNISHED FOR IT.
WE CAN EXPLAIN--
WHO SAID ANYTHING ABOUT CHARLOTTE BEING PUNISHED? DOESN'T SEEM LIKE ANY OF MY BUSINESS HOW YOU LIVE YOUR LIVES.
AND YOU I NEVER LIKED, ANYWAY.
BUT, YOU KNOW, NOW THAT I THINK ABOUT IT, I DO HAVE AN OBLIGATION TO REPORT ACTIVITIES LIKE THIS. DON'T I?
BUT I COULD BE PERSUADED OTHERWISE.
I MEAN, IF MIRANDA WANTS TO GO, I DON'T SEE WHY I SHOULD STAND IN HER WAY. RIGHT, CHARLOTTE?

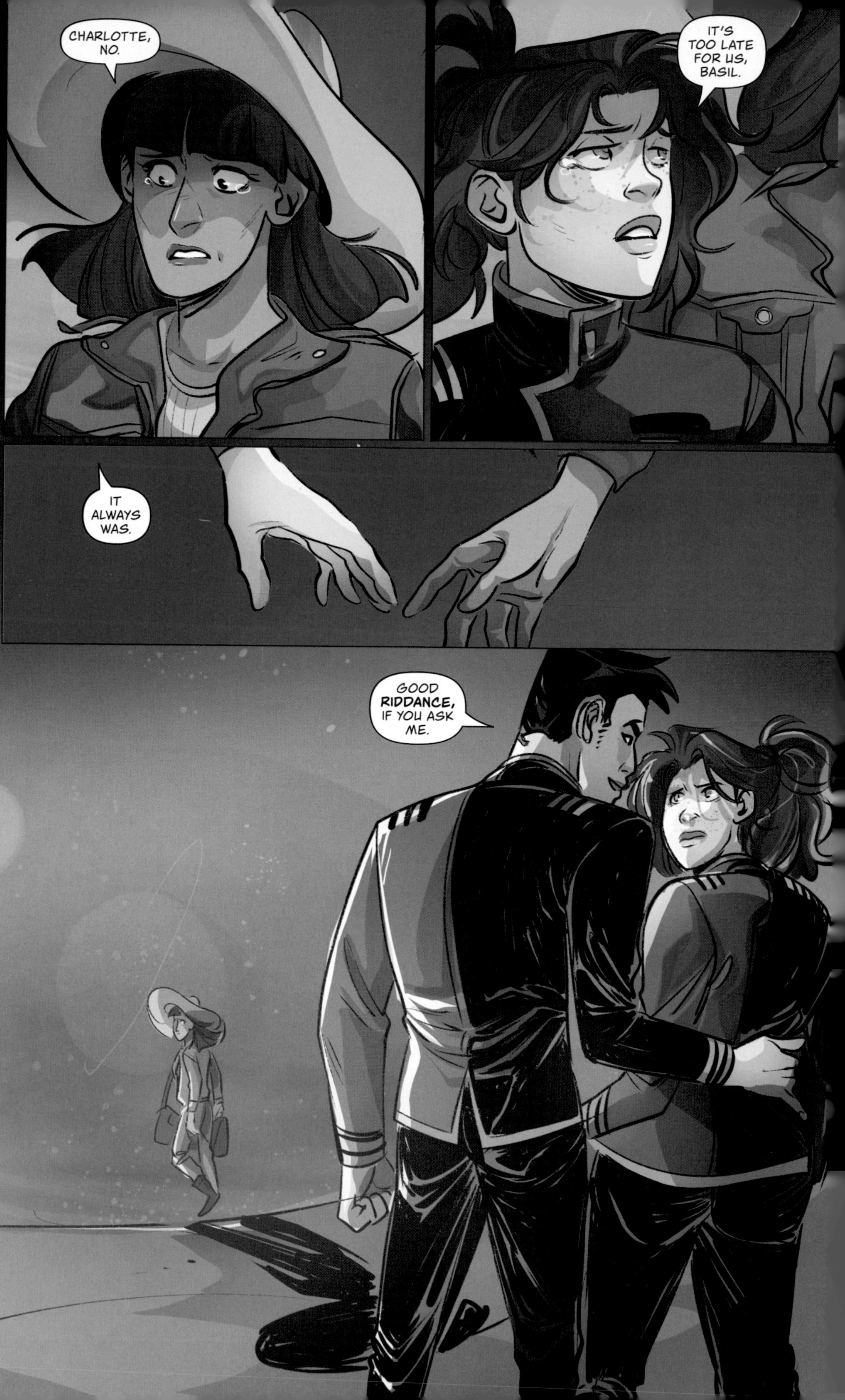
CHARLOTTE, NO.
IT'S TOO LATE FOR US, BASIL.
IT ALWAYS WAS.
GOOD RIDDANCE, IF YOU ASK ME.

Chapter **Five**

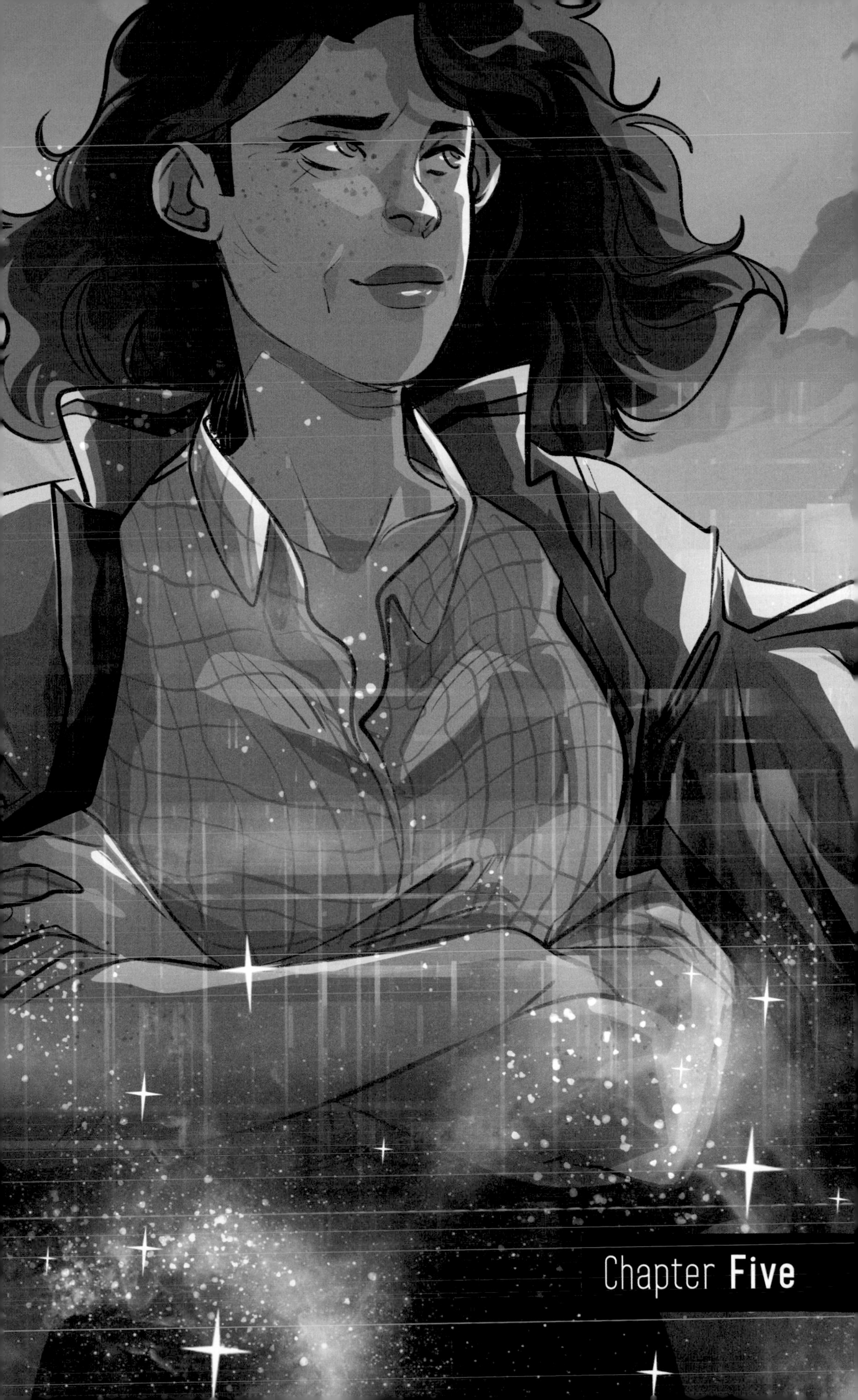

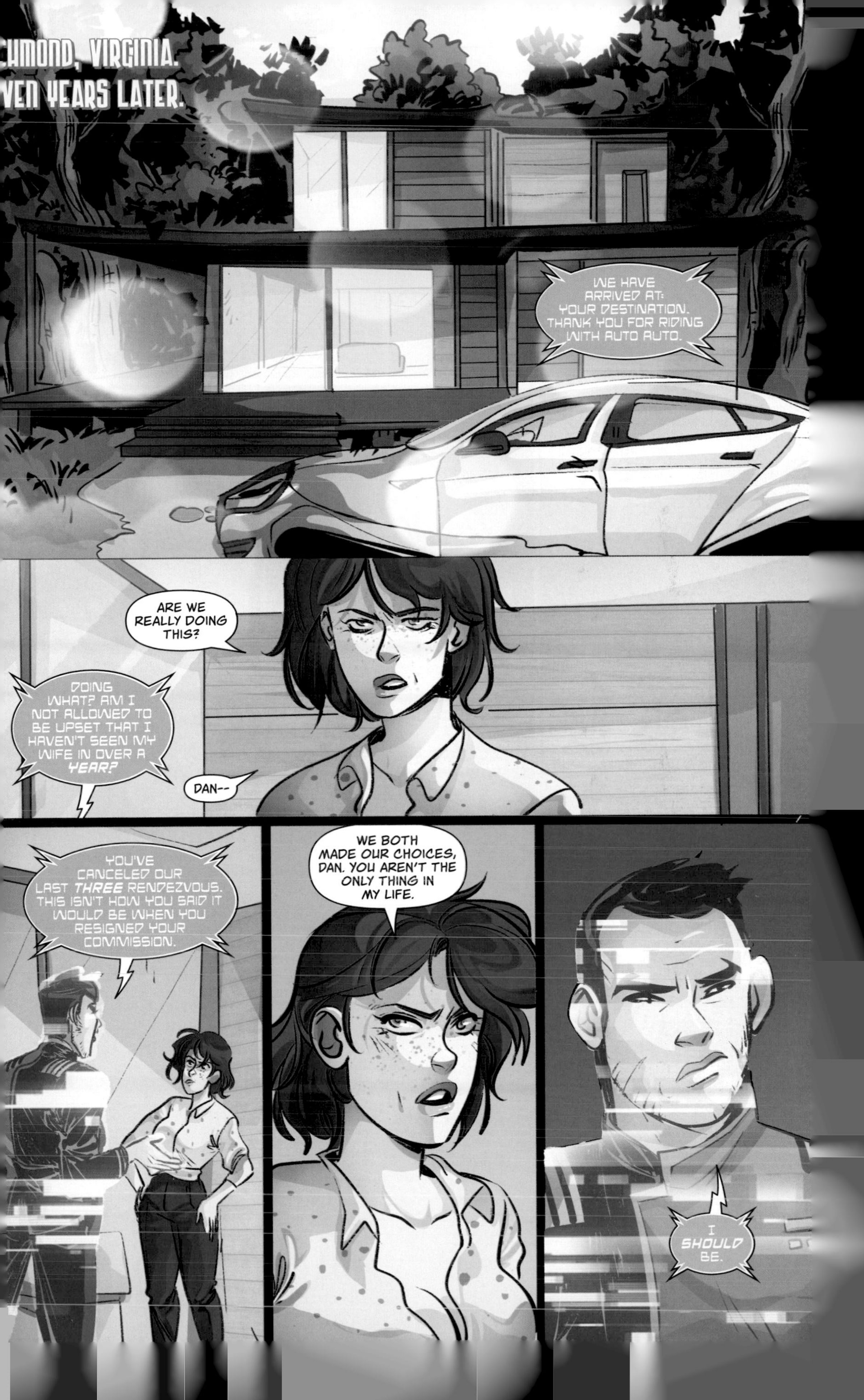

CHMOND, VIRGINIA.
VEN YEARS LATER.
WE HAVE ARRIVED AT: YOUR DESTINATION. THANK YOU FOR RIDING WITH AUTO AUTO.
ARE WE REALLY DOING THIS?
DOING WHAT? AM I NOT ALLOWED TO BE UPSET THAT I HAVEN'T SEEN MY WIFE IN OVER A YEAR?
DAN--
YOU'VE CANCELED OUR LAST THREE RENDEZVOUS. THIS ISN'T HOW YOU SAID IT WOULD BE WHEN YOU RESIGNED YOUR COMMISSION.
WE BOTH MADE OUR CHOICES, DAN. YOU AREN'T THE ONLY THING IN MY LIFE.
I SHOULD BE.

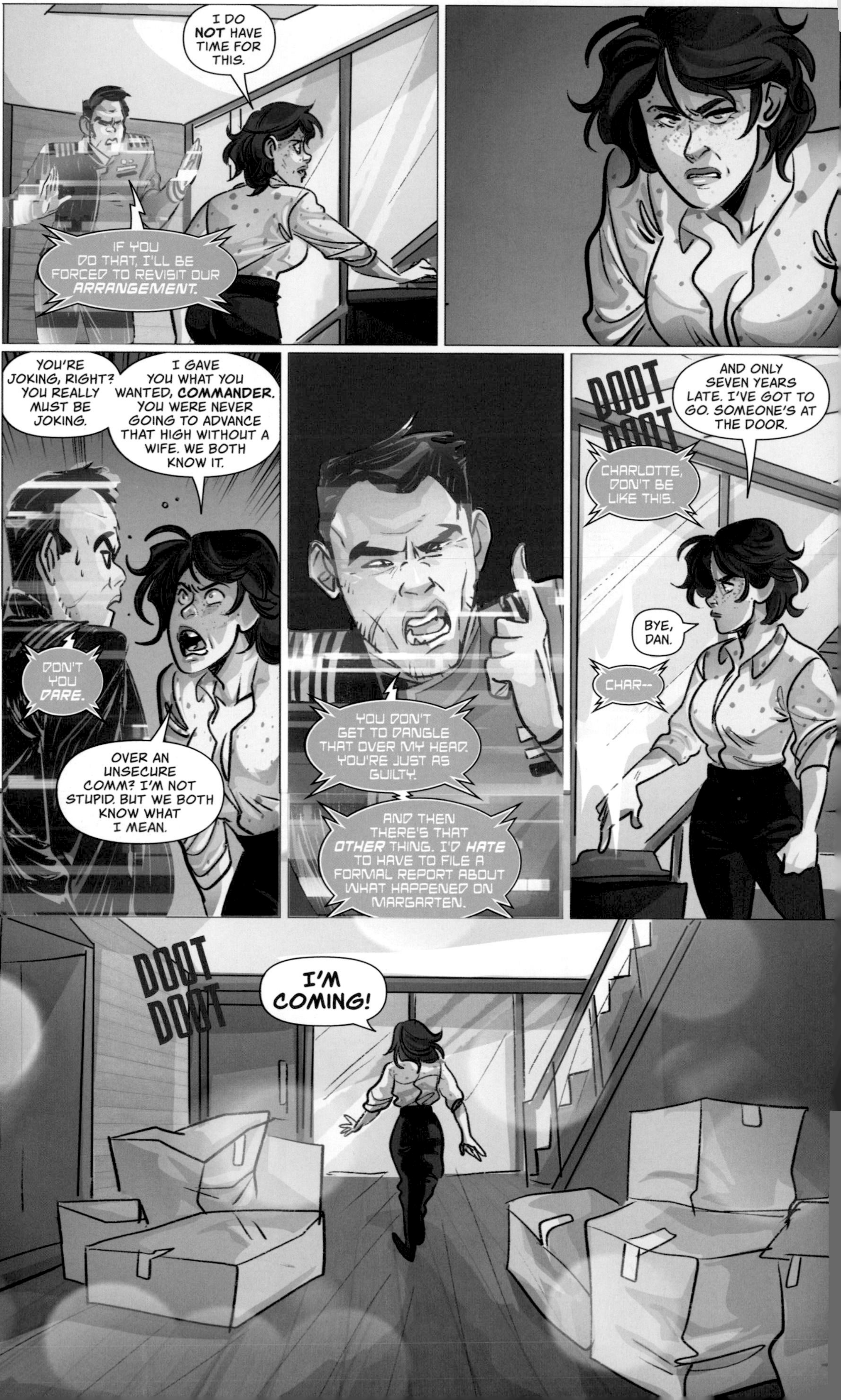
I DO **NOT** HAVE TIME FOR THIS.
IF YOU DO THAT, I'LL BE FORCED TO REVISIT OUR ***ARRANGEMENT.***
YOU'RE JOKING, RIGHT? YOU REALLY MUST BE JOKING.
I GAVE YOU WHAT YOU WANTED, **COMMANDER.** YOU WERE NEVER GOING TO ADVANCE THAT HIGH WITHOUT A WIFE. WE BOTH KNOW IT.
DON'T YOU *DARE.*
OVER AN UNSECURE COMM? I'M NOT STUPID. BUT WE BOTH KNOW WHAT I MEAN.
YOU DON'T GET TO DANGLE THAT OVER MY HEAD. YOU'RE JUST AS GUILTY.
AND THEN THERE'S THAT ***OTHER*** THING. I'D ***HATE*** TO HAVE TO FILE A FORMAL REPORT ABOUT WHAT HAPPENED ON MARGARTEN.
DOOT DOOT
AND ONLY SEVEN YEARS LATE. I'VE GOT TO GO. SOMEONE'S AT THE DOOR.
CHARLOTTE, DON'T BE LIKE THIS.
BYE, DAN.
CHAR--
DOOT DOOT
I'M COMING!

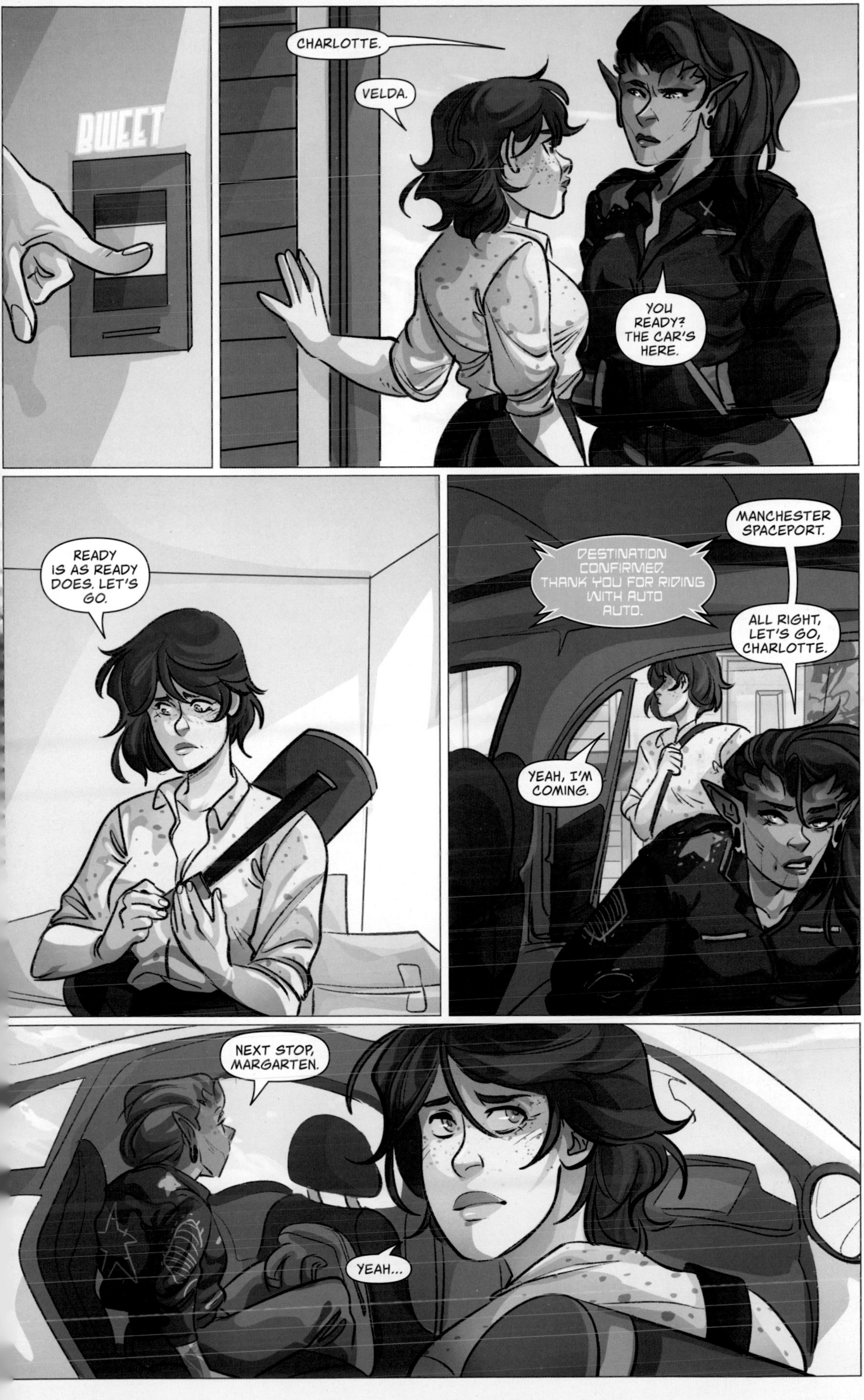
BWEET
CHARLOTTE.
VELDA.
YOU READY? THE CAR'S HERE.
READY IS AS READY DOES. LET'S GO.
MANCHESTER SPACEPORT.
DESTINATION CONFIRMED. THANK YOU FOR RIDING WITH AUTO AUTO.
ALL RIGHT, LET'S GO, CHARLOTTE.
YEAH, I'M COMING.
NEXT STOP, MARGARTEN.
YEAH...

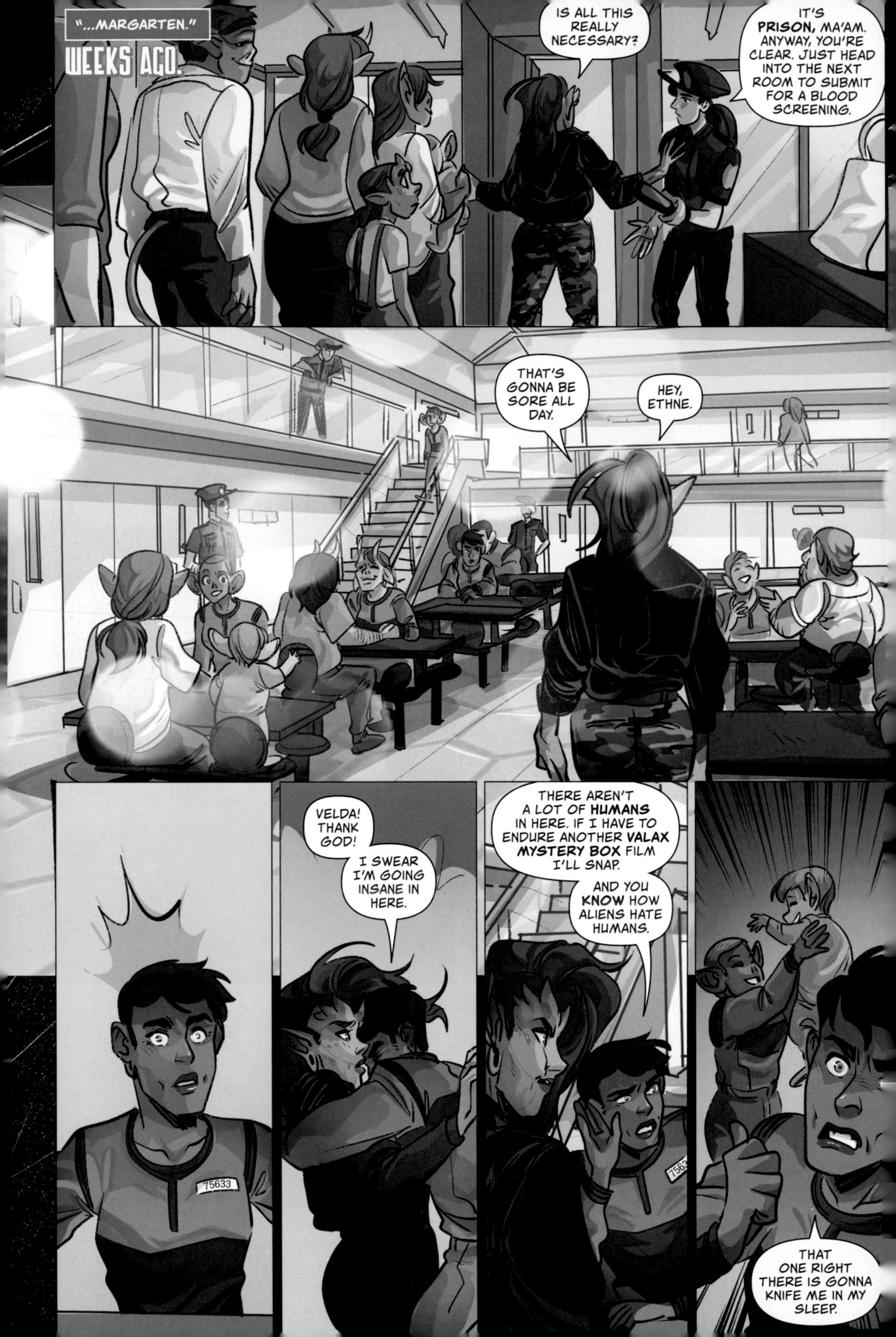
"...MARGARTEN."
WEEKS AGO.
IS ALL THIS REALLY NECESSARY?
IT'S PRISON, MA'AM. ANYWAY, YOU'RE CLEAR. JUST HEAD INTO THE NEXT ROOM TO SUBMIT FOR A BLOOD SCREENING.
THAT'S GONNA BE SORE ALL DAY.
HEY, ETHNE.
75633
VELDA! THANK GOD!
I SWEAR I'M GOING INSANE IN HERE.
THERE AREN'T A LOT OF HUMANS IN HERE. IF I HAVE TO ENDURE ANOTHER VALAX MYSTERY BOX FILM I'LL SNAP.
AND YOU KNOW HOW ALIENS HATE HUMANS.
THAT ONE RIGHT THERE IS GONNA KNIFE ME IN MY SLEEP.

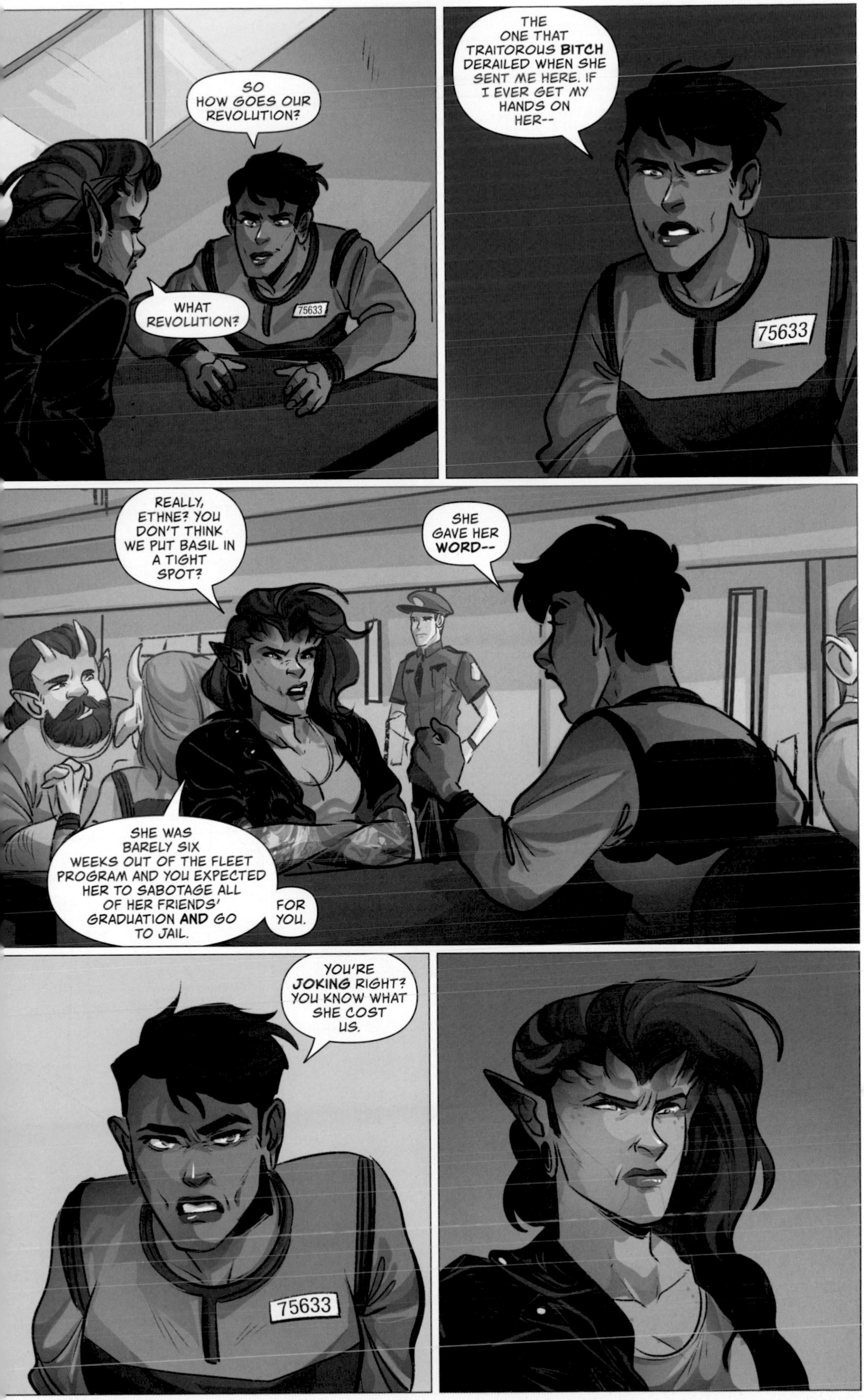
SO HOW GOES OUR REVOLUTION?
WHAT REVOLUTION?
THE ONE THAT TRAITOROUS BITCH DERAILED WHEN SHE SENT ME HERE. IF I EVER GET MY HANDS ON HER--
REALLY, ETHNE? YOU DON'T THINK WE PUT BASIL IN A TIGHT SPOT?
SHE GAVE HER WORD--
SHE WAS BARELY SIX WEEKS OUT OF THE FLEET PROGRAM AND YOU EXPECTED HER TO SABOTAGE ALL OF HER FRIENDS' GRADUATION AND GO TO JAIL.
FOR YOU.
YOU'RE JOKING RIGHT? YOU KNOW WHAT SHE COST US.
75633

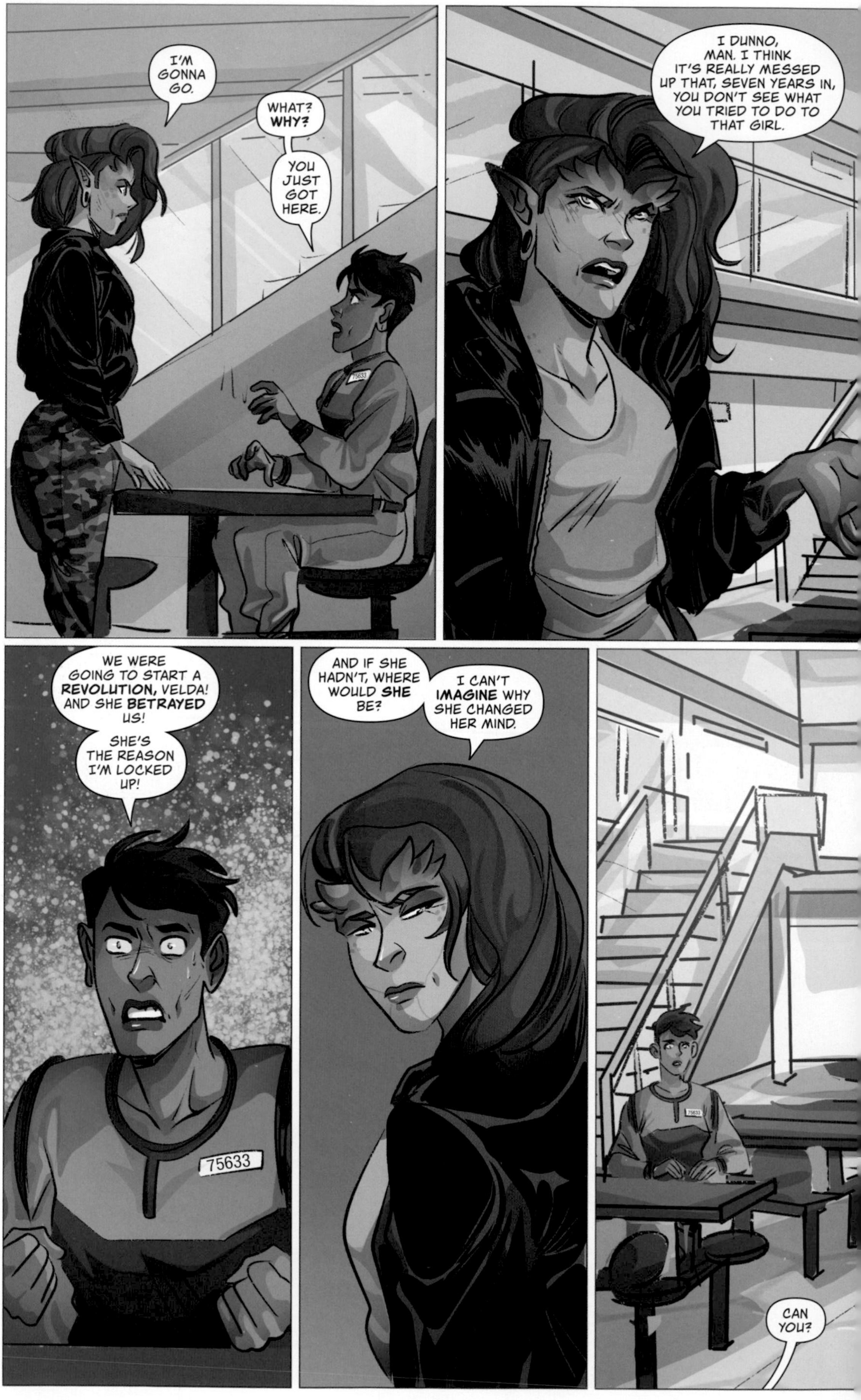
I'M GONNA GO.
WHAT? WHY?
YOU JUST GOT HERE.
75633
I DUNNO, MAN. I THINK IT'S REALLY MESSED UP THAT, SEVEN YEARS IN, YOU DON'T SEE WHAT YOU TRIED TO DO TO THAT GIRL.
WE WERE GOING TO START A REVOLUTION, VELDA! AND SHE BETRAYED US!
SHE'S THE REASON I'M LOCKED UP!
75633
AND IF SHE HADN'T, WHERE WOULD SHE BE?
I CAN'T IMAGINE WHY SHE CHANGED HER MIND.
75633
CAN YOU?

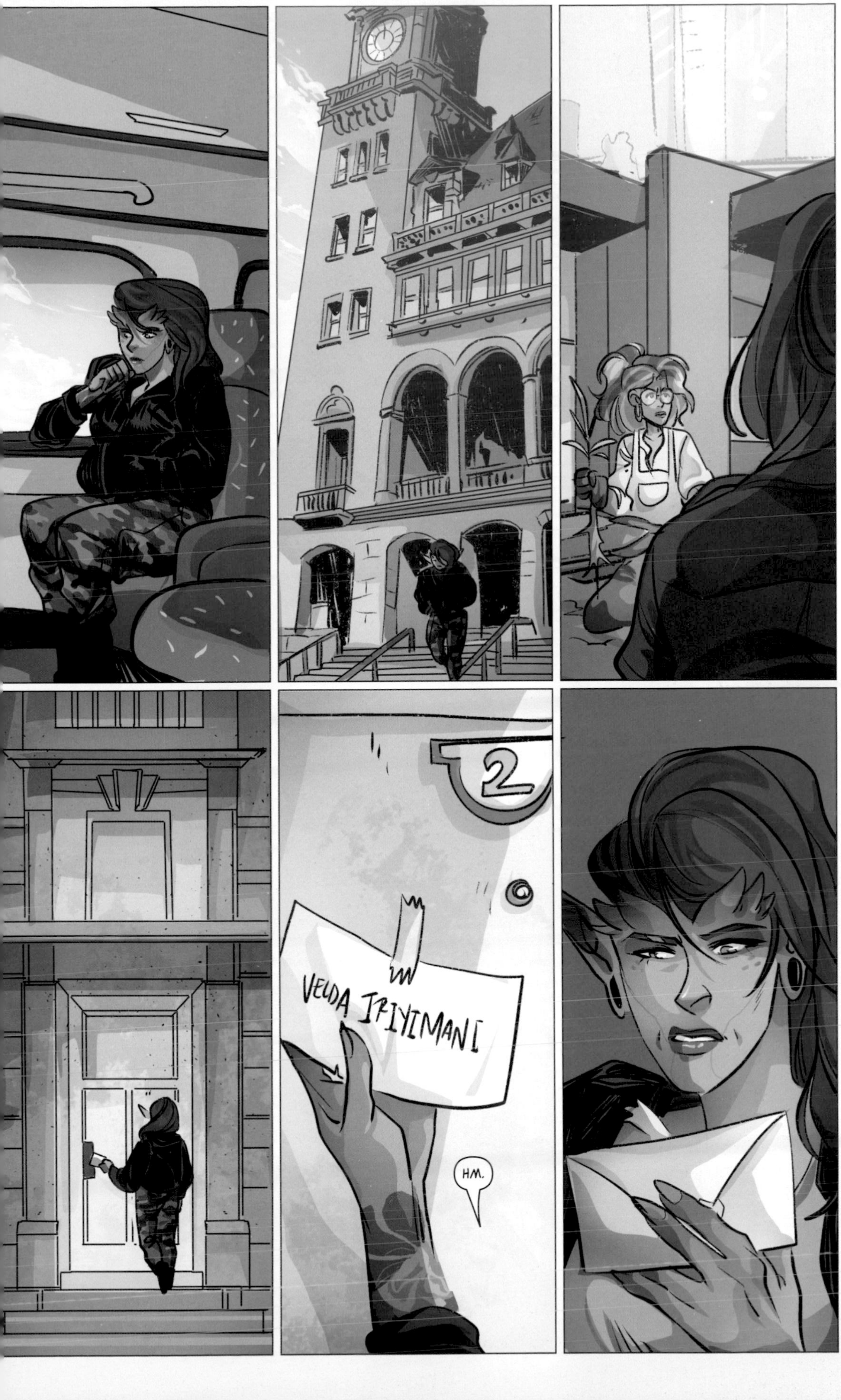
2
VELDA IRIYIMANI
HM.

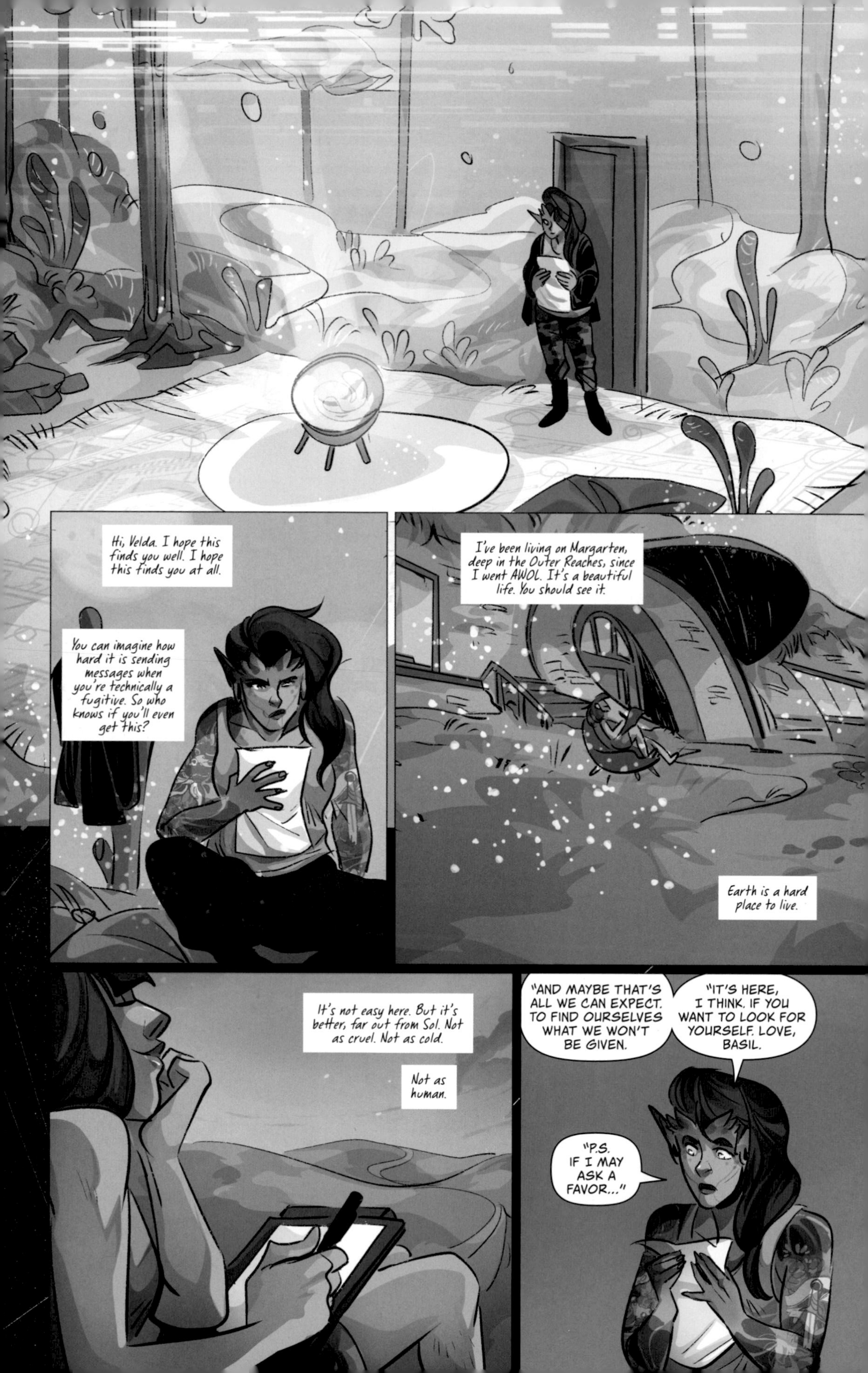
Hi, Velda. I hope this finds you well. I hope this finds you at all.
You can imagine how hard it is sending messages when you're technically a fugitive. So who knows if you'll even get this?
I've been living on Margarten, deep in the Outer Reaches, since I went AWOL. It's a beautiful life. You should see it.
Earth is a hard place to live.
It's not easy here. But it's better, far out from Sol. Not as cruel. Not as cold.
Not as human.
"AND MAYBE THAT'S ALL WE CAN EXPECT. TO FIND OURSELVES WHAT WE WON'T BE GIVEN.
"IT'S HERE, I THINK. IF YOU WANT TO LOOK FOR YOURSELF. LOVE, BASIL.
"P.S. IF I MAY ASK A FAVOR..."

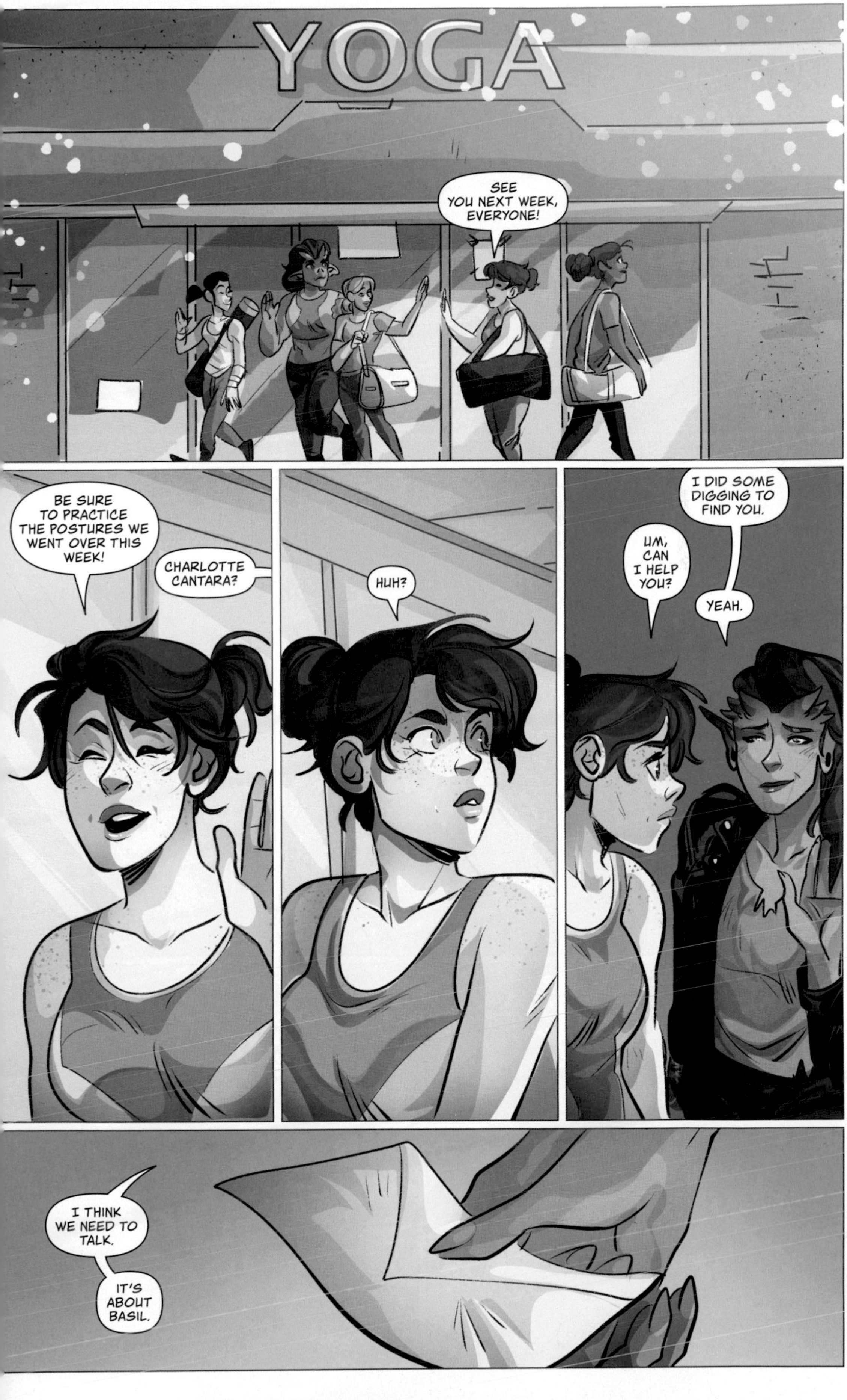
YOGA
SEE YOU NEXT WEEK, EVERYONE!
BE SURE TO PRACTICE THE POSTURES WE WENT OVER THIS WEEK!
CHARLOTTE CANTARA?
HUH?
I DID SOME DIGGING TO FIND YOU.
UM, CAN I HELP YOU?
YEAH.
I THINK WE NEED TO TALK.
IT'S ABOUT BASIL.

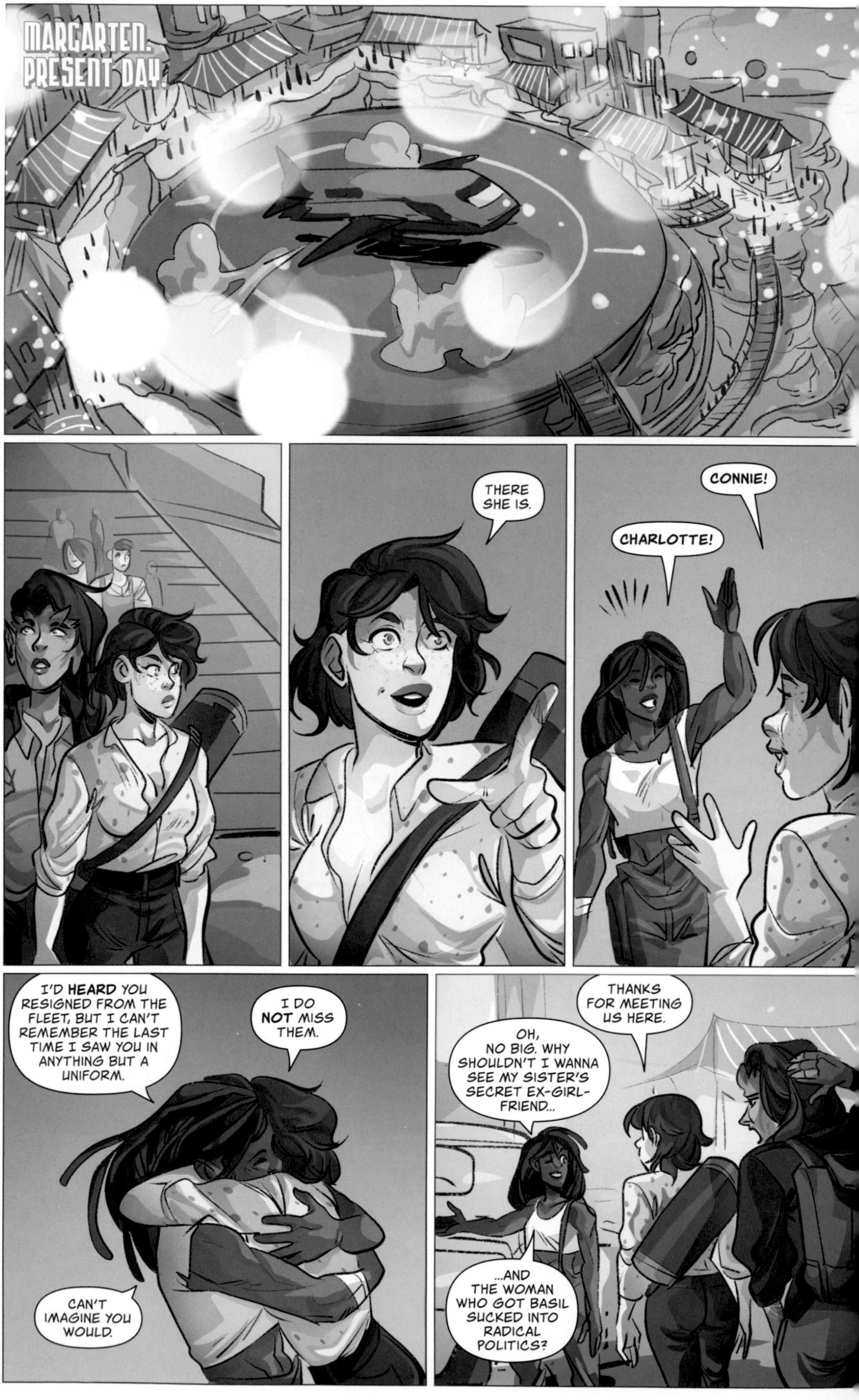
MARGARTEN.
PRESENT DAY.
THERE SHE IS.
CONNIE!
CHARLOTTE!
I'D **HEARD** YOU RESIGNED FROM THE FLEET, BUT I CAN'T REMEMBER THE LAST TIME I SAW YOU IN ANYTHING BUT A UNIFORM.
I DO **NOT** MISS THEM.
CAN'T IMAGINE YOU WOULD.
THANKS FOR MEETING US HERE.
OH, NO BIG. WHY SHOULDN'T I WANNA SEE MY SISTER'S SECRET EX-GIRL-FRIEND...
...AND THE WOMAN WHO GOT BASIL SUCKED INTO RADICAL POLITICS?

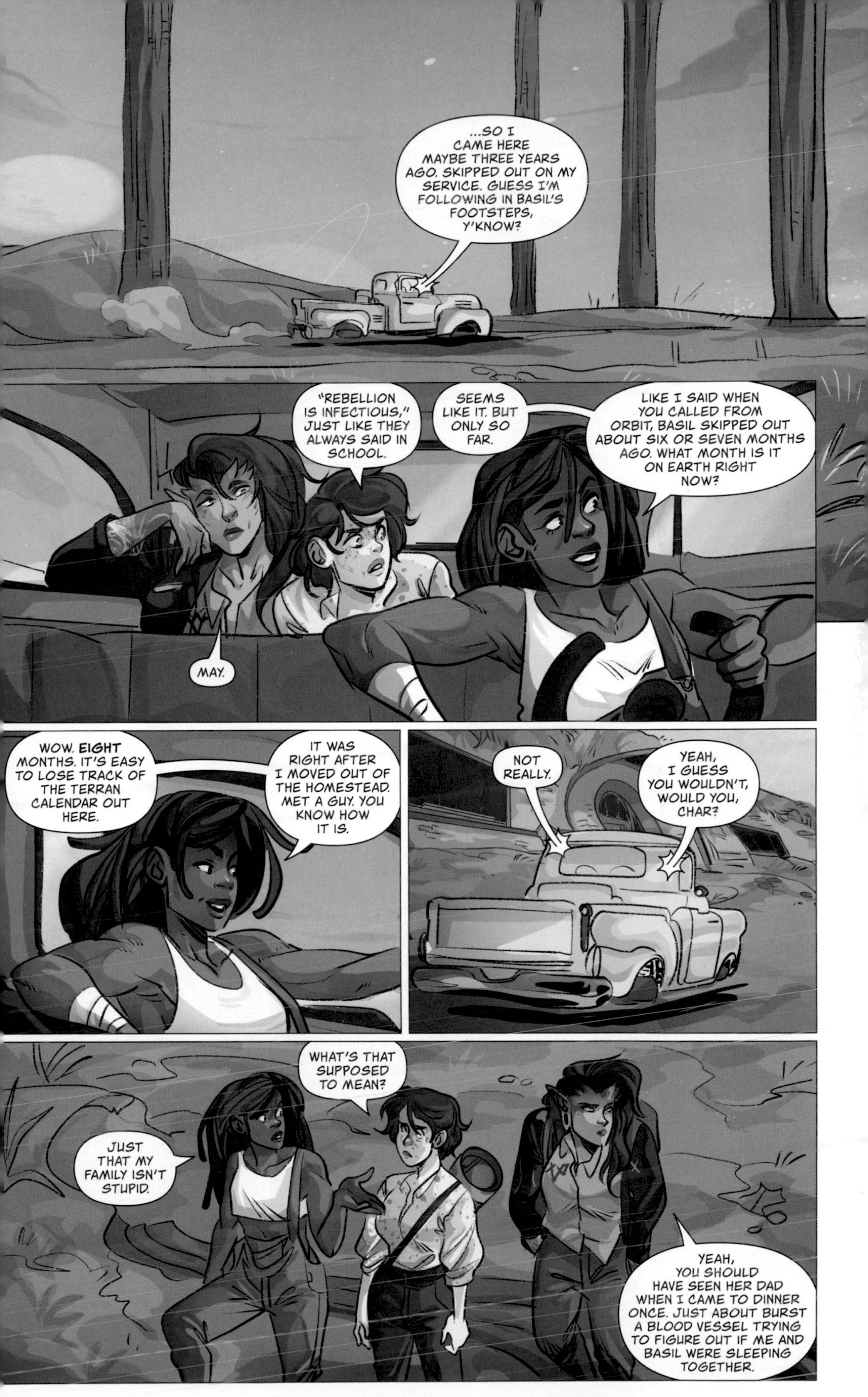
...SO I CAME HERE MAYBE THREE YEARS AGO. SKIPPED OUT ON MY SERVICE. GUESS I'M FOLLOWING IN BASIL'S FOOTSTEPS, Y'KNOW?
"REBELLION IS INFECTIOUS," JUST LIKE THEY ALWAYS SAID IN SCHOOL.
SEEMS LIKE IT. BUT ONLY SO FAR.
LIKE I SAID WHEN YOU CALLED FROM ORBIT, BASIL SKIPPED OUT ABOUT SIX OR SEVEN MONTHS AGO. WHAT MONTH IS IT ON EARTH RIGHT NOW?
MAY.
WOW. **EIGHT** MONTHS. IT'S EASY TO LOSE TRACK OF THE TERRAN CALENDAR OUT HERE.
IT WAS RIGHT AFTER I MOVED OUT OF THE HOMESTEAD. MET A GUY. YOU KNOW HOW IT IS.
NOT REALLY.
YEAH, I GUESS YOU WOULDN'T, WOULD YOU, CHAR?
WHAT'S THAT SUPPOSED TO MEAN?
JUST THAT MY FAMILY ISN'T STUPID.
YEAH, YOU SHOULD HAVE SEEN HER DAD WHEN I CAME TO DINNER ONCE. JUST ABOUT BURST A BLOOD VESSEL TRYING TO FIGURE OUT IF ME AND BASIL WERE SLEEPING TOGETHER.

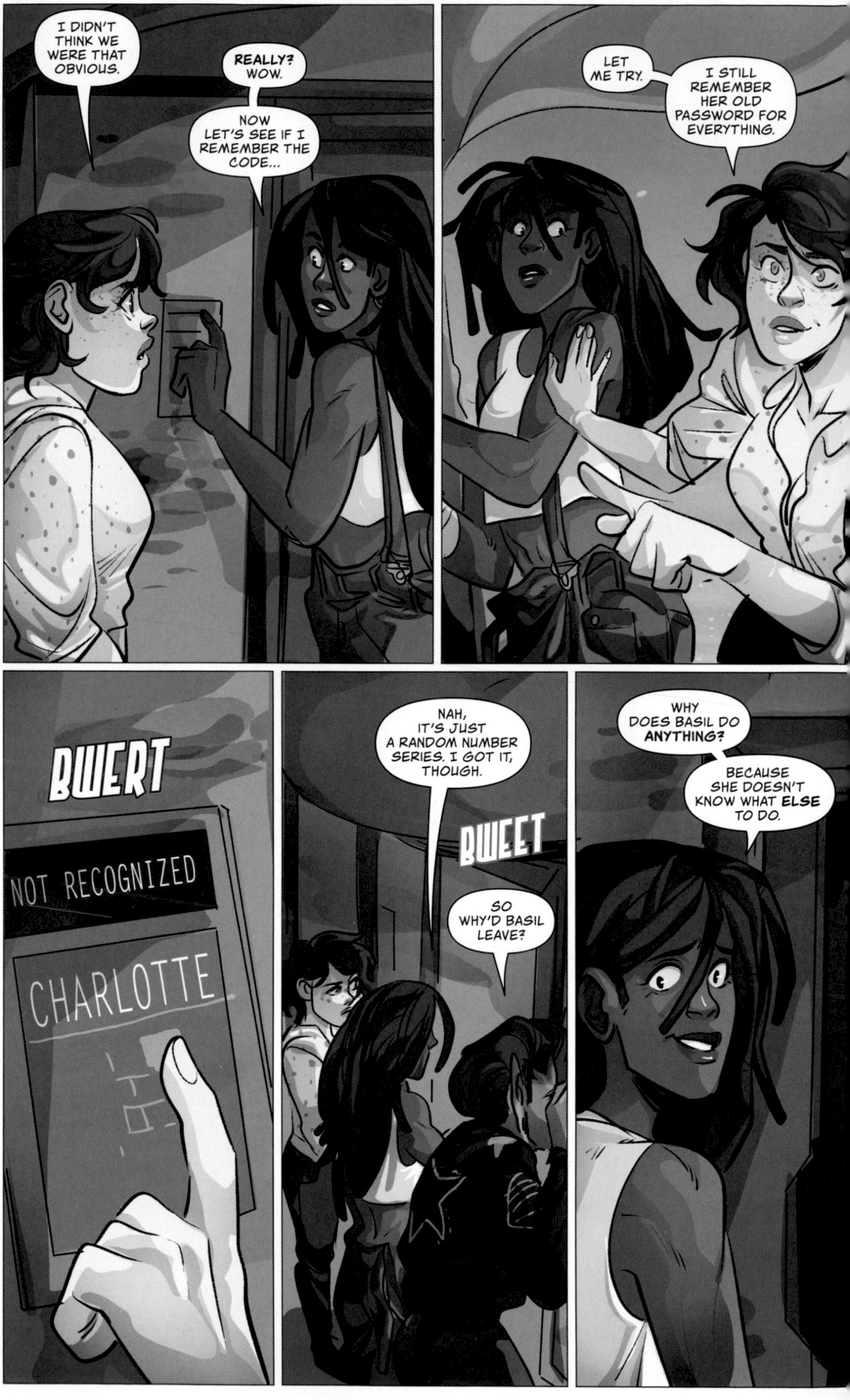
I DIDN'T THINK WE WERE THAT OBVIOUS.
REALLY? WOW.
NOW LET'S SEE IF I REMEMBER THE CODE...
LET ME TRY.
I STILL REMEMBER HER OLD PASSWORD FOR EVERYTHING.
BWERT
NOT RECOGNIZED
CHARLOTTE
NAH, IT'S JUST A RANDOM NUMBER SERIES. I GOT IT, THOUGH.
BWEET
SO WHY'D BASIL LEAVE?
WHY DOES BASIL DO ANYTHING?
BECAUSE SHE DOESN'T KNOW WHAT ELSE TO DO.

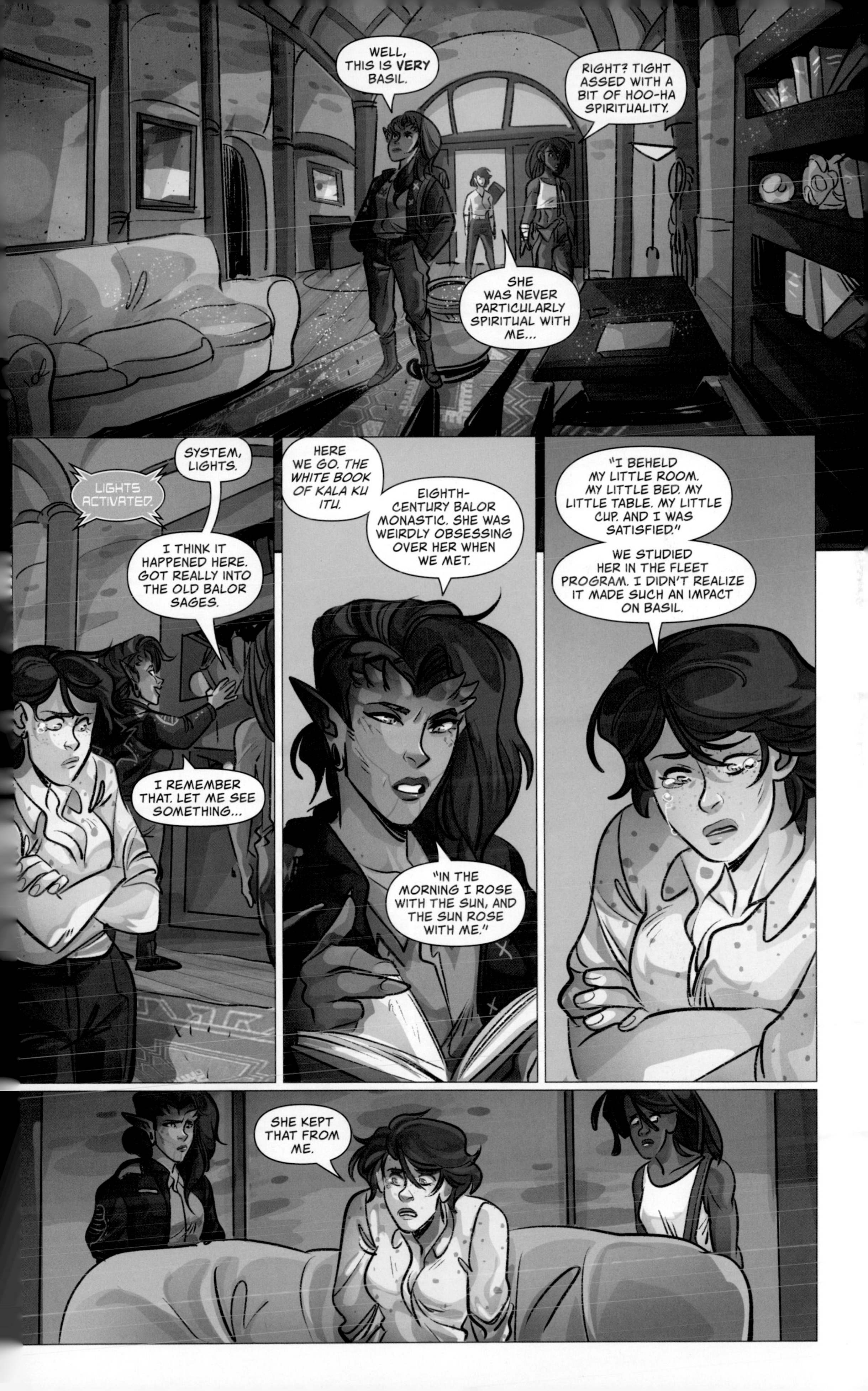
WELL, THIS IS VERY BASIL.
RIGHT? TIGHT ASSED WITH A BIT OF HOO-HA SPIRITUALITY.
SHE WAS NEVER PARTICULARLY SPIRITUAL WITH ME...
SYSTEM, LIGHTS.
LIGHTS ACTIVATED.
I THINK IT HAPPENED HERE. GOT REALLY INTO THE OLD BALOR SAGES.
I REMEMBER THAT. LET ME SEE SOMETHING...
HERE WE GO. THE WHITE BOOK OF KALA KU ITU.
EIGHTH-CENTURY BALOR MONASTIC. SHE WAS WEIRDLY OBSESSING OVER HER WHEN WE MET.
"IN THE MORNING I ROSE WITH THE SUN, AND THE SUN ROSE WITH ME."
"I BEHELD MY LITTLE ROOM. MY LITTLE BED. MY LITTLE TABLE. MY LITTLE CUP. AND I WAS SATISFIED."
WE STUDIED HER IN THE FLEET PROGRAM. I DIDN'T REALIZE IT MADE SUCH AN IMPACT ON BASIL.
SHE KEPT THAT FROM ME.

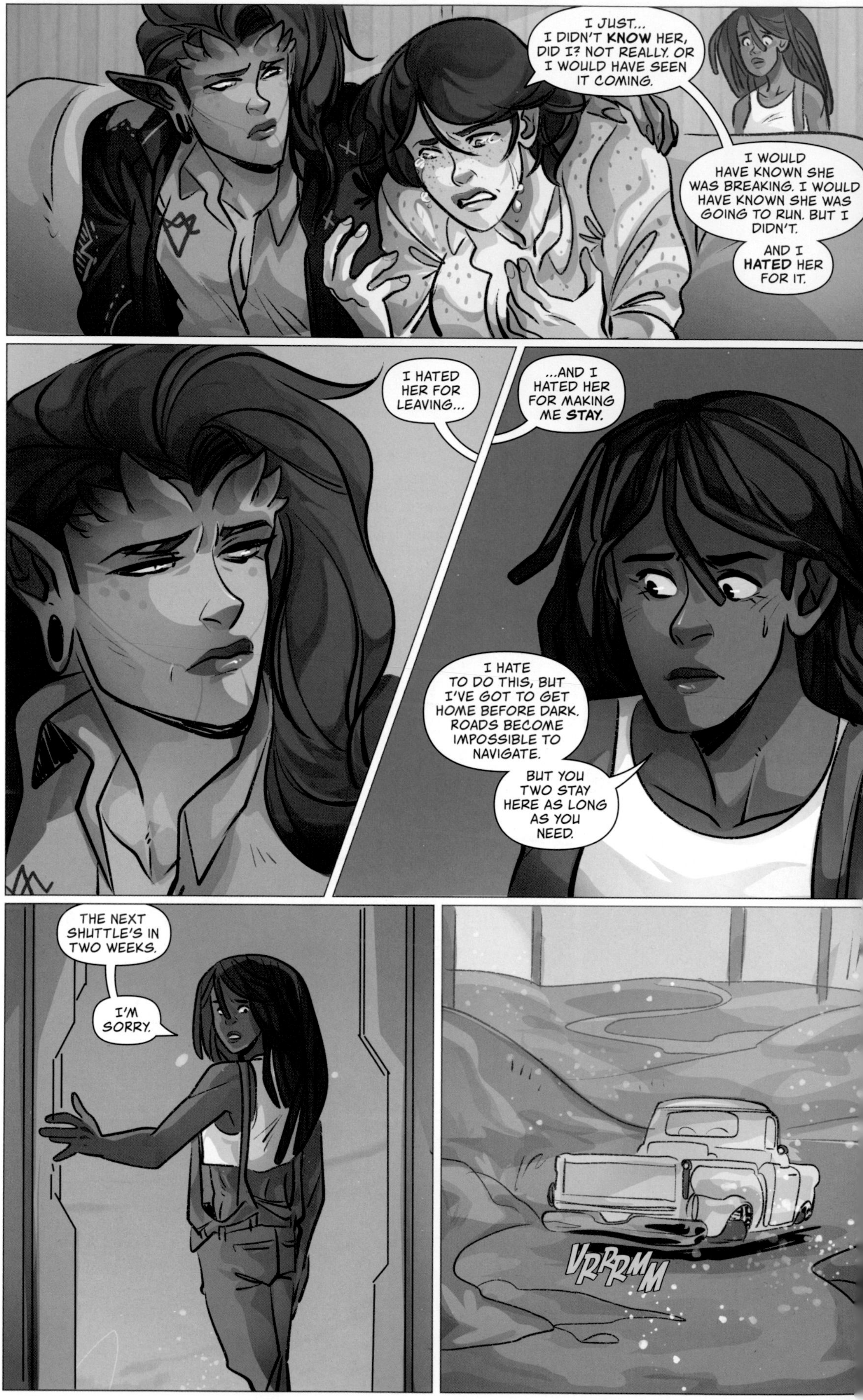
I JUST... I DIDN'T KNOW HER, DID I? NOT REALLY. OR I WOULD HAVE SEEN IT COMING.
I WOULD HAVE KNOWN SHE WAS BREAKING. I WOULD HAVE KNOWN SHE WAS GOING TO RUN. BUT I DIDN'T.
AND I HATED HER FOR IT.
I HATED HER FOR LEAVING...
...AND I HATED HER FOR MAKING ME STAY.
I HATE TO DO THIS, BUT I'VE GOT TO GET HOME BEFORE DARK. ROADS BECOME IMPOSSIBLE TO NAVIGATE.
BUT YOU TWO STAY HERE AS LONG AS YOU NEED.
THE NEXT SHUTTLE'S IN TWO WEEKS.
I'M SORRY.
VRRRMM

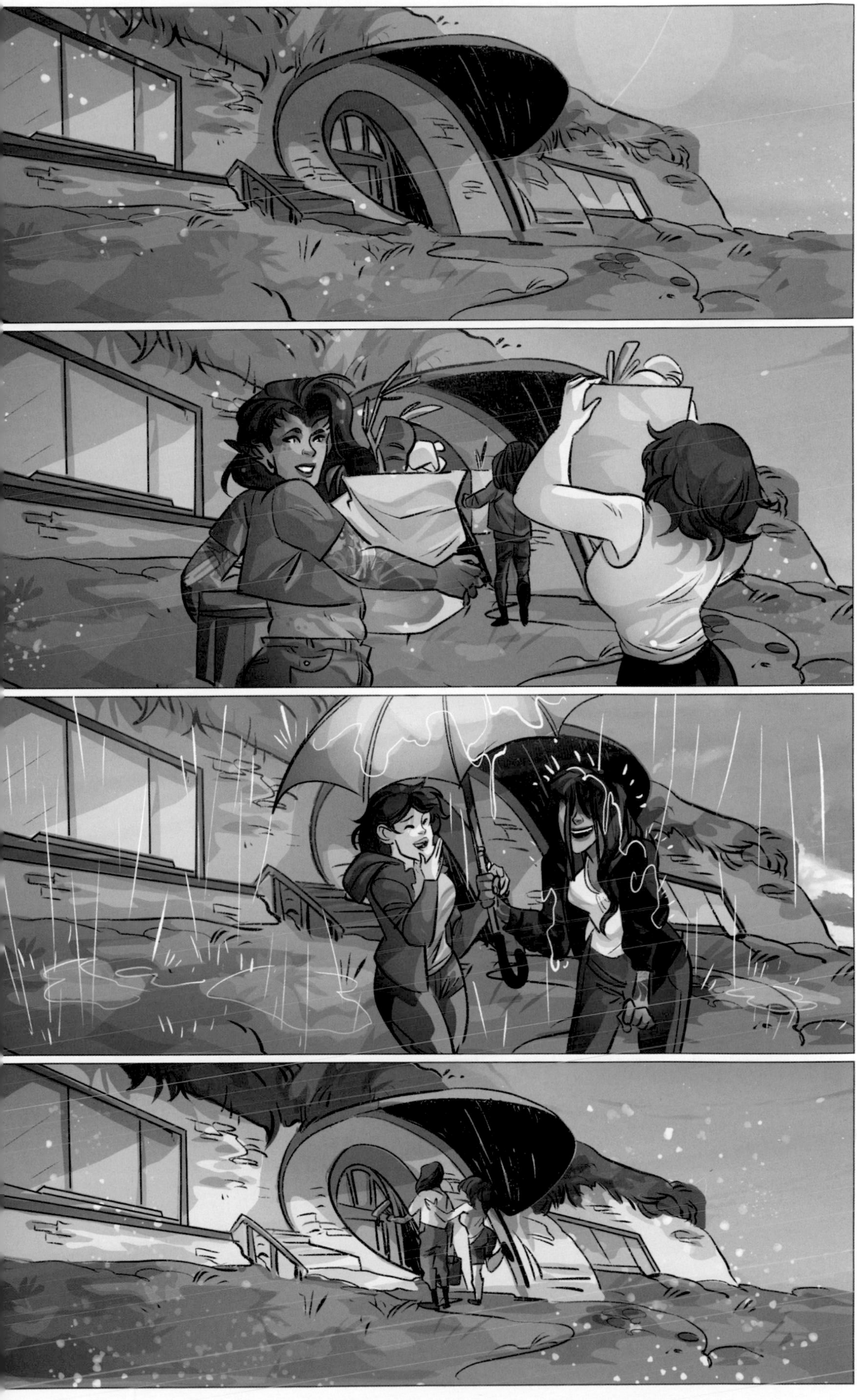

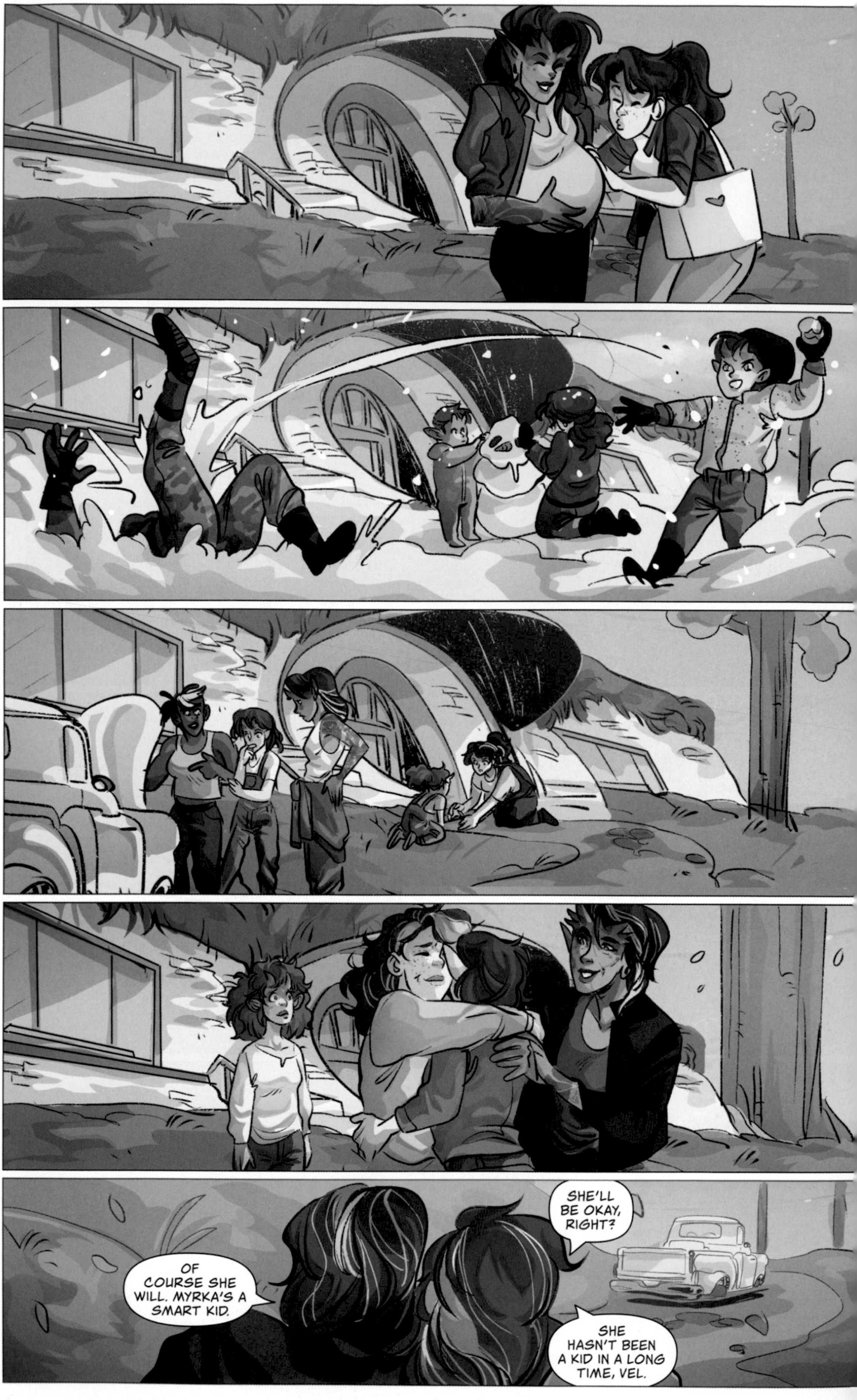
SHE'LL BE OKAY, RIGHT?
OF COURSE SHE WILL. MYRKA'S A SMART KID.
SHE HASN'T BEEN A KID IN A LONG TIME, VEL.

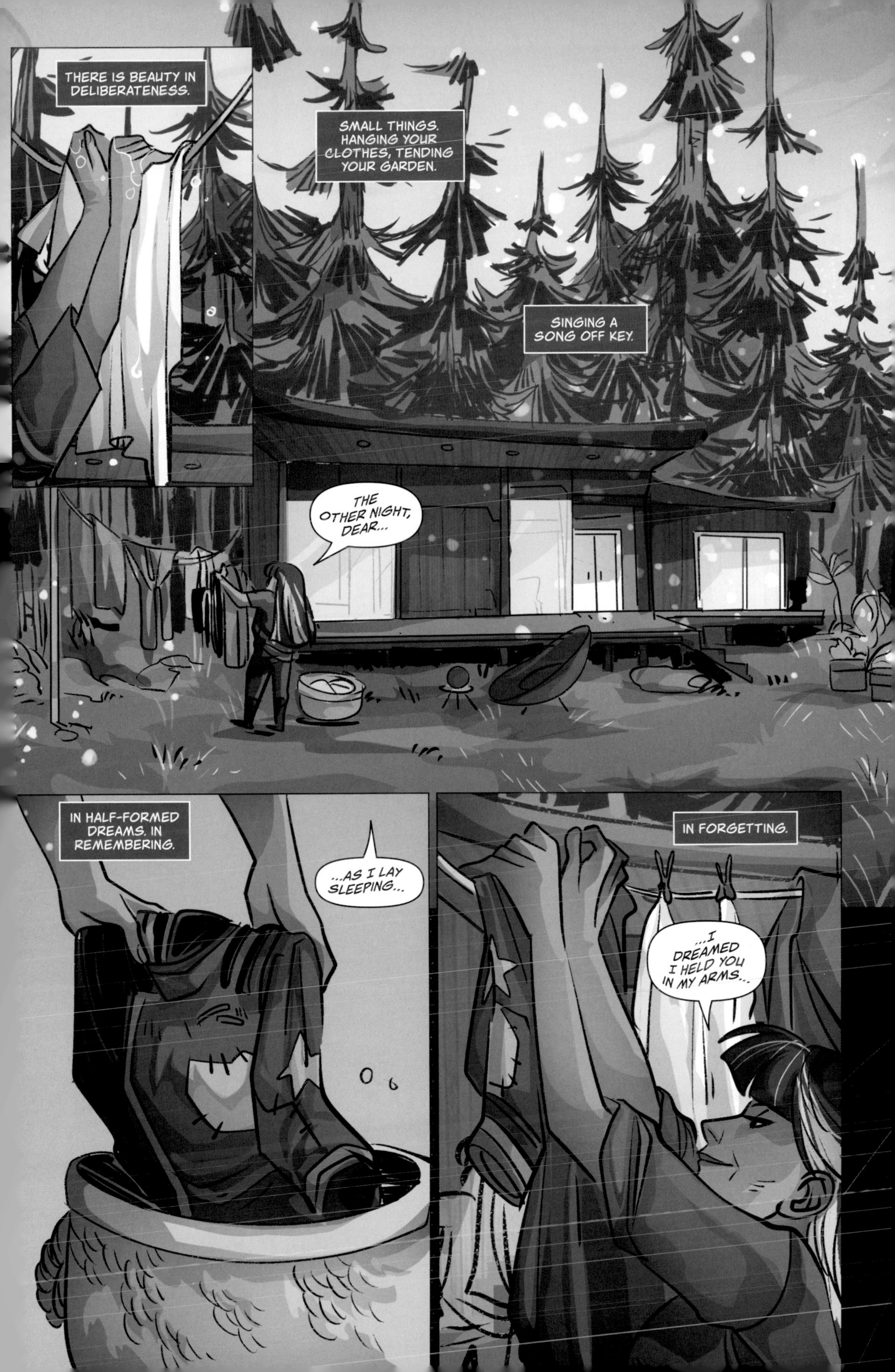
THERE IS BEAUTY IN DELIBERATENESS.
SMALL THINGS. HANGING YOUR CLOTHES, TENDING YOUR GARDEN.
SINGING A SONG OFF KEY.
THE OTHER NIGHT, DEAR...
IN HALF-FORMED DREAMS. IN REMEMBERING.
...AS I LAY SLEEPING...
IN FORGETTING.
...I DREAMED I HELD YOU IN MY ARMS...

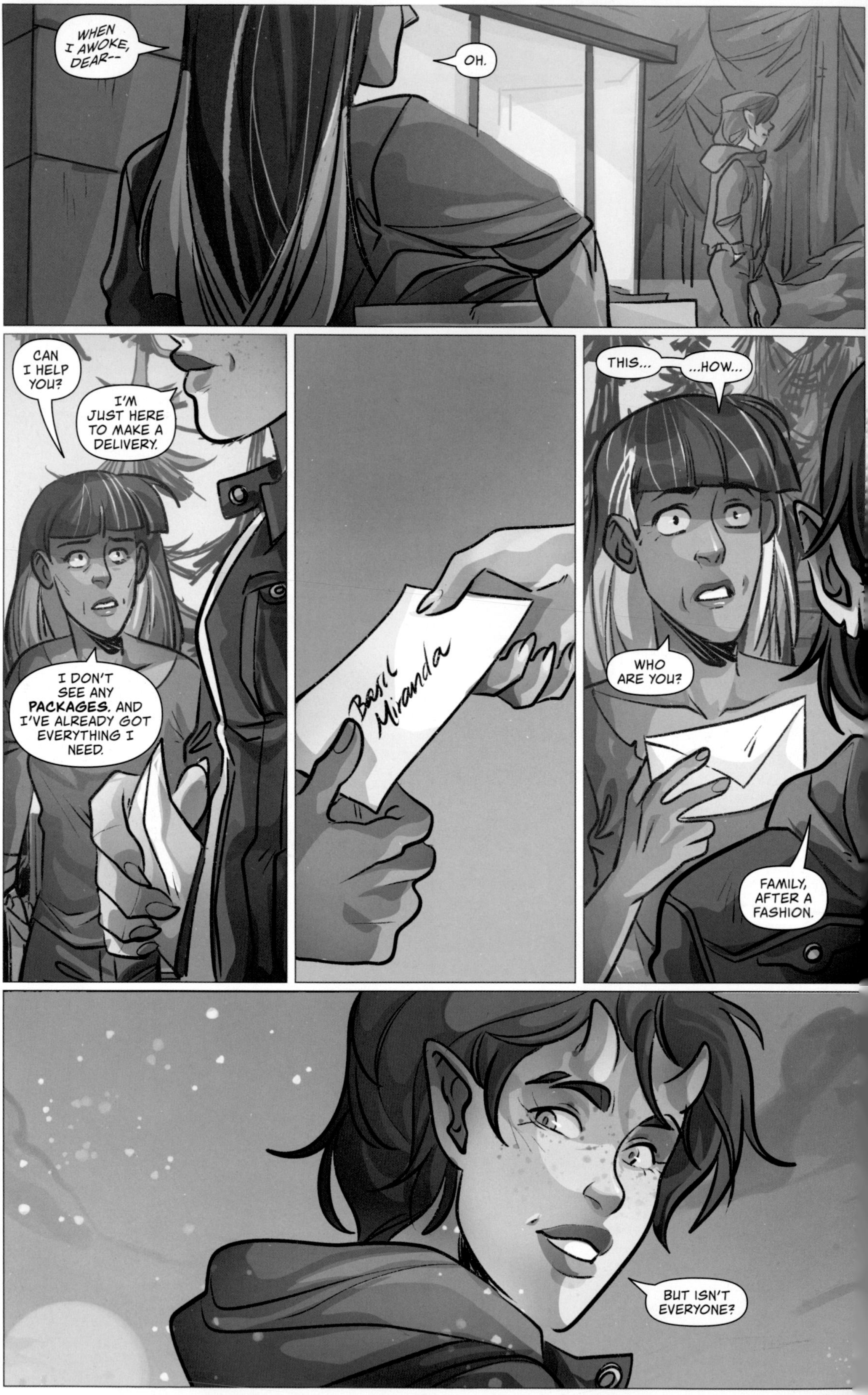
WHEN I AWOKE, DEAR--
OH.
CAN I HELP YOU?
I'M JUST HERE TO MAKE A DELIVERY.
I DON'T SEE ANY **PACKAGES.** AND I'VE ALREADY GOT EVERYTHING I NEED.
Basil Miranda
THIS...
...HOW...
WHO ARE YOU?
FAMILY, AFTER A FASHION.
BUT ISN'T EVERYONE?

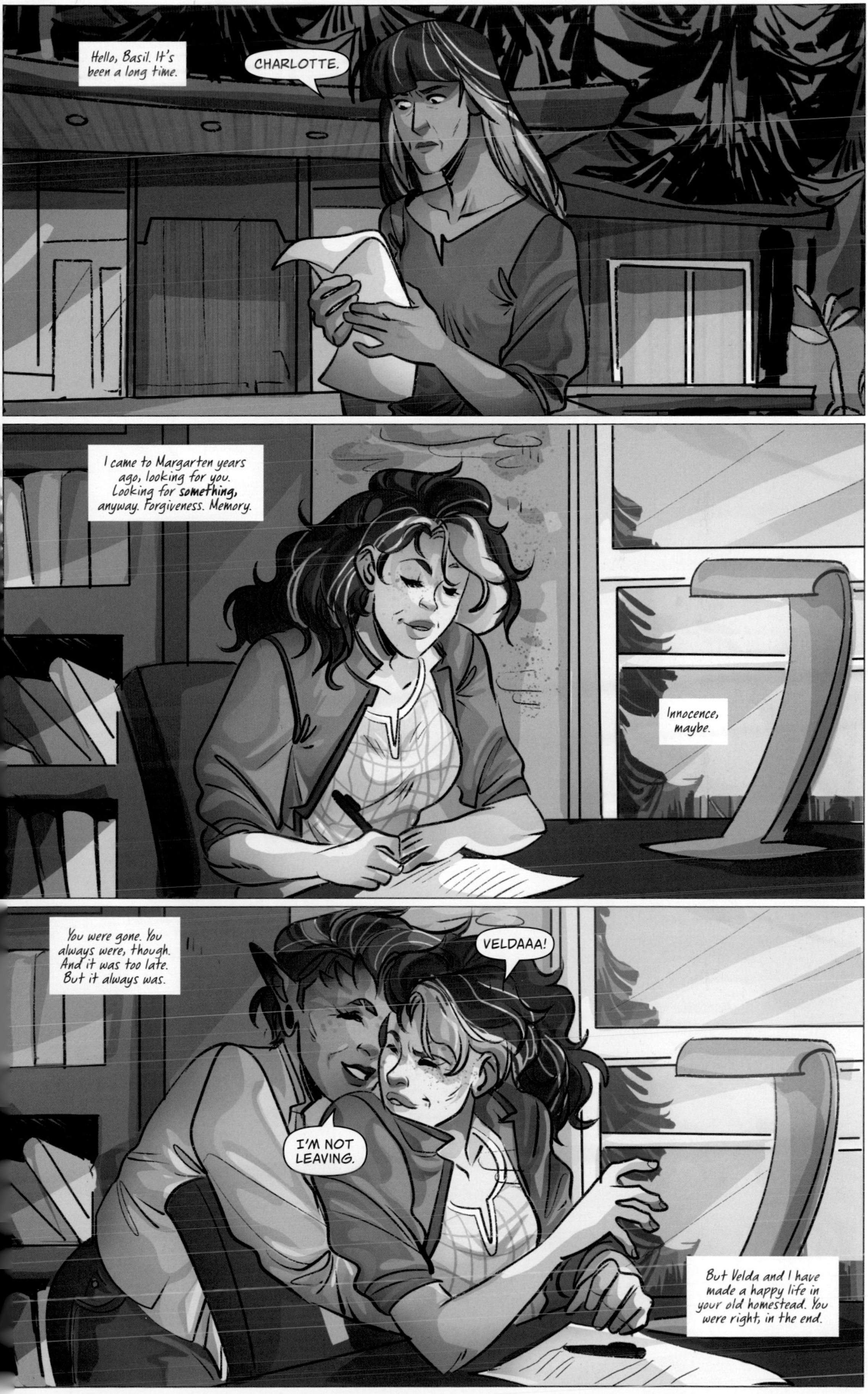
Hello, Basil. It's been a long time.
CHARLOTTE.
I came to Margarten years ago, looking for you. Looking for **something,** anyway. Forgiveness. Memory.
Innocence, maybe.
You were gone. You always were, though. And it was too late. But it always was.
VELDAAA!
I'M NOT LEAVING.
But Velda and I have made a happy life in your old homestead. You were right, in the end.

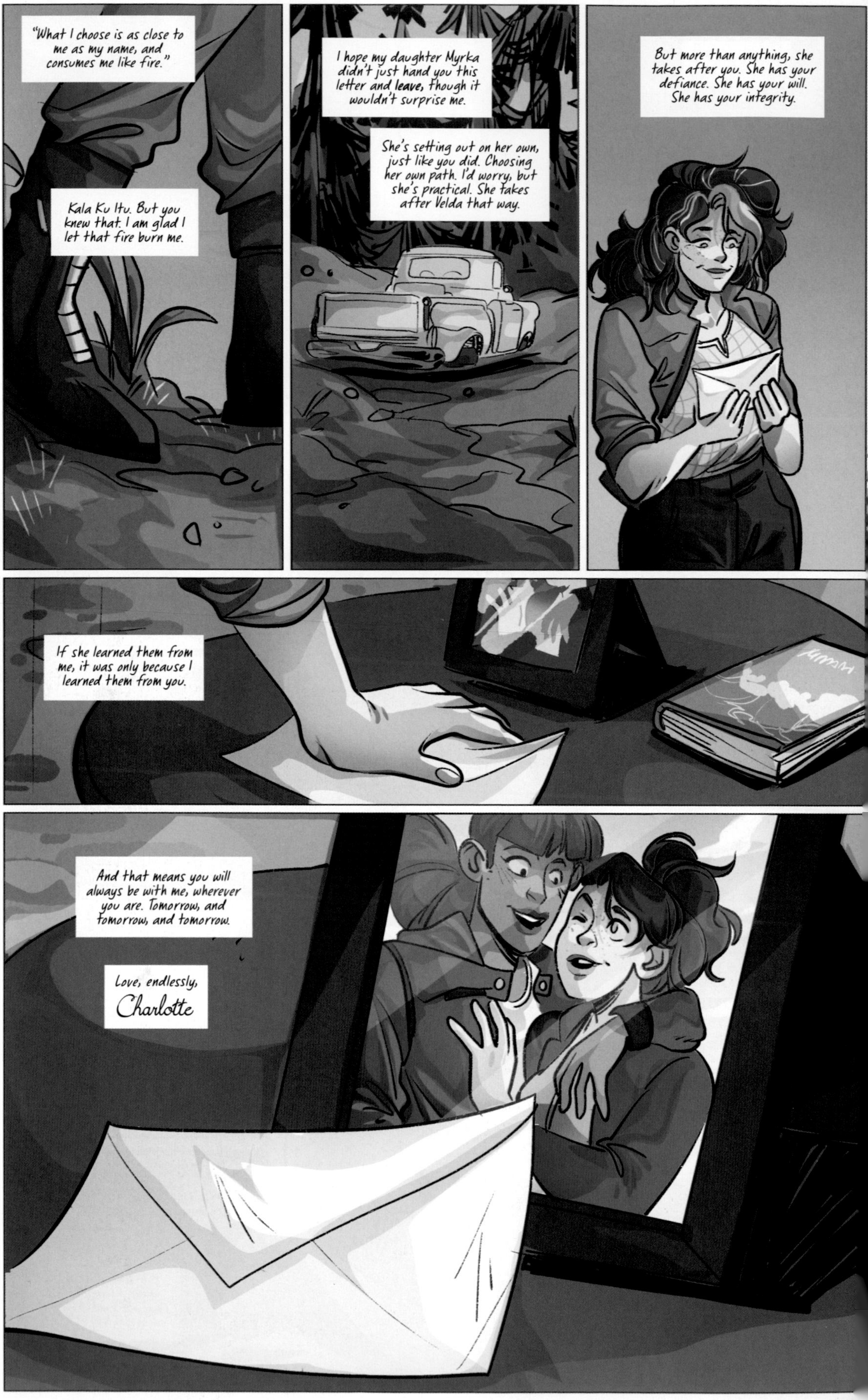
"What I choose is as close to me as my name, and consumes me like fire."
Kala Ku Itu. But you knew that. I am glad I let that fire burn me.
I hope my daughter Myrka didn't just hand you this letter and leave, though it wouldn't surprise me.
She's setting out on her own, just like you did. Choosing her own path. I'd worry, but she's practical. She takes after Velda that way.
But more than anything, she takes after you. She has your defiance. She has your will. She has your integrity.
If she learned them from me, it was only because I learned them from you.
And that means you will always be with me, wherever you are. Tomorrow, and tomorrow, and tomorrow.
Love, endlessly,
Charlotte

The art of

CLAUDIA AGUIRRE

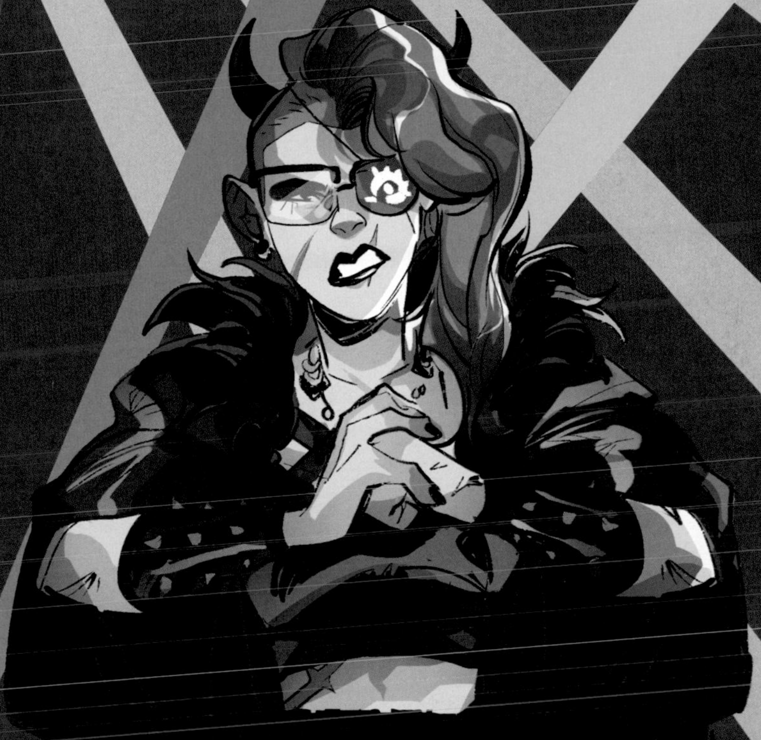

The following pages include the original character designs for our core cast of characters, detailed layouts from issue 1, pages 1 through 8, and an unused cover that's so good that we have to share it. All of this was done by *Lost on Planet Earth* cocreator **Claudia Aguirre.**

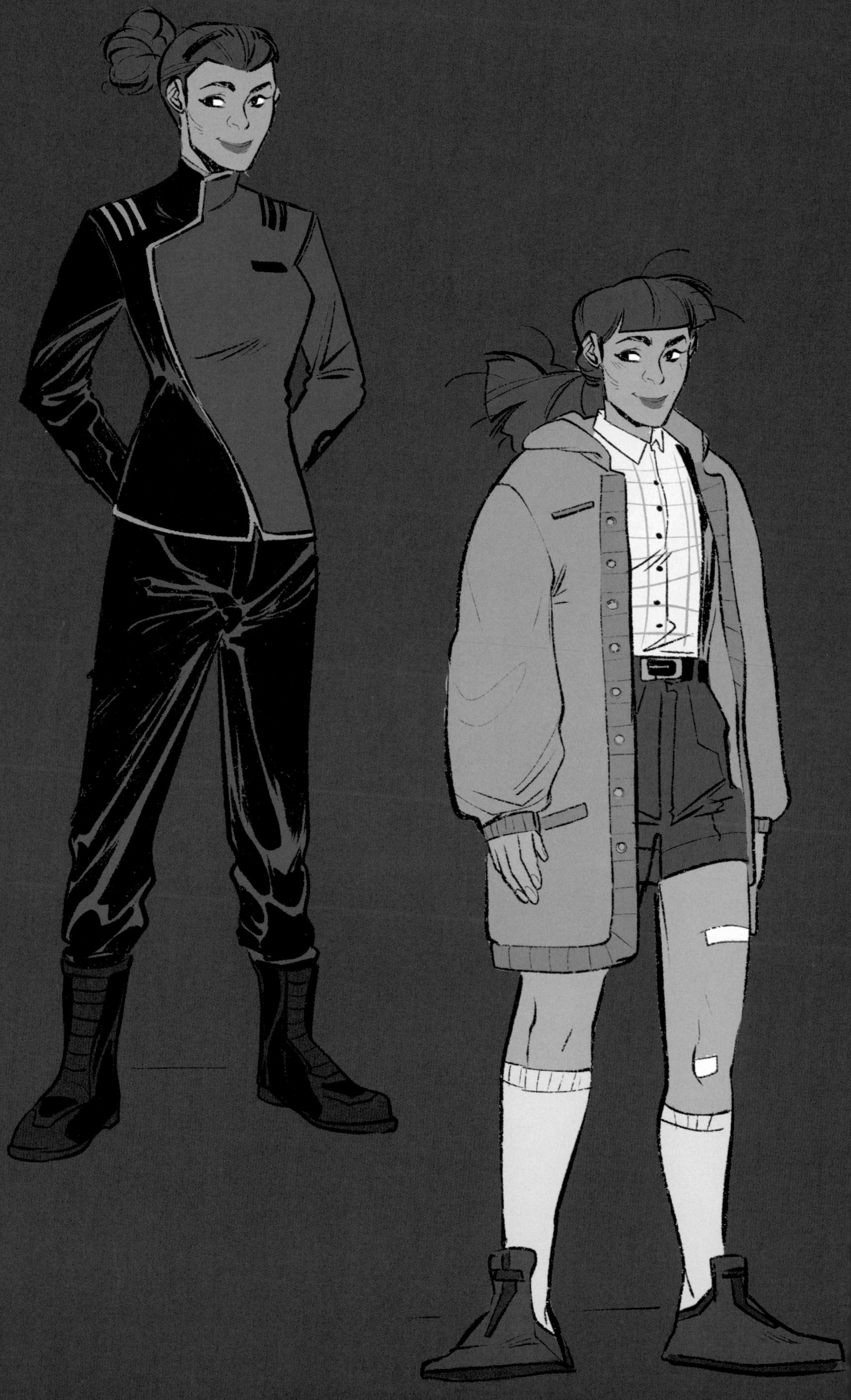

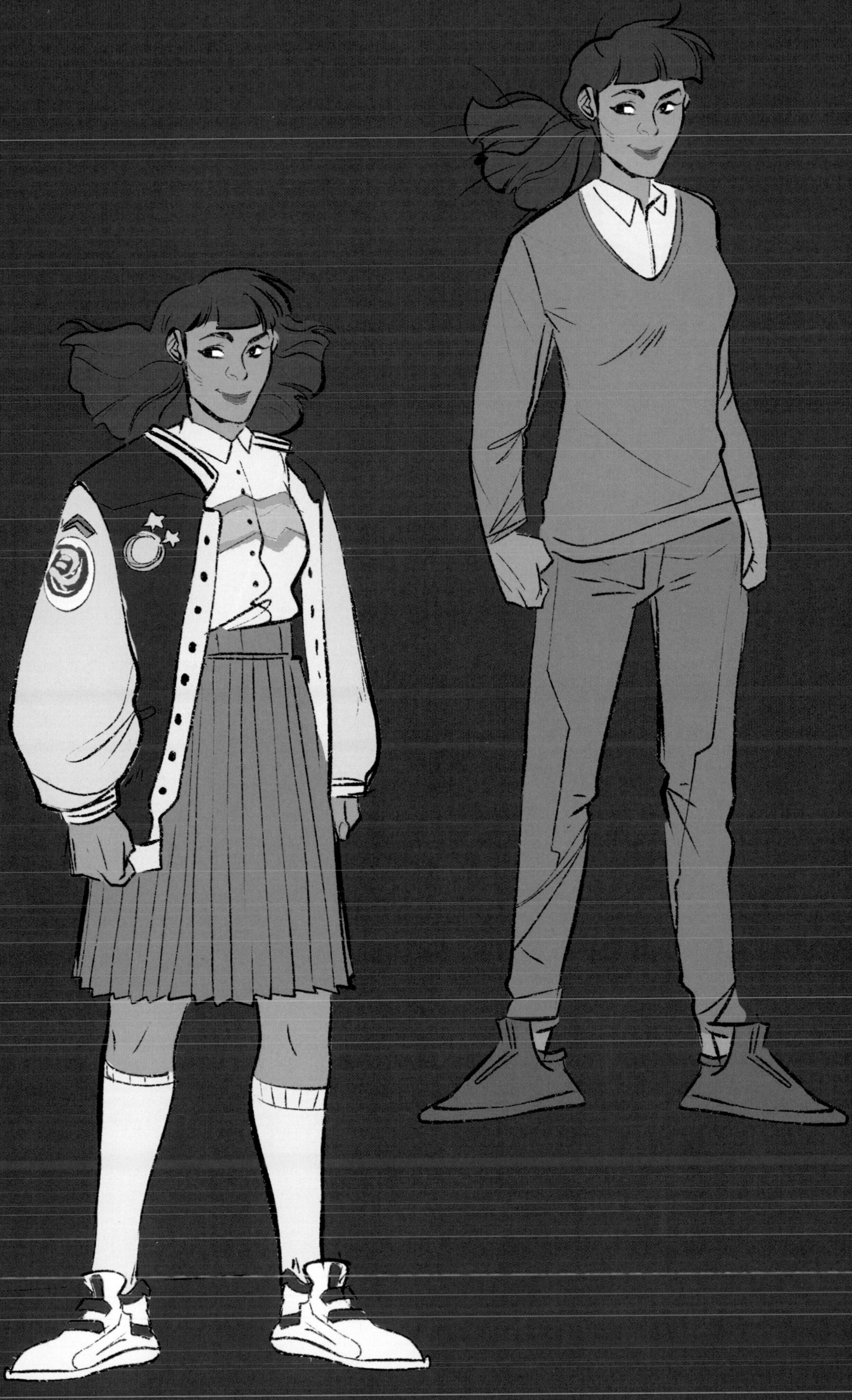

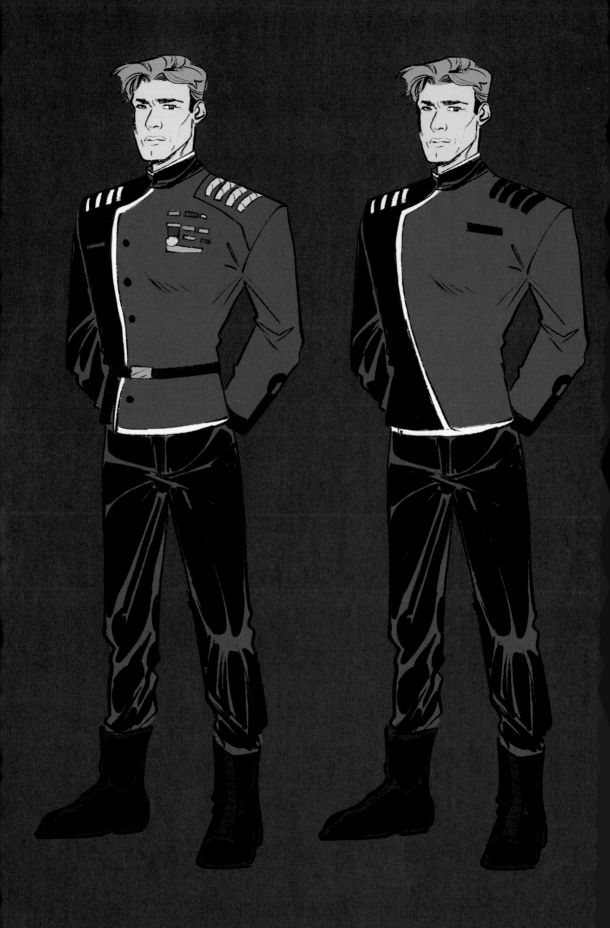

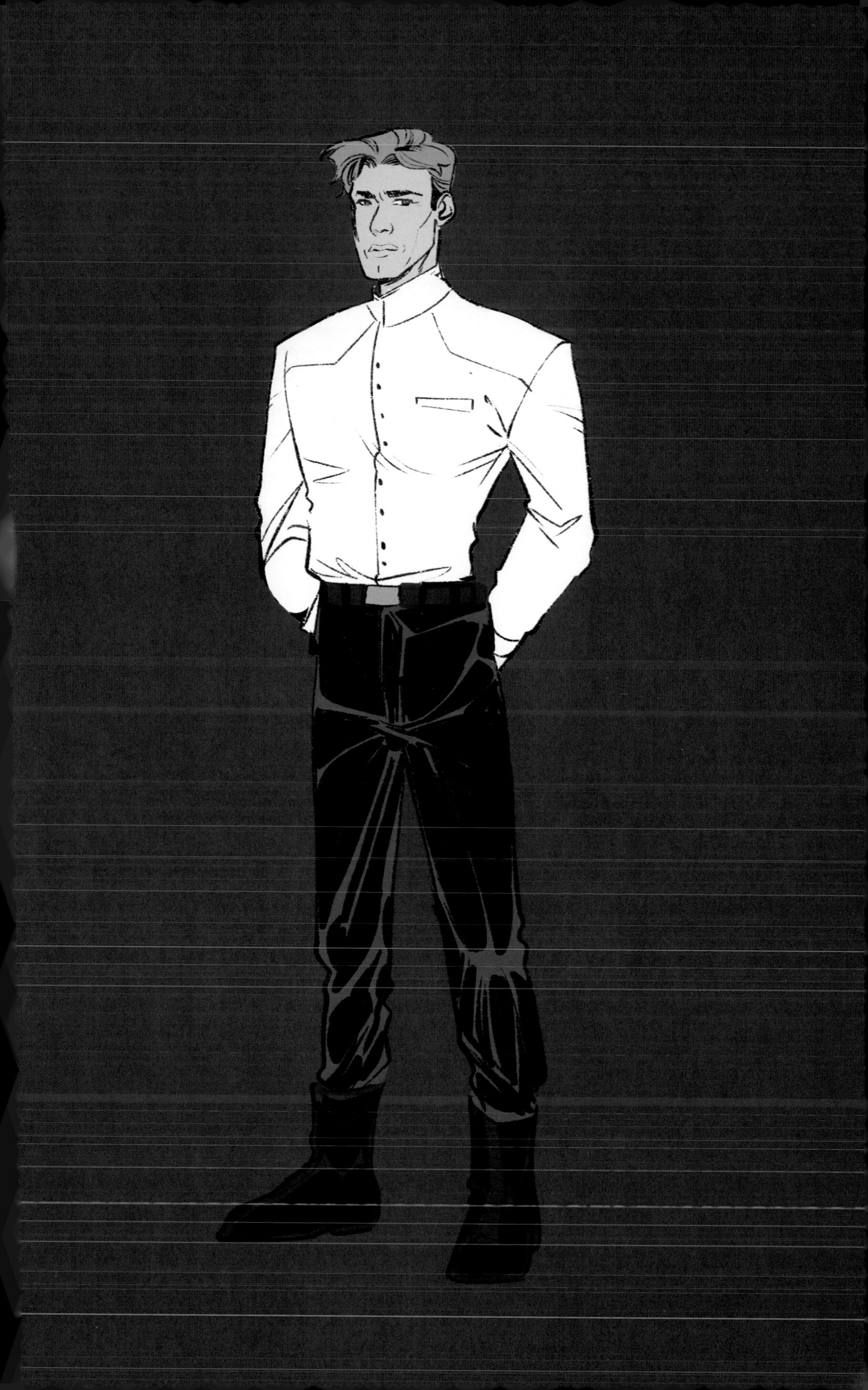

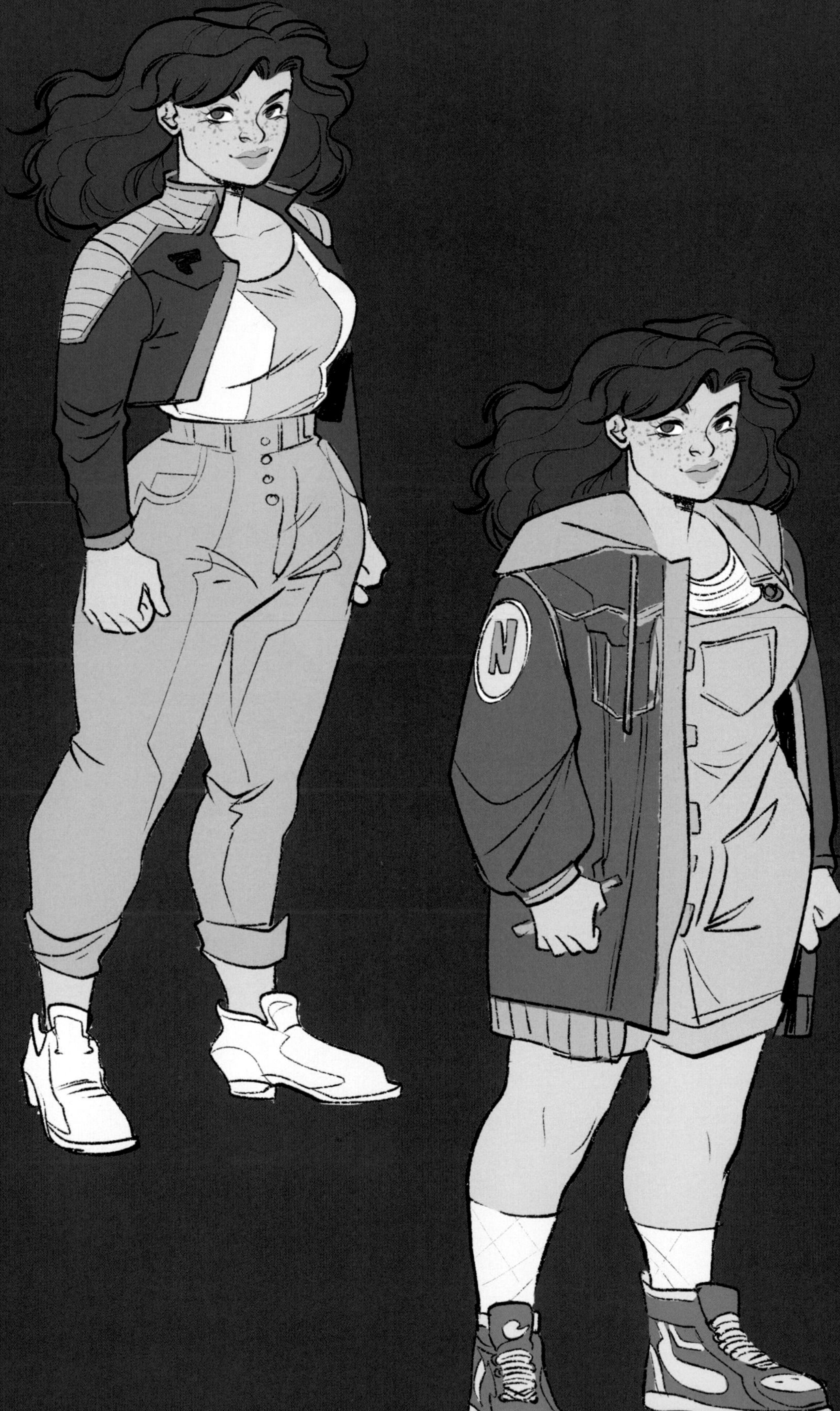
N

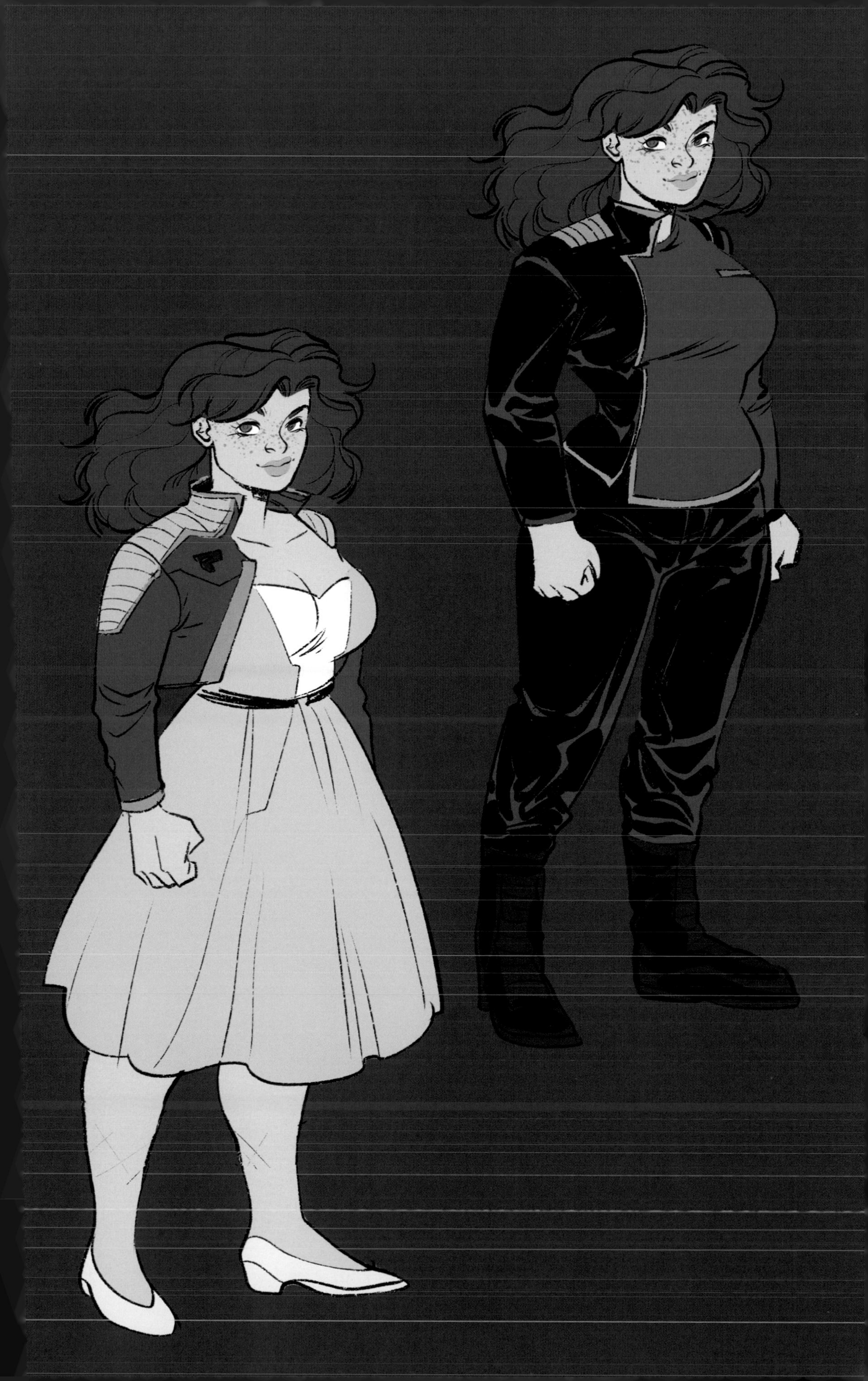

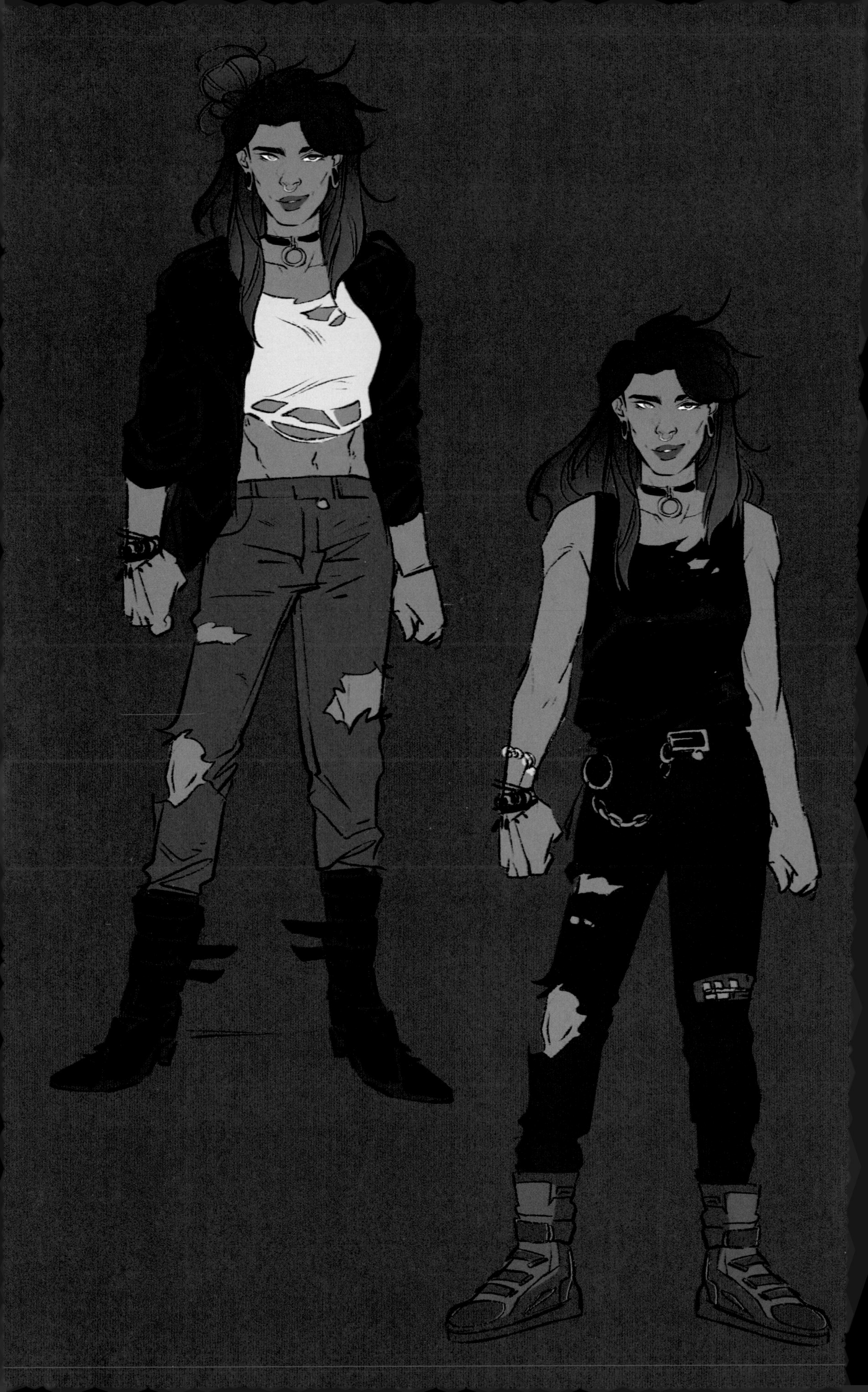

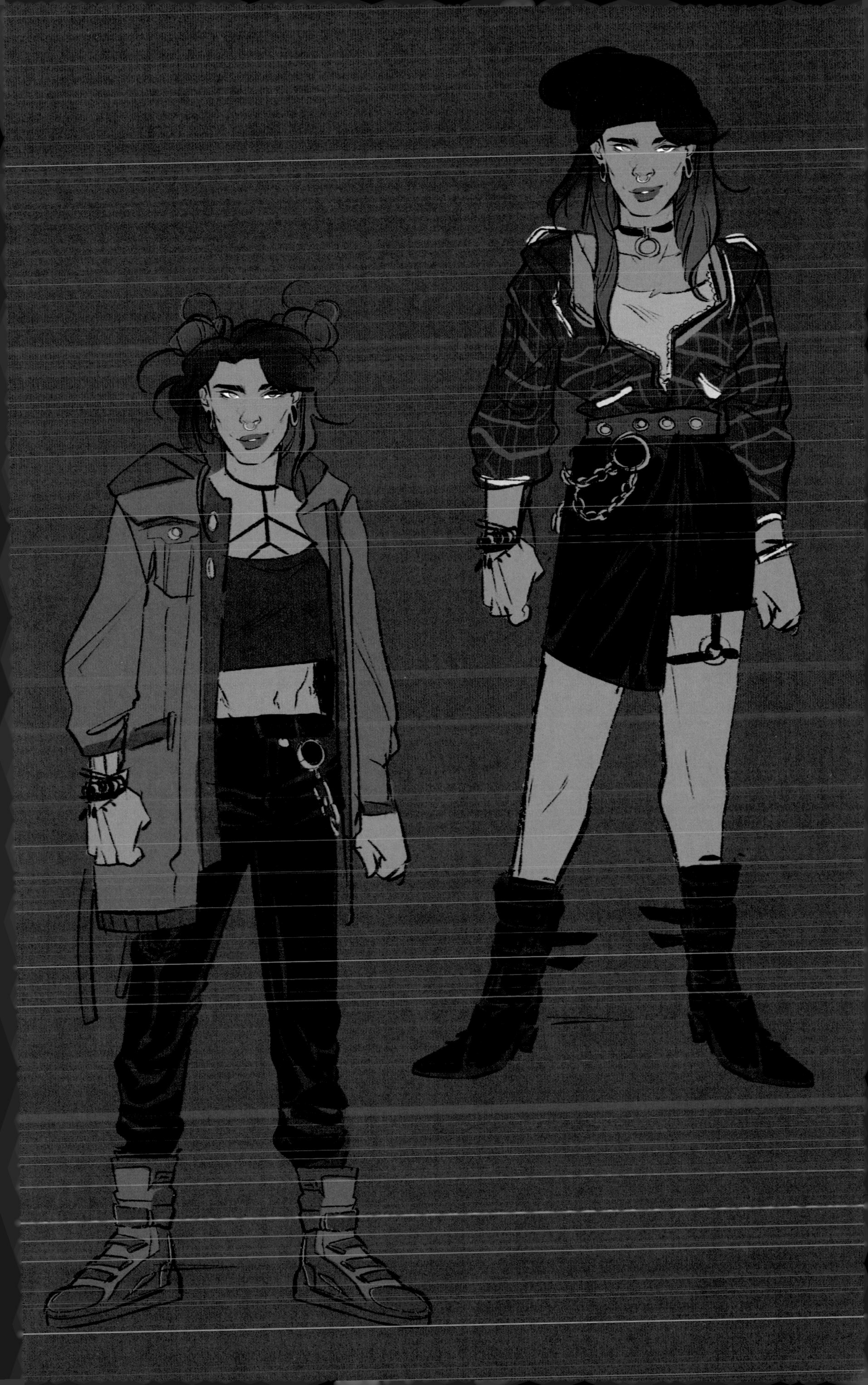

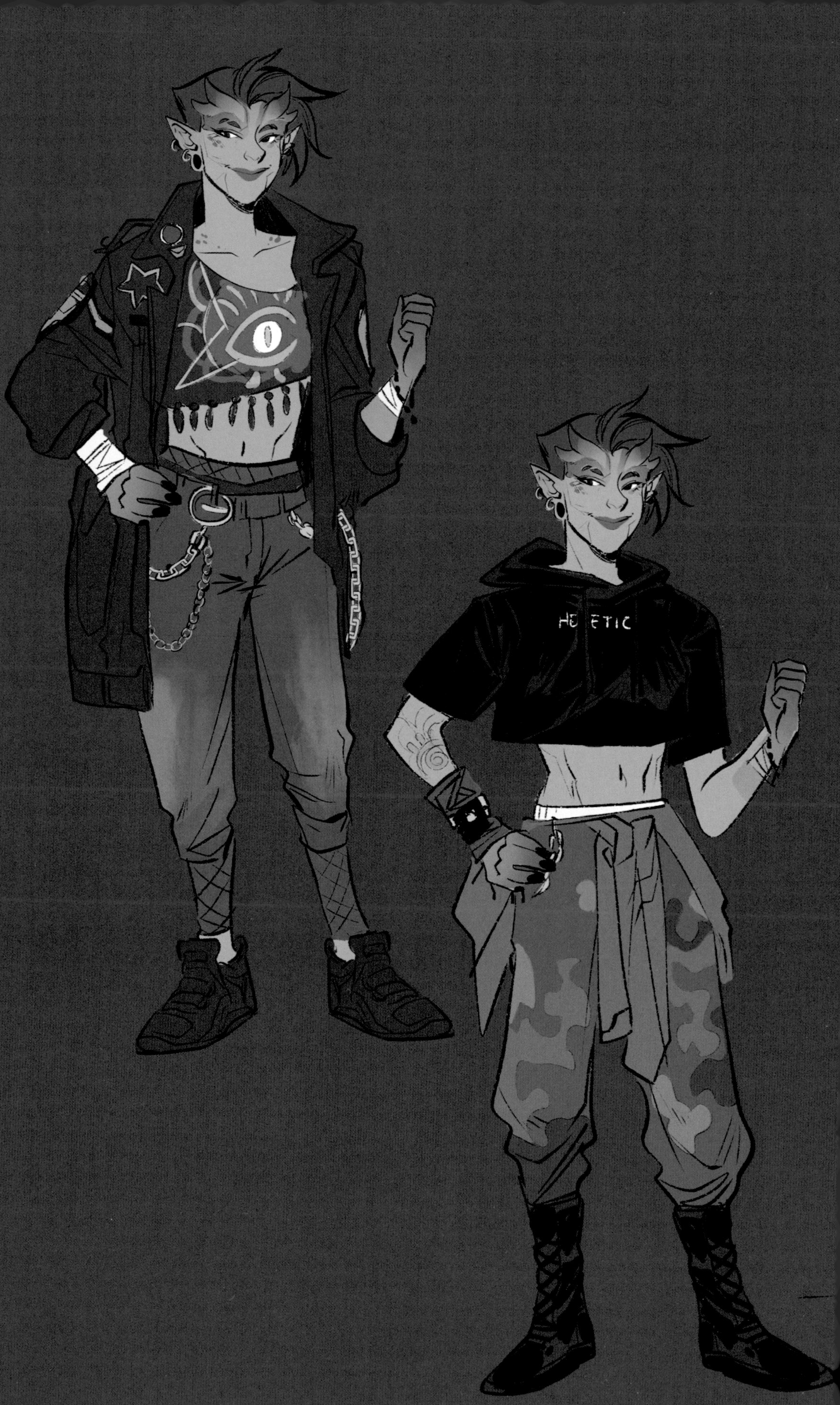
HE ETIC

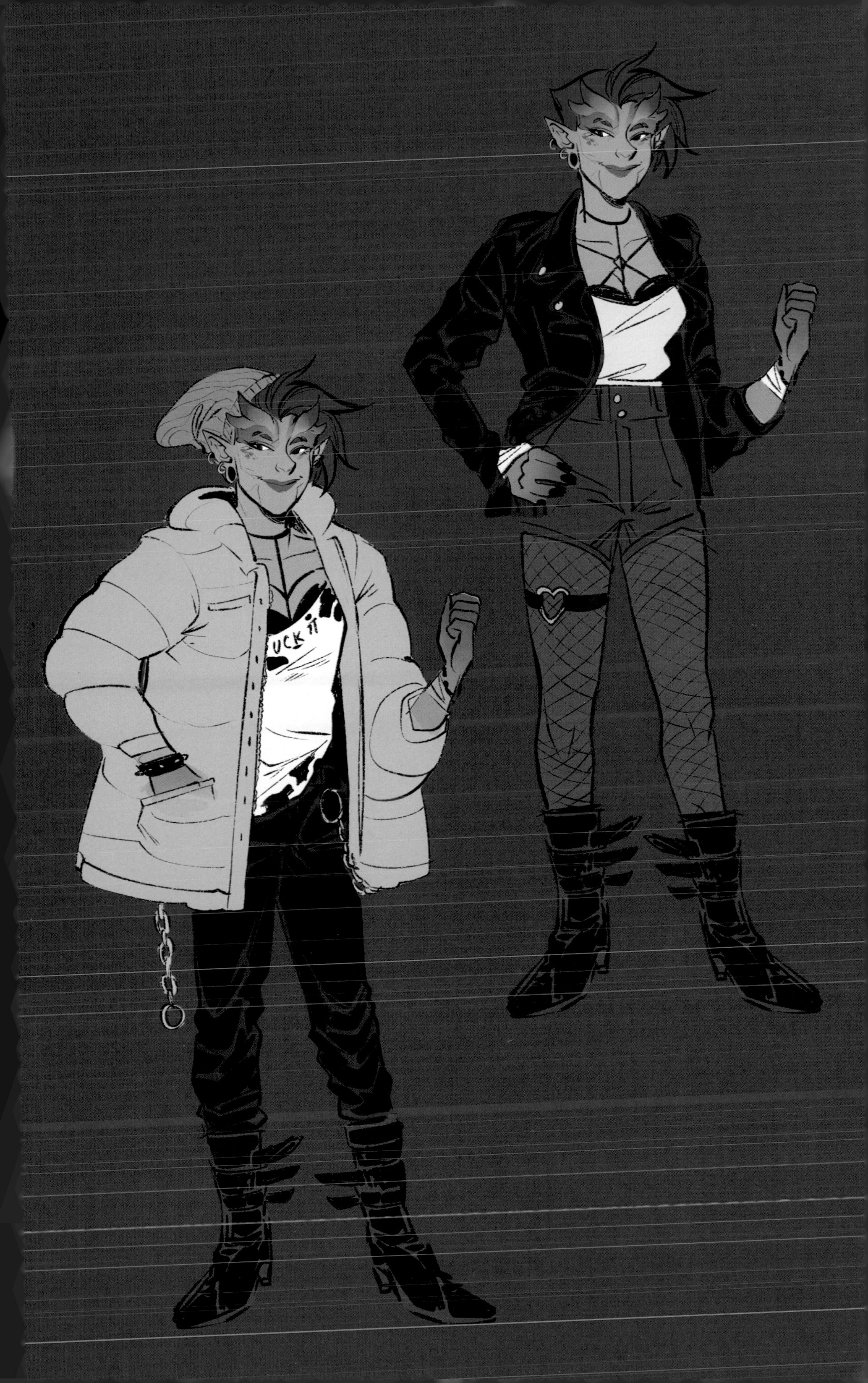
UCK IT

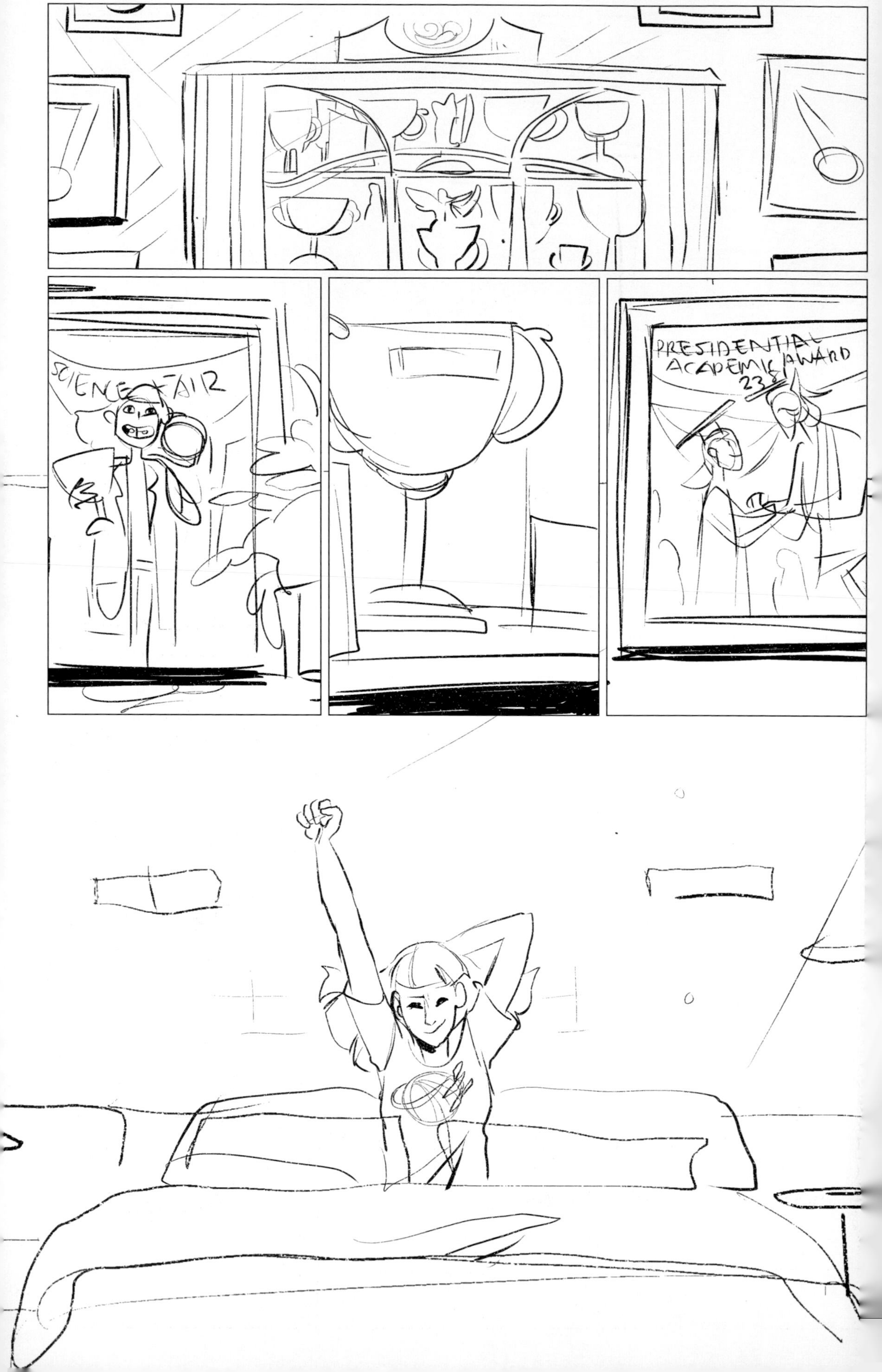

SCIENCE FAIR
PRESIDENTIAL ACADEMIC AWARD
2381

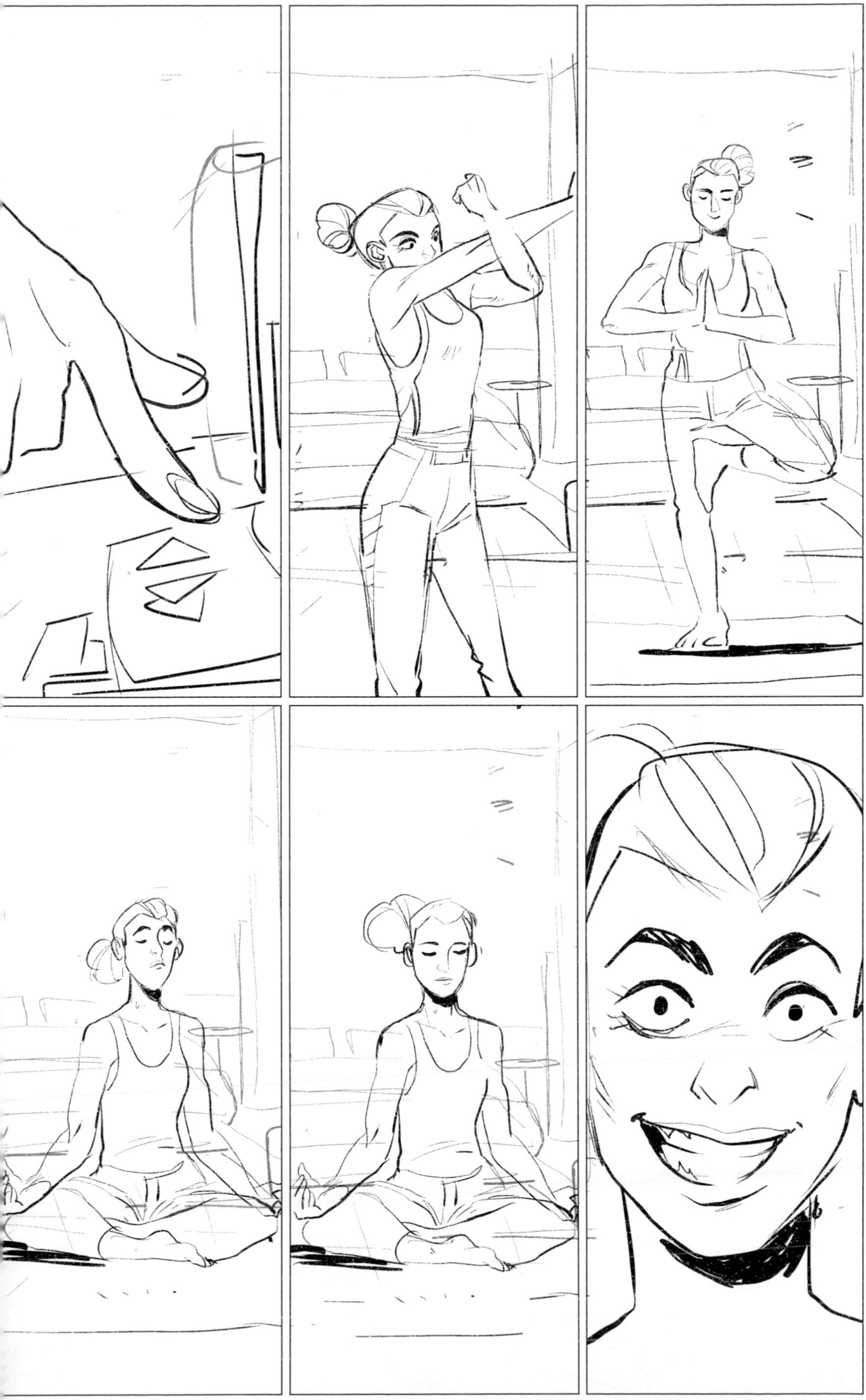

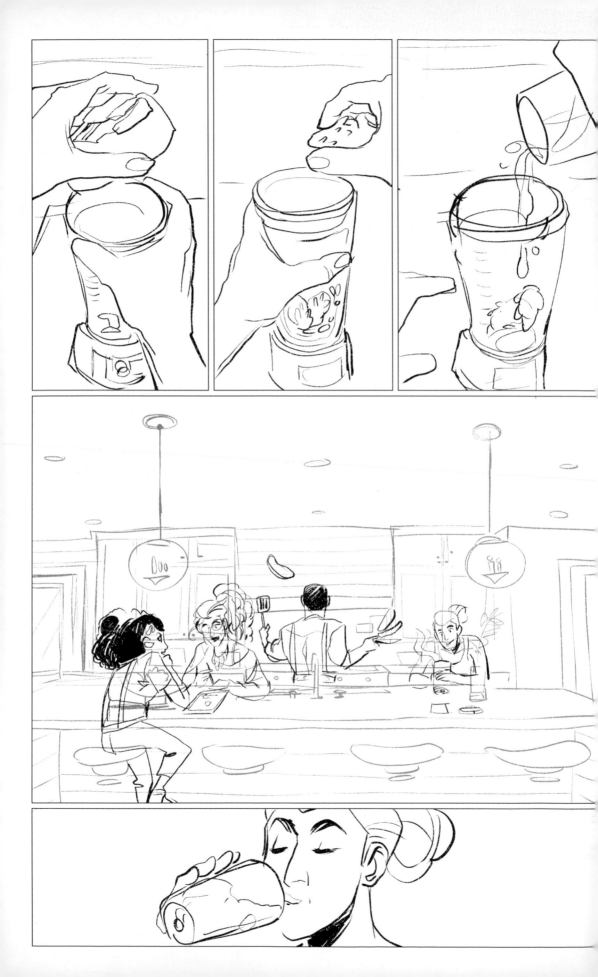

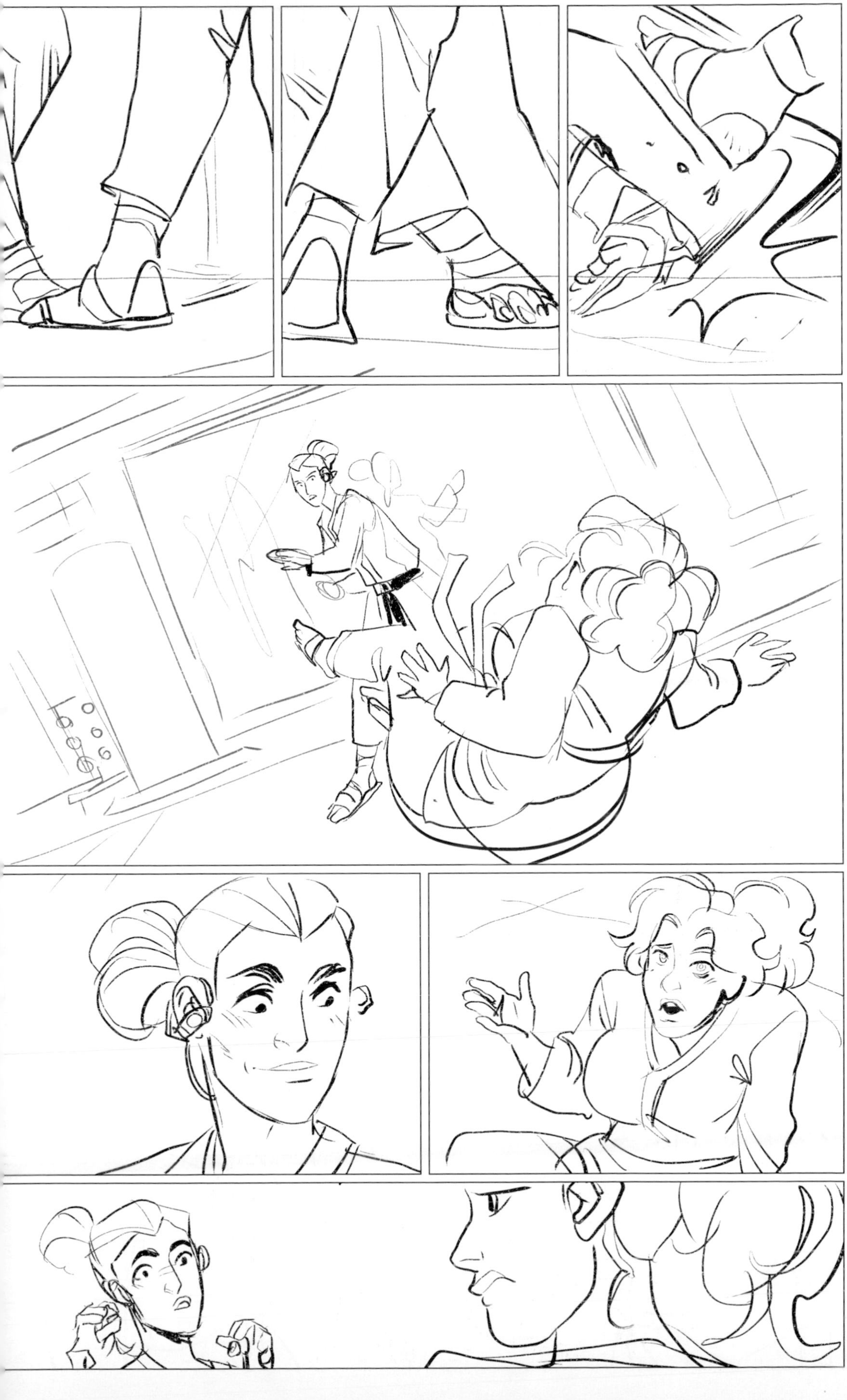

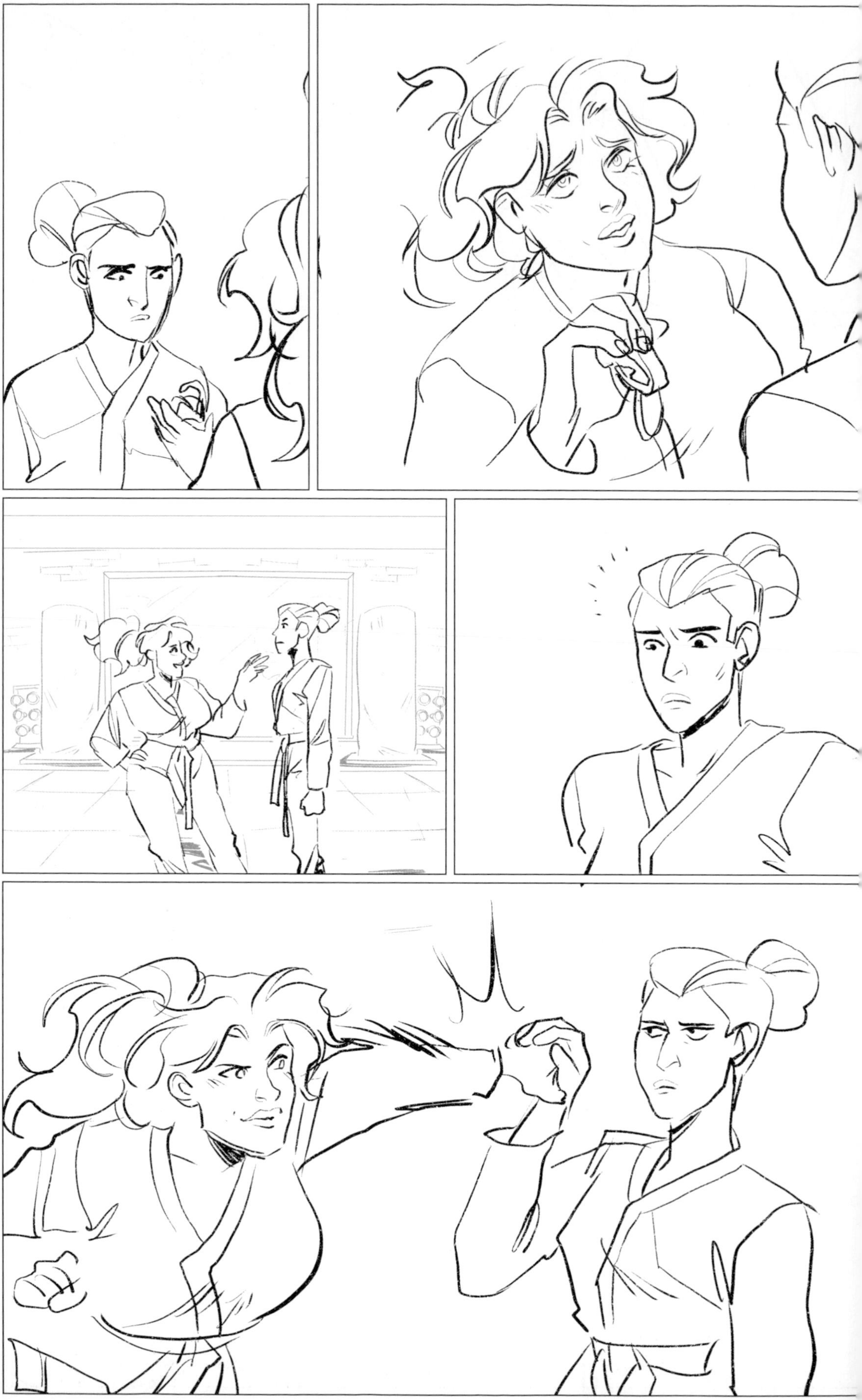

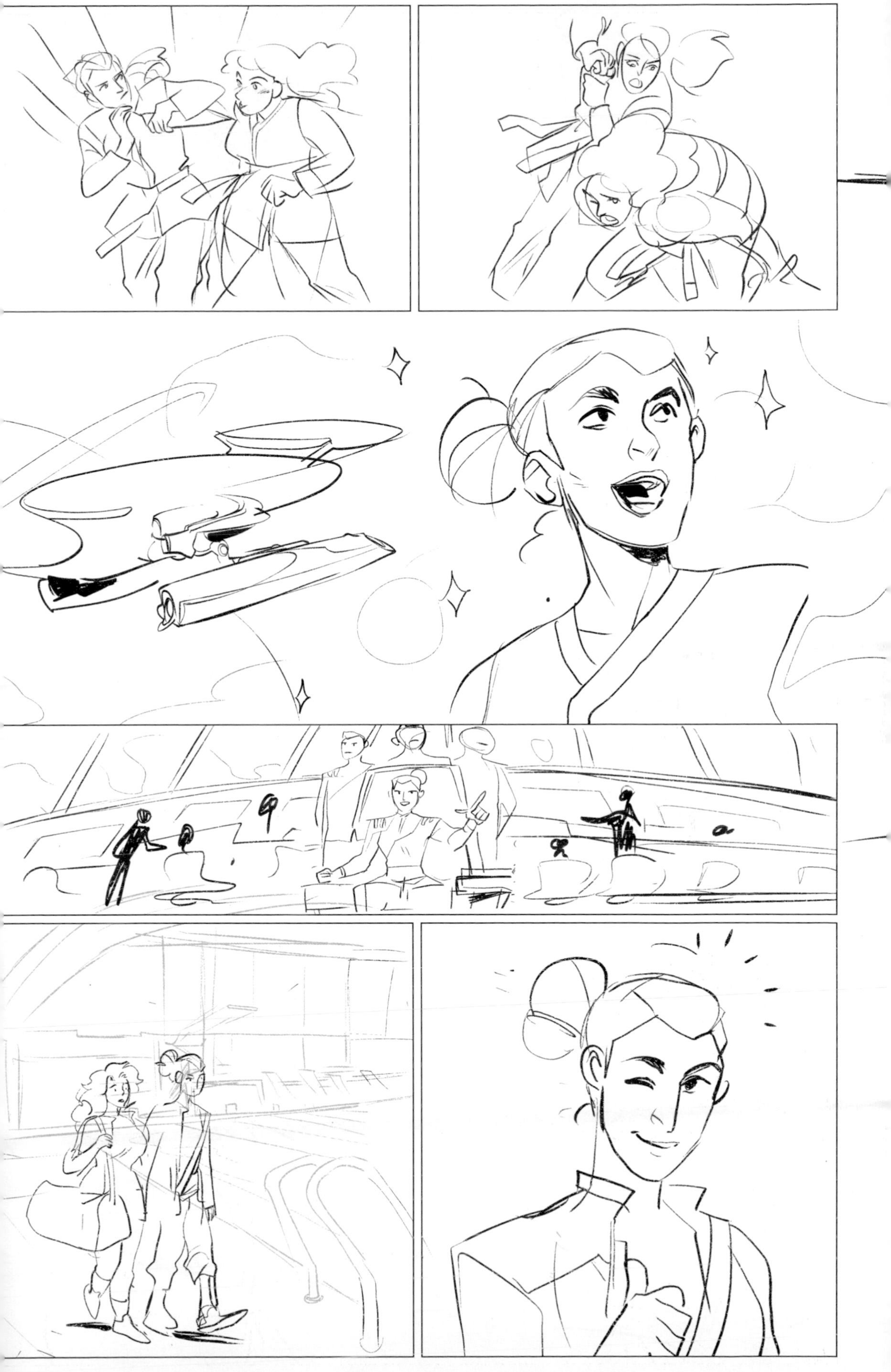

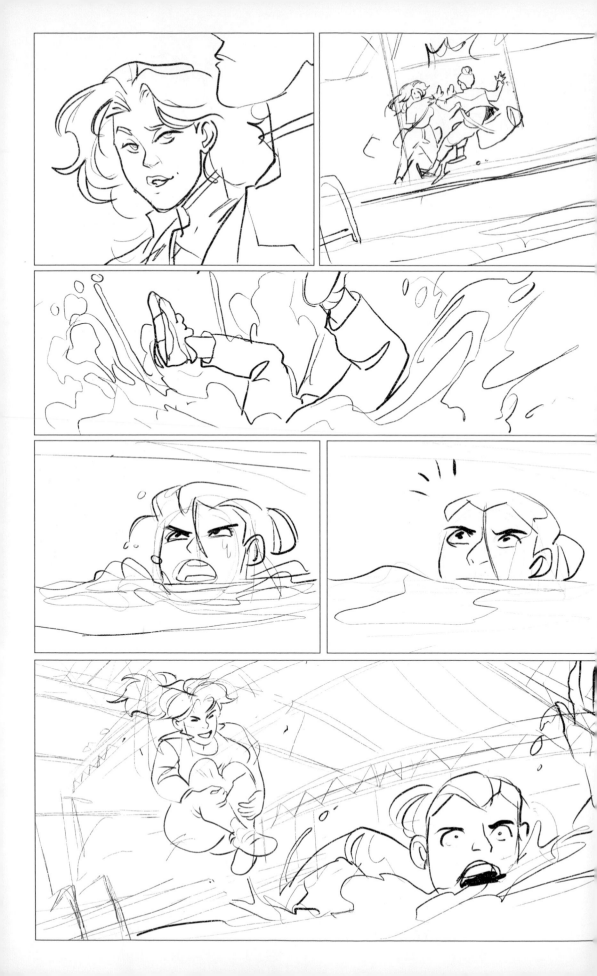

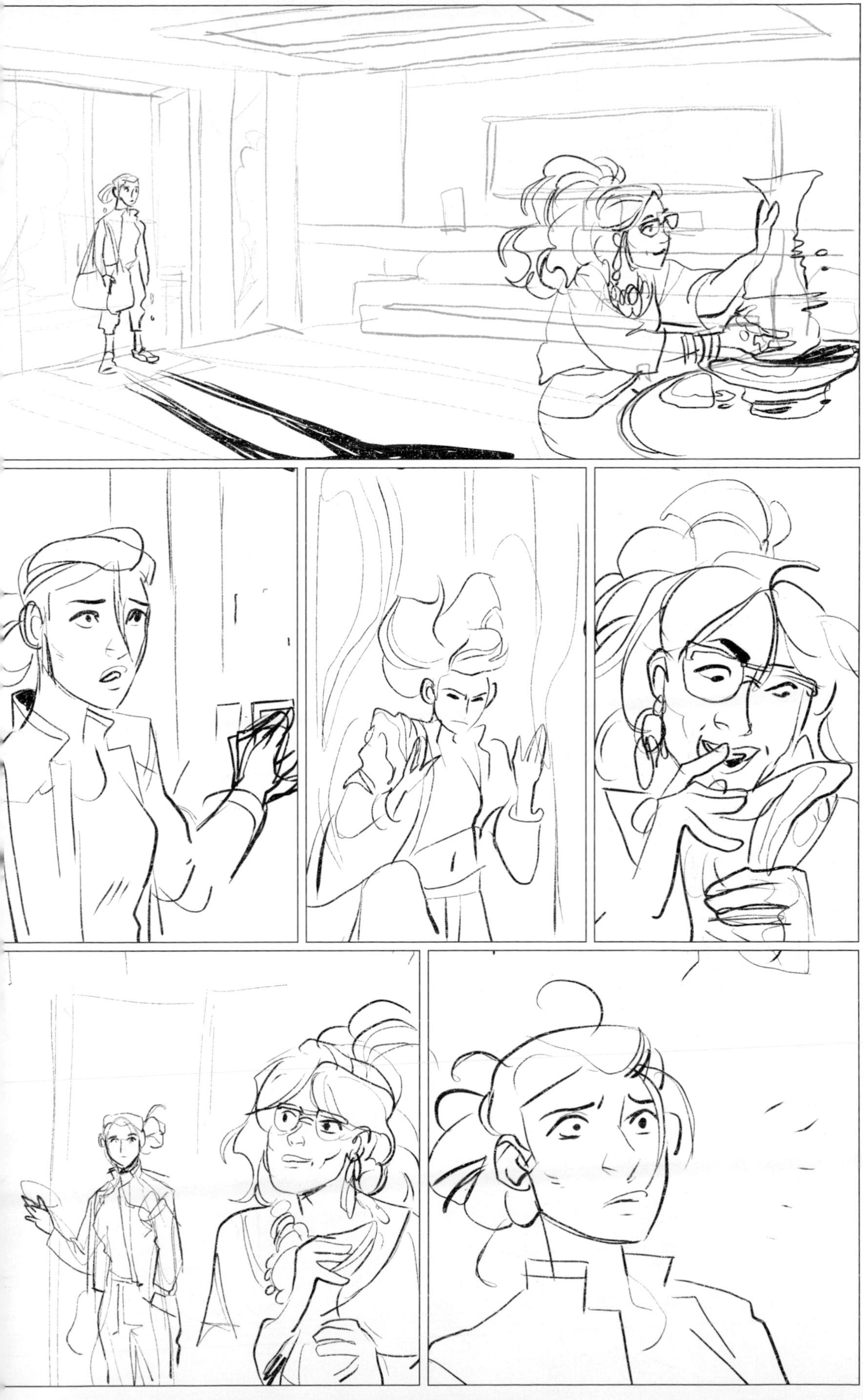

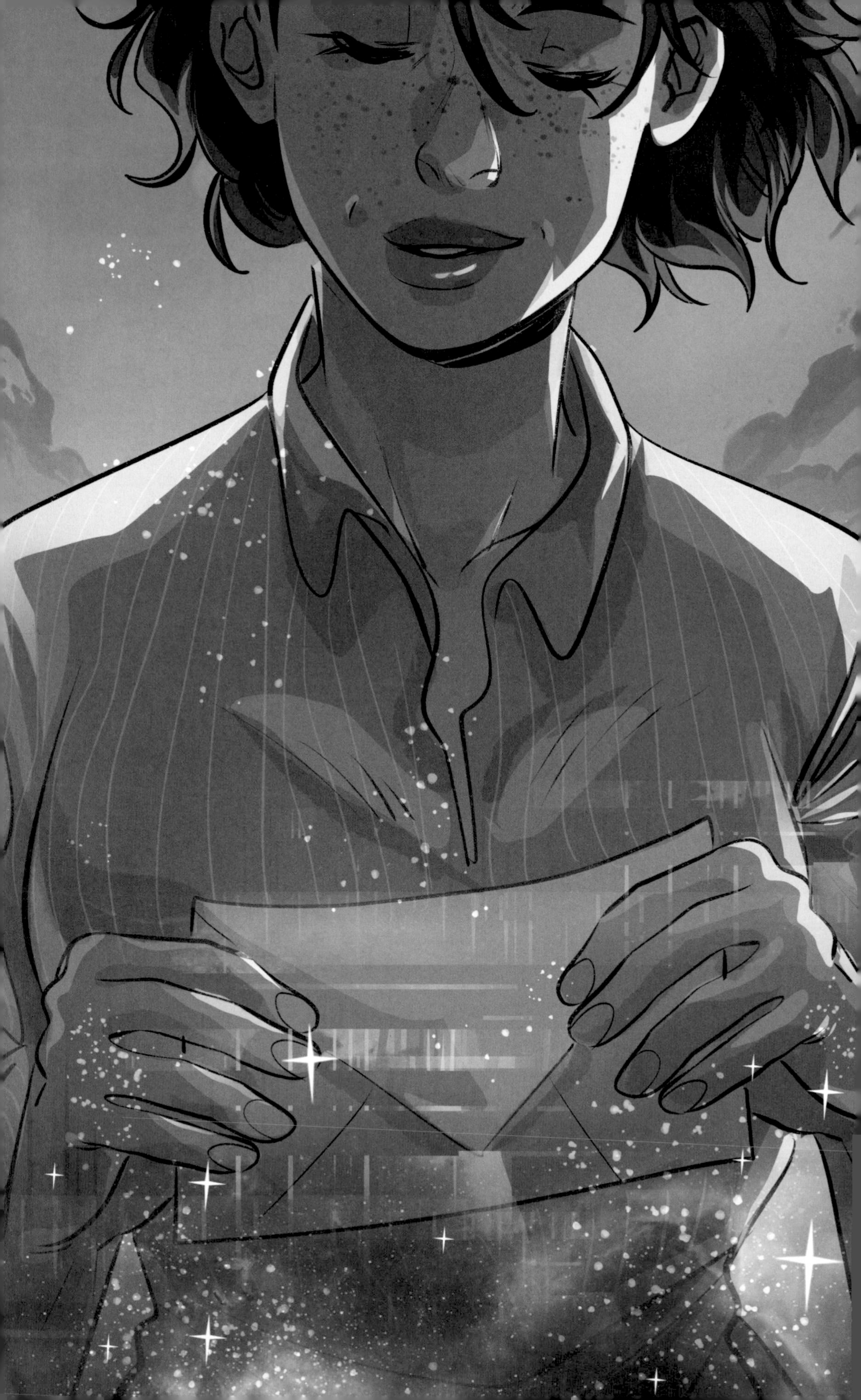

COMIXOLOGY COMES TO DARK HORSE BOOKS!

ISBN 978-1-50672-440-9 / $19.99

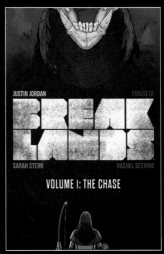

VOLUME 1: THE CHASE

ISBN 978-1-50672-441-6 / $19.99

"Bold, genre-defying and heartfelt. Youth hit a reader like the meteor in its own pages: an angry, wondrous and transformative book." —Scott Snyder (Batman, Justice League)

ISBN 978-1-50672-461-4 / $19.99

Named one of the "5 New Comic Book Series for the End of Summer" by the New York Times

Named One of "10 Comics to Celebrate Pride" by the New York Times

ISBN 978-1-50672-446-1 / $19.99

ISBN 978-1-50672-447-8 / $29.99

VOLUME 1: FIGHT OR FLIGHT

ISBN 978-1-50672-458-4 / $19.99

AFTERLIFT
Written by Chip Zdarsky, art by Jason Loo

This Eisner Award–winning series from Chip Zdarsky (*Sex Criminals*, *Daredevil*) and Jason Loo (*The Pitiful Human-Lizard*) features car chases, demon bounty hunters, and figuring out your place in this world and the next.

BREAKLANDS
Written by Justin Jordan, art by Tyasseta and Sarah Stern

Generations after the end of the civilization, everyone has powers; you need them just to survive in the new age. Everyone except Kasa Fain. Unfortunately, her little brother, who has the potential to reshape the world, is kidnapped by people who intend to do just that. *Mad Max* meets *Akira* in a genre-mashing, expectation-smashing new hit series from Justin Jordan, creator of *Luther Strode*, *Spread*, and *Reaver*!

YOUTH
Written by Curt Pires, art by Alex Diotto and Dee Cunniffe

A coming of age story of two queer teenagers who run away from their lives in a bigoted small town, and attempt to make their way to California. Along the way their car breaks down and they join a group of fellow misfits on the road. travelling the country together in a van, they party and attempt to find themselves. And then . . . something happens. The story combines the violence of coming of age with the violence of the superhero narrative—as well as the beauty.

THE BLACK GHOST SEASON ONE: HARD REVOLUTION
Written by Alex Segura and Monica Gallagher, art by George Kambdais

Meet Lara Dominguez—a troubled Creighton cops reporter obsessed with the city's debonair vigilante the Black Ghost. With the help of a mysterious cyberinformant named LONE, Lara's inched closer to uncovering the Ghost's identity. But as she searches for the breakthrough story she desperately needs, Lara will have to navigate the corruption of her city, the uncertainties of virtues, and her own personal demons. Will she have the strength to be part of the solution—or will she become the problem?

THE PRIDE OMNIBUS
Joseph Glass, Gavin Mitchell and Cem Iroz

FabMan is sick of being seen as a joke. Tired of the LGBTQ+ community being seen as inferior to straight heroes, he thinks it's about damn time he did something about it. Bringing together some of the world's greatest LGBTQ+ superheroes, the Pride is born to protect the world and fight prejudice, misrepresentation and injustice—not to mention a pesky supervillain or two.

STONE STAR
Jim Zub and Max Zunbar

The brand-new space-fantasy saga that takes flight on comiXology Originals from fan-favorite creators Jim Zub (*Avengers*, *Samurai Jack*) and Max Dunbar (*Champions*, *Dungeons & Dragons*)! The nomadic space station called Stone Star brings gladiatorial entertainment to ports across the galaxy. Inside this gargantuan vessel of tournaments and temptations, foragers and fighters struggle to survive. A young thief named Dail discovers a dark secret in the depths of Stone Star and must decide his destiny—staying hidden in the shadows or standing tall in the searing spotlight of the arena. Either way, his life and the cosmos itself, will never be the same!

AVAILABLE AT YOUR LOCAL COMICS SHOP OR BOOKSTORE / To find a comics shop near you, visit comicshoplocator.com / For more information or to order direct, visit darkhorse.com

CIMIXOLOGY ORIGINALS